MYTHIC CULTIVATION

The Great Desolation

By
D.C. Haenlien

Mythic Cultivation
Book One: The Great Desolation

ISBN (print): 979-8-88993-087-7
ISBN (e-book): 979-8-88993-086-0

Published 2025 by MoonQuill
Arlington, VA

www.moonquill.com

Table of Contents

Chapter 1

Pangu Forms Heaven and Earth

In the chaos devoid of color, light, or darkness existed an egg. It floated above a thirty-six-petaled green lotus, a chaos spiritual artifact known as the Thirty-Sixth Ranked Jade Lotus of Chaos.

Here space was immeasurable, and time flowed irregularly. Had any living creature existed in this bedlam, it would have perished instantly; only the egg floated above the Thirty-Sixth-Ranked Jade Lotus of Chaos, unaffected by its merciless environment.

A small crack on its surface was the only warning given before the egg shattered and a humanoid creature burst forth. The creature was born with two chaos spiritual artifacts: the Heaven-Opening Ax and the Jade Butterfly Disk of Good Fortune, which formed from the shell fragments.

The creature raised his head and spread out his arms triumphantly. "I am Pangu!"

His voice echoed throughout the void, alarming the 3,000 chaos fiendgods born before him. As his first act, Pangu raised his ax above his head and cleaved the space below him in two. The chaos exploded in waves, but only momentarily before imploding back into itself. At the point he struck, a small pearl formed.

Pangu Heaven Opening First Art - Chaos Splitter

Pangu's strike sent ripples throughout the chaos, and the other chaos fiendgods realized the danger the newcomer posed.

The newly born chaos fiendgod planned to use the chaos to fuel the creation of a new world, one that could help him achieve his vision.

Most chaos fiendgods were incarnations of the myriad laws, making the eldest the most powerful. Pangu subverted that truth. The firstborn among them, the Chaos Fiendgod of Time, instinctually knew he had no hope of defeating Pangu.

He nonetheless rushed toward Pangu along with the other chaos fiendgods, driven by a desire to stop him. He had a feeling that if he allowed Pangu to continue, chaos would be destroyed.

All chaos fiendgods lived in the primal chaos they were born into. If it was destroyed, it was akin to severing their path to ascension. They charged at Pangu, aware they were likely charging toward their demise.

The Chaos Fiendgod of Time reached him first, but he did not attack. Instead he observed Pangu, waiting for a chance.

The weakest chaos fiendgods were the first to confront Pangu. Snorting derisively, he killed most of them with a single swing of his ax.

"All who obstruct my path shall perish!" Pangu bellowed.

Light flew from the fallen chaos fiendgods' bodies and was absorbed by the Jade Butterfly Disk of Good Fortune. The once-small pearl absorbed the corpses and swelled.

Pangu glanced at the rest of the chaos fiendgods cowed by his demonstration. He snorted with disdain, raised his ax once more, and cleaved another tear in space. The second strike rang like a bell in all the chaos fiendgods' minds.

Pangu Heaven Opening Second Art - Open Heaven

"Haha, I don't care if your path is obstructed or not. I just want to battle!" a fearless voice shouted. The challenger resembled Pangu, but his arms were slightly longer, and fur covered his entire body. He was the Chaos Ape Fiendgod.

The Chaos Ape FiendGod swung his cudgel down on Pangu, who retaliated with his ax. "Scram!"

The Heaven-Opening Ax clashed against the seemingly ordinary cudgel, and the Chaos Ape Fiendgod's body was sent flying. To the shock of all those present, he survived the blow and spat out a mouthful of blood at his opponent. His weapon reflected his state as it now bore a deep gash.

The other chaos fiendgods were inspired to resume their attack, but like the first batch, Pangu unceremoniously killed them with one swing.

The Chaos Ape Fiendgod was relatively young, but he was among the hundred most powerful because he was the incarnation of the Law of War. The more battles he fought, the more powerful he became.

The next two waves of chaos fiendgods were easily dealt with. The chaos pearl absorbed their corpses while the Jade Butterfly Disk of Good Fortune absorbed their laws, and Pangu resumed his creation of the new world.

Between each swing, Pangu had to stop another batch of chaos fiendgods. Each swing increased the panic within the mob, so even if they knew they were sending themselves to die, they still recklessly charged.

Pangu was not unaffected either. Although the death of each chaos fiendgod increased the foundation of the nascent world, his strength waned with each new kill.

Pangu Heaven Opening Third Art - Dividing Earth

Pangu Heaven Opening Fourth Art - Yin-Yang Severance

Pangu Heaven Opening Fifth Art - Five-Element Foundation

Pangu Heaven Opening Sixth Art - Myriad Life Birth

Pangu Heaven Opening Seventh Art - Heavenly Ascension

Finally, right after the seventh cleave, the Chaos Fiendgod of Time struck.

An immense body resembling Pangu's emerged. It was similar, but unlike Pangu, the new creature had two large wings sprouting from his back. Floating next to him was a giant clock, the Chaos Clock.

He was flanked by the Chaos Fiendgod of Karma, the Chaos Fiendgod of Space, the Chaos Fiendgod of Five Elements, the Chaos Fiendgod of Yin-Yang, and the Chaos Fiendgod of Samsara. All were prepared to end Pangu, and all were among the top ten most powerful chaos fiendgods!

The Chaos Fiendgod of Five Elements struck first. "All things are born of fire, water, earth, wood, and metal! Five-element destroys all, Five-Element Disintegration!"

A ray of light containing five colors struck Pangu. He paused as a piece of skin flaked off, but recovered swiftly, to the horror of those around him.

"An ant is still an ant no matter how much bigger it gets!" Pangu said as he brought the Heaven-Opening Ax down upon the Chaos Fiendgod of Five Elements.

The others didn't have the luxury of worrying about the Chaos Fiendgod of Five Elements as they each displayed their most powerful techniques.

"All things exist in space. Without space, nothing exists. Thus, space is king! Spatial Severance!" the Chaos Fiendgod of Space shouted, pointing at Pangu.

A crescent-shaped ripple flew toward Pangu. It sliced a wide gash along his chest, but that too healed as quickly as it appeared. The

Chaos Fiendgod of Time capitalized on this moment and unleashed his technique.

"All things have time," he said. "Without time, there is no progress. No progress means no past, present, or future. Thus, time is venerated! Temporal Erasure!"

An arrow seemingly formed of flowing silver pierced Pangu's chest in the same spot as the last attack. A hint of blood dripped down Pangu's mouth. He roared and cut down the Chaos Fiendgods of Time and Space.

"All things have cause and effect. Without cause, there is no effect. With effect, there must be a cause. Pangu, you selfishly obstructed our paths. Thus, you must pay! Karmic Shackles!" a chaos fiendgod shouted.

All around Pangu, apparitions of all the chaos fiendgods he slew appeared. They shouted in fury and fear and grabbed at Pangu, wanting to rip him to shreds and drag him to hell.

"Ants should behave like ants!" Pangu said. With a wave of his arms, he destroyed all the specters.

The punch landed squarely on the Chaos Fiendgod of Samsara, obliterating him in an instant. The others froze in stunned silence, but their shock quickly gave way to understanding as they noticed a strand of his soul spiraling into the chaos pearl.

Pangu didn't care about the Chaos Fiendgod of Samsara's actions. As long as none impeded his ambition, they would be ignored. He turned toward the other chaos fiendgods and resumed his offensive.

The chaos fiendgods used all their tricks and trump cards, but they fell one by one until only Pangu remained. He turned back to his nascent world and raised his ax once more, but something gave him pause.

A giant silver river composed of time appeared, and a figure fell out. It was the Chaos Fiendgod of Time. Compared to his first emergence, he was in a sorry state. He'd lost two of his limbs, both his wings, and injuries littered his body. Even his lifebound spiritual artifact, the Chaos Clock, was in pieces.

"Pangu, do you think you'll succeed? I tell you now that you'll also fall under the machinations of the Great Dao!"

Something flickered in Pangu's eyes, but he still raised his ax and brought it down.

That was the last thing the Chaos Fiendgod of Time saw.

Chapter 2

Birth of the Three Purities

After fighting off 3,000 chaos fiendgods, Pangu did not have the energy to complete his creation. The birth of the world represented his way, his Dao, so he was not willing to give up.

Pangu sacrificed his body to complete the new world, just as the 3,000 chaos fiendgods had been forced to.

His breath formed the wind and clouds. His voice made lightning and thunder. The sun came from his left eye, and the moon his right. He molded the five regions from his limbs and torso, shaped his blood into rivers. His meridians became roads, his muscles formed fertile lands, his hair shifted into the stars of the night sky. His fur became vegetation, his bones and marrow turned to minerals and precious jewels, and his sweat turned to rain.

The whole process lasted 129,600 years, and so that became the length of each eon.

The new world took the name Great Desolation.

When he finished, Pangu's consciousness faded. His body still carried twelve drops of blood and parts of his spirit. The twelve drops of blood fell near the base of the Buzhou Mountain formed from Pangu's spine, the pillar separating heaven and earth.

As for Pangu's spirit, it turned into three azure qi that flew to

Kunlun Mountain. If Buzhuo was the Great Desolation's greatest mountain, Kunlun was a close second.

At first, the world was barren and lifeless, but as the eons passed, life began to appear. Over a hundred different species were born, but the most prominent ones were the dragon, phoenix, and qilin. They, along with the other creatures, became known as the Hundred Clans.

As the Hundred Clans prospered and fought for hegemony, the Great Desolation's tribulation began. The grudges and malice left behind by the slain chaos fiendgods conglomerated and birthed the fiends, fierce beasts that knew only destruction and havoc. The five most powerful became the Fiend Kings.

First was Shenni, the strongest of the fiends. The second was Taotie, who delighted in swallowing everything, even heaven and earth. Then Qiongqi, who reversed good and evil. The fourth was Hundun, who distorted right and wrong. Lastly, Taowu, arrogant and stubborn to the extreme.

Shenni had ambitions of destroying the Great Desolation and soon defeated the other four Fiend Kings to become the Fiend Emperor. The only ones who could fight them were the congenital gods born from the remnant fiendgods. These remnants and fiends were akin to two sides of a coin.

Even among the congenital gods, two stood out. First was Rahu, born from the remnant of the Fiendgod of Destruction. Second was Hongjun, but no one knew which fiendgod he was before Pangu slew him.

Left with no choice, the Hundred Clans allied themselves with Rahu and Hongjun. Only then, did they manage to exterminate the fiends in an event that came to be called the Fiend Tribulation.

After the Fiend Tribulation, the Way of Heaven was born. Hongjun and Rahu disappeared, on a journey to break through their current cultivation realm. The dragons, phoenixes, and qilins took advantage by absorbing the other Hundred Clans to fight for dominance once more.

They split the Hundred Clans into three factions. The Dragon Clan controlled the scaled creatures, the Phoenix Clan controlled the feathered creatures, and the Qilin Clan controlled the furred creatures.

Three azure qis on Kunlun Mountain remained unaffected by all of this. Born from Pangu's spirit, they could be considered Pangu's descendants, and thus his world protected them.

The rocks, vegetation, the spiritual veins, and even Kunlun Mountain itself formed a protective array that shielded them from the outside world and ensured their safe development. Not even the tribulation could disturb them.

The three azure qis hovered inside a cave, exuding the auras that came to be their names. The first was the Grand Pure Qi, the second was the Jade Pure Qi, and third was the Supreme Pure Qi.

Where am I? The thought echoed inside the consciousness inhabiting the Supreme Pure Qi.

It was puzzled for a moment as a scene replayed itself in its mind. *Pangu opening the heavens? The scene stopped after the Chaos Fiendgod of Time died. Does that mean I'm the Chaos Fiendgod of Time? No, I shouldn't be. I recall living in the twenty-first century! But, what's my name? How did I even get here?* the consciousness thought. It yearned to explore, but it couldn't even speak aloud, much less move.

Eh, there are two other balls like me? Grand Pure Qi and Jade Pure Qi? Does that mean I'm the Supreme Pure Qi? The consciousness's mind blanked for a moment. *I was somehow transported into the mythological era and became the Heavenly Venerable of Numinous Treasures?!*

The Supreme Pure Qi began to vibrate and blast waves of energy. The other pure qis responded in kind, calming down the consciousness.

Okay, this isn't too bad. The two others—I mean, my brothers— should also have developed consciousness, but we can't do anything yet since we haven't transformed. Even if I don't have all my memories, I know I became one of the Three Purities, so I should be okay.

A moment of silence passed.

Pei! I don't want to laze around, I want to do something! Although I'm not too familiar with Investiture of the Gods, I know that Tongtian, the Supreme Purity (a.k.a. me) got ganged up on by my brothers Laozi and Yuanshi. After my defeat, Hongjun locked me up till who knows when. Fuck, that's a terrible ending, I'll have to prevent that.

While the Supreme Purity organized what it knew, it felt a fluctuation inside itself. Upon searching for the source, it discovered a gray shard. *This didn't come from the three pure qis. Rather, it resembles a shard of the Chaos Fiendgod of Time's lifebound spiritual artifact. Did it carry a trace of his soul, and I happened to absorb it?*

Whatever. Since it came from a chaos fiendgod, it's definitely not ordinary. Right now, I shouldn't be distracted by it. I should build my foundations first.

After calming down, the consciousness discovered a cultivation method in its mind, the Supreme Pure Scripture. Its brothers must have had the Grand Pure Scripture and Jade Pure Scripture.

Father God is actually quite generous, the consciousness thought, not realizing that it had changed how it referred to Pangu.

It began to cultivate the Supreme Pure Scripture, and the azure light of the Supreme Pure Qi became brighter and denser. Its brothers also cultivated their own methods, their radiance also illuminating the cave.

After some time, the Grand Pure Qi flew out of the cave, causing tribulation clouds to form above it. All creatures that transform must undergo heavenly tribulation.

The lightning streaked across the clouds as it gathered power and roared. The Grand Pure Qi stayed calm as if it didn't hear the thunderous roar. Just before the first bolt of lightning struck, an exquisite pagoda flew out from the azure qi.

The Heaven and Earth Pagoda was the Grand Pure Qi's lifebound spiritual artifact. It was formed of the Xuanhuang Qi birthed at the creation of the world. The top-grade cardinal spiritual artifact possessed an unrivaled defense. If it claimed to be number two in defense, no spiritual artifact would dare claim to be number one.

It was cardinal because it was born from the creation of the world and contained the law within. Even if a spiritual artifact with more extraordinary powers appeared later, it could only be an innate spiritual artifact at best.

Even under the nine sets of nine bolts of tribulation lightning, the pagoda did not shudder in the slightest. After the final bolt descended, the heavenly clouds dispersed, and the Grand Pure Qi transformed.

Standing where the ball of azure qi had once been was an elderly man with long white brows and hair dressed in white robes. He had slight bags under his eyes, but his skin was tender and pale, like a baby's.

He stretched out his hand, and the Heaven and Earth Pagoda shrunk to fit snugly atop his palm.

"I am Laozi, the Grand Purity. Descendant of Father God Pangu's orthodox lineage!" he declared, his words defying physics and echoing throughout the Great Desolation.

The Supreme Pure Qi couldn't help but think, *Must you be so ostentatious? Don't you know how to be low-key? Ugh, well, it's not like Eldest Brother could help it. There's no way his voice could travel so far, so it must be the Way of Heaven.*

After announcing his presence, Laozi stepped aside for the Jade Pure Qi that flew out of the cave. Although the Jade Pure Qi had no lifebound treasure, it still withstood the heavenly tribulation without a scratch.

With the heavenly tribulation over, the Jade Pure Qi transformed into a middle-aged man with long black hair wearing a black robe. His forehead had a few wrinkles, giving him a severe appearance despite his fair skin.

"I am Yuanshi, the Jade Purity. Descendant of Father God Pangu's orthodox lineage!"

Yuanshi nodded to Laozi and stepped out of the way. Both looked inside the cave and waited for the Supreme Pure Qi, who stalled nervously. It had human memories, so it naturally feared being struck by lightning.

Steeling its heart, the Supreme Pure Qi exited the cave, and the tribulation clouds gathered once more. Luckily, it was a ball of azure qi. Otherwise, it would have been sweating buckets.

After several tense moments, the first bolt of tribulation lightning descended. To the Supreme Pure Qi's surprise, it didn't hurt at all. If anything, it created a warm and soothing sensation all over its body.

It was not only the first bolt that felt so comfortable, but all the other subsequent bolts of tribulation lightning as well. Finally, the Supreme Pure Qi realized the truth. *I'm one of the three pure qis formed from Father God's spirit, so it's normal to have special treatment from the world. Our extraordinary strength is proof.*

No mortals currently existed in the Great Desolation, so all creatures were born as congenital gods and immortals. Gods received the chaos fiendgods' inheritance—be it mind, spirit, or body—while immortals were naturally born lifeforms of the Great Desolation. Immortals had six stages: Earth Immortal, Sky Immortal, Profound Immortal, Golden Immortal, Golden Immortal of the Great Unity, and Golden Immortal of the Great Firmament.

Aside from the Three Purities, perhaps no other creatures had the right to be born as Golden Immortals of the Great Firmament. The titans born from drops of Pangu's blood couldn't really be categorized as immortals.

The Supreme Pure Qi also successfully crossed its heavenly tribulation and transformed.

"I am Tongtian, the Supreme Purity! Descendant of Father God Pangu's orthodox lineage!"

Tongtian turned around to look at Laozi and Yuanshi. "Greetings, Eldest Brother, Second Brother."

Laozi and Yuanshi had shocked expressions on their faces. They both gazed at Tongtian with unblinking eyes. Tongtian stared at his hands, perplexed.

When he'd spoken earlier, the voice hadn't been that of a young man's, it was too crisp and melodious. He noticed his jade-white hands were smooth and unblemished. Robes of vibrant red covered the arms and body, but there was one feature Tongtian couldn't ignore.

Two mounds on his chest.

Sucking in a breath, Tongian's hands reached for his crotch. He, or rather she, let go and took a deep breath.

"MOTHERFUCKER!"

Chapter 3
Way of Allheaven

The woman appeared to be in her late teens or early twenties. Her ink-black hair reached past her waist. Her red robes complemented her ivory skin. This woman was precisely the type that could make Tongtian's heart beat, but there was just one slight problem.

The woman was him! Or rather, her!

"Third Bro—Third Sister, calm—urk!" Yuanshi nearly bit his tongue at the lethal glare leveled by Tongtian.

"Second Brother, call me that again, and I'll slice off yours too," Tongtian said. Needles coated each of her words.

Yuanshi wanted to be angry, but upon seeing the tears pooling at the corner of Tongtian's eyes, his anger dissipated. Tongtian's beauty and teary eyes made her appear too harmless and adorable.

"All things are split into yin and yang. Although we were formed from Father God's spirit, it wouldn't be strange for one of us to be a woman," Laozi said.

"Then how about you turn into a woman and let me be a man? Huh?" Tongtian asked through gritted teeth.

Laozi coughed into his fist. "Third Sister, that isn't something I can decide. It's our innate nature."

What do you mean innate? I remember clearly that the Three Purities were brothers!

Tongtian scratched her head and clenched her teeth. With a huff, she stomped back inside the cave. Laozi and Yuanshi shared a look, and each saw helplessness in the other's eyes. After a moment, they followed Tongtian.

Inside, all three sat down in a lotus position facing each other. As the eldest, Laozi spoke. "Virtuous brothers, since we have just transformed, we should quickly seize the chance and discuss the way and consolidate our foundation."

The corner of Tongtian's lips twitched. *What a cultivation maniac. Not that I don't understand. In this world, there's not really much to do except cultivating, and we've been together for eons. There's not much else to talk about. Honestly, I'm holding up surprisingly well for someone who's been alive for eons. My memories as a human barely make up less than one percent of all my memories, though I was pretty sure I was a man.*

Laozi manifested green clouds behind him. Above them were three budding flowers. Laozi opened his mouth, and numerous mystical illusions appeared. Most prominent were the black and white fishes representing yin and yang.

As Tongtian listened to the Way of Inaction spoken by Laozi, she couldn't help but sigh in his heart—as expected of the head of the Three Purities.

Tongtian had thought she'd had a massive advantage over her two brothers, but she'd underestimated them and overestimated her own abilities. She discarded her contempt and focused wholeheartedly on Laozi's explanation of his way.

After Laozi finished, Yuanshi began his speech. Like Laozi, green clouds and three budding flowers manifested behind his head. Yuanshi's way was the Way of Primordial Beginning.

When Yuanshi finished speaking, Tongtian closed her eyes. When she opened them, green clouds appeared behind her head. Like her two brothers, her three flowers were mere buds.

Tongtian did not speak of her way like Laozi and Yuanshi had. Instead, she spoke of her insight into the Law of Time. As she spoke, the Chaos Clock shard in her mind thrummed as if resonating with her words.

She did not speak of the way because she didn't know her way. When she finished, the green clouds above the three's heads grew and began to interact with each other. All three closed their eyes as they digested their gains.

Laozi gained the most. Two of his three buds bloomed into flowers, and both had nine petals. Nine represented supremacy and perfection. Only one of Yuanshi's buds bloomed into a nine-petaled flower, and he suppressed the other bud that showed signs of opening. If he opened it in this state, it would have at most seven or eight petals, and Yuanshi refused to accept anything but perfection.

Tongtian's buds refused to bloom.

Yuanshi turned to Laozi helplessly. "Eldest Brother…"

"Third Sister has already started comprehending the laws," Laozi said. "This is not good for her. Perhaps she had a fortuitous encounter, or it might be because of her transformation into a woman, but Third Sister has lost her way. This isn't something we can help with. Believe in her."

Yuanshi nodded, but his face still held worry. Eyes on Tongtian, he started to explain his Way of Primordial Beginning again.

Who am I? Tongtian thought. *Am I the Chaos Fiendgod of Time slain by Pangu, possessing the Supreme Pure Qi? Or am I a soul from Earth that happened to get lucky and traveled to the Great Desolation to occupy Tongtian's place? Or maybe I'm just Tongtian, who happened to get the memories of the Chaos Fiendgod of Time and a future soul.*

Tongtian furrowed her brows as she sunk deeper and deeper into her own thoughts. Her green clouds began to dissipate and turned almost translucent. Her three flower buds showed signs of withering.

Upon seeing this, even Laozi had traces of worry on his face and started to preach his Way of Inaction. Tongtian was bombarded with the sound of her brothers' ways.

Unable to bear another moment, she opened her eyes and glared at the two. "AH! Shut up! How can I concentrate with both of you yapping in my ears?!"

Laozi and Yuanshi were stunned into silence by her outburst. Their wide eyes just stared at Tongtian, who closed her own again.

Does it matter who I am? All that matters is that I live this life to the best of my ability. Tongtian, Chaos Fiendgod of Time, future soul? None of that matters, I am just me. I want to live free and unfettered. Whoever dares to block my path, I will decapitate! This is the Way of Allheaven!

Tongtian opened her eyes. Only this time, her dissipating clouds condensed again, and one of her buds bloomed into a nine-petaled flower. Her aura turned sharp like a drawn sword.

Laozi and Yuanshi sighed in relief. "Congratulations to Third Sister for discovering your way."

"Many thanks for Brothers' aid. Had it not been for you two, I would not have figured out my path," Tongtian said with a smile, as if she hadn't just yelled at them.

Laozi and Yuanshi felt the corners of their lips twitch at Tongtian's blatant lie. Nevertheless, they began the second round of discussions, concluding them much faster this time.

With their gains, they began their individual secluded meditations to progress on their paths. After countless years, the three opened their eyes once more.

"I feel I've reached a bottleneck," Laozi said. "Staying in Kunlun Mountain won't help me progress anymore. It's time to explore the Great Desolation, but first, let me calculate the situation."

Laozi used his fingers to deduce the secrets of heaven. "The Great Desolation's next tribulation is still a bit off, but the secrets are starting to become obscure. The three protagonists of this tribulation should be the Dragon Clan, Phoenix Clan, and Qilin Clan. As long as we are careful, we should have no danger."

Yuanshi snorted. "Aren't they just flat-furred beasts? I don't believe that they can stop us once we act together."

"Second Brother," Tongtian chided. "Although we are from Father God Pangu's orthodox lineage, we cannot underestimate them. They are also born from Father God's world, who knows what tricks they have?"

"Third Sister, your aura is the sharpest out of the three of us. Why are you so cowardly? Is it because you are a woma—"

Tongtian stared at Yuanshi, and he snapped his mouth shut.

"Being cowardly and being careful are two different matters. You'd be wise to remember that, *Second Brother*," she said.

"Moving on, where do you think we should travel to in the Great Desolation?" Laozi asked, drawing their attention back to the matter at hand.

"Is there any need to ask?" Tongtian queried.

"Buzhuo Mountain," Yuanshi affirmed.

"Since we all have already decided in our hearts, let's go," Laozi said.

Before they left, Tongtian reinforced the protective array around Kunlun Mountain. The natural protection array had deteriorated with time and, without any external aid, would've disappeared after a few eons. Among the three, she was the best at formations, while Laozi excelled in alchemy and Yuanshi shined when artificing.

The three left Kunlun Mountain for the first time in their lives. Both Laozi and Yuanshi betrayed no emotion as they flew through the Great Desolation. Tongtian, with only her memories of Earth, observed everything through shining eyes.

Although the density of essence was subpar compared to Kunlun Mountain, it still shocked her. Everything was grander and more colorful than how she remembered Earth.

Along the way, they occasionally stopped to collect some unique and wondrous treasures formed by heaven and earth. Tongtian, in particular, took many of the connate and innate materials of this world, knowing they'd never form again. If they didn't collect any now, they could only regret it in the future.

Of course, they also encountered blind idiots who wanted to rob or kill them for their treasure. The Three Purities naturally showed them what it meant to be frogs in the well, but the price of the lesson was their lives.

"Aren't these guys too poor?" Tongtian griped. "Only one of them had a low-grade innate spiritual artifact, and the rest of them only had unrefined materials or low-grade artifacts. Worse, they aren't spiritual, and the process they used to refine these artifacts wasted the materials!"

"How common do you think spiritual artifacts are?" Yuanshi asked. "The Heaven and Earth Pagoda is all that we, the Three Purities, have. Do you expect this rabble to have them?"

Tongtian pondered Yuanshi's words and nodded. As Pangu's orthodox lineage, they had been innately endowed by the world. The other gods and immortals born alongside them were inherently inferior.

It took over 10,000 years to reach Buzhou Mountain. Tongtian sighed. With the time and speed they had spent traveling, it would have been enough to circle the Earth a thousand times over.

They didn't directly fly up Buzhou Mountain. Instead, they descended onto a piece of land near the mountain and walked up it step by step, like ordinary mortals.

Even a thousand li away, all three of them felt powerful coercion emitting from Buzhou Mountain. Perhaps, even if they'd tried flying up, they would be smashed back into the ground by the force.

"As expected of Father God," Laozi said admiringly. "Just his spine alone is enough to suppress all living beings."

Tongtian, who had witnessed Pangu's slaying of the 3,000 chaos fiendgods, couldn't help but frown. She knew how powerful Pangu was. Even the Three Purities combined could never defeat the weakest of the chaos fiendgods, so how could Pangu have died so easily? She banished the thought, too weak to solve it. Maybe when she reached the level of a chaos fiendgod, she could investigate.

They eventually neared the base of the mountain, but a few creatures stood in the way.

"Stop," one called. "This is the territory of the Qilin Clan. Leave immediately or face the consequences!"

Seeing the horde of qilins interrupting their pilgrimage, Laozi and Tongtian frowned.

Yuanshi was even less polite, saying, "Hmpf, you're just a bunch of furred beasts who haven't even transformed. How dare you stop Kunlun's Three Purities?"

Fury colored the lead qilin's face. "Good, good! Only the Dragon Clan and Phoenix Clan dare to humiliate the Qilin Clan like this. I'll make an example of you!"

Reality was cruel to the qilins stationed at the Buzhou Mountain.

The strongest of the qilins was only at the Early Great Unity Realm. How could they hope to stop the Three Purities who were at least in the Early Great Firmament Realm? The qilins were slaughtered, their bodies taken for materials by the Three Purities.

Tongtian's eyes lit up when she saw a qilin with snow-white fur and scales of white jade. "You're very beautiful and to my tastes. If you become my mount, I'll let you live. How about it?"

The white qilin sneered. "Even if you kill us, the Qilin Clan won't let you go!"

Tongtian rolled her eyes. "Is this your only trick? You make trouble with us, and now you want to rely on your elders. You have guts, I'll give you that."

She closed her fist and straightened her pointer finger like a blade. Sword aura coated it, and she pointed at the white qilin's forehead. A burst of light later, the qilin collapsed with a hole between its eyes.

CHAPTER 4

Twelfth-Ranked Green Lotus of Good Fortune

The clash with the qilins was only a minor setback for the Three Purities, who resumed their pilgrimage up Buzhou Mountain. The further they ascended, the greater the coercion. Even Golden Immortals of the Great Firmament felt weak under it. However, the Three Purities also felt a sense of gratification the higher they scaled.

If Tongtian had had to name the feeling, it was akin to the warmth of a mother. The coercion suppressed them, but it also purified and refined them. The further they walked, the purer the energy in their bodies became.

The green clouds in their consciousnesses began to roll and grow, and even the buds showed signs of flowering, but they didn't pay any attention to any of that. They just focused on slowly ascending the mountain and strengthening their daohearts.

Laozi was the first to reach the peak. When he did so, green clouds manifested behind him, and his third flower bud bloomed into a nine-petaled flower. The coercion suddenly disappeared, and he relaxed. The second to reach the peak was Yuanshi, whose second flower bud likewise bloomed into a nine-petaled flower.

Tongtian was the last to arrive. She closed her eyes and straightened her back. Green clouds appeared behind her head, and her second flower bud also bloomed into a nine-petaled flower. Yuanshi smiled.

"Congratulations to Third Sister for reaching the Intermediate Great Firmament Realm," Laozi said.

Are you praising yourself or me? Tongtian inwardly rolled her eyes. Still, she clasped her hands together and said, "Congratulations to Eldest Brother for reaching the Advanced Great Firmament Realm, and congratulations to Second Brother for reaching the Intermediate Great Firmament Realm."

After congratulating them, Tongtian surveyed her surroundings. Below her, she could see all of the Great Desolation, and above her, she could see the Starry Sky, where the 365 great stars resided among the millions of lesser stars.

She sighed and wondered what Pangu's thoughts were when he looked at all of this. Was he satisfied or discontent?

The Three Purities decided to descend the mountain after the baptism. It had taken them over an eon to climb all the way to the top, and Laozi could sense the secrets of heaven becoming murkier and murkier, signifying the coming of the tribulation.

A tenth of the way down, the sky suddenly brightened unnaturally. All three stopped and gazed at the Supreme Yang Star in the Starry Sky.

"Born of the Supreme Yang Star, I am Di Jun!"

The sun seemed to have transformed into a giant three-legged crow with red feathers. It unfurled its wings and cried out. This was the apparition of the golden crow. Simultaneously, a deep purple star's brightness increased as if resonating with Di Jun's birth. It was the Purple Majesty Star, also known as the emperor's star.

Yuanshi snorted. "Just a flat-feathered beast, and it still has ambitions to rule?"

Although Laozi didn't say anything, he also had his pride. As the orthodox lineage of Pangu, he was unwilling to submit to anyone or anything. Tongtian felt the same, but she had long expected Di Jun's arrival. She even looked forward to the birth of Taiyi.

Di Jun's apparition disappeared, and the sun returned to its original appearance, shining brilliantly again.

"Born of the Supreme Yang Star, I am Taiyi!"

Unlike Di Jun, no other star in the Starry Sky resonated with Taiyi's birth, but the ringing of a bell echoed throughout the Great Desolation. Laozi and Yuanshi were furious.

After Pangu formed heaven and earth, the Heaven-Opening Ax had split into three top-grade cardinal spiritual artifacts. Its blade turned into the Taiji Diagram, the handle turned into the Pangu Banner, and the ax poll transformed into the Chaos Bell. The Three Purities weren't present to witness this, but their inheritance allowed them to know.

These artifacts were on par with the Heaven and Earth Pagoda formed by Xuanhuang Qi. Because they were once part of the Heaven-Opening Ax, each one was bestowed with a large amount of Heaven-Opening Merit.

These three artifacts and the Three Purities were among the few in the Great Desolation with Heaven-Opening Merits. They could also be held by the twelve drops of Pangu's blood, Jade Butterfly Disk of Good Fortune, and Thirty-Sixth-Ranked Jade Lotus of Chaos.

They weren't that useful now, but soon, much would depend on them.

"Dammit, how could a mere beast have Father God's treasures?" Yuanshi demanded angrily. In his eyes, the three artifacts formed from the Heaven-Opening Ax should belong to the three of them, the orthodox descendants of Pangu. And Laozi agreed.

Tongtian remained calm. She knew that in the future, Laozi would gain the Taiji Diagram and Yuanshi would gain the Pangu Banner.

As for her? She would possess the Four Immortal Extermination Swords.

"Elder Brothers," Tongtian said. "Don't worry about it. What's ours will eventually return to us." Inwardly, she made a vow. *Taiyi, I'll let you borrow it for now, but I'll be sure to collect the Chaos Bell from you in the future, with interest.*

That was enough to placate her brothers. "Third Sister is right," said Laozi. "What's ours will eventually return to us."

"Hmpf, I'll let that flat-feathered beast be prideful for now," Yuanshi said.

*　*　*

"Elder Brother, should we go to the Great Desolation?" a young man asked. He appeared to be in his mid-twenties and wore red robes.

Next to him was a man who looked about five years his senior holding a book. He wore purple robes and a crown on his head.

Di Jun opened his eyes and closed his book. "I just calculated the secrets of heaven with the Celestial River Diagram. Our time to unify the Great Desolation hasn't come. Our chance will come after the tribulation ends. For now, we should improve our strength as much as possible."

Taiyi nodded. He sat down, and a bronze bell flew out of his mouth to enlarge and float above his head. Di Jun also sat down and started flipping through the Celestial River Diagram, and the Milky Way appeared above his head.

*　*　*

Halfway down the mountain, the Three Purities felt something attracting them. They shared a look and decided to check it out. It wasn't like it was the first time.

Buzhou Mountain was a treasure trove. On the way down, they had already collected quite a bit of material and many spiritual roots. As they got closer, it felt as if something was calling them.

They reached a cave entrance, where they saw an azure mist blocking their way. Laozi turned to Tongtian and said, "Third Sister, it's up to you."

She nodded and used her energy to penetrate the array guarding whatever treasure was behind it. It took over 29,000 years to break. She could have broken it earlier, but she spent the extra time comprehending the array.

Once the array broke, all three entered. Inside the cave was a small pond so clear it looked like air. Flashes of light blinked rapidly, but it was what was floating on the pond that caught the Three Purities' eyes.

"Twelfth-Ranked Green Lotus of Good Fortune!" Yuanshi exclaimed.

After Pangu created the world, the Thirty-Sixth-Ranked Jade Lotus of Chaos had fractured into six lotus seeds. Tongtian knew of the Twelfth-Ranked Green Lotus of Good Fortune, Twelfth-Ranked Black Lotus of Destruction, Twelfth-Ranked Golden Lotus of Merit, and the Twelfth-Ranked Red Lotus of Karma that grew from those lotus seeds, but she had never heard of what happened to the last two lotuses.

The Three Purities had a dilemma on their hands. The Twelfth-Ranked Green Lotus of Good Fortune was comparable to a top-grade cardinal spiritual treasure, but there was only one. How should they split it?

"I see that the green lotus has three parts: the flower, leaf, and stem. How about we each take one?" Laozi suggested.

Yuanshi and Tongtian both agreed. But just as Laozi was about to pluck the flower, Tongtian stopped him.

"Eldest Brother, I see that the green lotus is full of vitality. It should be about to produce some seeds. How about we split it after the seeds come out?"

"Don't you know that the vitality of the lotus will drop after producing the seeds?" Yuanshi asked. "The Twelfth-Ranked Green Lotus of Green Fortune's grade will degrade after being split by the three of us. The thirds might even drop to middle-grade artifacts after producing the seeds."

"No, Third Sister has a point," Laozi said. He pointed at the pond below. "This is Threelight Divinewater. It can heal and nurture all things. As long as we spend a bit of time and materials, we can restore the lotus to its peak after it produces its seeds."

Yuanshi's eyes lit up, and after thinking about it for a moment, he agreed.

Tongtian erected a new protective array to prevent others from discovering the cave.

It didn't take long for nine seeds to form from the Twelfth-Ranked Green Lotus of Good Fortune. The spiritual light coating it dimmed a bit, but it was still a top-grade spiritual root.

"Not bad. Since there are nine, each of us can get three," Laozi said as he took his portion. Yuanshi and Tongtian followed suit.

Yuanshi cupped his hands. "We will have to rely on Eldest Brother to restore the green lotus's foundation."

"We're siblings. No need to be polite," Laozi said. Several materials flew out of his sleeve. Using his alchemical prowess, he refined them into vitality-restoring elixirs and fed them to the Twelfth-Ranked Green Lotus of Good Fortune.

It took 100,000 years before the good fortune green lotus returned to its peak condition. During this time, Tongtian had to sigh. *Time really is the most worthless thing in the Great Desolation.*

Laozi plucked the lotus flower, and it transformed into a horsetail whisk. "From now on, it will be the Void-Refining Whisk."

Yuanshi was next. He plucked the lotus stem, and it turned into a jade scepter encrusted with violet, gold, and silver gems. "The heaven has three treasures: sun, moon, and stars; the earth has three treasures: water, fire, and wind; and man has three treasures, too: qi, essence, and spirit. From now on, it will be called the Three-Treasured Jade Scepter."

Do you have to be so dramatic? Tongtian thought. She waved her hand, and the lotus leaf transformed into a cyan-colored three-foot sword. The more she looked at it, the more pleased she became.

A thought suddenly occurred to her. What if she merged the Chaos Clock shard with the sword in her hand? Would it evolve from a high-grade cardinal spiritual artifact into a top-grade cardinal spiritual artifact?

Tongtian wanted to try, but she did not have the ability right now. She took out a salvaged slab of wood and refined it into a simple sheath. After sheathing the sword, she said, "From now on, you'll be called the Qingping Sword."

The sword thrummed in Tongtian's grasp as if in acknowledgment.

After getting three high-grade cardinal spiritual artifacts, the siblings did not immediately leave. They had to refine the artifact in hand first.

All spiritual artifacts had a set number of restrictions. Spiritual artifacts with 12 or fewer restrictions were low-grade spiritual artifacts; middle-grade spiritual artifacts had 13 to 24 restrictions; high-grade spiritual artifacts had 25 to 36 restrictions; top-grade spiritual artifacts had 37 to 49 restrictions.

Perhaps the Twelfth-Ranked Green Lotus of Good Fortune was destined for the Three Purities, because its refinement took less than a thousand years.

They only stopped because they felt it would take too long to refine all the restrictions. The walk down was quicker than the walk up, but they again met with an obstacle at the base of the mountain. Ten qilins of the Great Firmament Realm stood defiantly before them.

"All who offended the Qilin Clan will perish!"

Chapter 5

Qilin Ancestor

Laozi moved first. He waved his hand, and the horsetail whisk's fine hairs elongated and struck four of the qilins. Once struck, the four qilins froze mid-air. They tried to struggle, but the light in their eyes dimmed.

He was in the Advanced Great Firmament Realm, not to mention his deep foundations. Ordinary Golden Immortals of the Great Firmament were no match for him, much less these qilins still in the Early Great Firmament Realm.

"As expected of Eldest Brother," Yuanshi said. Unable to admit inferiority, he sent out his Three-Treasured Jade Scepter.

The jade scepter flew out and sent one of the qilins crashing into the ground. Then, two lights shot out of its jewels and struck the other two qilins.

"Don't forget about me!"

Holding the scabbard in her left hand, Tongtian appeared in front of the last three qilins. She gripped the Qingping Sword's handle, and a flash later, the qilin in front of her split into two halves. Before Tongtian had the chance to slay the other two, a powerful pressure shrouded the entire area.

"Three brats, you dare kill the members of my Qilin Clan!"

Goddammit. Who do you think you are, some xianxia miniboss?

After you defeat one, a more powerful one comes out. Wait, aren't I the future Heavenly Venerable of Numinous Treasures, aren't I one of the biggest bosses?

Despite her gripes, Tongtian immediately retreated to her elder brothers. They too had stopped attacks to cautiously observe the newly arrived qilin.

It wasn't the largest qilin they'd seen, but it was the noblest by far. They knew even a Peak Golden Immortal of the Great Firmament could not pressure them so. This could only mean that the qilin in front of them had exceeded the Great Firmament Realm.

"You are Qilin Ancestor?" asked Tongtian.

"At least you aren't blind," the first qilin in the world replied.

Hearing this, Tongtian sighed. No wonder the Qilin Clan had become one of the three overlords of the Great Desolation. Such strength had allowed them to carve out a decent territory. The Dragon Ancestor and Phoenix Ancestor should possess similar or greater strength.

"Now, die obediently!" Qilin Ancestor ordered, charging at the three of them.

Tongtian was stunned for a moment by Qilin Ancestor's direct brutish method, but she quickly commanded the Qingping Sword to fly at him. Yuanshi also covered his Three-Treasured Jade Scepter in three different-colored lights and sent it flying at Qilin Ancestor.

Laozi flicked his whisk, and the white hairs grew and wrapped around Qilin Ancestor. Thanks to his move, Qilin Ancestor lost his momentum for a second, allowing Tongtian's and Yuanshi's artifacts to land.

The Qingping Sword only left a shallow, white mark on Qilin Ancestor's black scales. The Three-Treasured Jade Scepter didn't fare much better, only bloodlessly cracking a few scales.

Tongtian and Yuanshi recalled their artifacts with shaken hearts. Those were nearly their strongest attacks, but they only scratched Qilin Ancestor's scales. A second later, he broke the horsetail binding him and resumed his charge.

Unknown to the Three Purities, Qilin Ancestor's heart also shook. Aside from Dragon Ancestor and Phoenix Ancestor, no one had injured him ever since he broke through the limits of the Great Firmament Realm.

This only reinforced Qilin Ancestor's will to kill the Three Purities.

At this time, a pagoda flew out of Laozi's mouth. The pagoda had 33 levels and shone with gold-black brilliance. It enlarged itself and hid the Three Purities within.

Upon seeing the Heaven and Earth Pagoda, Qilin Ancestor's eyes lit up with greed. Even among the Qilin Clan's treasury, no, all of the Great Desolation, perhaps only Dragon Ancestor's Dragon Pearl could compete with it.

"Break for me!" Qilin Ancestor roared, smashing his horn into the pagoda.

The Heaven and Earth Pagoda shivered under the attack, but there was nary a scratch on it. In fact, Qilin Ancestor's assault only sent it flying into the distance.

"Want to escape? Dream on!"

As Qilin Ancestor pursued, a rainbow-colored aurora appeared above the pagoda. The aurora sent streams of light at Qilin Ancestor that he could not dodge.

The streams of light didn't harm Qilin Ancestor, but he felt as if he was stuck in a quagmire. Every movement took a tremendous amount of effort, and he only moved little by little. He could only watch helplessly as the Heaven and Earth Pagoda flew farther and farther away.

Qilin Ancestor angrily returned to the foot of Buzhou Mountain. Upon landing, his face darkened further when he realized the Karmic Merits he'd attained from becoming the lord of all furred creatures had decreased. Even part of his Karmic Luck had disappeared!

Karmic Luck was ephemeral and seemingly useless in battle, but he knew its importance to all creatures. Karmic Luck represented the blessing of the world, and without it one would constantly struggle to fend off death.

He recalled the battle and couldn't think of why his merits and luck had decreased. Was it due to the three people who'd attacked him? Qilin Ancestor shook his head. If they'd had such methods, Qilin Ancestor would have discovered it with his superior realm.

The problem could only be the Way of Heaven or himself. Did his luck decrease because he attacked them? Or did the Way of Heaven punish him for attacking them?

Either way was bad news for him. He wondered who these strangers were.

* * *

In the distance, Laozi, Yuanshi, and Tongtian did not look pleased. Although Laozi put on an air of indifference and was mild-mannered, the pride in his bones was not one bit less than Yuanshi's.

Yuanshi himself had a belly full of anger. Forget the fact that they were the orthodox lineage of Pangu, all three had been defeated by a beast! A beast! Nothing more than the fleas on Pangu! Yuanshi vowed that he would get revenge one day.

Tongtian sighed at how low her vision had been. She had thought the qilin at the Great Unity Realm had been a frog in the well, but so was she. There were always heavens above heavens. Even if she was one of the Three Purities, she shouldn't underestimate others.

The Heaven and Earth Pagoda soared through the sky at maximum speed. Laozi didn't immediately return to Kunlun Mountain but made a detour in case Qilin Ancestor chased after them.

When they reached the East Sea, they finally stopped, and Laozi stored the Heaven and Earth Pagoda. "We should return. I've already divined that the tribulation should begin in less than an eon."

"Just like this?" Tongtian asked. "We're at the East Sea. Should we take a look? Maybe we'll find some treasures."

"Didn't you say it yourself?" Laozi retorted. "What's ours will eventually return to us. What's the use of seeking it out?"

"Grr. I don't care, I'm going to look around first. If you two don't want to explore, you can go back. Don't worry, I'll return before the tribulation begins."

"Third Sister," Yuanshi pleaded. "Stop being immature. The East Sea is under the control of the Dragon Clan. Their Dragon Ancestor isn't any weaker than Qilin Ancestor."

"I'll just avoid the Dragon Clan then," Tongtian said with a flippant shake of her hand. "You can't change my mind."

Laozi shared a helpless look with Yuanshi, saying, "Alright, make sure to prioritize your safety."

"I got it, I got it," Tongtian said, already leaving.

After her figure disappeared into the distance, the remaining two purities flew back to Kunlun Mountain.

Tongtian continued to venture deeper into the East Sea, keeping the sword aura on her body to prevent future conflicts.

If I recall correctly, she thought. *In the future, when the Three Purities separated, the Heavenly Venerable of Numinous Treasure went to the*

East Sea and settled on Jin'ao Island. Should I go looking for it now? Or shall I search for the Three Immortal Islands?

Tongtian continued to explore the East, but after several thousands of years, she found nothing. Of course, she didn't dare enter the sea, which would have raised her chances of finding the island and of the Dragon Clan discovering her.

She realized she had reached the border between the Great Desolation and chaos. As a Golden Immortal of the Great Firmament, she could survive the chaos, but not forever.

Tongtian was about to turn around, but she felt her green lotus seeds resonate with something. After a brief search, Tongtian still didn't discover anything, but she wasn't willing to give up.

She used the seeds as a sonar and tested out which direction gave the biggest reaction. Finally, she reached the immediate edge of the Great Desolation.

I'll just check it out. If I expend 30 percent of my essence, I'll immediately return, Tongtian thought as she stepped into the chaos.

Immediately, her face paled as the chaotic corrosion buffeted her. She held nothing back, and a sword aura burst out of her body, deflecting the corrosion.

"It's a bit hard to fly," Tongtian muttered, but she quickly adjusted. She was on a time limit since she couldn't absorb the essence of heaven and earth to replenish her spent energy.

She had underestimated the danger of the chaotic boundary. Even if her energy could repel the chaotic energy, her body wouldn't last long against the corrosion. However, Tongtian wasn't willing to give up and soldiered on.

Just as she felt her energy dwindle to about 85 percent, the chaotic energy weakened. Not just that, but she could feel the essence of heaven and earth, however faint it was.

Eyes lighting up, Tongtian flew forward, the green lotus seed resonating even more. After some time, she saw a giant floating island.

Tongtian smiled and approached. The farther she flew, the more essence she felt, and the chaotic energy dwindled. At the edge of the landmass, an array blocked her path. Formations were her forte, so she immediately set to work. After a thousand years, Tongtian opened an entrance into the island. She would have liked to further her study the array, but she had promised that she would return before the tribulation started.

Stepping onto the island, Tongtian felt the abundant essence of heaven and earth. Although there were no animals, it was filled with numerous immortal herbs and spiritual roots. This place was comparable to Kunlun Mountain.

After walking for a little while, she saw a stele with the word Fangzhang carved onto it.

This is Fangzhang Immortal Island? She was disappointed that it wasn't the most famous Penglai Immortal Island, but that was only a minor nitpick. Tongtian continued on her way; she wanted to know what had made the green lotus seeds so excited.

When she reached the center of the island, she saw a black pond that exuded a sinful aura. This was the Abyssal Sinwater, one of the top ten truewaters, like the Threelight Divinewater. Any who entered would drown in evil thoughts.

More eye-catching than the black water was the unsullied flower growing out of the pond. It had twelve white petals and exuded a pure, soothing aura. Just by being near it, Tongtian's unnecessary thoughts eased.

The Abyssal Sinwater might be the greatest poison to most, but for the Twelfth-Ranked White Lotus of Purification, it was the best source of nutrients.

Chapter 6

Qiankun Ancestor

Tongtian laughed. She had only gotten a high-grade spiritual artifact when they'd split the Twelfth-Ranked Green Lotus of Good Fortune, but now, she'd found its equal all for herself.

She could see a few more lotuses in the pond: three Ninth-Ranked White Lotuses of Purification, six Sixth-Ranked White Lotuses of Purification, and nine Third-Ranked White Lotuses of Purification.

Tongtian waved her arm, and the Twelfth-Ranked White Lotus of Purification trembled. Tongtian frowned and increased her strength, and it finally flew into her hand. Even so, the lotus struggled in her grip.

She didn't delay any longer and sat down to refine the Twelfth-Ranked White Lotus of Purification. One hundred years later, Tongtian succeeded.

Tongtian couldn't help but sigh. Although the two lotuses were of the same rank, she now saw that the Twelfth-Ranked Green Lotus of Good Fortune was a bit superior. The purification lotus didn't have the ability to become three high-grade cardinal spiritual artifacts. At most, it would be three high-grade innate spiritual artifacts.

Still, the Twelfth-Ranked White Lotus of Purification had its own advantages. It had the ability to purify all things, even chaotic energy, and could quell unruly minds. Its defensive abilities were nothing to scoff at either. Tongtian placed more importance on the second ability. The mindset was incredibly important for cultivation. A calm temperament could be more useful than talent.

Although she had cultivated for over 100,000 years, that didn't mean she did it nonstop. She had to take breaks along the way too. The only time she persevered was during the baptism on Buzhou Mountain, and that was partly because she refused to lose to her two brothers.

With the Twelfth-Ranked White Lotus of Purification in hand, Tongtian had confidence her cultivation would become smoother. The only gripe she had was about the color. "If it had been the Twelfth-Ranked Red Lotus of Karma, that would have been best. Too bad it should already have an owner."

Still, Tongtian felt the trip had been worth it. She wanted to take the other three Ninth-Ranked White Lotuses of Purification, but when she moved them, the sinful aura from the black pond started to spill out.

It was clear Fangzhang Immortal Island would turn into a hellish place if she took the other lotuses. Tongtian shrugged. It wasn't like she wouldn't return.

After leaving a spiritual imprint on the island, Tongtian left.

Once she stepped into the chaos again, the Twelfth-Ranked White Lotus of Purification enlarged into a lotus throne for her to sit on. With the protection of the white lotus, she could replenish her energy while traveling through the chaos.

This made the return trip much faster, but as soon as she breached the Great Desolation, something attacked her. Thankfully, the white lotus's petals curled protectively in front of Tongtian and deflected the blow.

"Attacking me out of nowhere, don't you think you're a bit rude?" Tongtian asked, staring down her foe.

Surprisingly, it was a humanoid, unlike the Hundred Beast Clan. He carried a ruler in his hand and stared greedily at the Twelfth-Ranked White Lotus of Purification under Tongtian. Worse still was the fact that he had a Peak Great Firmament Realm cultivation base.

"Rude? I don't know what relationship you have with Pangu, but everything related to him must perish!" He raised his arm and a giant painting of the world appeared behind him. He brought his hand down, and the picture mimicked his palm, pressing down against Tongtian.

Tongtian felt like a whole world was crushing her. She quickly controlled the white lotus to resist, and the two artifacts entered a stalemate. The Twelfth-Ranked White Lotus of Purification was of a higher grade than the painting, but she hadn't refined it enough to display greater strength.

Her intestines turned green with regret. Her attacker didn't allow her time for self-pity or even thought as he charged at her with the ruler in hand. Tongtian decisively jumped off of her white lotus and unsheathed her Qingping Sword.

Clang!

It didn't feel like a ruler had clashed against her sword; it felt closer to someone smashing a rectangular planet against her!

She roared and fully unleashed the sword aura restrained in her body. The Qingping Sword hummed in response and gained a steely gleam. It moved forward and started to cut into the ruler.

The unnamed Daoist frowned and retreated. From the clash alone, he discovered that the Qingping Sword was a high-grade spiritual artifact, not something his middle-grade spiritual artifact could compete with. The greed in his eyes shone brighter.

Tongtian wasn't willing to stay on the defensive and pressed forward. Her Qingping Sword sang a song of blood and steel. With each strike, her speed quickened, and with each clash, her swordplay advanced. As the battle progressed, her strength increased despite the fact her realm remained unchanged.

The ruler in the humanoid's hand was littered with scars.

Tongtian brandished her sword at him. After repeated confrontations, she'd finally discovered her opponent's identity. "You are Qiankun Ancestor, the remnant of the Chaos Fiendgod of Qiankun."

Qiankun Ancestor sneered. "So what if you know? My strength is far beyond what you can understand. A junior like you doesn't have any chance of leaving alive, no matter what you inherited from Pangu!"

Tongtian returned his sneer. "Big words for a loser. You might have possessed strength beyond the Great Firmament Realm, but that was in your heyday. You're nothing more than a fossil that should have died long ago!"

Anger smoldered in Qiankun Ancestor's eyes. He flipped his hand, and a palm-sized cauldron appeared, but Tongtian wasn't afraid. She entered a stance and silver light coated her sword.

Just as the two were about to resume their battle, someone called out, "Fellow Daoists, please wait. What need is there to resort to violence? Can't we just talk it out?"

The newcomer was a man in his early forties or late thirties. He had long red hair and wore a red robe engraved with clouds.

"Nosy!" Qiankun Ancestor said, sending the giant painting crashing toward the man.

Red clouds appeared around the Golden Immortal of the Great Firmament and formed a large formation. "Hmpf, I just couldn't stand to see you bully a woman, and wanted to talk it out. But since you're so unreasonable, taste my Red Cloud Formation!"

Tongtian didn't know if she should slash Qiankun Ancestor or Redcloud Ancestor. According to her memories, Redcloud Ancestor was known as the nicest guy in the Great Desolation, but because of this, he made as many enemies as friends.

Forget it, he's here to help me, after all. I'll let his comment slide just this once. Tongtian took this chance to move the Twelfth-Ranked White Lotus of Purification above her head and shroud herself in a white light now that the giant painting no longer entangled it.

"Taste my sword!" Tongtian abandoned all defenses and focused all her attention on attacking.

Qiankun Ancestor sneered. "Do you think I can't deal with you without my Qiankun Map? Come forth, Qiankun Cauldron!"

Before the Qingping Sword could pierce Qiankun Ancestor, green clouds manifested behind him, and a cauldron flew out. Seeing that the tide had turned, Tongtian shot dim silver sword light from her blade. It was unnoticeable as it struck him in the chest, but in return, Tongtian was swallowed by the Qiankun Cauldron.

Inside the Qiankun Cauldron, she saw a vast world even greater than the one in the giant painting. She couldn't help but curse. *Qiankun Cauldron, Qiankun Ruler, and Qiankun Map are obviously your lifebound artifacts, while I wasn't born with a single one? Am I from the orthodox lineage of Pangu, or are you?!*

Worse still, she couldn't absorb any essence and replenish her energy. It wasn't like the chaos outside; the very will of the world rejected her. Tongtian began to unleash sword light after sword light in an attempt to break out, but all her efforts were in vain.

Outside, Qiankun Ancestor snorted. "Just an ant who hasn't seen the strength of chaos fiendgods."

He grimaced and clutched his chest, where a diamond slit continuously leaked blood. Since when did he have such a wound?

Qiankun Ancestor searched through his memories, and it seemed to have always existed. He was surprised that he'd allowed such a wound to continue to exist unhealed. Stranger still was that he'd actually ambushed someone with a wound. After he slayed Pangu's descendant, he'd find a secluded cave to heal himself in.

He glanced at Redcloud Ancestor, who was still entangled in his Qiankun Map. The Red Cloud Formation was powerful, but it wasn't enough to overcome the spiritual artifact. "After I solve her, you're next."

He suppressed the wound on his chest and began refining Tongtian inside the Qiankun Cauldron. The Twelfth-Ranked White Lotus of Purification could delay the process, but she knew, sooner or later, she would run out of energy and die.

Nothing she did would help her escape the confines of the Qiankun Cauldron. Perhaps if someone could disrupt Qiankun Ancestor's concentration, she might have a chance, but she doubted Redcloud Ancestor had the ability. Even if he did, she didn't want to rely on him.

Tongtian stored the Qingping Sword away, but she wasn't admitting defeat. She held out her hand, and a gray shard appeared. The shard could only be described as a crude sword without a handle or guard, but it exuded a timeless aura.

Her eyes gained a silver sheen as she began to resonate with the Law of Time contained within the Chaos Clock shard. Tongtian gripped the bottom with both hands and took a deep breath. Her hair fluttered as the air around her became turbulent. She raised the shard above her head and then brought it down.

"Temporal Severance!"

Outside, Qiankun Ancestor's face suddenly paled. A second later, he spat out a mouthful of blood.

Tongtian flew out of Qiankun Cauldron, but her face was bloodless too. She reached out and grabbed the rim of the Qiankun Cauldron, but Qiankun Ancestor could only stare at her with confusion. When he looked at the Qiankun Cauldron, he felt a sense of unfamiliar familiarity, like the Qiankun Cauldron should have been his but wasn't.

He didn't have time to ponder any longer as Tongtian came charging forward, Qingping Sword in hand.

Qiankun Ancestor quickly brought out his Qiankun Ruler to block the Qingping Sword. As the two weapons clashed, he couldn't help but wonder what he had been thinking. Although he possessed the Qiankun Map and Qiankun Ruler, two spiritual artifacts didn't guarantee him an absolute advantage over someone with the Twelfth-Ranked White Lotus of Purification.

His eyes focused on the cauldron in Tongtian's grasp. Perhaps he had discovered the Qiankun Cauldron and wanted to refine it but was interrupted by her? No, that didn't sound right either. Qiankun Ancestor knew there was something wrong with him. He couldn't fight any longer lest his injuries worsen. He recalled the Qiankun Map and moved to flee.

How could Tongtian allow him to escape? The white lotus flew off and stopped the map just as he'd done to her during their first clash.

"You!" Qiankun Ancestor roared.

Tongtian smirked. "Don't you know what goes around comes around? Since you wanted to kill me and steal my treasure, be prepared to lose your life!"

Qiankun Ancestor saw the unfavorable situation. Since he'd recalled the Qiankun Map, Redcloud Ancestor had been freed and was rushing toward him. Even without the Twelfth-Ranked White Lotus of Purification, Tongtian still had a high-grade spiritual artifact in hand, unlike him.

If he was dragged into battle, then he might really fall if she joined forces with Redcloud Ancestor. With one last unwilling glance at the Qiankun Cauldron in Tongtian's hand, Qiankun Ancestor decisively abandoned the Qiankun Map and fled.

"I'll remember this!" he yelled.

Tongtian didn't chase after him. She had spent almost all of her energy unleashing Temporal Severance, and she was putting up a strong front. Plus, she had another top-grade cardinal spiritual artifact to refine.

The Qiankun Cauldron in her hand shivered and tried to fly away, but Tongtian suppressed it. She turned toward Redcloud Ancestor, who also didn't pursue Qiankun Ancestor.

"Thank you, fellow Daoist, for your aid."

Redcloud Ancestor quickly waved his hands. "No thanks, no thanks, I didn't do much."

"Then I'll leave the Qiankun Map to you. If fate brings you across my path again, I'll repay this favor," Tongtian said. Without waiting for a response, she took back the white lotus and flew off.

Redcloud Ancestor hesitated for a moment but formed the Red Cloud Formation again and trapped the Qiankun Map. A middle-grade spiritual artifact was still quite attractive to him because he had no artifact in hand.

Chapter 7
Upgrading the Qingping Sword

Inside Three Purity Palace, Yuanshi's newly refined spiritual artifact, the brothers sat on prayer mats in the grand hall. Next to them was an empty prayer mat.

Laozi opened his eyes and looked at Yuanshi. "Second Brother, calm your heart. Third Sister will be fine. If anything had happened to her, we would have felt it."

Yuanshi opened his eyes. "I'm not worried about her. I'm simply pondering on the complexity of the myriad laws."

Laozi closed his eyes as if to say, "Whatever you say."

Time passed, but every once in a while, Yuanshi would open his eyes and stare out of Three Purity Palace. When he could take it no more, he suddenly stood up and flew out of the palace.

Laozi opened his eyes and frowned a bit but then smiled. He rose as well and left Three Purity Palace.

"Third Sister, you're finally back," Yuanshi said to the returning Tongtian.

Tongtian looked at the new addition to Kunlun Mountain and smiled. "It seems you guys weren't idle while I was gone."

"The secrets can no longer be divined. You almost got caught in the tribulation. What do you have to say for yourself?" Yuanshi asked sternly.

Tongtian rolled her eyes. "Who are you? My father? Hurry and show me my room, I have to sort out my gains and refine my Qingping Sword." .

Yuanshi gave Laozi an almost pleading look, but Laozi ignored him and followed their sister into the palace. If he hadn't had to maintain his image, Yuanshi would have stomped like a petulant child.

After being shown to her room, Tongtian locked herself in to recover her lost essence. Once she was in her peak condition, she took out the Qiankun Cauldron and began to refine its restrictions.

The Qiankun Cauldron had 42 restrictions already, and it took 100,000 years to refine 27 of them. Unlike the Qingping Sword, the Qiankun Cauldron did not have an innate connection with her. Not to mention she didn't practice the Law of Qiankun.

With the preliminary preparations done, Tongtiang took out the Qingping Sword and the Chaos Clock shard. She placed both of them into the Qiankun Cauldron and began to refine them.

Under her control, the Chaos Clock shard melted into a gray liquid. The molten artifact coated the sword and eventually submerged into it. Finally, a line appeared at the center of the sword.

The reborn Qingping Sword flew out of the Qiankun Cauldron and into Tongtian's hand. During the refinement process, the restrictions had reset, forcing Tongtian to refine it again, but she wasn't upset. The number of restrictions on the Qingping Sword had increased, and she could sense a timeless aura on it, which meant that it had successfully upgraded into a top-grade cardinal spiritual artifact.

However, when she saw the exact number of restrictions on the Qingping Sword, a strange expression appeared on her face. "Forty-four restrictions? That doesn't sound ominous. *Not at all.*"

Tongtian shook her head to clear those needless thoughts and took the time to restore all the essence she had used. Then, she calculated the total time it took for her to merge the Qingping Sword and Chaos Clock shard.

"Three hundred thousand years?!" Tongtian nearly shouted. She covered her face with her hand. "Time really is the most worthless thing in the Great Desolation."

She pinched her nose and worked on refining the Qingping Sword, all the while knowing the Twelfth-Ranked White Lotus of Purification was still unfinished.

Another 10,000 years later, Tongtian opened her eyes again. She'd finally finished refining the Qingping Sword, although she had only refined thirty-seven restrictions on the Twelfth-Ranked White Lotus of Purification.

Tongtian blinked when she realized she had reached the Advanced Great Firmament Realm. "Huh, not bad. But I really need to go out now."

When she left her chambers, she joined Laozi and Yuanshi in the grand hall on their prayer mats.

"Third Sister, you were cultivating for over 300,000 years. Just what did you gain?" Yuanshi asked.

Laozi didn't say anything, but he waited for her answer too.

"Oh, nothing much," Tongtian said. She floated in the air, and a white lotus appeared beneath her. "Just a Twelfth-Ranked White Lotus of Purification. It's not as good as the Twelfth-Ranked Green Lotus of Good Fortune, though."

It's not as good as the Twelfth-Ranked Green Lotus of Good Fortune, but it's better than my Three-Treasured Jade Scepter and Laozi's Void-Refining Horsetail Whisk! Yuanshi thought. He couldn't help but stare at Tongtian's white lotus in envy. If he already regretted not joining Tongtian, what she took out next practically made his eyes red.

"Oh, and just this Qiankun Cauldron," Tongtian said, holding it out casually. "It's only a top-grade cardinal spiritual artifact. Not only can it refine pills and artifacts, but it can also make cardinal spiritual artifacts. Unfortunately, I don't have the skill to do so. It's such a waste in my hand, but who told me to be its owner? Hahaha."

Hearing Tongtian's smug laughter, Yuanshi hated that he couldn't grab the Qiankun Cauldron in her hand. His intestines turned green with regret. Why did he insist on returning to Kunlun Mountain? He should have followed her. Even Laozi stared at the Qiankun Cauldron with a heated gaze.

After having her fun, Tongtian tossed the cauldron to Yuanshi, who just stared blankly at her.

"I've already used it," Tongtian said, showing her Qingping Sword. "I'm not skilled in refining, so it's better in Second Brother or Eldest Brother's possession. Since Eldest Brother already has a top-grade artifact, I figured you should have it."

Yuanshi pushed it back into Tongtian's hand. "I can't accept this. Third Sister, you got this by yourself. You should keep it."

Tongtian pushed the artifact back. "It will only end up collecting dust in my hands. It's better for you to hold it. If you really can't accept, then help me refine a few artifacts."

Yuanshi stared at the Qiankun Cauldron. He did want a top-grade cardinal artifact like his siblings, and it was a cauldron, which held great allure for him. "Alright, Second Brother will make whatever you want."

Tongtian lit up with a beautiful smile that Yuanshi reflected back. At least until Tongtian opened her mouth again. "I want 129,600 swords. They don't have to be cardinal or innate spiritual artifacts, but they have to be spiritual artifacts at the very least."

Yuanshi's face cramped up. He wanted to reject the request, but seeing Tongtian's happy face, he could only swallow this bitter pill.

"Second Brother, lend me the Qiankun Cauldron for a bit too," Laozi said.

"Scram!" Yuanshi yelled.

* * *

In the deepest, darkest depths of the East Sea, a magnificent palace built atop a coral reef gave off shimmering rainbow light. The reef was awe-inspiring, but the palace possessed even greater beauty. Its crystal walls, shingles crafted from red gems, and pillars of precious metal housed unimaginable treasures. This was the Crystal Dragon Palace, an acquired spiritual artifact crafted by the Dragon Clan from an exorbitant amount of materials.

Within a grand but dimly lit room lay Dragon Ancestor. His coiled body nearly filled the entire room.

"Enter," Dragon Ancestor said, and his voice reverberated through the shut doors and out into the halls. Moments later, the grand doors opened to reveal another dragon flying in.

The new arrival possessed dull silver scales and had the head of an old man with two gray horns. He might've seemed decrepit, but his two eyes resembled the solar and lunar stars and gave him an ancient yet noble aura.

"Zhuyin greets the Ancestor," the silver dragon said with a lowered head.

"No need for such courtesy," Dragon Ancestor replied. "Among the Dragon Clan, not even my sons are as close as you to reaching the same realm as me."

"I may be the closest, but the others are catching up. Despite the urgency I feel, I still cannot break through the last hurdle even with Ancestor's guidance."

"Cultivation cannot be rushed. Still, it'd be best if you could break through as soon as possible. Once you reach the same realm as me, the

Dragon Clan's victory will all but be assured, even if the Phoenix and Qilin Clans ally against us."

"I'll do my best."

Dragon Ancestor shook his head, knowing words were meaningless. If all it took to break the limits of the Great Firmament Realm were empty words, the three clans would have had members who surpassed Golden Immortals of the Great Firmament. "Enough. Speak, why have you interrupted my cultivation?"

"Answering Ancestor, many pure-blooded dragons have gone missing near the land to the South."

Golden light reflected off of Dragon Ancestor's serpentine form as he adjusted his position. After the Fiend Tribulation, the three overlords had split the Great Desolation into three territories. The Dragon Clan claimed the seas, lakes, and rivers; the Phoenix Clan claimed the South and skies; while the Qilin Clan claimed most of the land and forests.

"Have you questioned the Phoenix Clan?" Dragon Ancestor asked.

"We have, but..."

"What is it? Don't hesitate and speak."

Zhuyin stayed silent for a moment longer, needing to find the strength to open his mouth. "Before we could question the Phoenix Clan, they sent a message asking why we killed members of their clan."

For a moment, silence reigned in the grand hall. A sudden pressure emerged, crushing Zhuyin and forcing him onto the ground. "Dragon Ancestor, please quell your anger!"

Blinded by rage, Dragon Ancestor roared. "Do those birds forget their place? Had it not been for us, they would have perished in the Fiend Tribulation. We haven't even questioned them, and they dare to question us?!"

When Dragon Ancestor turned his slitted pupils onto him, Zhuyin's body was paralyzed by the sheer difference in power.

"Send a delegate to the Phoenix Clan. Tell them that if they don't give a satisfactory answer, the Dragon Clan will destroy them!"

"I beseech Ancestor to reconsider!" Zhuyin cried out.

The pressure remained, but the furious words of the Dragon Emperor halted. "Speak, why should I?"

"This situation isn't simple. I find it strange that the Phoenix Clan questioned us about their missing members just as we lost some of ours. There must be a hidden force inciting conflict between us."

"None of the clans under us would dare to revolt," Dragon Ancestor said with absolute confidence.

His words weren't without basis. Dragons had a lustful nature, and because of this, they interbred with many species. Over the years, the Dragon Clan's bloodline had merged with many other members of the Hundred Clans. If a beast could awaken the dormant bloodline, they transformed into a dragon and gained many of the benefits.

Not everyone succeeded, not even the Dragon Ancestor's own sons. He had numerous children who inherited his golden scales, but he also sired nine blights. Each of the nine possessed draconic attributes mixed with those of other beasts, like a turtle or tiger. The nine became taboo existences among the Dragon Clan.

Still, many wished to awaken their dormant bloodlines.

"Enough, dispatch an envoy. As I said before, if they cannot give us a satisfactory answer or punish the perpetrator, then the Dragon Clan will destroy them. Go and execute my will."

Zhuyin knew he could not alter Dragon Ancestor's mind. He left and personally selected ten dragons at the Great Firmament Realm. He would personally lead the delegation to avoid any accidents. After setting a date and location with the Phoenix Clan, he set out.

It took a few years to arrive at the designated patch of beach that connected the southern region and the South Sea. To Zhuyin's surprise, the Phoenix Clan had sent a mild elder that he recognized. As the talks continued, both sides agreed that a third force had likely interfered to incite conflict between the Dragon and Phoenix Clans. After a long discussion, both sides vowed to cooperate to flush out the secret mastermind.

With his goal partially accomplished, Zhuyin felt lighter. That feeling did not last long when he returned to the Dragon Clan. The Phoenix Clan's delegates never made it back—at least not fully. The only survivor pointed his claws at Zhuyin and the Dragon Clan's delegation as the culprits.

Zhuyin knew it was over at this point. Even if the Dragon Clan denied this accusation, the Phoenix Clan would not believe it. As he predicted, the Phoenix Clan declared war on the Dragon Clan, and Dragon Ancestor only added fuel to the fire. He swore to exterminate the Phoenix Clan for their impudence.

The truth no longer mattered. As the war between the Dragon Clan and Phoenix Clan heated up, the Qilin Clan joined, claiming the dragons had killed members of their clan.

Once more, all three clans warred in the Great Desolation, only this time against each other and not united against a common foe.

CHAPTER 8

Phoenix and Qilin Clan United

A black-robed figure with an evil and indifferent bearing sat on a lotus atop Mount Sumeru. His seat was the Twelfth-Ranked Black Lotus of Destruction, an artifact formed from one of the six seeds the Thirty-Sixth-Ranked Jade Lotus of Chaos released before its destruction.

A moment later, a figure covered in black mist materialized in front of him. Five more mist-covered figures materialized, and one of them stepped forward. "Master, the conflicts between the three clans have increased and war is imminent."

The black-robed figure opened his eyes. The pupils, irises, and scleras were an indistinguishable endless void. He didn't look at his subordinates but gazed upward. To the casual observer, it was a normal day in which the sun, moon, and stars hung above them. Day and night intermixed to create a breathtaking image, but he was blind to the beauty of the world.

Unseen by anyone but him, thin lines of black mist stretched from the rest of the Great Desolation and congregated on Mount Sumeru. The black mist entered the core of the sacred mountain with no one but the black-robed figure realizing.

"It's too slow," he muttered. He focused his gaze on the first mist-covered figure. "Accelerate the plan."

One of the others couldn't help but say, "But, Master, the three clans are already suspicious. If we speed up, they might realize the truth. Won't it ruin Master's plan?"

The dark figure stared at his subordinate. Although his eyes had no pupils, his gaze was obvious.

The mist-covered figure felt a chill crawl up his spine, causing him to shout, "Wait, Mast—"

But it was too late.

The lackey slammed into the ground, dispersing the mist and revealing his true form. He was a qilin with blood-red eyes and dirty black scales. Unlike the noble aura most qilin radiated, he radiated an aura of sin and destruction. The qilin spat out a mouthful of blood filled with black dots. "F-Forgive me..."

"You should know what to do, right?"

The other shrouded figures shivered and quickly obeyed.

"Then, go."

All of his minions flew away, even the injured qilin. If his clan asked him who had injured him, he could always blame the Phoenix or Dragon Clan, anyway. Instead of closing his eyes and resuming his meditation, the black-robed figure and his lotus disappeared from the surface of Mount Sumeru.

When the Master reappeared, he was inside the mountain's core. As the center of the West, Mount Sumeru housed the largest spiritual vein that connected all the West. As such, it exuded a wonderfully dense essence that was only exceeded by Buzhou Mountain. This density allowed it to become a holy ground for cultivation.

The black-robed figure had had to slaughter numerous other creatures in order to lay claim to this wondrous land.

The essence density would only exceed that of a surface, but the black-robed man hadn't come to cultivate. No, he had come to inspect his embryonic trump card. Inside the core of Mount Sumeru was a massive formation diagram that was continuously absorbing the essence of heaven and earth.

Although faint, the black-robed figure could see thin streams of black mist streaming into the formation diagram. Four indistinct shapes were forming inside the diagram, all equal distances away from another. Despite their incomplete state, the black-robed figure could sense a heart-palpitating aura emanating from them.

As his hood fell back, Rahu's face permitted a rare smile. "Hongjun, oh, Hongjun. The day my four Immortal Extermination Swords are completed is the day I step into the next realm and regain my place as a chaos fiendgod!"

He and Hongjun had been the two protagonists of the Fiend Tribulation. These modern names were meant to hide their true identities as reincarnations of the chaos fiendgods Pangu slew to create the Great Desolation.

As the Chaos Fiendgod of Destruction, Rahu had been among the top thirty strongest chaos fiendgods. He didn't know which chaos fiendgod Hongjun was the reincarnation of, but he likely wasn't even in the top hundred.

Many other chaos fiendgods had sent a part of their remnant souls into the unborn world, waiting to be reborn. Not all had succeeded. The fiends Shenni, Taotie, Qiongqi, Hundun, and Taowu could be considered incomplete chaos fiendgod reincarnations.

Most fiends were just a mass of malevolent emotions and desires, and few could recall their memories as chaos fiendgods. Even though Fiend Emperor Shenni retained some of his memories, he was still driven by the desire to destroy the Great Desolation. In the end, the three overlords, Hongjun, and himself allied together to eliminate the fiends.

Rahu's realm had exceeded the Golden Firmament Realm, so even if the three overlords united against him, he would not fear them. His main concern now was that he had reached a bottleneck and, no matter what he did, he could break through. He had a feeling that Hongjun would soon become his biggest obstacle. In order to progress further on his path, he wouldn't mind destroying the Great Desolation, much less killing Hongjun.

The former Chaos Fiendgod of Destruction gazed at the incomplete artifact with a gaze that could only be described as loving, but within that gaze was an endless abyss of slaughter and sin. "Dragon Clan, Phoenix Clan, Qilin Clan, kill each other. Kill all those that disobey you, extinguish all other life! The more slaughter, the better. How else can I speed up the creation of my trump card?"

Rahu's smile turned cruel, but it quickly vanished as he regained his indifferent bearing. He disappeared from the core of Mount Sumeru and appeared on the mountainside once more. Just as he was about to leave the West to personally take action, he stopped.

He turned his attention to a towering tree with branches that continuously split. The leaves that grew from those branches seemed to contain all the profundities in the world. Rahu flew toward the tree, and his eyes lit up with delight.

"It seems that my luck is quite good. I didn't expect to find one of the top ten connate spiritual roots, the Bodhi Tree, growing in my territory."

The Bodhi Tree hadn't opened its spirituality yet, so it still had instincts akin to a beast. When Rahu neared it, it started to vibrate, as if to warn him. If the Bodhi Tree could have, it would have plucked its roots out of the ground and run away.

"Stop resisting and obediently obey this seat, or else face destruction!" Rahu commanded.

The vibrations formed an invisible force to assault those nearby and make them dizzy. Although it didn't have much effect on the former chaos fiendgod, it still annoyed him.

The Bodhi Tree didn't understand Rahu's words, but its instinct told it that if it continued, it would undoubtedly suffer, so it stilled.

"At least you aren't stupid."

Rahu sat down at the base of the tree, closed his eyes, and started to meditate. Slowly, the corners of his lips curled upward. Although the shackle preventing him from breaking to the next realm didn't loosen, he could still feel his strength increasing, giving him more confidence to deal with Hongjun.

After some consideration, a triangular shard appeared in Rahu's hands. If Tongtian were here, she would have recognized the broken jade disk as a fragment of the Jade Butterfly Disk of Good Fortune. Even broken, it was still a top-grade cardinal spiritual artifact. The current Jade Butterfly Disk of Good Fortune had below-average offensive and defensive capabilities, but it was Rahu's most precious treasure.

Upon taking it out, Rahu opened his eyes and gazed toward the East. In a palace on Jade Spirit Mountain, an old Daoist held a fragment of the Jade Butterfly Disk of Good Fortune that was twice as large as Rahu's. Their eyes met for a brief moment before they both looked away as if neither had seen anything.

"Hmpf, safeguard your piece well, Hongjun, because it will soon belong to me," Rahu said, closing his eyes once more.

As time passed, an evil, baleful black mist began to shroud Rahu's body. If those without strength were to glance at it, they would have immediately gone crazy. While Rahu cultivated, Hongjun waited.

* * *

Inside the Violet Heaven Palace, Hongjun clutched his fragment of the Jade Butterfly Disk of Good Fortune. It had absorbed the laws of the chaos fiendgods Pangu had slain, so all 3,000 laws that formed the Great Desolation were recorded within.

Because it was shattered, however, the law records were incomplete. Hongjun possessed the largest piece, and Rahu had obtained the second-largest. Since the Fiend Tribulation, they'd both been collecting as many fragments as possible. Now all of its pieces were accounted for.

Both congenital gods had surpassed the Great Firmament Realm and were only a step away from the Primordial Origin Realm, but they could not break through. Each had a feeling that only after the other fell would they be able to progress.

The Jade Butterfly Disk of Good Fortune disappeared as Hongjun waved his hands for the doors of the Violet Heaven Palace to open. Two godss flew in, one in a black and white robe, the other in a light green robe. They too were reincarnations of chaos fiendgods.

"Fellow Daoist Yin-Yang, fellow Daoist Kunwu," Hongjun greeted them.

Yin-Yang Ancestor and Kunwu Ancestor nodded in greeting.

"Since both of you have arrived, you've agreed to my proposal?" Hongjun said.

"This is natural," Yin-Yang Ancestor said. "But after Rahu is defeated, you won't forget what you promised us, right?"

"Since I have promised you two, I will naturally keep my word," Hongjun said.

Upon hearing this, both Yin-Yang Ancestor and Kunwu Ancestor's eyes flashed with yearning and excitement.

Hongjun waved his hands and two prayer mats appeared next to him. Daoists Yin-Yang and Kunwu sat down to iron out the details of their cooperation. Three months later, the two former chaos fiend-gods left. The day Rahu took action would be the day the three of them besieged him.

* * *

The battle between the Dragon Clan and Phoenix Clan intensified. The small frictions exploded into all-out war. It no longer mattered whether the Dragon Clan or Phoenix Clan had offended the other. All that mattered were the piling grievances and corpses of their clan members.

It soon became clear that the Dragon Clan's members were stronger and more numerous than those of the Phoenix Clan. Compounded by their lustful nature, the Dragon Clan possessed many dragon-blooded descendants further bolstered their strength and numbers.

In light of the situation, the Phoenix Clan sought an ally.

Atop the tallest Parasol Tree in the South, the strongest experts of the Phoenix Clan gathered.

"Does anyone have a good idea?" Phoenix Ancestor asked.

One phoenix at the Great Firmament Realm suggested rounding up the remaining beast clans that had not sworn allegiance to any of the overlords. The Dragon Clan controlled the scaled beasts, the Phoenix Clan controlled the feathered beasts, and the Qilin Clan controlled the furred beasts. The beast clans that did not fall under the three criteria were few in number, and even if they joined the Phoenix Clan, they could not reverse the situation.

Another suggested gathering a large number of experts and ambushing a squad of dragons. With their greater numbers, they would surely bury the dragons with minimal losses, if any. This was also rejected because that would require relocating phoenixes from one battle to another. If they had possessed greater numbers, the plan might have been feasible. In fact, they had to be wary of the Dragon Clan using such tactics.

Idea after idea flowed out of the phoenixes' beaks, but none of them perfectly solved the problem. Finally, a member wreathed in blue flames suggested, "How about allying with the Qilin Clan?"

The Qilin Clan were the third overlords, and though their numbers equaled the Phoenix Clan's, they'd somehow managed to stay out of the conflict. While the Phoenix Clan and Dragon Clan warred, the Qilin Clan watched from the sides, their intent obvious.

"The Qilin Clan is an appropriate ally, but we will have to pay a price for them to take action. For them, the best situation would be for us and the Dragon Clan to suffer major losses, paving the way for their supremacy," Phoenix Ancestor explained.

Her subjects fell silent. Although a disparity existed between them and the Dragon Clan, the same wasn't the case with the Qilin Clan, who were surely watching the situation with devious expectations. Once the Phoenix Clan was weakened enough, they could swoop in to create a very unequal alliance.

Naturally, the Phoenix Clan had to think of a method to drag the Qilin Clan into war. Treasures were almost useless. As overlords of equal strength, whatever the Phoenix Clan had, the Qilin Clan also possessed. If they sent half or even a quarter of their treasures, the Qilin Clan might join the war, but it would also severely weaken the Phoenix Clan. Not all members of the Phoenix Clan possessed the pure bloodline of the Phoenix, so they needed resources to strengthen themselves.

Finally, a phoenix with black feathers wreathed in gray flames said, "Why don't we create a conflict between the Qilin Clan and Dragon Clan?"

"What do you mean, Mofeng?" Phoenix Ancestor asked.

Mofeng sneered. "We already know the accusations made by the Dragon Clan are weird. If they weren't so arrogant, they would know who the true enemy is. I suspect that this conflict was instigated by the qilins to weaken our clans."

His words aroused the approval of his fellow phoenixes.

Mofeng continued, "In that case, we'll pay back the Qilin Clan by using their own scheme against them!"

"Are you sure that is a wise option? If we expose traces of our involvement, it will only make the Qilin Clan attack us and hasten our destruction," Phoenix Ancestor cautioned.

"Great Ancestor, I will personally take charge of this operation." Mofeng's stance and words exuded confidence, bringing an inexplicable sense of reassurance. Of course, if Mofeng weren't so capable, the other phoenixes would have just called him arrogant. He wasn't one of their strongest, but if he wanted to hide, then not even Phoenix Ancestor could follow his traces.

"Since you will take charge of the operation, I'll leave it in your capable hands," Phoenix Ancestor said. Contrary to her words, she still couldn't shake the feeling of unease. She shook her head and chalked it up to the pressure from the Dragon Clan.

"Ancestor, I have another suggestion," a fiery-red phoenix said.

"What is it?"

"Why don't we recruit those two golden crows that live in the center of the Supreme Yang Star? As feathered beasts, they should obey the summoning of the Phoenix Clan."

Phoenix Ancestor sighed. "Anyone with eyes can see this war will be as tragic as the battle with the fiends. Who would want to join unless there was no choice?"

"It should be the two crows' honor to be valued by the Phoenix Clan."

"It won't work," Phoenix Ancestor said with a shake of her head. "Not even we phoenixes can ignore the power of the Solar Truefire of the Supreme Yang Star. Only those two golden crows can."

"Not even Great Ancestor can withstand the Solar Truefire?" Mofeng blurted out, shocked.

"It's not that I can't, but the price is too high. The Supreme Yang Star is an integral part of the Great Desolation. If I forcibly break into the core, ignoring the damage to my body, I would negatively affect the world, making our clan sinners. This isn't something I nor the Phoenix Clan can take at this moment."

"That's too bad," Mofeng said.

After this, the discussion came to an end. Mofeng left with a squad of ash-feathered phoenixes to carry out the plan while the other experts returned to the battlefield. Phoenix Ancestor did not budge. As the sole phoenix above the Great Firmament Realm, her only job was to counter Dragon Ancestor.

The battle raged on, and more than 100 phoenixes fell in as many years. It was clear now that the Dragon Clan possessed an overwhelming advantage, which emboldened them to move out of the sea and encroach upon the South.

Just as it seemed that the Dragon Clan would kill their way to the heart of the Phoenix Clan, a shocking piece of information spread like wildfire. At the juncture between the Dragon Clan's and Qilin Clan's territory, both sides had stationed a number of guards However, over 90 percent of the Dragon Clan's guards no longer existed because the Qilin Clan had suddenly invaded.

Blinded by rage, the Dragon Clan declared war on the Qilin Clan, dividing its attention. Although the Phoenix Clan and Qilin Clan had not allied, the Dragon Clan was now forced to fight a war on two fronts, greatly alleviating the pressure on the former.

****

"Dammit! Who schemed against my Qilin Clan?! Once I find out, I'm going to hang the culprit by their entrails and have birds slowly eat away at them!"

The top echelons of the Qilin Clan shivered as Qilin Ancestor stamped the ground, shattering the ground. All but one backed away for fear of drawing his ire.

A lone brave qilin with sea-blue scales, Qihai, stepped forward. "Ancestor, it must have been those despicable birds who wanted to drag us down."

Qilin Ancestor glared at Qihai. "Nonsense, do you think I don't know?! It's those damn dragons. Even a child could see this is a scheme, yet he still declared war on us? Does he have no brains?!"

After a bit more ranting and raving, Qilin Ancestor finally settled down with a final gnashing of his teeth. Like the Phoenix Clan thought, he wanted to be the oriole watching the mantis stalk the cicada. As they say, Qilin proposes and the Way of Heaven disposes.

"Speak. What ideas do you have?" Qilin Ancestor asked.

This time, an azure-scaled qilin exuding a calming aura spoke. "How about allying with the Dragon Clan?"

Everyone stared at him in shock and anger over such an outrageous proposal. The Dragon Clan had already declared war on them. Did they have to swallow their pride and beg them to reconsider? However, their leader still hadn't said anything yet, so these other experts of the Qilin Clan didn't speak out and rebuke the azure-scaled qilin.

"Go on," Qilin Ancestor said.

"Yes. As long as the Dragon Clan publicly states that the dragons killed were casualties of the Phoenix Clan, and they reimburse us for the damages they caused, we will ally with them against the Phoenix

Clan. Naturally, we won't send our full force. The best-case scenario would be for the Phoenix Clan to grind down the Dragon Clan's expert and make it easier for the Qilin Clan to become the sole hegemon of the Great Desolation."

"Your idea is good, but impossible."

"Why, Ancestor?" the azure-scaled qilin asked. In his view, the Dragon Clan should want to quickly exterminate the Phoenix Clan to focus on the Qilin Clan. Why waste effort on dealing with both at once?

"Hmpf, you, Qinglin, were born after the Fiend Tribulation, so you don't know how prideful those dragons are," Qilin Ancestor said. His eyes glazed over as he recalled the calamitous war that determined the fate of the world.

At this time, a qilin with ink-black scales and a man of ghastly flames stepped forward. Those near him backed away. Qilins liked purity, and this included members of their own kind. The soiled aura surrounding the ink-black qilin made them uncomfortable.

"Ancestor, how about allying with the Phoenix Clan?" the inky qilin proposed.

A frown appeared on Qilin Ancestor's face, but he didn't directly reject it. "Tell me your reasoning, Molin."

Molin paused. He feared that if he didn't give a satisfactory answer, Qilin Ancestor might punish him. He smiled helplessly. He'd only sought refuge with Rahu because his clan had alienated him for something that wasn't his fault. He didn't ask to be born as a sinful qilin.

"Answering Ancestor, instead of letting emotions cloud our minds, why not think logically? It's a given that the Dragon Clan will attack us. Even if the Phoenix Clan plotted against us, it's pointless at this stage. Instead of stalling and letting the Dragon Clan ravage our territory, why not ally with the Phoenix Clan? Revenge won't be too late after defeating the Dragon Clan."

Qilin Ancestor fell silent and digested Molin's words.

Seeing his hesitation and the pride in his eyes, Molin inwardly sneered. "Ancestor, we can also ask for some compensation from the Phoenix Clan. We know they attacked us, they know they attacked, and only the Dragon Clan would be so foolish as to blame us. If they don't compensate us adequately, we can threaten to attack them."

The qilins stamped their feet nervously. Although they weren't as arrogant as the Dragon Clan, pride was embedded in their bones, and they disliked such trickery. Still, they couldn't put their pride before the future of their clan.

Noting the hushed support for Molin's proposal, Qilin Ancestor made up his mind. "Send someone to contact the Phoenix Clan."

CHAPTER 9

End of the Dragon-Phoenix Tribulation

As Rahu schemed, the Qilin Clan and Phoenix Clan allied against the Dragon Clan. The battlefield became leveled and blood dyed the land red. The density of baleful air increased, causing a violet haze to shroud the skies of the Great Desolation. Black qi rose into the sky and condensed into streams that flowed toward the West, specifically Mount Sumeru. All three overlords turned a blind eye to these things, as if they couldn't sense the phenomena.

High above the Great Desolation, in the chaotic boundary that separated the world from the harsh chaos, was a small island. The small patch of land did not have a residence of any sort. Instead, a willow tree grew from the center of the island, and under the branches was a stone table. Inscribed into the surface was a series of dots and lines that formed a playing board.

Two figures sat on either side of the table, staring at the table filled with black and white pieces. One was an old Daoist wearing white robes, and the other was a man with brows longer than his beard. He wore plain gray robes and seemed almost undetectable, as if he and the space were one and the same.

The plain-robed Daoist placed a white piece onto the table. "You lost, Hongjun."

Hongjun's eyes flickered, and he sighed. "You're right, fellow Daoist Yangmei."

Yangmei waved his hands and the black and white pieces on the table disappeared. "Do you want to go another round?"

"There's no need," Hongjun said with a shake of his head. "This is already the fourth time I lost."

"No need to demean yourself. You and I pursue different paths. Your path is much harder than mine, and at the same level, I am not your match."

Hongjun didn't answer and faced that Great Desolation. "Are you really unwilling to take action against Rahu? You must know that once he wins, none of us can live in this world."

Yangmei shook his head with a knowing smile. "Is there a difference between being suppressed and killed by Rahu or you?"

Hongjun said nothing.

"There's no need to convince me anymore. No matter which one of you wins, it makes no difference to me or the other reincarnated chaos fiendgods. The Way of Heaven wants to exterminate us. The only difference is when and how."

"That's not necessarily true," Hongjun said. "With your talent, as long as you gain a strand of Grandmist Violet Qi, you can become a Saint of Heaven."

"Becoming a Saint of Heaven might be worth it for you, but it would only chain me down," Yangmei said. He turned his gaze away from the Great Desolation and toward the unending chaos. "However, I want to know if there's something else beyond here. I've always felt something strange since I was born, but I didn't know what it was. Even now, I still don't know, but I've vaguely sensed something."

"If that's the case, then I won't stop you," Hongjun said. "When do you plan to leave?"

"Now."

"So soon?"

"I've already waited long enough. Now, I finally have the power to roam the chaos."

Hongjun's eyes widened, his wizened face openly shocked. "You've already reached that step?"

"What's so amazing about this? I was already in this realm before Pangu killed me," Yangmei said without an ounce of pride. "I've simply regained some of my power back."

Without waiting for Hongjun to reply, he disappeared. Without him, the island began to shake and break apart, revealing the willow tree and its root. The tree transformed into a silver streak of light that flew away from the Great Desolation.

Hongjun floated in the chaotic boundary, unmoving, but his gaze never strayed from the direction Yangmei flew. After a while, he sighed. "You and I are different. Since birth, you've stood high and mighty as one of the top ten chaos fiendgods, but I, along with many others, could only scrape by at the bottom."

With a wave of his hand, Hongjun stored the stone table and disappeared.

* * *

The battle between the three clans raged on for tens of thousands of years. And not only did the battle's intensity not dwindle over time, it intensified instead. It was as if madness had blinded the three clans, and they would stop at nothing short of absolute destruction of their foes.

Originally, the Phoenix Clan and Qilin Clan had been equals, but after a period of time, both Phoenix Ancestor and Dragon Ancestor realized that Qilin Ancestor had fallen behind. Although all three were at the same level, both Phoenix Ancestor and Dragon Ancestor considered him the weakest. Qilin Ancestor knew it, too. After the battle with the Three Purities, Qilin Ancestor discovered that his cultivation had slowed down. He'd once rivaled Phoenix Ancestor, but now, he was weaker. It was more important than ever for the Dragon Clan to weaken the Phoenix Clan.

Still, Qilin Ancestor's ranking did not change the general direction of the global war. As rage and hatred continued to build, it eventually exploded into the climactic battle between the three overlords.

The ground quaked as it devolved into a wasteland from the clash of the three ancestors. Below them, their clan members slaughtered each other, dyeing the land red.

"Dragon Ancestor, obediently accept your death!" Phoenix Ancestor shouted as she flapped her scarlet wings and spewed flames from her mouth. As the phoenix ruler, she controlled the Nirvana Truefire, one of the top ten truefires of the Great Desolation.

"With just you?" Dragon Ancestor retorted. Burns and gashes littered his golden scales, but he still bravely charged through Phoenix Ancestor's flames and slashed at her with his claws.

"Don't look down on me!" Qilin Ancestor shouted as he charged toward the old dragon's back. His wounds were similar to those of Dragon Ancestor, though not as severe.

Dragon Ancestor roared and used his tail to whip Qilin Ancestor into the ground. After climbing out of the crater, he flew up to Phoenix Ancestor.

Five claw marks marred Phoenix Ancestor's body, but a flash of fire later, the scars completely disappeared. She had no injuries because she used the innate ability of the Phoenix Clan, Nirvana Rebirth, to heal herself. It came at a cost, however, as she had expended the most energy.

Still, none of the three had any thoughts of backing down. The fierce battle that consumed the world continued. Finally, after more than a hundred years, the three overlords collapsed onto the ground. They all struggled back to their feet, each determined to end the others' lives.

As they wobbled up, devilish laughter echoed in their ears. "Hahaha, this seat thanks you for your contribution!"

Flying out of Mount Sumeru was a middle-aged man with long black hair, wearing black robes. His eyes emitted slaughterous intent and exuded an evil aura.

With the appearance of Rahu, it was as if the veil of madness had been lifted from Dragon Ancestor, Phoenix Ancestor, and Qilin Ancestor's eyes. They shared a look and observed their surroundings. Everywhere, they saw the corpses and broken bodies of their fellow clansmen. Tears of grief streamed down their faces as they glared hatefully at Rahu.

"You schemed against us! The Phoenix Clan didn't kill my son, you did!" Dragon Ancestor roared.

"Haha, no need to thank this seat!" Rahu said. He opened his arms, absorbing the dense murderous intent that had suffused the battlefield. His aura grew until it left Dragon Ancestor, Phoenix Ancestor, and Qilin Ancestor numb with shock.

"As thanks for helping this seat, I will send you on your way," Rahu said as a plain black spear appeared in his hand. Just as he was about to pierce the three overlords, he stopped and stared into the distance.

An old Daoist flying on a golden lotus appeared. Next to him were Yin-Yang Ancestor and Kunwu Ancestor.

"You still dare to show yourself in front of this, Hongjun? You've had your chance, but you wasted it. Unlike Pangu, I won't give you a chance to rise again!"

Four swords appeared around Rahu. They had no embellishments on their hilts or blades, but they exuded a dangerous crimson light. Rahu clasped his hands together and the swords began circling around him as he spoke.

"Hidden under Mount Sumeru, they are neither copper, iron, nor steel.

"The reversal of yin-yang could smelt them. How can its edge be quenched without water and fire?

"Exterminate immortality, slaughter immortal monarchs, crimson light confines all immortals.

"Transforms all immortals into limitless miracles, golden immortal of the great firmaments shall be dyed red.

"Four Immortal Extermination Sword Formation, rise for me!"

Red and black qi formed from bloodlust emerged. The two qis expanded into a giant red and black lotus that covered the entire area, trapping Hongjun, Yin-Yang Ancestor, and Kunwu Ancestor in separate areas.

Inside the formation, Hongjun used the Twelfth-Ranked Golden Lotus of Merit to protect himself against the slaughterous sword lights flying about with the Four Immortal Extermination Sword Formation. He summoned a golden staff bearing nine dragons coiling around it as he stared warily at his surroundings.

"Hongjun, oh, Hongjun," Rahu mocked. "If you had brought another helper, this seat would have been vigilant, but you can't face the Four Immortal Extermination Sword Formation without four people at the same level. This is your loss. Wait patiently for this seat to send you off and achieve the primordial origin!"

* * *

Kunwu Ancestor's face paled as he resisted the vicious sword lights by covering his body in a protective light. A sword that resembled a spine with twenty-eight segments appeared in his hand.

This was his top-grade innate lifebound artifact, the Kunwu Sword. He had other artifacts, but they were too weak to be of much use here.

Kunwu Ancestor's expression turned ugly when the sword light parted to reveal Rahu. Above his head was a lotus, the Twelfth-Ranked Black Lotus of Destruction, and in his hand, a plain black spear. The spear was formed from the stem of the Thirty-Sixth-Ranked Jade Lotus of Chaos. Both were top-grade cardinal spiritual artifacts.

"You'll be the first sacrifice," Rahu said as he charged forward with a spear thrust. "Taste my Godslayer Spear!"

Kunwu Ancestor backed off and slashed the Kunwu Sword at the usurper. The sword's twenty-eight segments split and elongated, turning almost whip-like.

Rahu snorted and continued his charge. The Godslayer Spear struck the Kunwu Sword head-on. Under Kunwu Ancestor's disbelieving eyes, his lifebound spiritual artifact shattered instantly from the confrontation. Of the twenty-eight segments, only thirteen remained attached.

Kunwu Ancestor had no time to mourn his broken artifact as a black spear pierced his chest. His eyes widened as he opened his mouth to spit out blood, but nothing came out. He pushed Rahu and the spear from his body, but he still clutched his chest.

"My soul, you damaged my soul!" Kunwu Ancestor roared desperately, hysterically. He could already feel his memories fading as madness set in.

Rahu raised the Godslayer Spear above his head and smashed it down like a cudgel.

From another quadrant within the Four Immortal Extermination Sword Formation, Yin-Yang Ancestor sensed Kunwu Ancestor's death. Although Kunwu Ancestor was the weakest out of the three, that didn't mean he could be so easily defeated.

Suddenly, the sword light separated, and Rahu flew out. "You're next."

Yin-Yang Ancestor didn't waste his breath on needless words and summoned his artifact. A yin-yang symbol appeared behind him. This was the Taiji Diagram formed from a third of Pangu's Heaven-Opening Ax.

Under the black and white symbol, Rahu felt his consciousness and mind split. He roared and forced his mind and body to connect once more. The space around his speartip distorted, diverting the monochrome lights.

Yin-Yang Ancestor's eyes reflected Kunwu Ancestor's disbelief. Eyeing the nearing spear, Yin-Yang Ancestor quickly blocked the attack with the Taiji Diagram. Black light exploded from the speartip, launching Yin-Yang Ancestor and his spiritual artifact backward. Once he stabilized, Yin-Yang Ancestor stared at the Godslayer Spear in Rahu's hands with naked fear.

"Your spear can damage the soul too?"

"So what if you know? Your ending will not change!" Rahu boasted. He exploded forward again, spear poised to kill.

Yin-Yang Ancestor quickly retreated. He raised his hands above his head, and the Taiji Diagram floated above him. Golden Radiance shot of the Taiji Diagram as an illusory golden bridge came forth.

Rahu felt the space inside the Four Immortal Extermination Sword Formation change, and his expression shifted. A black light shot out from his speartip toward the golden bridge, but it harmlessly phased through.

The next thing he knew, Hongjun had appeared next to Yin-Yang Ancestor.

"I was wondering what you were trying to do, but just because you added another person doesn't increase your chances of survival. It'll only speed this up!"

Rahu reduced the range of the Four Immortal Extermination Sword Formation, causing the slaughterous sword light to condense and increase in density. In the outside world, the red and black lotus shrunk noticeably until it was only a tenth of its former size.

Dragon Ancestor, Phoenix Ancestor, and Qilin Ancestor shared a look. In unspoken agreement, all three started to attack the Four Immortal Extermination Sword Formation from the outside.

Rahu sneered. He sensed the external attacks, but he paid them no heed. Why should he acknowledge three pawns abandoned by the Way of Heaven?

"Now, shall we get back to our battle?" Rahu asked, his killing intent soaring.

"Don't presume victory so soon, Rahu. I still have a few tricks up my sleeve," Hongjun said.

"Oh? Then bring them out. This seat will break them all," Rahu proclaimed.

"Come forth, my three Corpses!" Hongjun called.

Green clouds appeared behind Hongjun, ridden by three figures bearing a striking resemblance to their summoner.

One of the three figures jumped off the green clouds, and a banner the color of chaos appeared in his hands. The second figure jumped off, holding a mirror in one hand and a flag in the other. When the third figure jumped off, it also held a flag in one hand, but it held a sword in the other.

"Pangu Banner, Apricot Flag of Central Infinity, Plain-Colored Flag of West Clouds?" Rahu was taken aback by the three spiritual artifacts of Hongjun's Corpses. Although the mirror and swords were still a threat, he had to eliminate the more powerful artifacts first.

Rahu no longer dared to underestimate his opponents. He rushed forward with his spear aimed at the three Corpses.

The one holding the Pangu Banner flew forward to block the Godslayer Spear. The Corpse was blown back but was otherwise unharmed.

The second Corpse shone the mirror on Rahu, issuing forth a silver light to capture him. Rahu felt as if everyone around him had sped up. The third Corpse came charging forward, golden sword in hand.

Rahu grabbed the sword. His skin sizzled and emitted a foul odor, but Rahu didn't care as he thrust his spear forward. The third Corpse waved the Plain-Colored Flag of West Clouds and blocked the thrust. The spiritual light dimmed and the Corpse's face paled, but he survived the blow.

Rahu was shocked to discover that all three Corpses were only slightly weaker than Hongjun himself. Madness erupted from his eyes, and he charged forward.

Either he killed Hongjun and stepped into the Primordial Origin Realm, or Hongjun killed him and ascended instead. There was no other possible outcome.

* * *

Dragon Ancestor, Phoenix Ancestor, and Qilin Ancestor found that the Four Immortal Extermination Sword Formation's defense had suddenly weakened. They redoubled their efforts and blasted the red and black lotus with all their strength.

Finally, their efforts bore fruit as a single crack appeared on the lotus. That single crack multiplied into uncountable fissures covering the whole formation. With a final bang, the lotus shattered, revealing the black-robed Rahu and Hongjun and his three Corpses.

"Hongjun!" Rahu madly bellowed.

Although Hongjun had won the confrontation, he didn't appear victorious. All three of his Corpses were clutching their chests with pale expressions—their foundation had been damaged.

Green clouds appeared behind Hongjun once more. His first Corpse holding the Pangu Banner returned, along with his second Corpse holding the mirror and Apricot Flag of Centered Infinity. Of note was his third Corpse. It had lost the golden sword and now held the Plain-Colored Flag of West Clouds and the Taiji Diagram.

"You've damaged my Corpses' source and hindered my way! You deserve death!" Hongjun roared, almost a mirror image of Rahu.

Suddenly, Rahu smiled and laughed as if understanding something. "In the end, we find that the Way of Heaven has schemed against us. You and I treated the three overlords as chess pieces, but are we not chess pieces of the Way of Heaven?"

Hongjun suddenly had a bad feeling, so he retreated, but Rahu ignored it.

Rahu's aura suddenly rose, exceeding his rival's by a large margin, but it was only the twilight before death. His body continued to grow and grow until it reached over 1,000 li. Above his head, a world manifested. Inside, there was no life, no prosperity, only destruction.

"So, this is the Primordial Origin Realm," Rahu whispered to himself. He raised his hands above his head and stared at the sky. "The Way of Heaven above, I, Rahu, see that the Great Desolation is incomplete. I will sacrifice my body to supplement the deficiencies. From now on, as long as one undergoes a heavenly tribulation, they must face the Inner Devil Tribulation! As long as the Immortal Path exists, the Devilish Path will remain forever eternal!"

As if in response, golden clouds of merit appeared above Rahu and descended upon him. He directed one last smile at Hongjun and then self-detonated.

Although he had reached the Primordial Origin Realm by force and would die within hours, he would still die a Golden Immortal of the Primordial Origin. His self-detonation shattered the Western Region.

All the spiritual veins broke, mountains shattered, the land split, and prosperity left. The West had become a barren land.

When the smoke cleared, a taiji symbol appeared. The symbol faded away to reveal a golden lotus. Hongjun floated beneath the Twelfth-Ranked Golden Lotus of Merit, looking haggard.

Clouds of merit ten times larger than the ones Rahu had summoned descended from the sky. Eighty percent of them flew directly toward Hongjun, but he remained sullen.

He had gained a lot from this battle, but he had to bear half the cause for the West's destruction. In the future, he would have to pay back the effect. The karma could hinder him from reaching the Primordial Origin Realm.

Ten percent of the clouds descended on the barren land, revitalizing it slightly so that life could appear once more. The final ones split amongst the three overlords. Qilin Ancestor wanted to curse the heavens when he received the fewest.

The other two weren't happy either. They had received tremendous merit, but it could not offset the destruction to the Great Desolation the three clans had caused during the war for supremacy. Because of the war, almost all the Karmic Luck their clans had gathered disappeared. If nothing was done, extinction would follow them.

Dragon Ancestor acted first. He sighed and then spat out the Dragon Pearl, which flew off toward the East Sea. It wasn't an artifact, but in the hands of a dragon, it could display the powers of a top-grade innate spiritual artifact.

Then, the Dragon Ancestor stared at the sky, much like Rahu had done. "The Way of Heaven above, from now on, the Dragon Clan is willing to guard the Four Seas and regulate the Wind and Rain. I am willing to offer my body to supplement the damaged lands!"

Dragon Ancestor's words echoed throughout the Great Desolation. His body exuded a brilliant light and transformed into countless tiny motes of golden light that disappeared into the skies.

"The Way of Heaven above, from now on, the Phoenix Clan is willing to quell the South's Undying Volcano. I am willing to offer my body to supplement the damaged lands!"

Seeing Phoenix Ancestor disappear into motes of red lights, Qilin Ancestor sighed. "The Way of Heaven above, the Qilin Clan is willing to transform into auspicious beasts and bring prosperity to the world. I am willing to offer my body to supplement the damaged lands!"

As Qilin Ancestor transformed into motes of black light, the tribulation came to an end.

* * *

Hongjun sat in the great hall of the Violet Heaven Palace on Jade Spirit Mountain with furrowed brows. He turned his half of the Jade Butterfly Disk of Good Fortune over in his hands. Because of the self-detonation, he had failed to recover Rahu's half, only looting a few treasures and the Four Immortal Extermination Swords, but not the formation diagram.

He fiddled with the disk for a bit and muttered, "Do I really have to become a Saint of Heaven?"

Chapter 10

The Titan Tribe

After the Dragon-Phoenix Tribulation ended, peace and quiet returned to the Great Desolation. It took seven eras for the damage brought about by the war between the three clans to slowly heal.

This ushered in the birth of a new generation of congenital gods. Their origin wasn't as pure and powerful as those born in the previous era—the Three Purities, Di Jun, Taiyi—but they were still born as Golden Immortals.

In the Darknorth Sea, farther than the North Sea, a leviathan swam through the icy waters. Its thousand-li body leapt gracefully into the air, transforming into a giant bird. With a flap of its wings, hurricanes formed.

Its name was Kunpeng.

Inside a cave on Buzhou Mountain, two eggs cracked and out slithered two figures. One was a man with the lower half of a snake, and the other was a woman with the lower half of a snake.

Their names were Fuxi and Nuwa.

At the base of Buzhou Mountain, hidden within a valley, existed a temple. Formed from Pangu's heart, this was the Pangu Temple!

The pool of blood in the center of the temple began to churn, and multiple beings crawled out of it.

The first creature resembled a yellow sac with six legs and four wings. His name was Di Jiang, created from the Law of Space mixing with Pangu's blood.

The second being had a red serpentine body and the head of a man. He was Jiuyin, born from the Law of Time mixing with Pangu's blood.

The third had the body of a bird and a human head, and he sat atop two dragons. He was Jumang, and he was born from the Law of Wood mixing with Pangu's blood.

The fourth had the body of a tiger but the head of a man. Instead of fur, silver scales lined his body, and two snakes slithered out of his ears. He was Rushou, formed from the Law of Metal mixing with Pangu's blood.

The fifth had the head of a snake, black scales, a dragon under his feet, and a blue python wrapping around his arm. He was Gonggong and he was born from the Law of Water mixing with Pangu's blood.

The sixth had red scales instead of black, the body of a man with the head of a beast. Two snakes pierced his ears, and he rode atop a fire dragon. His name was Zhurong, and he was born from the Law of Fire mixing with Pangu's blood.

The seventh possessed the body of a tiger, eight heads, and ten tails. His name was Tianwu, and he was born from the Law of Wind mixing with Pangu's blood.

The eighth had a human body, a snake in his mouth, a tiger's head in his hand, hoofed feet, and long arms. He was Qiangliang, and he was born from the Law of Thunder mixing with Pangu's blood.

The ninth came in a bird's form, with a human head, green snakes around his ears, and a red snake in his talons. His name was Jizi, and he was born from the Law of Lightning mixing with Pangu's blood.

The tenth had a man's head but long dog-like ears and a beast's body. He was Shebisi, and he was born from the Law of Storm mixing with Pangu's blood.

The eleventh had the body of a beast covered in spikes. Her name was Xuanming, and she was born from the Law of Rain mixing with Pangu's blood.

The last had a snake's lower half and a woman's upper half. In addition to her two arms, seven more sprouted from her back, each holding a serpent. Her name was Houtu, and she was born from the Law of Earth mixing with Pangu's blood.

These were the titans, beings that gained life from the twelve drops of Pangu's blood, akin to how his spirit formed the Three Purities. They announced their presence to the Great Desolation, aided by the Way of Heaven.

In the barren West, where Rahu had once made his headquarters in Mount Sumeru, a Bodhi Tree shivered. A bald man wearing golden-yellow robes calmly walked up to the top ten spiritual root of heaven and earth. "Don't be afraid, I'm here to enlighten you."

He sat down and began to preach to the Bodhi Tree. Many years later, the Bodhi Tree passed the heavenly tribulation and transformed. He clapped his hands together and thanked the golden-robed man. "Zhunti thanks Senior Brother Jieyin."

Near the Undying Volcano in the South were two bird eggs. One was golden with green light emitting from it, while the other was blue but shone with the light of five different colors.

The second egg wobbled and cracked as a beak pushed through, with the rest of its body following soon after. What emerged was a peacock with five tails; one each of red, black, yellow, white, and green.

The peacock seemed confused, as if it had just woken up from a dream. But the sight of black tribulation clouds forming above its head made everything clear. It spread its wings and fanned out its tails. "I am Kong Xuan!"

The tribulation clouds stopped gathering and, with one thunderous roar, disappeared.

Kong Xuan sighed in relief and turned its gaze toward the golden egg.

* * *

Inside the Three Purity Palace, Tongtian opened her eyes. She could sense that the secrets of heaven were no longer obscured. Plus, she'd have had to be deaf not to hear the heavenly oaths of Rahu and the three overlords eras ago.

She closed her eyes and began to calculate with her fingers again. Her fight with Qiankun Ancestor had proven that her battle methods were too crude and needed improvement. Since she specialized in sword arts and formation, she'd create a supreme sword formation.

Tongtian called it the Myriad Sword Formation because it primarily relied on the number of swords used to form it. She had already deduced three levels: the Ten Sword Formation, the Hundred Sword Formation, and the Thousand Sword Formation.

She was still working on the fourth level, the Ten Thousand Sword Formation. According to her estimation, its power would surpass Golden Immortals of the Great Firmament like Qilin Ancestor.

While creating this formation, Tongtian's cultivation did not stagnate, and she reached the peak of Advanced Great Firmament Realm.

Years of hard work got Tongtian no closer to the fourth level of the Myriad Sword Formation. She decided to leave it at that and left her room.

Entering the grand hall, she saw Yuanshi sitting alone. When she sat down next to him, Yuanshi opened his eyes and waved his hand. Hundreds of sword-shaped spiritual artifacts appeared in the air.

Tongtian accepted all of them and closed her eyes to cultivate. She could smell a medicinal fragrance, so Laozi had probably borrowed the Qiankun Cauldron to concoct some pills or elixirs again.

Many years later, Laozi exited his room. He returned the Qiankun Cauldron to Yuanshi and sat down on his prayer mat. While Tongtian tried to create her Myriad Sword Formation, both Yuanshi and Laozi focused more on their cultivation and reached the Peak Great Firmament Realm.

Tongtian took this time to speak. "Let's leave Kunlun Mountain and explore the rest of the Great Desolation. Last time, we had to return because of the tribulation, but the next tribulation should be far off into the future."

"We have reached a bottleneck in our way. Perhaps we may find inspiration in this trip," Laozi said.

Since Laozi had already agreed, Yuanshi nodded.

"Should we visit the Titan Tribe then?" Tongtian asked.

"Hmpf." Yuanshi turned his head. "Who are they to claim the orthodox lineage in front of us?"

"Don't say that. Since they are born from Father God's blood, they must have their own unique traits," Tongtian said. "I noticed this previously when I entered the chaotic space to search for Fangzhang Island, but our bodies are too weak. We may gain something out of it."

"Third Sister's words have some merit. Let's visit the Titan Tribe and see their abilities." As soon as Laozi spoke, the decision was already set in stone. The three departed from Kunlun Mountain and arrived at the base of Buzhou Mountain.

It wasn't hard to find the exact location of the Titan Tribe because they had eliminated every beast within 10,000 li. The Three Purities had chanced upon a member of the Titan Tribe exploring the land with a bow and arrow in hand. Unlike the twelve titans, the Titan Tribe members were not formed from any laws. They only inherited a fraction of their strength, so they became known as giants.

The giant archer looked up to see the Three Purities looking down on him. Although he could discern that he was weaker than them, he still notched an arrow and aimed it at them. "Who are you? Don't you know this is the territory of the Titan Tribe?"

Yuanshi snorted. The giant below him wasn't an immortal, but he had the power of a Golden Immortal of the Great Unity. Before he could punish the fool, Tongtian raised her hand to stop him.

Tongtian looked at the giant with interest. She could feel a vague sense of familiarity like that of a family member, although it was closer to a nephew than a cousin. "Take us to your leaders. Tell them that the Orthodox Lineage of Pangu, the Three Purities, are here."

The giant immediately said, "Impossible. The titans are the only descendants of Father God! Scram, or don't blame me for being rude!"

Not only did Laozi and Yuanshi frown, but so did Tongtian. All three released the aura hidden in their bodies. It pressed down upon the giant, causing him to fall onto his knees.

The giant's eyes widened in shock. He had felt this sensation before when he'd interacted with the twelve titans—but instead of the sensation of boiling blood, he felt something deeper originating inside him.

"Are you titans that were born outside the tribe?" the giant asked deferentially after they hid their aura again.

"We aren't titans, but the Three Purities," Yuanshi repeated impatiently. "Now, take us to your leaders."

The giant nodded. "Please follow me."

Along the way, Tongtian asked, "What's your name?"

The giant paused for a bit and said, "Houyi."

An explosion went off in Tongtian's mind. *He's that Houyi? The one that shot down nine out of ten suns?*

Though shocking, Tongtian quickly recovered from the revelation. No matter who she met, could it beat the shock of the moment she'd discovered that she had become the future Heavenly Venerable of Numinous Treasures?

As they ventured deeper into the Titan Tribe's territory, the Three Purities saw more and more giants. Not all of them possessed the power of a Golden Immortal of the Great Unity, but the weakest were still on the same levels as Golden Immortals. If you ignored the Qilin Ancestor, the Titan Tribe was capable of equaling or even surpassing the Qilin Clan.

Before they even reached the core of the Titan Tribe, Tongtian already felt a sense of danger. Even more than that, there was something calling out to her, attracting her. Laozi and Yuanshi clearly felt it too.

They entered a valley and were greeted by twelve towering titans. Tongtian realized what was calling out to them: the titans themselves. Or more specifically, the blood in their bodies.

All things are divided into yin and yang. Pangu's spirit is yin while his blood is yang. If they could absorb the titans' blood essences, they would be able to enrich their source and foundation.

Outright asking for their blood essences was impossible, of course. A war might directly erupt. Although, judging from a few of their belligerent expressions, a battle might be unavoidable.

As the eldest and leader of the Three Purity, Laozi stepped forward. "We have long heard of your fame. We are the Three Purities, the orthodox lineage of Pangu—"

He never had a chance to finish as Zhurong stepped forward and jabbed his finger at them, growling, "Shut up! What orthodox lineage of Pangu? We are his only inheritors. Fakes like you should scram while you still can."

Yuanshi sneered. "Who are you calling fakes, you fraud? I don't mind showing the difference between a real and a fake."

Tongtian sighed. It was evident that both of them felt the traces of Pangu on the other, yet they still clung to their false beliefs out of pride. She watched helplessly as Yuanshi sent his Three-Treasured Jade Scepter at Zhurong, who met it with a fiery punch.

Her eyes brightened when she saw Houtu, who exuded a down-to-earth and motherly aura. Tongtian was quite interested in this titan, who would sacrifice her life to form the Six Paths of Reincarnation and the Underworld.

Chapter 11

No Spirit

The moment Zhurong's fist connected with Yuanshi's Three-Treasured Jade Scepter, a shockwave echoed throughout the valley. The resulting explosion sent the jade scepter flying back several meters toward Gonggong.

Yuanshi's face remained impassive, but he inwardly raised his guard. Zhurong had the power of a Golden Immortal at the Advanced Great Firmament Realm. He would have to be careful without his artifact in hand.

Zhurong retreated over a hundred steps. His face turned ugly as he glared at Yuanshi. He prepared to charge, but halted at the sound of a taunting voice.

"Haha, Zhurong, you're too weak," Gonggong said as he rushed forward. "Watch me."

A watery veil covered Gonggong's fist as he knocked away the incoming Three-Treasured Jade Scepter. This clash vaulted it even farther away, but Yuanshi somehow still recalled it into his hold. Surprised, Gonggong took nearly fifty steps back.

"Haha, what are you so proud of?" Zhurong asked. "If I'd used my flames, I wouldn't even have taken a single step back."

"I'd like to see how you would fare!" Gonggong roared.

Zhurong didn't reply with words but with action. Fire shrouded his entire body as he charged forward. Yuanshi sent the Three-Treasured Jade Scepter at him again, but this time, it absorbed the flames on Zhurong's body and encased itself in red light.

Zhurong was knocked back a hundred steps again. Yuanshi sneered. "Is that all? You still dare claim to be the orthodox lineage of Pangu?"

"Don't get arrogant, we'll show you our true abilities now!" Zhurong retorted.

Zhurong and Gonggong used their innate abilities to rush Yuanshi. He still had a calm expression, but it took all he had to entangle them and prevent them from reaching him.

The two titans displayed abilities stronger than the average peak Golden Immortal of the Great Firmament, despite not using any artifacts. Wielding such powerful artifacts could've turned the tables, and yet neither did. Instead, Tianwu and Xuanming, the Titans of Wind and Rain, joined the fight against Yuanshi.

The Three-Treasured Jade Scepter absorbed Gonggong's and Xuanming's waters and Tianwu's wind, increasing its power, but that was not enough to hold off all four. Two finally broke past his jade scepter and reached him.

Yuanshi frowned. Fighting the titans was a bit troublesome. Not only did each of them have a powerful innate ability, but all of them were comparable to advanced Golden Immortals of the Great Firmament.

Just as two titanic fists hurdled toward Yuanshi, a cauldron appeared in front of him. The Qiankun Cauldron did not budge under the attack. The artifact attempted to swallow the two titans, but they resisted, retreating to regroup with their brethren.

The battle between Yuanshi and the four titans reached an equilibrium after this.

"They really are powerful." Tongtian said. "Second Brother would have been in trouble if they'd used their artifacts. Why don't they use artifacts? Do you not have any?"

While Yuanshi fought Zhurong, Gonggong, Tianwu, and Xuanming, Tongtian had flown next to Houtu's head. Of the twelve titans, she was the least belligerent and had a benevolent temperament.

"We have discovered some artifacts, but they are useless to us." Houtu's voice was deep yet gentle, bringing a sense of comfort. "We titans don't possess spirits, so we can't refine and leave a spiritual imprint on artifacts of any grade or type."

Normally, the soul was composed of three parts truesoul and seven parts spirit. The spirit protected the truesoul and added an additional layer of protection and abilities. If a living being did not possess a soul, they couldn't use those abilities and they would disintegrate after the body died.

Tongtian tilted her head. "This must be the price for your tyrannical bodies, but are you sure you should be telling me this? Our siblings are still fighting, after all."

Houtu smiled. "It's no big deal. You'll eventually learn of it. What's the harm in letting you know now?"

Tongtian nodded. Made sense. She turned her gaze onto Di Jiang and Jiuyin. Of all the twelve titans, Di Jiang radiated the strongest aura. If she'd had to guess, he should have been equivalent to a peak Golden Immortal of the Great Firmament.

As if noticing her stare, Di Jiang turned toward her. Tongtian smiled and observed Jiuyin. He was the one she was truly interested in, as she had already embarked on the path to understanding the Law of Time. Jiuyin's blood essence would not only increase her comprehension but aid her in creating a method to strengthen her body.

After it became clear that victory and defeat could not be decided without fatal injury or death, Di Jiang stepped forward and said, "Enough."

Zhurong, Gonggong, Tianwu, and Xuanming obediently stopped and returned to their position. Their indignant expressions made them look like children who'd just realized that they weren't the best.

Yuanshi snorted and stored the Qiankun Cauldron. He appeared pleased as he grasped his scepter once more. Since he could fight four of them at once, didn't that mean he was better?

"I acknowledge you have the strength to back up your claims as Father God's orthodox lineage, but we are the true inheritors of Father God," Di Jiang said. His words contained no arrogance, only supreme confidence, as if he was stating a fact.

"That remains to be seen. As one, I can fight four of you, and so can my two other siblings," Yuanshi said, not willing to appear weak.

Di Jiang shook his head. "No, it's true that the three of you might be able to fight the twelve of us, but we have a trump card. Once we unleash it, only death will await you."

"What's the trump card?" Tongtian asked curiously. Even if they did, couldn't they hide in Laozi's Heaven and Earth Pagoda? Its title as the number-one defensive artifact was not for show.

"I can't say," Houtu said.

"Figures," Tongtian muttered.

After that, the Three Purities left. Although both parties acknowledged the other's strength, coexistence was impossible. As the saying goes, two tigers cannot coexist on one mountain.

Per Tongtian's suggestion, they decided to scale the mountain again a few years later. In her words, "Since the tribulation is over and so are those pesky qilins, let's take some time to scour Buzhou Mountain for treasures."

No one thought they had too much wealth, so Laozi and Yuanshi agreed.

When they returned to Buzhou Mountain, they noticed the coercion had weakened. Perhaps in a few hundred eons, it would completely vanish.

Tongtian sighed. She didn't know what her brothers thought, but she could still recall Pangu's stalwart figure as he'd cleaved the chaos with his ax. Even now, she could not comprehend or understand the complexity of his ax strikes. To think that even such a mighty figure was not immune to decay.

The essence radiating off Buzhou Mountain had noticeably weakened as well. Perhaps in the future, it might no longer be the number-one spiritual mountain of the Great Desolation.

They found only a connate spiritual root, the Banana Tree. It bore several aromatic bananas and four leaves corresponding to earth, air, fire, and wind.

"Since I practice alchemy, I'll take the fire banana leaf," Laozi, storing it.

"I'll take the earth leaf," Yuanshi said.

"Then, I'll take the water leaf," Tongtian said. "What should we do with the final leaf? We can split the banana fruits but not the wind banana leaf."

After some deliberation, Laozi decided to take it. Because the fire leaf could control the flames for his alchemy, the wind banana leaf could be used to increase its strength.

"You don't mind if I take the rest of the banana tree, right?" Tongtian asked.

"Go ahead, but what are you going to use it for?" Yuanshi asked. "It won't grow any more leaves, and without the leaves, it won't grow any more fruits."

"It still has a good connate spiritual root. I'm thinking of fashioning the trunk into a sword," Tongtian said.

"How are you going to turn it into a sword?" Yuanshi asked, already dreading the answer.

Tongtian gave a brilliant smile and handed the banana tree to Yuanshi. "Thank you very much for volunteering."

Yuanshi opened his mouth to reject Tongtian's solicitation, but upon seeing her smiling face, he could only swallow his bitterness. Out of the three of them, Tongtian had the most artifacts—mostly because of his years of hard work.

Further searching yielded no treasure, so the Three Purities decided to leave and visit Fangzhang Immortal Island. Tongtian couldn't help but look back.

"Did you sense something, Third Sister?" Yuanshi asked.

"No, it's nothing," Tongtian said, averting her gaze. *I'll meet her in the future. There's no need to see her now.*

* * *

Inside a cave on Buzhou Mountain sat two figures, one female and one male. Both had the lower halves of a snake. This was no ordinary cave but a miniature world with a vast valley full of plants and animals—an immortal grotto.

"Brother, have they left?" Nuwa asked, turning to Fuxi.

Fuxi's face was deathly pale, and his fingers were moving so fast that they seemed like blurs. When they stopped, Fuxi wiped off the trail of blood that dripped from the corner of his lip. "They left."

"Did we have to hide from them? They didn't seem hostile," Nuwa said.

"But we can't leave it to chance. What if they are? In this world, there are many beings more powerful than us. The only way we can guarantee safety is to gain strength. We should enter the Great Firmament Realm as soon as possible."

"Then let's make haste. I want to leave this cave as soon as possible."

* * *

The Three Purities traveled to the East Sea and entered the boundary between the Great Desolation and the chaos outside. With the protection of Laozi's Heaven and Earth Pagoda, they quickly reached Fangzhang Immortal Island.

Tongtian led her brothers to the lotuses at the center of the island. While she'd been away, the three Ninth-Ranked White Lotuses of Purification had reached the peak of their power. Without a miraculous encounter, their ranking would never increase.

"Last time I was here, I didn't have enough time to fully refine and control the array," Tongtian said. "We'll talk about splitting the white lotuses after I take full control of Fangzhang Immortal Island."

"I'll take some of this Abyssal Sinwater and see what I can do with it," Laozi said, storing it in a gourd-shaped artifact he'd refined. He shook it experimentally. "The water is too corrosive for the container. If I'm not careful, the artifact will be destroyed or corrupted."

Yuanshi also found a spot and began refining the banana tree, as he still owed Tongtian more than 100,000 swords. Briefly, he wondered if he could even refine that many before dispelling that thought, lest he give in to despair.

Many years later, Laozi and Yuanshi stopped what they were doing and looked up. They could feel the island moving. Not long after, it entered the Great Desolation, and the chaotic sky that once shone above it turned into the sky of the Great Desolation.

Tongtian hadn't thought about it much, but day and night existed at the same time. Or more accurately, there was no day or night, only a single sky, which made for a strange sight.

"Okay," Tongtian said. "I've fully controlled Fangzhang Immortal Island. Even if you take out all the white lotuses that restrained it, the Abyssal Sinwater won't corrupt anything with the formation I placed above it."

The other two just stared incredulously.

"Well, what are you waiting for? Take your pick," Tongtian directed. "Oh, but leave a ninth-ranked, two-sixth ranked, and three third-ranked white lotuses for me, okay?"

"Third Sister, this is what you found, there's no need to split it with us," Laozi said.

"What's the harm? Aren't we siblings? Good things are meant to be shared," she said. "Now, hurry and pick some. They don't mean much to me since I already have the Twelfth-Ranked White Lotus of Purification."

At Tongtian's insistence, Laozi took a sixth-ranked white lotus. Yuanshi followed suit.

"Second Brother, take a few more. You've helped me refine so many artifacts, after all. You deserve them," Tongtian said.

Yuanshi's heart soared at Tongtian's words, a warm and fuzzy feeling rising in his chest. "Thank you, Third Sister. It's only natural that you found the Twelfth-Ranked White Lotus of Purification; it fits you perfectly."

"Hah?" Tongtian's face darkened. "Are you trying to call me a white lotus?"

Under her angry gaze, Yuanshi quickly apologized. *What did I do wrong? I just complimented her. I don't understand women.*

"Okay, since everyone got a share, let's search for Penglai and Yinzhou Immortal Islands," Tongtian said. "Since Fangzhang Immortal Island had Abyssal Sinwater and the Twelfth-Ranked White Lotus of Purification, I wonder what the other two have."

Laozi's and Yuanshi's hearts moved at Tongtian's suggestion. They quickly agreed and moved out.

"Oh, don't forget to share the treasures found on the island like I did, hehe," she said with a smile, causing her brothers to not know whether to laugh or cry.

The three immortal islands should have been connected. Tongtian used her control over Fangzhang Immortal Island to search for the others, but something was blocking their connection. They searched for many years, but they couldn't find hide nor hair of the other two.

"Unless they are also in the chaotic boundary like Fangzhang Immortal Island?" Tongtian muttered to herself. It made sense. After all, she'd only found Fangzhang Immortal Island thanks to the lotus seed in her possession. Suddenly, she looked up and turned her gaze toward the east.

A cloud of purple qi more than 30,000 li long arrived from the east. Following it, 10,000 flowers bloomed, their fragrance filling the Great Desolation. Beasts roared and chirped in unison as if to worship it while musical notes unlike any other descended, each filled with the sound of the 3,000 laws that formed the world. The voice of Hongjun rang out.

"High above the nine clouds, the truth floats free.

"Within heaven and earth, I shall enlighten all beings.

"Pangu, born of Taiji, formed the two rites and four cardinal directions.

"One way passes to three peers, two lights illuminate all seekers.

"The founder of the Immortal Path, one Qi transformed to Hongjun."

Chapter 12

Six Prayer Mats

After Hongjun's song drifted into everyone's ears, an immense coercion descended. In the first breath, almost every life-form kneeled under it. At the second breath, the third breath, more and more life kneeled, unable to keep their backs straight.

On the fifth breath, in the Darknorth Sea, Kunpeng couldn't resist it anymore and kneeled. In the South, the transformed Golden-Winged Great Roc knelt in his gilded robes. In West Kunlun Mountain, Xi Wangmu, the Queen Mother of the West, fell to her knees.

By the sixth breath, Minghe Ancestor fell from the Twelfth-Ranked Red Lotus of Karma and into the Blood Sea. In Firesource Grotto, Redcloud Ancestor collapsed onto his knees. In a cave on Buzhou Mountain, Fuxi genuflected.

The seventh breath brought down Di Jun in the Supreme Yang Star. Next to him, Taiyi continued to resist. In the West, Zhunti could no longer resist the coercion and fell to the ground. In the South, next to the transformed Golden-Winged Great Roc, Kong Xuan used all his might to try and rise. Nuwa reluctantly joined her brother Fuxi in kneeling.

On the eighth breath, the Chaos Bell above Taiyi's head continued to ring, albeit weakly, as he was brought to the ground. In the West, Jieyin put his hands together and knelt as if in prayer. On

Penglai Island, Dong Wanggong, the King Duke of the East, followed suit.

On the ninth breath, the only life still resisting was the Three Purities. Above Laozi's head was the Heaven and Earth Pagoda, above Yuanshi's head was the Qiankun Cauldron, and above Tongtian was the Twelfth-Ranked White Lotus of Purification. Still, they could not hold on a moment longer and fell onto their knees. Just as they kneeled, the coercion disappeared on the tenth breath.

"I, Hongjun, have become a Saint of Heaven! I have established my abode in the chaotic boundary. I will preach three times, and each sermon will last 3,000 years. The first sermon will begin in a thousand years. Those who have fate with me can come to Violet Heaven Palace."

After Hongjun's proclamation, the purple qi and all the natural phenomenons vanished as if they'd never existed. But every being in the Great Desolation knew it was not an illusion, because they were still kneeling!

"Who was that?" Yuanshi asked. "Even we, the Three Purities, had to kneel." They were the transformation of Pangu's spirit, no one in the Great Desolation had the honor or status to make them kneel, yet reality proved different.

"A Saint of Heaven, is that the next stage after the Golden Immortal of the Great Firmament?" Laozi asked, more to himself than anyone else.

"Whatever the reason, it's obvious that he is above us. Shall we attend his sermon?" Tongtian asked, even though she already knew the answer. Everything was playing out as in the tales from her memories.

"Of course," Laozi said.

Yuanshi was perhaps the most eager of the three of them. He

wanted to understand who could stand above them. Tongtian hid Fangzhang Immortal Island and, the three quickly flew toward the chaotic boundary.

When they reached the edge of the Great Desolation, hundreds of thousands of people were already there, ranging from normal Golden Immortals to Golden Immortals of the Great Firmament.

The Three Purities entered the chaotic boundary without giving the other people another glance.

"Feh, how long do you think they will last?" a Golden Immortal of the Great Unity asked.

"Who knows, but they don't strike me as simple," his compatriot said.

"Wait, they seem familiar," one immortal said. His eyes widened. "Those three are Kunlun Mountain's Three Purities!"

During their travels, the Three Purities name had spread far and wide. They didn't deliberately spread it, but their fame still rose. Upon learning of the three's identities, everyone present watched with anticipation to see how they would deal with the chaotic energy.

Laozi summoned the Heaven and Earth Pagoda over his head and covered himself in black and yellow light. Tongtian summoned her Twelfth-Ranked White Lotus of Purification and sat on it.

Yuanshi surprised everyone, even Tongtian and Laozi. He didn't take out the Qiankun Cauldron but instead directly absorbed the chaotic energy into his own body, which increased his speed the longer he was in the chaotic boundary.

"Kunlun Mountain's Three Purities, not simple at all," another Golden Immortal of the Great Firmament piped up.

"Second Brother, how are you absorbing the chaotic energy?" Tongtian asked. *How strong is your body?!*

"Third Sister, do you think you're the only one embarking on the path to comprehension? I've already started to comprehend the Law of Chaos," Yuanshi said, a slight proud smile on his face.

"As expected of Second Brother," Tongtian said, causing Yuanshi to preen under her praise. She turned toward Laozi. "What about Eldest Brother?"

Laozi continued to look forward as he replied, "Law of Infinity."

Tongtian sighed. Sure enough, none of the Three Purities were simple. She had thought she was amazing for starting to comprehend the Law of Time, but her two brothers were even more amazing. *Should I try to understand the Law of Spacetime? It seems that I'll need to get Di Jiang's blood too.*

The three searched the chaotic boundary for 500 years. Along the way, they saw many other gods and immortals, but mainly Golden Immortals of the Great Firmament, since those weaker almost all perished. Survival here was a coin flip even for those in the Great Firmament Realm.

Not everyone had treasures like they did or could absorb the chaotic energy like Yuanshi.

Finally, nearing the 600th year, the Three Purities found Violet Heaven Palace. It was situated on Jade Spirit Mountain, long-removed from the Great Desolation.

They discovered that they could only reach the foot of the mountain and couldn't fly up anymore. Just as on Buzhou Mountain, they were forced to walk.

A solemn palace awaited them at the top. The plaque above its entrance said Violet Heaven Palace. When they read those words, all three entered a trance. The intricacy of 3,000 laws was engraved onto it, yet it also gave off a sense of simplicity.

Tongtian first searched for the Law of Time and comprehended as much as she could. Afterward, she searched for the Law of Space, but she couldn't find it no matter what. *Am I not talented in the Law of Space?*

Finally, she could only give up. When she looked at her brothers, she saw they had already awakened.

"We appear to have arrived first. We can only wait for the gate to open," Laozi informed her.

Tongtian nodded, and the three sat in the lotus position, cultivating while waiting. To live in the Great Desolation, one must have the ability to enter a state of meditation at a moment's notice.

As time passed, more and more people arrived. Unlike the Dragon Clan, Phoenix Clan, or Qilin Clan, they all had humanoid forms. However, each one also bore non-human features: horns, fur, scales, or feathers on various parts of their bodies. Few, if any, were completely human-looking like the Three Purities.

All three siblings turned toward the two latest arrivals. It wasn't as if they recognized the two, but they felt a familiar sensation from one of them, the Chaos Bell.

Tongtian's gaze intersected with Taiyi's. As if time had stopped, neither broke the gaze. Yuanshi finally couldn't stand it anymore and moved in front of Tongtian, blocking Taiyi's line of sight. Tongtian frowned. Did that mean that she lost?

Taiyi started to walk forward, but a hand on his shoulder stopped him. He looked back to see Di Jun shaking his head at him, so he gave one last look at the Three Purities and turned to the plaque.

The two of them sunk into comprehension upon seeing the words Violet Heaven Palace. Few newcomers had been so absorbed by the plaque. Most of them just gave it a short glance and, aside from feeling it was profound, didn't think much more. Only Di Jun, Taiyi, Minghe, Nuwa, Fuxi, Dong Wanggong, and a few others gained anything from it.

"Fellow Daoist, we meet again."

Yuanshi frowned as he saw a red-haired man wearing red robes with clouds on them approaching.

Tongtian smiled. "Yes, we meet again, Daoist Redcloud." She introduced him to her brothers. "He helped me defeat Qiankun Ancestor, who I got the Qiankun Cauldron from."

"Haha, it's nothing, I only helped a little. Strictly speaking, I profited more."

Hearing Tongtian's introduction, Yuanshi's expression softened. "I'll thank you in place of Third Sister. If there is a chance in the future, I'll pay you back for this grace."

"It's nothing," Redcloud Ancestor repeated. "Still, I didn't expect fellow Daoist to be the famous Supreme Purity Tongtian. The fame of your beauty has reached far and wide."

Tongtian's expression darkened. *My beauty became famous, not my strength?*

Yuanshi glared. *This fellow isn't thinking of getting together with Third Sister, right? If he is, I'll teach him a lesson he'll never forget because it will be the last lesson of his life!*

Only Laozi's expression stayed the same. Redcloud Ancestor nonchalantly pulled over a Daoist with long white hair and beard wearing earth-yellow robes.

"This is my bosom friend, Zhen Yuanzi," Redcloud Ancestor introduced. "His Ginseng Fruits are the most delicious. Fellow Daoists should visit Wuzhuang Temple on Longevity Mountain sometime."

"Don't just invite other people into my home," Zhen Yuanzi snapped.

Redcloud laughed. "Why not? It's not like those Ginseng Fruits affect you anymore. What's the harm in sharing?"

Just as the conversation became heated again, mostly between Re-cloud Ancestor and Zhen Yuanzi, the door to the Violet Heaven Palace opened.

Two children came out, one boy and one girl. Both appeared as if they had been carved out of white jade and painted with rosy cheeks and ink-black hair. Just seeing them made Tongtian want to take them back to Kunlun Mountain with her.

These two must be Haotian and Yaochi, the famous Jade Emperor and Jade Empress of the future. Tongtian thought. Although they appeared like children, they were Golden Immortals of the Great Unity.

"Fellow Daoists," the immortals said in unison. "The thousand-year period is nearing its end, and Teacher will start his sermon soon. Please come into Violet Heaven Palace. Remember, do not make a ruckus."

Everyone rushed to the door, but the Three Purities were the fastest. Inside, there were 3,000 prayer mats, and the front row had six larger, conspicuous prayer mats.

The three immediately set their sights on them. Using their abilities and strength, they seized the first three mats. Laozi sat on the first, Yuanshi on the second, and Tongtian on the third.

The other guests greedily set their sights on the remaining three positions of honor. So as to not offend Hongjun, they did not directly clash and used their various skills and abilities to fight for the remaining spots instead.

With Fuxi's aid, Nuwa secured the fourth prayer mat. Just as Fuxi was about to fight for the fifth mat, a green-robed figure swooped in. He had a gloomy aura, narrow eyes, and a hooked nose.

Just before he took his stolen seat, a five-colored light erupted behind him, knocking him, Fuxi, and the others away from it. While everyone was delayed, a golden-robed figure sat on the fifth prayer mat, and the one who knocked everyone away sat behind him.

During the melee over the fifth mat, Redcloud Ancestor quietly occupied the sixth spot. Upon seeing this, everyone sighed and gave up. Some had ill intent in their eyes, but after remembering where they were, they gave up.

Tongtian, her brothers, and Nuwa all looked at the person sitting on the fifth mat and his companion. He really was daring, attacking people in Violet Heaven Palace and offending the majority of the 3,000 guests inside.

The golden-robed man bore some similarities to the azure-robed man who released the five lights. Her eyes pierced through his outer appearance and into his roots—a giant golden roc. In the front row, where everyone was at least advanced Golden Immortals of the Great Firmament, he stood out with his Early Great Firmament Realm cultivation base.

Tongtian sized up the man behind him. Where the golden-robed man had an aura like the wind, the man behind him had an aura of all five elements, and his original form was that of a peacock's.

Wait, a peacock with five tails corresponding to the five elements? Isn't that Kong Xuan, the Five-Tailed Element Peacock? Then the one in front of him should be the Golden-Winged Great Roc. They are the two children of the Phoenix Ancestor! Tongtian's gaze turned strange. *According to legend, those two aren't supposed to be born so soon, and the fifth prayer mat should go to Kunpeng. Did my arrival change matters so soon?*

Before Tongtian could finish that thought, her attention was drawn away by Haotian and Yaochi.

"The time is up. Close the doors to Violet Heaven Palace."

Haotian and Yaochi moved to shut the gates, but before they could, a voice called out.

"Hold on a moment, wait for us!"

Chapter 13

The Saint's Sermon

Haotian and Yaochi paused for a slight moment, and that was all it took for two yellow-robed figures to slip through. They made for a sorry sight with tattered robes and wounded bodies.

So these are the famous Jieyin and Zhunti, Tongtian thought as she observed them. *Yep, their heads are very shiny. Did Buddhists shave their heads because of them?*

She turned her sights on the fifth and sixth prayer mats. According to legend, the Three Purities sat on the first three, Nuwa sat on the fourth, Kunpeng sat on the fifth, and Redcloud Ancestor sat on the sixth—but the fifth and sixth eventually transferred to Jieyin and Zhunti.

Now that the Golden-Winged Great Roc was sitting on the fifth prayer mat, would things play out like the legends said?

Zhunti stared at the full room, zeroing in on the six occupied prayer mats in the front. He shared a quick look with Jieyin and burst out in tears.

"Ah, Senior Brother," he wailed. "We rushed as fast as we could from the West, but the journey was long and fraught with danger. The West is barren and we didn't have any protective artifacts. We almost died in the chaotic boundary. I can't believe that we rushed with all our strength, only to see this."

Jieyin sighed. Anyone who heard it would feel a sense of bottomless sadness welling from within them. "Speak no more, Junior Brother. It is already our fortune to be here and listen to the Saint's preaching."

"But we are the only gods from the West. With only the two of us, how can we bring prosperity back to the West and free all creatures of suffering?"

Wow, so shameless, Tongtian thought. She wasn't the only one. Although many showed sympathetic faces, few considered getting up. Some even showed outright disdain for their act.

Tongtian spared a glance at Redcloud Ancestor, who was clearly torn.

Sensing the need to turn it up a notch, Zhunti started sobbing. "I c-can't live knowing that the West is s-still suffering from the devilish aura. If that is the case, I might as well die here!"

To the shock of all the gods present, Zhunti actually charged toward one of the walls, seemingly intending to shatter his head on it. No one expected him to be so daring and rash. If he made the Saint unhappy, wouldn't it cause more misery for the West?

Unnoticed by anyone, a cloudy look appeared in Redcloud Ancestor's eyes for the briefest of moments. "Fellow Daoist, please wait!"

Zhunti's body slowed down, allowing enough time for Jieyin to grab and secure him. They both looked to Redcloud Ancestor, who continued, "There is no need to go so far. I'll give you my seat."

Tears continued to leak from Zhunti's eyes as a smile blossomed on his face. He quickly sat down on Redcloud Ancestor's spot. "Thank you, fellow Daoist. I'll never forget this kindness."

Redcloud Ancestor smiled back, but internally, he already regretted his decision as he felt a sense of unknown loss. Ignoring the disdainful gazes of the other gods and immortals, he sat down next to Zhen Yuanzi.

"You, ah you! Why did you give up your seat?" Zhen Yuanzi asked with exasperation.

Redcloud Ancestor only smiled back. He also questioned what had come over him.

Tongtian thought, *As expected of the Number-One Nice Guy of the Great Desolation.*

Zhunti's smile disappeared. He had a seat but Jieyin, the greatest benefactor of his life, didn't. Greed knows no bounds, and he turned his sight to the other prayer mats.

He had never heard of the fame of the Three Purities, but just from a single glance, he knew they wouldn't budge. In addition, all three were linked, so targeting one meant he would earn the ire of all three.

On the fourth prayer mat was a woman. Zhunti could tell that her cultivation and strength were not one bit weaker than his own. Furthermore, he saw another person supporting her from behind, so she was out of the question.

That only left the fifth prayer mat. The golden-robed man was an early Golden Immortal of the Great Firmament, the weakest one present. Even the one behind him that seemed to be linked with him was only an intermediate Golden Immortal of the Great Firmament.

"Who are you? How can you be qualified to sit with us?" Zhunti bellowed.

"Wha?" the Golden-Winged Great Roc let out dumbly, having never expected Zhunti to question him.

At this moment, Taiyi spoke up. "Fellow Daoist is right. What qualifications do you have to sit in the front with your strength?"

Di Jun wordlessly agreed. The two had grand ambitions, and they didn't want the Golden-Winged Great Roc to gain an advantage over them, especially since they were both avian creatures.

Under the pressuring gazes of all the gods present, the Golden-Winged Great Roc felt sweat drip down his face. Just as he was about to vacate his seat under pressure, a voice spoke up.

"Hmpf, my brother gained the seat with his abilities. Stop using your own failure to pressure him!" Kong Xuan said as he glared at Zhunti and the two golden crows.

"Your own abilities? Hmpf," Kunpeng derided. Out of all the gods present, he hated those two the most. He was just one step away from the prayer mat, but because of Kong Xuan's unexpected attack, he'd lost his chance. "It's true everyone competed fairly, but you broke the rules. Aren't you afraid of offending the Saint by attacking guests in his palace?"

Kong Xuan also snorted, not willing to show weakness. "Rules, I don't recall any rules about not attacking. Stop blaming others for your own stupidity."

"No, Fellow Daoist has a point," Nuwa said. Originally, Fuxi should have had a chance, but Kong Xuan's attack had injured him, causing her to hold a grudge. "Not attacking in the Saint's palace is basic respect. If you can't even understand that, neither of you deserves that seat."

Nuwa's reproach was the straw that broke the camel's back. As one of the six in the front, her words held great sway. The Golden-Winged Great Roc was about to move, but Yuanshi cut in.

"Flat-feathered beasts like you aren't worthy to sit with us, the Three Purities."

The Golden-Winged Great Roc caved and moved to sit behind his brother. Kong Xuan aimed a withering gaze at everyone, especially the Three Purities. He then glared at the Golden-Winged Great Roc, hating iron not becoming steel.

Jieyin seamlessly slid into the vacant prayer mat. He greeted Zhunti, Nuwa, and the Three Purities, but Laozi ignored him, and Yuanshi only snorted. He'd only spoken up because he found the Golden-Winged Great Roc displeasing to the eye. Gold feathered? Red feathered? What was the difference? To him, all those feathered beasts deserve eternal damnation for coveting his sister!

Tongtian wanted to kick Yuanshi in the shin. The Golden-Winged Great Roc was already going to leave, why did he have to muddy the waters? Not only did they earn the disdain of Kong Xuan, but Di Jun and Taiyi were glaring at them now too. Di Jun was going to become the Heavenly Emperor until Haotian could reign as the Jade Emperor.

Tongtian wasn't afraid of them, but that didn't mean she wanted to make enemies needlessly. Thankfully, there was a powerful ally who drew away their ire.

"This isn't right," Kong Xuan said, unwilling to give up. Finding that no one was on his side, he looked to Haotian. "Haotian, how can you let them get away with this? You should be ashamed as the Saint's servant."

Haotian's face darkened. Correct, he was Hongjun's attendant, but that didn't mean anyone could just call his name out like this—not to mention degrading him as a mere servant. "Fellow Daoist, be mindful of your words. I already turned a blind eye to your actions earlier. If you couldn't keep the prayer mat, you aren't destined for it."

"Haotian, you brat," Kong Xuan cursed.

At this moment, the air in the hall changed, and everyone turned their gazes toward the front, where a white-robed Daoist sitting on a cloud throne appeared. It was as if he had always been there, despite just appearing.

Hongjun scanned the room and observed each and every one of the gods present. Tongtian didn't know if she'd imagined it, but she felt as if Hongjun's gaze had paused on her for the slimmest of moments.

"From now on, the seating will not be changed," he said, staring at Kong Xuan.

Kong Xuan's expression froze, and a drop of sweat appeared on his forehead, but it soon returned to normal. He bowed his head and reverentially said, "As the Saint wills," along with the other guests at Violet Heaven Palace.

"Haotian, ring the bell."

Haotian nodded. After fully closing the gate to the palace, he walked up to the Purple-Gold Bell and struck it with a small golden hammer. The ring echoed throughout the hall, and everyone felt refreshed and focused.

"In the first sermon, I will preach the Immortal Path and the 3,000 laws. The Immortal Path is the method I created to refine essence into qi and refine the spirit with qi to promote the self and break through your limits."

The gods were overjoyed. Of all the guests present, less than half were Golden Immortals of the Great Firmament. Most were Golden Immortals of the Great Unity, and a rare few were Golden Immortals who'd managed to reach Violet Heaven Palace by luck.

They weren't like the Three Purities. All their inherited knowledge only reached the limit of the Great Unity Realm, and few, if any, of them could create a method to break into the Great Firmament Realm.

Hongjun's sermon was like an oasis for a man dying of thirst in a desert.

"Earth Immortals are the beginning of the Immortal Path. Earth Immortals refine yin essence and strengthen their spirit. However, their bodies are still weak and easily destroyed."

"Sky Immortals refine yang essence and strengthen the body, bringing balance between the spirit and the body. Once yin and yang are balanced, Sky Immortals are ready to ascend to the next realm."

"Profound Immortals merge yin and yang to transform their spirits and souls to achieve eternity and share longevity with Heaven and Earth. But their bodies are not strong enough, tipping the balance between yin and yang."

Hongjun suddenly paused, much to the confusion of everyone present. He opened his mouth, but it wasn't a continuation of his previous words.

"The Dao must not be transmitted to Liu Er!"

Hongjun's words didn't just echo inside Violet Heaven Palace. It also spread through the chaotic boundary and entered the Great Desolation, reaching every corner. In a certain mountain, a white-haired macaque with three pairs of ears on his head doubled over, clutching his bleeding ears.

Liu Er? Six Ears? The Six-Eared Macaque of the Four Celestial Primates? Tongtian thought, but she didn't have time to ponder more as Hongjun resumed his sermon.

"Golden Immortals refine their bodies with their spirits to achieve an unaging body and attain true immortality. They will not age, nor will they weaken with the passage of time."

"Golden Immortals of the Great Unity refine the five qis of fire, water, earth, wood, and metal in their dantian. When they merge all five, they achieve perfection. They will no longer be harmed by anything still trapped within the five-elements."

"Golden Immortals of the Great Firmament have jumped out of the River of Time. They are no longer bound by any constraints, allowing them to perceive the laws of heaven and earth. Only Golden Immortals of the Great Firmament who comprehended a law can lay the foundation to embark on the Great Dao."

Hongjun no longer spoke about the realms between Earth Immortal to the Golden Immortal of the Great Firmament, launching into a preliminary introduction to the 3,000 laws that formed the foundation of heaven and earth.

In the front, green clouds appeared behind Laozi. His three flowers released an unfathomable aura as his clouds changed from green to nothingness. They were present but indiscernible, nowhere yet everywhere.

Yuanshi's clouds changed from green to black with countless tiny motes of light. They exuded a chaotic aura yet radiated order—anyone who observed it would feel as if they had been transported into the chaos.

The clouds behind Tongtian turned silver and exuded a timeless aura. The petals that formed Tongtian's three flowers sharpened into blades that sliced through the silver clouds and controlled them. Any weak-willed being who stared into them would find themselves drowning in memories of their past and even see branching illusions of their future.

Nuwa's green clouds turned azure and exuded an aura of life and prosperity, bringing joy to any who basked in it.

Both Zhunti's and Jieyin's green clouds turned a golden yellow, but Jieyin's glowed with a brighter sheen. Anyone who observed the golden clouds would feel goodwill toward Jieyin, as if they were life-long friends.

Di Jun's and Taiyi's clouds turned a fiery red, like the surface of the Supreme Yang Star. Redcloud Ancestor's cloud now matched the eponymous one that he had transformed from. Zhen Yuanzi's cloud turned into an earthly yellow and exhibited a steady and firm aura.

The Golden-Winged Great Roc's green cloud didn't change, but his aura rose, and he opened his second flower.

Kong Xuan's cloud split into five. One of them kept the green color but exuded an aura of wood. The others turned red for fire, black for water, yellow for earth, and white for metal.

While everyone was still basking in the Saint's sermon, it suddenly stopped. Everyone reluctantly opened their eyes, like they had been awakened from a wonderful dream.

"The 3,000 years have come to an end. The next sermon will begin in 30,000 years."

Chapter 14

The Immortal Gourd Vine

Hongjun's figure disappeared just as mysteriously as he appeared, leaving many gods hanging. Several, including Laozi and Yuanshi, wanted pointers, but Hongjun never gave them a chance. Still, this did not give rise to any discontent.

"We thank the Dao Ancestor for this grace!"

Without Haotian's or Yaochi's intervention, all the guests dispersed by themselves. Everyone sought to seclude themselves and digest the knowledge they'd gained from the sermon.

The Three Purities didn't even bid anyone farewell, but that was par for the course. Only Redcloud Ancestor had the time, but only Zhen Yuanzi bothered with him.

"Zhen Yuanzi, am I hated?" Redcloud Ancestor asked.

Zhen Yuanzi covered his face with his palm. "No, you just can't read the room."

* * *

On the way back to Kunlun Mountain, the Three Purities paused near Buzhou Mountain. Tongtian felt something inside calling out to her. Judging from Laozi's and Yuanshi's reactions, she wasn't the only one.

"Should we check it out?"

"I do not see the harm. It's only a detour," Laozi said.

With that, the three of them made their way to the source of the calls, where they found remnants of an array. It must have been a natural array that dissipated recently, so they could just sense it.

At the center of the former array was a vine. It was not tall, but it had seven different-colored gourds hanging from it. Each one had yet to mature, yet they already emitted a purple-gold radiance.

"Third Sister," Yuanshi said.

Tongtian nodded and reconstructed the array that had been guarding the gourd vine. While she was at it, she added a few more defensive and concealment features.

The three had to wait until the gourds matured before plucking them. Tongtian stared at the vine for a moment before she realized what it was. "Could this be one of the top ten connate spiritual roots, the Immortal Gourd Vine?"

"If that's the case, then it is destined for us," Yuanshi said.

Tongtian nodded. The Immortal Gourd Vine produced seven gourds, and each one could be used to create a cardinal spiritual treasure. Of course, the grade depended on the artificer's skill and materials. She only felt a connection to one of them, and according to legend, her brothers would each take only one as well, which meant that the other four were destined for others.

The purple-gold colored gourd would become Laozi's. He'd mainly use it to store pills, but it could also absorb people and melt them down like the Gold-Horned and Silver-Horned Kings had tried to do to Sun Wukong. Although he escaped in the end, even trapping the Monkey King was a feat.

The second was the white gourd taken by East Emperor Taiyi. He'd later refine it into the Immortal Beheading Flying Blade, a top killing weapon. It would be used by Daoist Lu Ya during the Investiture of the Gods.

Redcloud Ancestor would refine the red one into the Nine-Nine Soulscatter Gourd.

The fourth was an orange gourd to be obtained by Nuwa. She'd merge it with the Demon Banner to create the Demon-Summoning Banner. Any demon who placed a strand of their truesoul into it would be at the mercy of the wielder.

The black fifth gourd contained an inner space filled with chaotic energy. Yuanshi had never parted with it once he got it, so not much was known about it.

The cyan sixth gourd was Tongtian's, and it contained the power of fire and water. Truth be told, she preferred Taiyi's white gourd for its affinity for metal, the element closest to the sword. She even preferred the color of Laozi's purple and gold gourd.

Tongtian didn't know what would happen to the final one. It was gray-colored and exuded a mysterious aura.

The Three Purities waited patiently for the Immortal Gourd Vine to mature. Some time later, Tongtian frowned and looked into the distance.

"What's wrong, Third Sister?"

Yuanshi's question was soon answered by the unmistakable ringing of the Chaos Bell. Not long after, seven figures arrived. In the front was Di Jun, followed by Taiyi with the Chaos Bell above his head, and five other guests from Violet Heaven Palace.

The two parties stared at each other in a stalemate. Di Jun was the first to step up and speak. "Fellow Daoist, I feel that this spiritual root has fate with my brother and me. What do you think?"

Yuanshi snorted. "Three of the gourds have fate with us three siblings. If you dare to take what is ours, be prepared for the consequences."

Detecting an arrogant tone, Di Jun couldn't help but frown. He quickly glanced toward Taiyi, but to his surprise, his brother showed no anger.

"What fellow Daoist said is right. The gourds will go to those fated with them."

Di Jun wondered if his proud brother had somehow been swapped with an identical stranger.

Taiyi saw Di Jun's strange look but ignored it. Instead, he took discreet glances at the goddess in red. Unfortunately, his line of sight was soon blocked by a black-robed middle-aged man who glared at him.

As the gourd neared maturity, two more uninvited guests came: Fuxi and Nuwa.

"Fellow Daoists," Di Jun greeted Fuxi and Nuwa, who responded in kind. Nuwa's eyes kept drifting toward the orange gourd, worrying Di Jun.

Upon seeing this, Di Jun's mind spun. "Daoist Nuwa, the Three Purities have claimed three of the seven gourds, as have we demons. If you don't mind, I can give one slot to you."

Fuxi's eyes narrowed. Nothing was free in this world, there was always a price. Still, he nodded to his sister.

"Then I'll thank Daoist Di Jun for your gift," Nuwa said. "But what are demons?"

"Demons are all the creatures born in heaven and earth. The Hundred Clans, you, I, and everyone are demons," Di Jun explained.

Yuanshi was already annoyed when Di Jun arbitrarily claimed three of the immortal gourds, but it seemed from his words that he considered the Three Purities demons too?

Unforgivable.

"Don't group us with you flat-furred beasts," Yuanshi said, radiating displeasure. "We are the orthodox inheritors of Pangu's lineage. We are different from you."

Di Jun frowned. "Daoist Yuanshi, don't you think you are too arrogant? All beings are born from Pangu; that means every one of us is an inheritor of Pangu's lineage."

All Three Purities now looked ready to start a war. Even Tongtian felt this, although she was stymied as to where the anger originated from.

Di Jun was shocked by the aura radiating off of the Three Purities. Tongtian had only been an advanced Golden Immortal of the Great Firmament when she entered Violet Heaven Palace, but now, she was a peak Golden Immortal of the Great Firmament.

More astounding was the energy coming from the siblings. After hearing Hongjun's sermon, Di Jun had converted half the essence in his body into qi, but it seemed that the Three Purities had already converted all their energy into qi!

Qi and essence were different on two levels. Even with nine of them present, including Nuwa and Fuxi, Di Jun wasn't sure they could defeat the Three Purities. The strongest member present was his brother Taiyi, thanks to the Chaos Bell. However, of the five he'd convinced to follow him, their top combat strength was only at the intermediate Great Firmament Realm.

To his surprise, Taiyi stepped out at this moment. Just as Di Jun began to worry that Taiyi would aggravate the situation, he took a step back.

"You can choose not to accept the label of demon," Taiyi started. "However, the emergence of demons is unavoidable. If you join us now, I can guarantee that all three of you will be demon emperors."

Di Jun wondered if this was an imposter again. However, he also agreed with Taiyi's proposal. If the Three Purities accepted, then the fledgling demon force's strength would be greatly bolstered. He'd just have to worry about the Three Purities' influence overtaking his, but that wasn't likely. He at least had that much confidence in his abilities and charisma.

"Taiyi, Di Jun, are you looking down on us?" Laozi asked.

"We respect the Dao Ancestor for his strength and knowledge, but to make us submit to you? You overestimate yourself," Tongtian said.

Di Jun frowned at their stubbornness. Without a doubt, they would become a variable when he conquered the Great Desolation.

As both sides entered a stalemate, Fuxi stood protectively in front of Nuwa. Upon seeing this, Yuanshi frowned and stood in front of his sister.

Tongtian looked down at Yuanshi's shin, feeling a strong desire to kick it. Who was he trying to compete with?

As if the situation weren't fraught enough, another unwelcome guest entered.

"Oh? Fellow Daoist Tongtian and Fellow Daoist Di Jun are also here?" Redcloud Ancestor observed, laughing delightedly. "Did you sense something calling out to you too? And it seems they are about to mature, so I'll just go ahead and pick mine."

Sometimes, Zhen Yuanzi wondered if Redcloud Ancestor was as tactless as he appeared. Couldn't he feel the tension between the Three Purities and Di Jun's group?!

Yuanshi snorted. "Cease your movement this instant. We came first, so we should pick the gourds first."

Redcloud Ancestor stopped. He wasn't offended, for he felt Yuanshi's words had logic to them. He motioned toward the Immortal Gourd Vine. "Please, fellow Daoist."

Yuanshi froze at Redcloud Ancestor's words, having never expected him to be so amiable. He turned toward Laozi for guidance.

Laozi closed his eyes. "There's still time before the gourds mature. Wait a while."

After this farce, peace settled between everyone. Not long after, the seven gourds started to mature and emitted an aromatic fragrance.

Laozi stepped forward and plucked the purple-gold gourd. "This one is destined for me."

Yuanshi plucked the black gourd just before Tongtian stepped up. She hesitated between choosing the white or the cyan gourd. She felt the cyan one calling out to her, but she wanted the white one more. Plus, Di Jun and Taiyi had said they sensed something calling out to them too. That meant Taiyi might know that the white gourd was meant to go to him.

Tongtian started to reach for the cyan gourd, but just as she was about to take it, she plucked the white gourd. So what if Taiyi was meant to get it? If she wanted it, it would be hers, just like the Chaos Bell.

As she flew back to her brothers, she turned her head and her gaze connected with Taiyi's. *Does he know? Does he want to fight?*

In the end, Taiyi said nothing. Without waiting for Di Jun to speak, he stepped forward and took the cyan gourd—the one Tongtain had originally reached for. While walking back, a smile graced his lips.

Di Jun graciously said, "Please, Daoist Nuwa."
Nuwa nodded and took the orange gourd.

Di Jun paused. Truthfully, he didn't feel any of the gourds calling out to him, but he'd simply followed Taiyi. He turned toward Redcloud Ancestor. Although he felt Redcloud Ancestor was foolish, he couldn't deny that he had a wide range of contacts and friends.

He smiled. "Fellow Daoists, after you."

"Thank you." Redcloud Ancestor didn't feign politeness and walked up to pluck the red gourd. He stored it away, feeling satisfied.

At this moment, the seventh gourd, which was about to mature, started withering. Soon, it would lose its source and foundation and degrade.

Redcloud Ancestor sighed with lament. "I hadn't expected this. There wasn't enough energy for the Immortal Gourd Vine to nurture all seven gourds, so the seventh gourd couldn't mature."

Di Jun's face darkened. He couldn't help but glare at Redcloud Ancestor, but soon turned away. He was the one who'd said it, so he couldn't go back on his word. He walked forward and plucked the gray gourd. It couldn't become a cardinal spiritual treasure, and it was hard to say if it could even become an innate spiritual treasure without a heavy investment.

Tongtian stayed behind as the others prepared to leave. She stared at the Immortal Gourd Vine for a moment before uprooting it.

Yuanshi immediately guessed her thoughts as she did so.

She noticed that the soil around the vine was unordinary. Thinking about it, how could ordinary soil nurture one of the top ten connate spiritual roots?

"It turns out to be Ninesky Blessdirt," Tongtian announced. Feeling a sudden presence, she turned to see Nuwa staring at her.

"Daoist Tongtian, I feel the soil calling out to me. Would you be able to part with some of it?" Actually, Nuwa had felt a sense of loss when Tongtian had touched the Immortal Gourd Vine, but she didn't harbor any fantasies of getting that from Tongtian, so she asked for the soil.

Nuwa was fully prepared to pay a heavy price, but she didn't expect Tongtian to smile and say, "Daoist Nuwa, we sat next to each other in Violet Heaven Palace. That means there is fate between us. Take half, it's just some soil."

Nuwa smiled after getting over her shock. Where was the arrogance of Pangu's orthodox lineage? She would reciprocate Tongtian's goodwill. "Thank you, fellow Daoist."

The Three Purities then flew back to Kunlun Mountain while Di Jun asked Fuxi, Nuwa, Redcloud Ancestor, and Zhen Yuanzi to stay.

CHAPTER 15

Above the Great Firmament Realm

Goodbye, fellow Daoists," Di Jun said, bidding Fuxi, Nuwa, Redcloud Ancestor, and Zhen Yuanzi farewell. Of course, he'd already gotten the locations of their residences, such as Redcloud Ancestor's Firesource Grotto.

"Brother, why didn't you invite them to join the demons?" Taiyi asked.

"You don't understand, their strength is comparable to mine. If they joined now, it wouldn't be conducive to my rule over the demons."

Taiyi nodded. "I see. Still, it feels like they got the artifact embryo too cheaply."

"Call it an investment. Speaking of which," Di Jun said, staring at his brother. "What was that?"

"What was what?"

"You know what I mean. I'm thankful that you didn't aggravate the situation by attacking the Three Purities like you usually would."

"Like I usually would?!"

"But for you to take a step, what a rarity. Taiyi, have you...?" Di Jun asked as pride brightened his eyes.

Taiyi's whole body stiffened in anticipation of his elder brother's next words.

"Finally matured?"

"Yes," Taiyi finally said after a long pause. He was thankful that his brother didn't find out, but why did he feel slighted?

Di Jun patted Taiyi's shoulder and said, "Let's go."

The brothers and their five other guests from Violet Heaven Palace set off.

For Di Jun's plan to work, they'd have to form a powerful force known as the demons. Unlike the Hundred Clans or the three Overlord Clans, all things are demons, so Di Jun could recruit every being who accepted the label of a demon.

Of course, to do so, he would need something to attract them. Just pure strength would not do. Thankfully, he'd attained the Dao Ancestor's cultivation method. He would use it as a reference to create a cultivation method suitable only for demons.

With the allure of the cultivation method, demons would flock to him. Sure, he would be losing precious time on cultivation, but this was related to his Way of the Emperor. He was already in the Advanced Great Firmament Realm, so it wouldn't take long for him to reach the Peak Great Firmament Realm. Besides, Taiyi was better at combat with him, so he would let Taiyi focus on cultivating.

Twenty thousand years later, demons began flocking to Buzhou Mountain, hoping to learn the Demon Scripture created by Di Jun based on Hongjun's sermon. This act earned the ire of the Titan Tribe. Soon, small-scale conflicts flared on Buzhou Mountain as both forces laid claim to the Great Desolation's best mountain.

The Titan Tribe went as far as to attack and kill any demons on sight, even if they weren't part of the Demon Clan. Before, they'd merely hunted demons for sustenance to fuel their daily activities and growth, but now it was war.

Di Jun didn't stop them. First, because the Titan Tribe had more powerful combatants, although they had fewer members overall. Second, an enemy like the Titan Tribe was conducive to the Demon Clan's unity. Third, the more tyrannical the titans were, the more demons flocked to him for protection.

* * *

The Three Purities secluded themselves in Kunlun Mountain and sealed it off, forbidding anyone from disturbing their peace. They'd gained the most from Hongjun's sermon and there was important work ahead.

All three had already embarked on the path to understanding the laws. Hongjun's sermon only scratched the surface of all 3,000 laws, but it provided a general direction to pursue further comprehension.

Before they could do that, they'd need to change their cultivation. Hongjun's cultivation method was broad and all-encompassing, but it was not tailored to them; they needed to create their own.

Only when their cultivation was truly their own could they advance to the next step.

Laozi created the Grand Purity Scripture, Yuanshi created the Jade Purity Scripture, and Tongtian created the Supreme Purity Scripture.

After that, Tongtian began to comprehend the Law of Time. She was born as a Golden Immortal of the Great Firmament, so she didn't need to use qi to upgrade her realm—which was both an advantage and disadvantage.

It was an advantage because it gave Tongtian strength. In the Great Desolation, strength was the key to survival. If they hadn't displayed their power, the twelve titans would have likely killed them on the spot to cement their claim as Pangu's orthodox lineage.

It was a disadvantage because she'd never experienced the breakthrough of rising from a lower realm. She could simulate the procedure, but there would always be deficiencies. Tongtian still would have chosen to start off strong, however.

Who would want to be born weak?

Tongtian didn't think she would have failed to reach the same height if she'd been born weaker, but being born strong had its perks. Had she been born as anything else, her origin wouldn't have been Pangu's spirit, which would have significantly weakened her potential.

In the future, when humanity was created, they were said to have more extraordinary talents than demons and congenital gods like her, but how many were able to reach the same heights? It was considered very impressive if they could become mere golden immortals.

According to Hongjun's Immortal Path, to ascend, you must refine qi. Since a Golden Immortal of the Great Firmament already merged the five elements into their qi, how should she upgrade the qi in preparation for her ascension?

The answer was the law.

Hongjun said that only the Golden Immortals of the Great Firmament could comprehend the law to form a foundation. That meant the key to improving lay among the 3,000 laws.

Tongtian placed her Qingping Sword on her lap and began to resonate with it. Although it only contained a part of the Law of Time, it was still more than what she understood at this point. In the future, once she surpassed the Qingping Sword, she would infuse her understanding of time into it to increase its strength.

During the sermon, Tongtian had focused mainly on Hongjun's explanation of the Law of Time, but she'd also memorized his explanation of the Law of Space for later.

Silver clouds appeared behind Tongtian as her sword hummed in resonance. The flow of time around Tongtian blurred as a timeless aura radiated from her.

In another part of the Three Purities Palace, Laozi opened his eyes and looked in Tongtian's direction. He held the Void-Refining Whisk in his arms, and his aura flickered in and out of existence as if he was an illusion.

"Third Sister is much further along than me in comprehending the law. I mustn't fall behind, or my title as eldest of the Three Purities would shackle me with shame," he said. He closed his eyes to ruminate on the Law of Infinity.

In another room, Yuanshi smiled in Tongtian's direction. Behind him were black clouds filled with tiny motes of light exuding an aura of chaos. He'd also come up with a method to upgrade his qi and improve his realm.

"Third Sister is doing well, but I can't fall behind. Otherwise, where would my prestige as an elder brother go? If I improve even further, Third Sister might even ask me for advice." Just imagining the scene made his smile widen. Yuanshi closed his eyes and doubled his efforts.

Time flowed like water as the silver clouds behind Tongtian slowly changed shape until they resembled a river of silver light.

At the head of the river, 3,000 monsters surrounded a single man. At the edge of the river's center, there was a blurry image of a violet palace atop a mountain with 3,000 gods listening to an old Daoist atop a cloud throne. The farther the river traveled from the source, the more it split until it resembled a tree branch.

Beginning from the source, a white ball bobbed along its waters. With each split in the silver river, the white ball also split into tinier balls.

After more than 15,000 years, the white balls no longer appeared, and Tongtian was clad in an argent aura. Her hair billowed as a powerful pressure emanated from her.

Her brothers soon opened their eyes as they felt the pressure. "Third Sister was a step faster."

The pressure exceeded Three Purity Palace and passed Kunlun Mountain's boundary. One thousand li, two thousand li, three thousand li, five thousand li, ten thousand li, fifteen thousand li, twenty thousand li, finally stopping at thirty thousand li.

Di Jun, Taiyi, Nuwa, Fuxi, Di Jiang, Jiuyin, Zhurong, Gonggong, Xuanming, Houtu, and all the nearby gods felt Tongtian's pressure. Grave expressions appeared on their faces as they felt Tongtian's strength exceeding the Great Firmament Realm.

Sitting in front of ten thousand demons, Di Jun glanced in Kunlun Mountain's direction.

"Did one of the Three Purities reach the same level as the Dao Ancestor?" Di Jun asked aloud. "No, although the pressure is strong, it hasn't reached the Dao Ancestor's level. And there are no miraculous changes between heaven and earth, so just what did they do?"

In a secluded chamber, Taiyi opened his eyes and experienced the pressure with his body. A renewed determination entered his eyes as he closed them once more. The Chaos Bell above his head rang.

At the core of the Titan Tribe, the twelve titans gathered in a circle inside Pangu Temple.

"We should head to Kunlun Mountain and kill them immediately," Zhurong, with his ever-present fiery temper, said.

"Don't be an idiot. Yuanshi was enough to fight four of us. Although we have gotten stronger, one of them has exceeded the limit of our level. Attacking them now will only bring us losses," Gonggong said.

"What, are you afraid?" Zhurong accused.

"I'm just thinking calmly, unlike a brain-dead fool!" Gonggong roared.

"Huh, you want to fight?"

"I don't come looking for fights, but I'll be sure to finish them!"

"You wanna say that again?"

"As many times as you want!"

"Enough!" Di Jiang said, glaring at his brothers. He then addressed the wisest of the Titans, Jiuyin. "What do you think?"

Jiuyin shook his head. "Now is not the time. Although we suppress the Demon Clan, they far outnumber us. If we take out the Pangu Genesis Formation now, it'll only cause the whole world to target us."

Di Jiang nodded. "For now, we will ignore them. Once we eliminate the Demon Clan and claim our birthright, we can eliminate the Three Purities if they don't know what's good for them."

All the other titans agreed, but Di Jiang saw that Houtu was deep in thought. "What are you thinking, Sister?"

"I'm debating whether or not to listen to Hongjun's sermon. The Three Purities achieved this only after returning, so there must be some secret."

"Alright, go, but take Jiuyin with you." Di Jiang wasn't stupid. Although they only worshiped Pangu, they wouldn't ignore the strength of the other party. If it came down to it, he believed they could kill Hongjun with their Pangu Genesis Formation, but the price would be too high.

* * *

Three days later, the pressure receded, and everyone sighed in relief, but just seven days later, the pressure appeared again. This time, it wasn't only from one source, but two!

Both Laozi and Yuanshi had surpassed the limit of the Great Firmament Realm!

The many gods of the Great Desolation wanted to curse. Did they listen to the same sermon? Why were they so different?

Those who learned of the matter redoubled their efforts to close the gap. Some even traveled to Kunlun Mountain, hoping to seek guidance. One such god was Burning Lamp Daoist.

He hadn't been lucky enough to attend the first sermon, but he had heard wondrous tales. Burning Lamp Daoist wanted to worship the Three Purities as teachers. Unfortunately, he couldn't enter Kunlun Mountain with his powers as a Golden Immortal of the Great Unity, so he could only lurk outside.

As the time until Hongjun's second sermon slowly approached, a heavy pressure came once more—this time from within Buzhou Mountain. Accompanying it was the ringing of a bell.

Tongtian, Laozi, and Yuanshi stopped their discussion in the main hall of the Three Purities Palace and glanced toward the source.

It seems I can't rest on my laurels for too long, Tongtian thought.

Chapter 16

Titans and Demons Clash

"What is the meaning of this?!" Nuwa shouted as she flew out of her immortal grotto.

Fuxi followed with a furious expression, clutching the Fuxi Qin, his lifebound innate spiritual artifact.

The two had been quietly minding their own business and digesting their gains from the Dao Ancestor's sermon. They'd even created their own unique methods of refining essence into qi.

Fuxi and Nuwa had attempted to comprehend one of the 3,000 laws expounded upon by the Dao Ancestor. They knew it was the foundation for the next step, so they wanted to prepare for the next sermon.

Nuwa was even under greater pressure than the rest. As one of the six people sitting in the front, she couldn't show any signs of weakness in front of the other guests of Violet Heaven Palace. She had thought she'd prepared quite well, but then she'd felt the advancement of the Three Purities in Kunlun Mountain.

Even Fuxi had to sigh at the Three Purities' talent and admit they deserved to sit on the first three prayer mats. Nuwa didn't say anything and just tripled her efforts. She wanted to break through the Great Firmament Realm before the Dao Ancestor's second sermon.

The pressure on her shoulders only increased when she felt a fourth pressure originating from somewhere on Buzhou Mountain. It was impossible for this fourth person to be another from the front row, unless Jieyin and Zhunti had traveled to Buzhou Mountain for some unknown reason.

Nuwa estimated she could attempt to break the limit before the second sermon, but fate was not on her side. She'd never expected the Titan Tribe to discover their immortal grotto and attack them at this point in time, ruining her plans.

The attacking army was composed of over a hundred giants, each at least equal to a Golden Immortal of the Great Unity. They were led by Zhurong and Qiangliang, the Titans of Fire and Thunder.

"Buzhou Mountain belongs to the Titan Tribe," Zhurong declared without an ounce of mercy. "All trespassers must leave or die!"

"You bullying oafs!" Nuwa shouted as the lower half of her body elongated into that of a snake. "We were born here, this is our home!"

"Who cares whether you are born here or not? If I say you are trespassing, you are trespassing! Trespassers must leave, and demon trespassers must die!" He spewed a fiery-hot flame from his sneering mouth.

She took out a lantern with a lotus pattern on it, the Treasured Lotus Lantern. Light shone out from the high-grade innate spiritual artifact and fell onto the giants behind Zhurong and Qiangliang. The light entrapped them in bubbles, leaving them unable to move or escape.

Fuxi held the Fuxi Qin vertically and started playing with one hand. The notes turned into crescent blades that soared straight at the two titans.

Qiangliang rushed forward. His roar shattered the land and rang like thunder. Fuxi's crescent blades all shattered under the sheer impact of his shout.

Fuxi grunted and retreated behind his sister. He placed the Fuxi Qin horizontally on his lower half and started playing with both hands. Musical warriors bearing blades sprung forth.

Qiangliang roared again, but although cracks appeared on the musical warriors, they did not shatter. Zhurong stepped forward and spewed a fiery breath that evaporated the incoming soldiers, forcing Nuwa to use her Treasured Lotus Lantern to block his attack.

With Nuwa's focus diverted, the treasured light on the giants weakened. Coupled with Qiangliang's roar, the bubbles popped, freeing the trapped giants.

With the addition of the hundred giants, Nuwa and Fuxi were slowly forced into a disadvantageous situation. Left with no choice but death, the two fled. Not only did Zhurong and Qiangliang chase them out of their birthplace, they wanted to exterminate them now.

"Do they really think we are so easy to bully?" Nuwa asked as she ran away with Fuxi.

"Sister, conserve your strength. If they send another titan at us, I'm afraid we won't be able to escape unharmed," Fuxi said.

It was as Fuxi feared, for the Titan Tribe sent Tianwu to pursue them. It should have been easy to escape just one titan, but he was the fastest among his siblings.

"I'll take your life, demons!" Tianwu shouted as he flew toward them with cyclones shrouding his fists.

Nuwa and Fuxi were trapped. They couldn't defeat Zhurong, Qiangliang, and the hundred giants, and they couldn't escape with Tianwu cutting them off.

"Sister, escape first. I'll come after you later," Fuxi said as he stood protectively in front of Nuwa.

"No, I won't leave without you! We were born together, and I won't abandon you."

"Stop being so stubborn! Only one of us has a chance to escape. You sat on one of the first six prayer mats, your accomplishments in the future will be limitless!"

"I only sat on that seat with your help! If it hadn't been for me, you would have sat on one of them."

"Stop being so stubborn and leave!" Fuxi shouted as sweat dripped down his face. "If you don't leave now, it'll be too late!"

"I want to see if the two of you are able to escape under my watch!" Tianwu bellowed, blocking their only escape.

Fuxi sighed. "It's too late now, sister."

"I have no regrets," Nuwa said as she faced off against the Titan Tribe.

The titans were powerful, but their moves were rough and unsophisticated, which allowed Nuwa and Fuxi to deflect their attacks with their superior skill. But one advantage of pursuing pure power was that it did not tax the mind as much. All it would take was one moment of carelessness for everything to go south.

After valiantly defending for hundreds of moves, Nuwa slipped up. She was knocked to the ground and spat out a mouthful of blood.

"Sister!" Fuxi shouted.

The instant he was distracted, Qiangliang appeared in front of him and struck him to the ground too. He vomited a mouthful of blood and bits of internal organs. Although he only appeared bruised from the outside, Qiangliang had used a sound attack to pulverize his insides. Had Fuxi not been knowledgeable in this aspect, his injuries would have been far worse.

"You're finished!" Zhurong shouted, closing in on the fallen with his comrades.

"You dare kill the members of my Demon Clan?" a proud voice shouted. Accompanying the voice was the ringing of a bell.

Zhurong, Qiangliang, and Tianwu were knocked onto their backs.

Taiyi slowly descended from the sky like an exalted ruler. "You damn brutes should perish."

Holding the Chaos Bell in hand, he charged at Tianwu, but Qiangliang quickly appeared in front of the downed titan to block the attack. The titan of thunder couldn't fully defend against the powerful strength behind it and was sent flying.

"Qiangliang!" Zhurong shouted. With eyes of fury, he expelled an incinerating column of red.

Taiyi snorted and placed the Chaos Bell in front of him, blocking the inferno. He promptly engaged the titans, brimming with killing intent. Although the titans were at an obvious disadvantage and were injured in each clash, Taiyi couldn't land a decisive blow.

He turned his gaze upon the hundred giants, and killing intent spilled out.

"Stop!" came Zhurong's furious cry, but Taiyi ignored him and set about killing the giants. In the end, Tianwu only managed to save less than twenty in addition to Zhurong and Qiangliang.

Taiyi didn't chase after them and instead focused his attention on Nuwa and Fuxi. "Are fellow Daoists alright?"

"Many thanks for Daoist Taiyi's aid," Fuxi said as he saluted Taiyi with a cupped fist.

"What's the courtesy for? I'm the East Emperor of the Demon Clan, it is only my duty to save all demons in danger. The Titan Tribe won't give up easily. How about coming back with me to the Demon Clan's headquarters?"

Nuwa and Fuxi shared a look. They knew what Taiyi wanted, but they nodded anyway. They could leave Buzhou Mountain and avoid conflict, but they wanted revenge!

* * *

With just 100 years until the Dao Ancestor's second sermon, the previous guests of Violet Heaven Palace traveled to the chaotic boundary.

The Three Purities were among the latest arrivals to Jade Spirit Mountain. Without talking to anyone, the siblings walked right up to the entrance and waited. Due to their superior strength, none of the congenital gods dared block them, only staring from afar with awe.

Twenty years later, Di Jun led a group of 500 demons to Violet Heaven Palace. The most eye-catching ones following behind him were Taiyi, Nuwa, and Fuxi. After Taiyi broke the limits of the Great Firmament Realm, many demons had willingly joined the brothers.

Tongtian didn't know if it was her imagination or not, but she felt that Taiyi was staring at her. However, whenever she turned to look, he was always talking to his brother. *Is it just my imagination, or is he holding a grudge over the gourd incident?*

Not long after, the two from the West came. They'd learned from their first mistake and left earlier this time. Tongtian's eyes widened slightly when she saw that Jieyin had also broken the limit of the Great Firmament Realm.

Sure enough, he has the talent and luck to become the Dao Ancestor's disciple. If the West weren't so barren, he might have equaled us, the Three Purities." Tongtian's thoughts halted to a jarring stop as she reviewed what she had just thought.

Although she admired Jieyin for his talent, that didn't mean she would praise him as her equal. The only ones capable of equalling them were the twelve titans, but she still thought she and her brothers were superior. Something had altered her thoughts.

Tongtian took another look at Jieyin and frowned. Whenever she looked at him, she felt as if she was looking at a long-lost friend or sword sibling. The more she looked, the greater the feeling became. *Just what law did Jieyin comprehend? It's terrifying to manipulate my emotions with just a look. Still, it's not enough.*

She wasn't the only one who had noticed. Laozi and Yuanshi did too, and they used their own methods to eliminate Jieyin's influence. An otherworldly and ethereal aura cloaked Tongtian's body. No emotion can stand the passage of time.

I can't underestimate him, but—Tongtian's eyes flashed toward Redcloud Ancestor, Kunpeng, Golden-Winged Great Roc, and Kong Xuan—*none of the others who originally sat in the front six seats and anomalies broke through their limits.*

She also looked at Nuwa with some disappointment.

Unbeknownst to her, Kong Xuan was also observing the ones who'd broken the limits of the Great Firmament Realm. The Three Purities breaking the limit was almost expected, but it was Jieyin's and Taiyi's breakthroughs that shocked him.

He and his brother, Jinchi, the Golden-Winged Great Roc, had also been invited by the Demon Clan with the promise of learning the method to break the limits of the Great Firmament Realm. Kong Xuan had scoffed and rejected the offer then and there, even clashing with the Demon Clan's messenger over it. He'd only left the messenger alive because it wasn't the time to have a falling out with the Demon Clan yet.

Kong Xuan correctly guessed that the method was nothing more than using a law to temper their qi. Once their qi broke the limits of the Great Firmament Realm, they used it to refine the self and break the limit.

He had already comprehended parts of the Law of Fire, Law of Water, Law of Wood, and Law of Metal. Now, he just needed to gain a glimpse of the Law of Earth to combine them into the Law of the Five

Elements. Still, he wondered what laws the Three Purities, Jieyin, and Taiyi had used to break through.

He didn't have time to ponder the question for much longer as the gate to Violet Heaven Palace opened. Haotian and Yaochi exited and welcomed everyone in. Haotian glared at him as he passed, but he didn't care.

After everyone sat down and Haotian rang the Purple-Gold Bell, Hongjun appeared on his cloud throne. Kong Xuan's fiery gaze focused on him.

"For the second sermon, I will explain the method to become a Quasi-Saint."

CHAPTER 17

Hongjun's Way of Three Corpses

Tongtian spared a glance backward upon feeling the familiar, intimate sensation. There, near the back, were Houtu and Jiuyin. Even with them there, there were still only 3,000 guests in Violet Heaven Palace. *Two gods must have fallen.*

Haotian rang the bell, recalling her attention to the front. Once Hongjun summarized what he would be teaching, a million questions ran through her head. As he wasn't taking any questions, she suppressed them and listened.

"Originally, the stage after the Golden Immortal of the Great Firmament was the Golden Immortal of the Primordial Origin. However, I created a method and a stage between these two, known as Quasi-Saint. To become a Quasi-Saint, you must sever the Three Corpses." Ignoring the confusion below him, Hongjun continued. "The so-called Three Corpses are the poison that exists in the body.

"The Upper Corpse is the Green Self. The Green Self causes blindness, creates bags under the eyes, forms wrinkles, and causes teeth to drop out. The Middle Corpse is the White Self. The White Self causes the body to never feel full, the bones to become brittle, and the flesh to wither. The Lower Corpse Corpse is called the Black Self. The Black Self causes concentration to dissipate, thoughts to diverge, and a desire to seek the company of others.

"The Upper Corpse resides in the upper third of the body known as the Jade Pillow Gate. The Middle Corpse resides in the middle third of the body and is known as the Narrow Ridge Gate. The Lower Corpse resides in the lower third of the body, known as the Hind Burden Gate.

"In addition to the Three Corpses, there are the Nine Worms. They block the three gates and nine orifices, absorbing misfortune and preventing ascension.

"The Nine Worms are the Crouching Worm, Dragon Worm, White Worm, Flesh Worm, Red Worm, Splitting Worm, Lung Worm, Stomach Worm, and Intestine Worm. The Nine Worms will distract you and burden your thoughts with material desires.

"To sever the Three Corpses, you must purge your body of the Nine Worms first. Then, the so-called severance of the Three Corpses is to cut off your good thoughts, evil thoughts, and obsessions using a spiritual artifact.

"Every time a corpse is severed, your Daoheart will rise a level. Your qi doubles and your comprehension of the law will become smoother. When all three corpses are cut, you will achieve the Awakened Mind State and be unaffected by unnecessary thoughts.

"From there, you will merge all Three Corpses back into yourself and achieve the peak of the Quasi-Saint Realm. You will only be a step away from a Saint of Heaven. From there, you only need a chance to enter Sainthood."

Once Hongjun finished, it was near the end of the 3,000 years, but he didn't leave or force others to do so.

Someone in the crowd asked, "Does the grade of the spiritual artifact affect the Corpse?"

"Any innate spiritual artifact can be used to cut the Corpses, but the grade of the spiritual artifact affects the strength of the Corpse.

The stronger the spiritual artifact, the stronger the Corpse," Hongjun said.

When they heard this, most of the gods present wailed in despair. Ignoring cardinal spiritual artifacts, only about one in ten of them had innate spiritual artifacts. Did that mean they could not become Quasi-Saints?

No, that wasn't right. They turned their heads to look at the Three Purities, Jieyin, and Taiyi. Hadn't those five entered the Quasi-Saint Realm?

"Is there any other way to enter the Quasi-Saint Realm?"

After a moment of silence, Hongjun answered, "Yes."

Before the 3,000 gods could rejoice, Hongjun elaborated: "The path is much harder than the method of Three Corpses. Without cutting any Corpse, you must comprehend a portion of the law and use that law to temper your qi. Using the tempered qi, refine yourself and enter the Quasi-Saint Realm."

While everyone was wallowing in the difficulty, Kong Xuan spoke up. "Is there a difference between entering the Quasi-Saint Realm using the law and the method of Three Corpses?"

"Yes. To enter the Quasi-Saint Realm using the law increases your foundation and chance of merging the Three Corpses."

"Asking the Dao Ancestor, what is a Saint of Heaven and what is a Golden Immortal of Primordial Origin?" Laozi asked.

"A Saint of Heaven is a Golden Immortal of Primordial Origin, but a Golden Immortal of Primordial Origin might not necessarily be a Saint. A Saint of Heaven can utilize the power of heaven and earth, while a Golden Immortal of the Primordial Origin cannot."

"Asking the Dao Ancestor, is the method of Three Corpses the only way to become a Golden Immortal of Primordial Origin?" Yuanshi asked.

"I know three methods to enter the Primordial Origin Realm. The first method is Pangu's method—use force to break the shackles and become a Golden Immortal of Primordial Origin."

Upon hearing this, most of the gods dismissed the idea. Pangu fell, didn't this mean he failed to enter the Primordial Origin Realm?

Unfortunately, they all had the wrong idea. Tongtian, who had the final memories of the Chaos Fiendgod of Time, knew that Pangu's strength exceeded that of a Golden Immortal of Primordial Origin. Even now, she couldn't discern his realm, so entering the Primordial Origin Realm with power was completely possible.

"The second method is my Way of Three Corpses. Sever the Three Corpses and merge the three. When the chance comes, you will become a Saint of Heaven. The third method is to use merit to become a Saint of Heaven. You also need a chance like the second method."

"Asking the Dao Ancestor, what is the chance?" Yuanshi asked.

"It will be revealed in the third sermon."

It was now Tongtian's turn to ask questions. "Asking the Dao Ancestor, does severing the Three Corpses affect our emotions?"

"You will still have your emotions, but they will no longer dictate your actions."

Tongtian nodded. "Asking the Dao Ancestor, I can sense the Three Gates but not the Nine Worms. Is there a problem?"

Hearing this, the people originally envious of the Three Purities couldn't help but gloat. Perhaps this was because they'd tempered their qi with the law and entered the Quasi-Saint Realm?

"The Three Purities are transformed from Pangu's spirit and thus do not possess the Nine Worms. You just need to discover your three thoughts to sever the Three Corpses."

The gods that had been gloating all choked on their spit. They initially thought it was a bane, but it turned out to be a boon. How can the world be so unfair?

"Dao Ancestor, we titans do not possess spirit and cannot comprehend the law. Are we not able to become Quasi-Saints?" Houtu suddenly asked.

All the other guests turned toward Hongjun. They had long heard of the Titan Tribe's ferocity. They dominated everyone at their level who did not possess spiritual artifacts.

"You can enter the Primordial Origin Realm with force," Hongjun said. "You are not of the Immortal Path; the Titan Tribe cultivates the Strength Path. Strengthen your flesh, and you will enter the Quasi-Saint Realm."

Houtu and Jiuyin inwardly sighed in relief. If they really couldn't become Quasi-Saints, they could only wait to be exterminated even with the Pangu Genesis Formation.

"I seek the consent of the Dao Ancestor. I, Di Jun, see that the Great Desolation is disorderly and full of hardship. I am willing to bear the burden to bring order and prosperity to the Great Desolation and unite all beings within."

Upon hearing this, the Three Purities' expressions darkened. Unite all beings. Didn't that include them? How could they willingly submit to Di Jun? Even the kindest titan, Houtu, was emitting killing intent at Di Jun, but her face remained impartial.

Hongjun stayed silent, making Di Jun nervous. He didn't need the Dao Ancestor's consent, but having it would legitimize his rule and increase the orthodoxy of the Demon Clan. Finally, Hongjun nodded. "You can."

Di Jun smiled as he and Taiyi kneeled and thanked Hongjun.

The Dao Ancestor's eyes revealed nothing as he focused his gaze on Dong Wanggong and Xi Wangmu.

"Di Jun will bring order and prosperity to the flood, but there must be leaders for the immortals. Dong Wanggong, you have great luck on your body and are transformed from the first strand of Yang Qi. You will be the leader of the male immortals. Xi Wangmu, you also have great luck on your body and are transformed from the first strand of Yin Qi. You will be the leader of the female immortals."

When Hongjun finished speaking, Di Jun struggled to hide his disappointment. The joy and elation on his face instantly evaporated. What did the Dao Ancestor mean by this?

Jiuyin and Houtu didn't care. They were titans, not immortals. The Three Purities didn't feel the same, as they were gods and immortals. They couldn't accept Di Jun's rule, so why would they accept another's?

Dong Wanggong and Xi Wangmu were oblivious to their anger. They were shocked by the Dao Ancestor's edict, and before they could react, he waved his sleeve. Two artifacts flew out and stopped in front of them.

In front of Dong Wanggong was a golden staff with nine dragons on it. "This is my former personal spiritual artifact, the Nine-Dragon Cane. Although it is only a top-grade innate treasure, it can rival a top-grade cardinal treasure and anchor your Karmic Luck."

In front of Xi Wangmu was a silver mirror that instantly drew Tongtian's attention. She could discern temporal and spatial fluctuations from the artifact. "This is the Kunlun Mirror. It can travel through space, trap your foes, and reveal the past, present, and future. Like the Nine-Dragon Cane, it is also a top-grade innate spiritual artifact."

Dong Wanggong and Xi Wangmu were dizzied by Hongjun's actions. They thought they had already reached the peak of their moods, but Hongjun had more to give. He flipped his hand, and a book flew toward them.

"This is the Ten Thousand Immortals Book. By itself, it is not an artifact, but it contains the Ten Thousand Immortals Formation. With it, you can repel all foes unless they have similar formations or are Saints."

Tongtian's eyes were glued to that book. Aside from swordplay, she was most skilled in formations, so the Ten Thousand Immortals Book was extremely attractive to her. She couldn't help but think that Hongjun was baiting her to attack Dong Wanggong and Xi Wangmu, but she quickly suppressed her rampant desires. Her eyes returned to their previous rippleless appearance.

Dong Wanggong accepted the Ten Thousand Immortals Book and kowtowed to Hongjun with Xi Wangmu. "We thank the Dao Ancestor for your trust. We will fulfill our duty and lead all immortals."

Hongjun nodded. "Alright, the sermon is over. The last sermon will be in 30,000 years."

All the guests left after this obvious dismissal. As Dong Wanggong and Xi Wangmu departed, many immortals—including Tongtian—eyed their newly gained treasures. None dared rob them of a direct bestowment from the Dao Ancestor, but things could change in the future.

Tongtian averted her eyes. She had a different target. She searched around and found a god covered in a bloody aura. He was Minghe, the lord of the Blood Sea.

The Blood Sea was formed from the turbid blood from Pangu's belly. As long as the Blood Sea existed, Minghe would never perish. This powerful god was so lowkey that only a few noticed his terrifying power.

"Fellow Daoist, please hold on a minute," Tongtian said as she walked up to him. Behind her, Laozi and Yuanshi followed, wondering what Tongtian's intentions were.

Contrary to her assumptions, Minghe wasn't ugly at all, and in fact, appeared rather otherworldly in his blood-red robes. He appeared in his mid-twenties, with pale skin and bone-white hair.

"So it's fellow Daoist Tongtian. To what do I owe the pleasure?" Minghe said rather pleasantly, if you could ignore his baleful aura.

"I have a transaction that you will be interested in," Tongtian said.

Minghe paused for a moment and nodded. "I'll hear you out."

The four flew back into the Great Desolation, stopping just short of the Blood Sea. Minghe wanted to escape if things went awry, but Tongtian pretended not to see his little actions.

She flipped her hand, and the high-grade Sixth-Ranked White Lotus of Purification appeared in her hand. "I want to trade this for three lotus seeds from your Twelfth-Ranked Red Lotus of Karma."

Chapter 18
Establishment of Violet Manor

When the Thirty-Sixth-Ranked Jade Lotus of Chaos shattered, it bore six lotus seeds. Of the six, Tongtian only knew of the Twelfth-Ranked Green Lotus of Good Fortune, Twelfth-Ranked Red Lotus of Karma, Twelfth-Ranked Black Lotus of Destruction, Twelfth-Ranked Gold Lotus of Merit, and Twelfth-Ranked White Lotus of Purification. All were cardinal treasures since they appeared during the birth of heaven and earth.

The lotus seeds born of these twelfth-ranked lotuses could not become cardinal, but they were connate. If they were refined into artifacts, they would be innate spiritual artifacts. In other words, they were perfect for severing Corpses!

Minghe stared at the Sixth-Ranked White Lotus of Purification in Tongtian's hand for a moment. He shook his head. "It's not enough. Once my red lotus bears three seeds, its vitality will be damaged."

"Then what if I add two Third-Ranked White Lotuses of Purification?"

Minghe's face struggled, but he still rejected Tongtian's offer. She wasn't mad as he said, "Unless Daoist Tongtian can offer an innate spiritual artifact, I can't part with any lotus seeds."

Tongtian could feel Yuanshi about to burst behind her, so she turned and glared at him. Her brother stopped and drooped his head like a kicked puppy.

She ignored him.

"Then what if I tell Daoist Minghe a method to make the Three Corpse Merging smoother?"

Minghe froze, as did Laozi and Yuanshi. If it related to proving their way, Minghe could even trade the Twelfth-Ranked Red Lotus of Karma if the price was high enough. "You aren't lying to me, are you?"

Tongtian smiled. "It's just conjecture, but I can guarantee that my guess is nine-tenths correct."

"Tell me," Minghe demanded.

"Don't be so impatient. Let's trade my three white lotuses for three red lotus seeds first," Tongtian chided. Seeing Minghe hesitate, she added, "I can vow on my identity as the Supreme Purity, I will not lie to you."

Minghe stared at Tongtian for a moment, ignoring Yuanshi's killing intent, and nodded. Blood clouds appeared behind, and a red lotus flew out of them and into his hand. The Twelfth-Ranked Red Lotus of Karma shuddered for a moment and produced three seeds.

After exchanging the white lotuses for the seeds, Tongtian smiled. "Fellow Daoist made a wise choice. Recall that the Dao Ancestor said we must cut off the Three Corpses with a spiritual artifact."

Minghe nodded. "Get on with it."

"Patience," Tongtian said. "After cutting them, you must merge them again. Once a Corpse is severed, it will take on the spiritual artifact's source. If all three Corpses are severed from the same source, won't the merging process be simpler?"

It was simple logic, but it thundered in Minghe's mind. Laozi and Yuanshi felt as if Tongtian's words had exploded in their heads too.

There was a fiery gaze in Minghe's eyes. He thanked Tongtian and flew back into the Blood Sea. The Sixth-Ranked White Lotus of Purification and the two Third-Ranked White Lotuses of Purification gave him a chance to produce a Ninth-Ranked White Lotus of Purification.

"Third Sister, is what you said true?" Laozi asked.

"It's just my theory, but it should be true. I actually suspect that if you used three spiritual artifacts with different sources, you might not be able to merge them in the end," Tongtian said.

Yuanshi sighed. "Third Sister is wise."

Tongtian smiled mischievously. "Brothers, do you still not want the two Ninth-Ranked White Lotuses of Purification?"

Hearing this, Laozi and Yuanshi were stymied. Laozi recovered first, saying, "No need. With my abilities, I can nurture it to the ninth rank."

"But are you better off investing the resources into the red and green lotus seeds? We need all three, after all," Tongtian said.

Laozi paused. "Then I'll thank Third Sister for this grace."

"Haha, what's the courtesy for? Aren't we siblings? We also need your help to nurture the lotus seeds. Isn't that right, Second Brother?" Tongtian asked, looking at Yuanshi.

He nodded. "Then I can only indebt myself to Third Sister and Eldest Brother for now. In the future, I will definitely repay it."

The three siblings happily flew to the East Sea, where Fangzhang Immortal Island was located. Once there, Laozi prepared to plant three red and three green lotus seeds .

Tongtian prepared to cut off her evil thoughts into her Evil Corpse. It might be difficult for others to sense their evil thoughts, but for Tongtian, it was easy.

* * *

Dong Wanggong led Xi Wangmu and several other gods who wanted to join him to his residence. They didn't follow Dong Wanggong because of his personal strength, but because the Dao Ancestor was backing him. He now had a brighter future than even Di Jun.

Di Jun took all of this in. A hint of ruthlessness flashed through his eyes as he led his followers back to Buzhou Mountain. Still, a few of the Violet Heaven Palace guests followed him. Since the Dao Ancestor acquiesced to Di Jun's rule, didn't this mean that the Dao Ancestor supported him too?

It was simply a difference between ruling the Great Desolation or immortals.

When Di Jun returned to Buzhou Mountain, he found the Demon Clan's headquarters half-demolished. Taking a deep breath, he curbed the urge to seek revenge and instead asked for the casualties. Luckily, it looked worse than it appeared. Di Jun had already been on guard for the Titan Tribe's attack while the Demon Clan's most powerful force was away listening to the Dao Ancestor's sermon.

Still, this situation could not remain. He summoned the Ten Demon Sages, the top ten most powerful demons of their clan.

"Tell me, where should the Demon Clan migrate to? We need a better place to live—someplace defendable," Di Jun said.

The Ten Demon Sages looked at another, not knowing what to say.

Finally Bai Ze, the wisest of them all, came forward. "Answering Your Majesty, why not search for one of the three immortal islands? I heard that Daoist Tongtian discovered Fangzhang Immortal Island. Why don't we search for Penglai or Yinzhou Immortal Island?"

"Your suggestion is feasible, but I heard that Fangzhang Immortal Island is less than 1,000 li large. It's impossible to fit all the demons on such a small piece of land."

Bai Ze, for all his wisdom, could not solve the demon emperor's problem.

Di Jun sighed and waved his hand. "Go back and instruct the Demon Clan to search for suitable land to inhabit. Oh, and summon Fuxi."

"As Your Majesty commands," Bai Zei said as he and the other demon sages retreated.

Not long later, Fuxi arrived. Although he and his sister both possessed strength that exceeded the Ten Demon Sages, Di Jun had yet to give them an official position. This was not because he didn't want to, but because the time wasn't right.

"Your Majesty summoned me?" Fuxi respectfully asked.

Di Jun nodded. "If I recall correctly, Daoist Fuxi is most skilled in formations."

"I have some minor achievements, but I have heard that Daoist Tongtian of the Three Purities has even higher achievements."

"You don't have to be so humble. In the near future, I believe you will surpass her," Di Jun said, much to Fuxi's confusion. Majestic purple clouds appeared behind him as he pulled out the Celestial River Diagram.

Di Jun caressed his lifebound artifact. He'd been born with two lifebound artifacts, but the Celestial River Diagram was a top-grade innate spiritual artifact, so he'd always favored it. The Gold Sun Wheel was only a high-grade innate spiritual artifact, after all.

"This is my lifebound artifact, and I have always kept it close. I noticed that there seems to be an embryonic formation hidden within, linked to the stars in the Starry Sky," Di Jun said, offering it to Fuxi. "I want you to decipher the formation within. I believe that it won't be inferior to the Ten Thousand Immortals Array spoken about by the Dao Ancestor."

"Your Majesty, you mustn't," Fuxi said. "This is Your Majesty's lifebound weapon. You must not hand it over to others."

"But the Demon Clan needs the formations as soon as possible. I cannot selfishly hoard it."

"Your Majesty can ruminate on the formation yourself."

"I said that it's for the future of the Demon Clan. I have confidence in your formation attainments, and I believe Daoist Fuxi's character."

Fuxi's eyes widened as he felt his emotions move. He no longer pushed the Celestial River Diagram back but accepted it. "I won't let Your Majesty down."

Di Jun smiled and began cultivating. He didn't need to micromanage the Demon Clan with the aid of the Ten Demon Sages. He planned to enter the Quasi-Saint Realm by severing his corpse using his Golden Sun Wheel.

After 100 years, his expression darkened. The Demon Clan had finally found traces of Penglai Immortal Island, but it already had an owner, and that owner was Dong Wanggong!

* * *

When Jiuyin and Houtu returned to the Titan Tribe with news of the Quasi-Saint Realm, Di Jiang had a headache. The original high spirits from raiding the Demon Clan's territory disappeared.

"Let's use the Pangu Genesis Formation and exterminate those three-legged crows," Zhurong, the war hawk, immediately suggested.

For once, Gonggong didn't contradict him, causing the Titan of Fire to shoot furtive glances at the Titan of Water, waiting for the inevitable conflict. But when Gonggong stayed silent, Zhurong felt a strange sense of loss.

In fact, many of the titans held the same opinion.

As the suggestion became more and more optimistic, Di Jiang

opened his mouth. "After we destroy the Demon Clan, can we continue to use the Pangu Genesis to destroy all the other Quasi-Saints?"

Everyone fell silent.

"Rather than delaying the inevitable, we must find a method to strengthen ourselves," Di Jiang continued. "The Dao Ancestor said we cultivate the Strength Path, and there must be a method to break into the Quasi-Saint Realm. If we don't know it, then there is only one place that holds the answer."

All of the titans knew Di Jiang was referring to the blood pool inside Pangu Temple that birthed them. After creating the twelve titans and the giants, the blood pool had lost much of its energy, so Di Jiang had ordered the Titan Tribe to hunt for creatures of flesh to restore the pool's vitality.

Without the blood pool, the Titan Tribe's reproduction speed was too slow. Di Jiang could resonate with the blood pool to create more giants, but they would only be at the Profound Immortal level.

When the twelve titans entered Pangu Temple, they returned to their original forms as a sign of respect to their Father God. They sat around the blood pool and began to think of ways to break through the limits of their bodies.

* * *

"I heard that Fangzhang Immortal Island fell into the Three Purities' hands, but I didn't expect Daoist Dong Wanggong to also possess one of the three immortal islands," Xi Wangmu said as she landed on Penglai Immortal Island.

Dong Wanggong laughed jovially. "I wasn't born on a blessed land like the Three Purities, but I had the good fortune of finding Penglai Island."

He led Xi Wangmu and the other guests from Violet Heaven Palace to the heart of the island. Within the first eon after he had found it, Dong Wanggong had already mastered all the formations on Penglai Immortal Island.

When Xi Wangmu entered the core area, she saw a violet mansion next to two connate spiritual roots. One of them was a top-grade connate spiritual root, the Fusang Tree. However, it was the other one that caught her eye.

The tree split into five branches, and each branch exuded an aura of fire, water, earth, wood, and metal. This was one of the top ten connate spiritual roots of the Great Desolation, the Five Elements Tree!

"Daoist Dong Wanggong's fortune makes one envious," she said.

He laughed, pleased with himself. Dong Wanggong invited all the gods and immortals into his abode, an artifact he had refined into the Violet Manor. From there, he spread the news of the Dao Ancestor's decree and began mass-recruiting immortals.

Gods and immortals who refrained from secular struggles came out to join Dong Wanggong and Xi Wangmu like moths to a flame. Many of them included the reborn remnants of chaos fiendgods.

A hundred years later, Dong Wanggong and Xi Wangmu officially announced the birth of Violet Manor, the home of 10,000 immortals.

Chapter 19

Era of Quasi-Saints

The establishment of Violet Manor, otherwise known as the Ten Thousand Immortals Alliance, sent ripples through the Great Desolation. The Titan Tribe and Demon Clan had already shown signs of becoming overlords of the world, and now a third force has joined their ranks. It reminded those that had lived through the Dragon-Phoenix Tribulation of the deadlock of the three past overlords.

Strangely, this began a time of peace. All three forces were content to stay in their own territories and accumulate strength. Of course, this was just the calm before the storm; one tiny spark could explode into war.

None of this bothered the Three Purities, however. After picking up the three Ninth-Ranked White Lotuses of Purification, they returned to Kunlun Mountain. Compared to Fangzhang Immortal Island, it felt more like home.

Yuanshi also expanded Three Purity Palace. Now, instead of just one grand hall and several rooms, the grand hall became the Three Purity Hall. He even added the Grand Purity Hall, Jade Purity Hall, and Supreme Purity Hall.

He also built a specifically prepared alchemy chamber where Laozi could concoct pills and nurture spiritual herbs and roots.

Planted in the center of all of this, with an array constructed by Tongtian to gather Kunlun Mountain's essence, was a pond formed from an elixir of Threelight Divinewater and other precious truewaters.

Three green lotus seeds and three red lotus seeds had taken root inside the pond and sprouted in the thousands of years since the second sermon at Violet Heaven Palace. Now, six buds peeked above the water.

They would bloom into first-ranked lotuses within a thousand years. After that, Laozi would slowly nurture them until they reached the ninth rank. None of the Three Purities were particularly in a rush for the lotuses to mature since they were still finding the three thoughts that made up their Three Corpses. That was what Laozi and Yuanshi assumed, anyway.

Inside the Supreme Purity Hall, Tongtian sat on the Twelfth-Ranked White Lotus of Purification. A branching silver river appeared behind her, and above the river bloomed three flowers. Slowly, they took the form of magnolia flowers.

Silver light emerged from the river and condensed on the left flower. The light formed a humanoid figure with no distinct features sitting in a lotus position.

The Ninth-Ranked White Lotus of Purification appeared in front of Tongtian, and she formed a seal with her hand.

"SEVER!"

The silver humanoid jumped out of the magnolia flower and into the Ninth-Ranked White Lotus of Purification. Once the white lotus fully merged with the silver humanoid, it began to hum and radiate light.

Like when the Three Purities had entered the Quasi-Saint Realm, an immense pressure spread far and wide to the surrounding lands. It ballooned rapidly, spreading out to reach 60,000 li.

All the life within its radius that did not possess enough strength knelt in reverence for Tongtian's supreme might. The Demon Clan and Titan Tribe felt this and increased their efforts to minimize the widening gap between the two forces—Taiyi especially.

When the light disappeared, the Ninth-Ranked White Lotus of Purification transformed into a white-robed man in his early twenties. Despite appearing young, he had a calm and mature air to him. His hair hung freely over his shoulders, and despite not having exquisite features, his face was perfect, and one could gaze at him for eternity.

Tongtian already had an urge to cave in her Evil Corpse's flawless face with her fist. Instead, she sighed and motioned for him to return, and he flew over to sit on her left magnolia flower.

She closed her eyes and sensed the changes. Her Evil Corpse already had the cultivation of an early Quasi-Saint, while her own cultivation had improved to the Intermediate Quasi-Saint Realm. The most important improvement was the heightened clarity with which she perceived the Law of Time.

A hundred years later, Tongtian exited Supreme Purity Hall and came to Three Purity Hall, where her two brothers waited for her. Yuanshi was the first to speak. "Third Sister, how is it? How do you feel? Is anything wrong?"

What are you, my mother? Tongtian thought, but she still explained all the changes and miraculous effects of cutting a Corpse.

Hearing this, Laozi sighed. "As expected of the Dao Ancestor. No wonder he could become the first Saint in the Grand Desolation."

Yuanshi nodded in agreement. "Yes, tell us how you discovered your evil thoughts so quickly."

A sinister smile graced Tongtian's lips. "It's simple."

Both Laozi and Yuanshi unconsciously leaned in.

"Just become a woman."

Laozi and Yuanshi's thoughts froze on their faces. An ominous aura emanated from Tongtian's body. "My evil thoughts are formed from my resentment over turning out this way while you two were male. That's why my Evil Corpse turned out to be a perfect man, so perfect that I want to destroy him myself."

Tongtian eyed her brothers. "Tell me, Eldest Brother, Second Brother, do you want me to help you devise a technique to change your gender? I'm sure you two could just as easily cut off your evil thoughts as I did."

"My way is that of inaction, to let all things develop naturally. I thank Third Sister for your offer, but I must decline," Laozi said, perhaps a bit too quickly.

"This is Third Sister's fortune. Second Brother can envy but not replicate," Yuanshi said, just as quickly.

Tongtian snorted. It was a cute little snort, almost coy, at least in Yuanshi's opinion.

She stood up. "Alright, I won't bother Eldest and Second Brother anymore. I'm going to wait at Fangzhang Immortal Island for a chance to grab the Kunlun Mirror when Violet Manor falls, since I won't be able to cut off my second corpse anytime soon."

"Violet Manor has the backing of the Dao Ancestor, it should not fall," Laozi said.

"I feel the Dao Ancestor's meaning in setting up the Ten Thousand Immortals Alliance should not be simple. Why would he support Dong Wanggong and Xi Wangmu right after giving Di Jun his consent?"

Laozi went silent. He also found the manner behind the establishment of Violet Manor suspicious.

Actually, Tongtian was just gambling on the legends she'd learned from her memories as a human. According to legend, Dong Wanggong, the master of Violet Manor, perished. Many generations later, he was reincarnated as Lu Dongbin, a famous poet of the Tang Dynasty who later became the leader of Eight Immortals.

"What if Violet Manor decided to attack you?" Yuanshi asked.

"No worries," Tongtian said. "Even if I can't defeat them, I can defend or run away with Fangzhang Immortal Island. As for the Ten Thousand Immortal Array, they can't set it up without long preparation, giving more than enough time for me to escape.

"Let me come with you. I'm worried," Yuanshi said, following Tongtian out of the hall.

Laozi watched this and sighed. He returned to Grand Purity Hall and started to meditate. At this rate, Yuanshi should be able to cut off his good thoughts soon. Although Tongtian had a unique circumstance regarding her Corpse Severing, Laozi didn't want to fall too far behind either.

Five thousand years later, another pressure spread 60,000 li out from Kunlun Mountain. Everyone nearby couldn't but sigh in envy, jealousy, and hate at the good luck of the Three Purities.

Everyone else, including Taiyi, was still trying to eradicate the Nine Worms in their body, while the Three Purities were already severing their three thoughts. Some had had more success than others, such as Jieyin and Nuwa, but they were still some distance away from completely dispelling all Nine Worms.

Another 5,000 years later, a pressure that reached 60,000 li emanated from Fangzhang Immortal Island. Yuanshi had severed his good thoughts and condensed his Good Corpse.

The news of all Three Purities severing off a Corpse spread throughout the Great Desolation. The Titan Tribe, Demon Clan, and Violet Manor were growing tense. As forces with the ambition to dominate the Great Desolation, a rogue power like the Three Purities brought unneeded variables into their eventual rule.

If they could, they might have already killed the Three Purities.

After stabilizing her realm, Tongtian realized that she could detect the invisible Karmic Luck in the world. It was faint, as if hidden by heaven, but she could still make out some secrets.

In her eyes, she and Yuanshi had an immense amount of Karmic Luck, condensed almost solid. It didn't grow or shrink, but it was always following them.

In contrast, the Karmic Luck of the Violet Manor was like a large pillar of gold. It was faint, almost transparent, like air. Most of it was concentrated on Dong Wanggong, whose luck took the form of a golden flower, and Xi Wangmu, whose luck appeared like a silvery-blue peach.

Although the luck of Violet Manor seemed glorious, it was without foundation. At its base, the pillar of light dissolved into a pale mist. It was like the manor itself, lacking solid support.

Right now, it seemed strong, but most of those immortals had only gathered due to the Dao Ancestor's words, not because of Dong Wanggong's or Xi Wangmu's charisma. Such weakness would fade with time, but the question was whether Di Jun would miss such an opportunity.

While Tongtian was meditating on the Law of Time and trying to discover her good thoughts and obsession, a pressure emanated from Penglai Immortal Island. She stopped to pay close attention. The pressure didn't originate from one person but two. Tongtian could feel the essence of yin and yang within the pressure, meaning Dong Wanggong and Xi Wangmu had broken through at the same time.

Solitary yang does not flourish; lone yin does not prosper.

Did Dong Wanggong and Xi Wangmu dual-cultivate? Tongtian maliciously wondered.

Regardless of what she thought, the Violet Manor instantly gained two early Quasi-Saints that propelled them to the top of the three forces. With the increase of their strength, the foundation for their pillar of luck stabilized a bit. It would need further accumulation for it to stabilize completely.

The Demon Clan went from the strongest force to the second-strongest, and the Titan tribe was even worse off. They were placed in third, with no signs of any of them breaking into the Quasi-Saint Realm.

A few hundred years later, Nuwa broke through into the Quasi-Saint Realm. A thousand years later, Di Jun followed suit, restoring the Demon Clan to its previous position.

The Titan Tribe was put in an awkward, unstable position.

* * *

Di Jun was in a good mood. He had severed his Good Corpse using the Golden Sun Wheel, increasing his strength. He would have preferred Nuwa enter the Quasi-Saint Realm later than him, as that would be more conducive to his rule over the Demon Clan.

Luckily, Fuxi was too busy deciphering the formation contained within the Celestial River Diagram to cultivate. Di Jun was broken out of his thoughts when a demon reported that Fuxi wanted to meet with him.

Fuxi had not reappeared since gaining the Celestial River Diagram. Di Jun's hopes couldn't help but rise as he quickly invited him in. "Daoist Fuxi, did you...?"

Fuxi appeared haggard, with bags under his bloodshot eyes. However, he had a small smile on his face. "Fortunately, I did not disappoint Your Majesty."

"The formation is called the Starry Sky War Array. With the Supreme Yang Star and the Supreme Yin Star at the center, the formation utilizes the power of the 365 major stars and 48,000 minor stars."

Hearing this, Di Jun frowned.

"You need Golden Immortals of the Great Firmament to command the two supreme stars and the major stars, and profound immortals to command the minor stars. The stronger the immortals commanding them, the stronger the formation."

Di Jun's head ached now. Forget the profound immortals, the Demon Clan didn't even have 300 Golden Immortals of the Great Firmament. Unfortunately for Di Jun, Fuxi wasn't done.

"You also need to extract the essence of each star and refine them into flags. This way, you don't need to be on the stars themselves to set up the array. Although it is called an array, it can unleash its power anywhere the starlight shines," Fuxi finished.

Di Jun's eyes lit up. If that was the case, that eliminated the greatest weakness of arrays. Arrays were stronger than formations, but they couldn't move.

"Dispatch the demons to collect the star essence as soon as possible," Di Jun ordered. He sent Bai Ze to supervise the operation and gave Fuxi time to rest.

Bai Ze came back 2,000 years later to report to Di Jun. "Your Majesty, we discovered a suitable place for the Demon Clan's new headquarters."

CHAPTER 20

Thirty-Three Heavens

Di Jun followed Bai Ze and the demon scouts up Buzhou Mountain. He had already traveled up the mountain once after discovering the pressure could aid his cultivation. He hadn't found anything at the peak and hadn't expected anyone else to either.

Now, it seemed that the timing just hadn't been right.

When Di Jun arrived at the peak of Buzhou Mountain, he saw a portal. After entering it with Bai Ze and the other demons, he saw a colossal gate named South Heaven Gate in Dao Script.

The essence here was denser and richer than even that of the mountain!

"Your Majesty, the scouts reported it immediately after discovering it," Bai Ze said. "This realm doesn't seem to have any life despite the favorable environment. It's almost like the heavens prepared it for Your Majesty."

Di Jun smiled at Bai Ze's flattery. Yes, wasn't this specially prepared for him? He was going to be the sole ruler of the Great Desolation, what greater place to rule than from atop Buzhou Mountain?

He entered through South Heaven Gate to discover grand yet solemn structures, radiant palaces, supreme halls, a jade throne, and much more. He discovered 33 levels in total, and at the very top was a magnificent palace.

Eminence Heaven Palace was written in Dao Script above the entrance.

Walking inside, Di Jun saw a grand throne that shone with a splendid golden luster. Nine golden dragons, each with nine claws, coiled around the throne and emitted heavy pressure. He sat down upon it with a smile.

The wise Bai Ze kneeled silently, and so did the demons behind him. Di Jun chuckled, and that chuckle transformed into deep laughter.

Di Jun didn't spend long on the Heavenly Throne. He and the other demons soon returned to their current headquarters to prepare. Under Di Jun's full support, the Demon Clan began to pack up and relocate.

Due to the immense size of their clan, this relocation process took hundreds of years. During this time, the Titan Tribe and Violet Manor caught news of the Demon Clan's movement. Still, neither of the two forces took action, prolonging this strange period of peace.

Once the Demon Clan finished relocating, they sent out invitations for the establishment of Heavenly Court a thousand years later to all major parties, even the Titan Tribe and Violet Manor.

For the Three Purities, he dispatched Bai Zei to Kunlun Mountain and Fangzhang Immortal Island as a show of respect. For the others, such as those who'd broken through to the Quasi-Saint Realm, he dispatched the other demon sages.

As the thousand-year mark neared, Di Jun received news of the Violet Manor hosting an Immortal Conference on the exact same date, and sending invitations to all immortals.

On the Heavenly Throne, Di Jun's eyes flashed with a sinister light. "Dong Wanggong, Xi Wangmu. Since you don't know what's good for you, then don't blame me for being ruthless."

Thanks to the emergence of the Thirty-Three Heavens, the Demon Clan's attempts to gather star essence were successfully hidden from prying eyes. It would not be long until they refined all the star flags and formed the Starry Sky War Formation.

* * *

Inside Violet Manor's central hall, Dong Wanggong and Xi Wangmu were sitting in front of each other. Dong Wanggong emitted golden energy that reached out and entwined with the blue energy of Xi Wangmu.

"Dong Wanggong, are you sure this is wise?" Xi Wangmu asked with her eyes closed.

"What is wise?"

"Holding the Immortal Conference at the same time as the Establishment of Heavenly Court."

"There is nothing wrong. The Dao Ancestor has already spoken. Di Jun will rule the Great Desolation, while we rule the male and female immortals. There is no conflict."

Xi Wangmu stayed silent for a moment. "Between you two, who rules the other?"

"Naturally, it is me. Di Jun may rule the Great Desolation and be a congenital god like us, but he is also an immortal. Therefore, he falls under my jurisdiction."

"But are immortals not also part of the Great Desolation? Doesn't this give Di Jun the right to rule over us? Will he submit?"

Dong Wanggong snorted. "Does he dare to disobey the Dao Ancestor's decree? Speaking of which, have the Three Purities responded?"

Xi Wangmu shook her head. "I already sent a messenger to Fangzhang Immortal Island and Kunlun Mountain, but I've received no reply."

Dong Wanggong's face darkened. "Hmpf, Laozi and Yuanshi are male immortals and should fall under my jurisdiction. Tongtian is female and should be under your control. Do they think that just because they are a bit luckier that no one will catch up?"

Xi Wangmu stayed silent.

"I want to see how long they can maintain their arrogance. Soon, more and more Quasi-Saints will appear, and the three of them won't amount to much. As the head of male and female immortals, both of us will become Saints of Heaven. I want to see how those three will fare afterward," Dong Wanggong said. His eyes exuded pride and supreme confidence.

Xi Wangmu sighed. She wasn't as optimistic as her yang counterpart.

"Right, have you discovered Yinzhou Island yet?" he asked. "I heard the Three Purities were also searching for it. It should belong to you. As for Fangzhang Immortal Island, it will eventually become Violet Manor's."

"There's still no news of Yinzhou Immortal Island. I'm more worried about the future. There are not enough spiritual artifacts to go around, and the Demon Clan already has three Quasi-Saints. We have to admit, they are much richer than us."

Dong Wanggong sighed. "You and I are quite lucky. I severed my Corpse with the Fusang Tree, while you had an innate spiritual artifact related to Yin Qi. We have plenty of innate spiritual artifacts, but they are all low-grades. None of them are willing to use subpar artifacts to sever their Corpses.

"There are two methods." He turned his gaze outside. "We can only wait until the Immortal Conference to invite loose immortals to join Violet Manor. We will teach them the Three Corpses method, but not the details pertaining to the grade of innate artifacts. Even if their Corpses aren't Quasi-Saints, their main bodies will be."

"And the second method?"

"Force a member of the Hundred Clans to join us. As survivors of the Dragon-Phoenix Tribulation, they should have amassed a large amount of treasures."

Xi Wangmu furrowed her brow. "But the Hundred Clans are all demons. Won't this step on Di Jun's bottom line?"

Dong Wanggong said nothing.

* * *

"Those bastards," Zhurong bellowed. "The Demon Clan invited us, but Violet Manor actually ignored us!"

"You can't say that," Houtu reasoned. "We are titans, not immortals, so it's only natural for them to skip over us."

Zhurong snorted.

The Titan Tribe had been under immense pressure for the last 10,000 years. After the Three Purities had entered the Intermediate Quasi-Saint Realm, there were at least ten Quasi-Saints! And yet, the Titan Tribe still hadn't discovered a method to break their bodies' limits and enter the Quasi-Saint Realm.

At this rate, they would only lose the advantage they once possessed and be abandoned by the times.

"We can't let this happen," Rushou, the Titan of Metal, said. "Even if we can't discover a method to enter the Quasi-Saint Realm, we have to weaken the Demon Clan so that their strength doesn't rise and leave us behind, no matter the cost."

"I agree," Jumang, the Titan of Wood, said. "Does Di Jun think he has already won? By coming to the establishment of Heavenly Court, wouldn't we implicitly agree to his rule? We titans bow to no one, only Pangu!"

"Di Jiang, let's use the Pangu Genesis Formation to attack them and show everyone the power of the Titan Tribe," Jizi, the Titan of Lightning, said.

"Jizi is right. We can't let the situation continue," Shebisi, the Titan of Storm, said.

Di Jiang silently glanced at Tianwu, Xuanmnig, Gonggong, Qiangliang, and Houtu before finally landing on Jiuyin. "What do you think?"

Jiuyin, the Titan of Time, nodded after a moment of consideration. "I think there is merit in Rushou's proposal."

Di Jiang closed his eyes for a moment, but when he opened them again, there was an unwavering light. "Alright, let's show the world that we titans are the true rulers of the Great Desolation!"

All the titans cheered, and a belligerent light shone in their eyes.

* * *

"Brother, why haven't you severed your Corpse and broken into the Quasi-Saint Realm?" Jinchi, the Golden-Winged Great Roc, asked. "I don't believe with Big Brother's talent, you are inferior to any of the six people at the front."

"Hmpf, had you persevered and not given up your seat, you would have been one of those six," Kong Xuan said, glaring.

After the second sermon at Violet Heaven Palace, the two brothers had returned to their territory near the Undying Volcano in the South. Due to the Phoenix Ancestor's sacrifice, most of the Phoenix Clan had migrated there.

Although the brothers were born from the Phoenix Ancestor's two eggs, they weren't born phoenixes, even if they'd inherited her bloodline. As such, the Phoenix Clan refused to acknowledge them.

Not that Kong Xuan thought that the Phoenix Clan had anything worth their attention. Jinchi was furious at the blatant disregard for what he perceived as their birthright, so he hated the Phoenix Clan.

Jinchi pouted. "It's not a good idea to make enemies of everyone."

Kong Xuan snorted. "In the future, you will know what great chance slipped through your wings. How is your progress in severing your first Corpse?"

"I'm still trying to discover my good or evil thoughts," Jinchi said, then he stopped and glared at Kong Xuan. "Brother, aren't we talking about you? You should have sensed your good and evil thoughts, right? Why haven't you severed them?"

"Short-sighted. Hongjun said that if you entered through the Quasi-Saint Realm by tempering your qi with the law, the foundation would be firmer than if you directly severed a Corpse."

"Then are you trying to comprehend the law? Do you think I can enter the Quasi-Saint Realm through the power of the law?" Jinchi's excited voice halted when he saw Kong Xuan's expression. "Don't look down on me so much! Haven't you been stuck at this step too? Hmpf."

"I'm stuck here by choice. I've already comprehended enough laws to enter the Quasi-Saint Realm. There's a difference, do you understand?"

"Yes, yes, Big Brother is the most amazing. Then why haven't you entered?"

"I comprehended the Law of Fire, Law of Water, Law of Earth, Law of Wood, and Law of Metal. But I want to merge them and comprehend the Law of Five Elements because that is the path most suited for me. Unfortunately, I'm stuck at the last step."

"Don't worry, I believe Brother will be able to merge the five laws."

"I naturally know that. I don't need you to spout useless words." Kong Xuan ignored Jinchi's pouting. "What I'm worried about is others. While I stagnate, everyone else is progressing. What is the difference between stagnation and regression?"

"Then what do you want to do?"

"I heard that Dong Wanggong and Xi Wangmu are hosting an Immortal Conference; I may need to visit and join them."

"Those two?" Jinchi asked with obvious disdain. "Just two lucky gods graced by the Dao Ancestor. They're even worse than Di Jun. At least he had the guts to conquer the Great Desolation without the Dao Ancestor's aid. They're still two stinky crows, though."

"Yes, but right now, we aren't their opponents," Kong Xuan said decisively. "But right now, I need the help of the Five Elements Tree they possess. You stay here and continue to try to sever your first Corpse. I'll be back before the Dao Ancestor's last sermon."

"But," Jinchi protested, seeing his brother leave.

"Listen to me," Kong Xuan said with finality. Jinchi nodded, however unwilling.

* * *

"Are you really going to go?" Yuanshi asked with displeasure as he and Tongtian flew toward Kunlun Mountain.

"Why not?"

"We are the Three Purities. How can we attend the establishment of Heavenly Court? Wouldn't it be acknowledging that they are the rulers of the Great Desolation?"

Tongtian smiled. "In the Great Desolation, it's always been strength that speaks the loudest. So what if we go? Are our strengths theirs? Besides, I think there is someone who doesn't wish to see the establishment of the Heavenly Court more than us."

Yuanshi's mind spun. "You are talking about the Titan Tribe. Did they discover a method to break through into the Quasi-Saint Realm? But that's not right, we would have sensed something."

"Who knows, but I'm curious about the trump card that they say can slay us easily," Tongtian said, anticipation in her eyes. "If we go to Thirty-Three Heavens, we might get a chance to witness it."

Chapter 21

Establishment of the Heavenly Court

Dong Wanggong laughed and smiled as he cupped his fist and greeted the newcomer. "Shangxia Ancestor, welcome to my Penglai Immortal Island. It's an honor to entertain you."

"No, it's my honor to attend the conference held by the head of the male immortals," Shangxia Ancestor said. Dong Wanggong's smile widened ever so slightly. He had one of the servants, an earth immortal transformed from one of the animals that originally inhabited Penglai Immortal Island, lead the congenital god to his seat.

Most of the guests so far were those unlucky few gods who could not make it to Hongjun's sermons, or those who'd refused to. Over a hundred Golden Immortals of the Great Firmament had arrived, hidden experts whom Dong Wanggong hadn't known existed.

As Dong Wanggong received more and more guests, his confidence also rose. Surely, the high-end combat power of the Violet Manor would exceed the Demon Clan soon. Before his fantasies could get the better of him, he brought himself back to reality.

The next guest surprised him. The label of demon would have fitted the new arrival more than that of immortal. "Fellow Daoist Kong Xuan, I didn't expect you to attend my Immortal Conference."

Kong Xuan plastered a polite smile on his face. "Daoist Dong

Wanggong, I've always considered myself an immortal, so of course, I would come. Or, are you saying you don't welcome me?"

"Haha, how can that be? Please enter and take a seat."

Dong Wanggong seated Kong Xuan near himself—right next to him, in fact. Although Kong Xuan was weaker than him, Dong Wanggong felt a peculiar aura emanating from him. His instincts told him that Kong Xuan wasn't far from the Quasi-Saint Realm.

He resolved to recruit Kong Xuan to Violet Manor, no matter the cost.

Not long after, the time came for the Immortal Conference to commence. Dong Wanggong sat on the right with Kong Xuan and all the male immortals. On the left sat Xi Wangmu and the female immortals.

Xi Wangmu's grip on her wine glass tightened as she glanced toward the lunar star. She had invited the two lunar goddesses, Xihe and Changxi, to the Immortal Conference, but neither showed up.

Each guest was seated in front of a table with plates of spiritual fruits and immortal wine placed in front of them. Dong Wanggong raised his cup to make a toast. "I thank all of you for giving me face today and attending my Immortal Conference. However, this is a conference and not a banquet, after all. So, I will hold a sermon, explaining my understanding of cultivation and the method to enter the Quasi-Saint Realm."

At this, silence descended. The majority of the guests not part of Violet Manor had come just for a chance to hear Hongjun's Way of Three Corpses.

Reading the atmosphere, Dong Wanggong didn't delay, preaching his understanding of cultivation starting from Earth Immortal, like Hongjun had during the first sermon in Violet Heaven Palace. Xi Wangmu would interject and take the lead from time to time, giving another viewpoint on cultivation unique to her and supplementing Dong Wanggong's insights, amplifying the effects.

Kong Xuan, who had heard Hongjun's first sermon, felt that although Dong Wanggong and Xi Wangmu couldn't replicate the charm of Hongjun's sermon, they managed to convey around 70 percent of it.

After finishing speaking about the Great Firmament Realm, then came the most crucial aspect. Dong Wanggong and Xi Wangmu started explaining their experiences in discovering their good and evil thoughts. They spoke about the process of severing them and turning them into a Corpse, but infuriatingly, Dong Wanggong and Xi Wangmu perfectly dodged mentioning the exact method.

When they ended their sermon, most of the guests felt as if something was scratching their hearts. They wanted to stop the itch, but they couldn't reach it.

Because of this, many of the factionless immortals, including Shangxia Ancestor, decided to stay. Dong Wanggong accepted them all, but his true goal was Kong Xuan.

After dealing with them, Dong Wanggong joined the son of the phoenix, who was staring at the top connate spiritual root, the Five Elements Tree, with yearning.

"Daoist Kong Xuan, does my Five Elements Tree interest you?"

He smiled at the host. "I won't hide from fellow Daoist, the Five Elements Tree does hold great appeal for me. I was wondering if Daoist Dong Wanggong could allow me to comprehend under the tree for a few thousand years."

Dong Wanggong made a troubled face upon hearing Kong Xuan's requests. "It's not that I don't want to allow fellow Daoist to cultivate under there, but the Five Elements Tree is part of the Violet Manor, and I can't just let outsiders use it."

Kong Xuan's eyes seemed to bore a hole in the Five Elements Tree, but he gave a long sigh and turned away. "If that's the case, I'm sorry for troubling fellow Daoist."

Seeing Kong Xuan turn to leave, Dong Wanggong gritted his teeth and reached out. "Please wait, fellow Daoist. If you join my Violet Manor, I can allow you to cultivate under it."

Kong Xuan's eyes lit up, but he immediately closed them and shook his head. He cupped his fist and said, "I'm sorry for failing Daoist Dong Wanggong's expectation, but I must decline."

"What about if I give you one of the five branches of the Five Elements Tree?"

The Five Elements Tree only had five branches, one for each element. Taking away a single branch of the Five Elements Tree would drop it from a top-grade connate spiritual root to a high-grade connate spiritual root. It would take many years to regrow it and even longer to restore it to its former grade.

Kong Xuan froze and looked at Dong Wanggong as if to confirm the veracity of his offer. After a moment of deliberation, Kong Xuan nodded.

Dong Wanggong's heart split as he thought about cutting off a branch, but upon remembering that Violet Manor would gain another Quasi-Saint, his mood lifted.

Before he could be happy for too long, Dong Wanggong's expression hardened as he stared in the direction of Buzhou Mountain. Kong Xuan, Xi Wangmu, and all the others close to or at the Quasi-Saint Realm likewise turned their heads.

Golden clouds of merits gathered above Buzhou Mountain, directly above the Thirty-Three Heavens. Next, Di Jun's voice echoed throughout the Great Desolation, aided by the Way of Heaven.

* * *

"Redcloud Ancestor, Zheng Yuanzi, welcome, welcome," Di Jun said as he personally stepped forward to greet his guests.

Redcloud Ancestor didn't consider himself a demon and would have preferred to attend Violet Manor's Immortal Conference. He came because he owed Di Jun, who'd graciously taken the half-matured gourd from the Immortal Gourd Vine and let him take the red one

"I came by to witness the establishment of Heavenly Court. Surely it will be a grand spectacle," Redcloud Ancestor said with a laugh.

Di Jun's smile deepened as he led the two into the Thirty-Three Heavens. He placed them near the front, where he would perform the ceremony of worshiping the Way of Heaven.

"Fellow Daoist, I've been meaning to ask, but are you willing to join my Demon Clan?" Di Jun asked. Seeing Redcloud Ancestor's hesitant expression, he added, "Of course, you'll be given the honored position of a demon emperor."

Redcloud Ancestor sighed. "I thank fellow Daoist Di Jun for your thoughts, but I prefer to roam free and unfettered. Joining a faction doesn't really suit me."

"I see, that's a shame," Di Jun said without showing any displeasure. After a few more pleasantries, he left.

"You shouldn't have rejected him so directly, at least say that you'll consider it," Zheng Yuanzi chastised.

"What's the point of prolonging it? It will only delay Daoist Di Jun," Redcloud Ancestor said without a care.

Zhen Yuanzi sighed.

Di Jun was pleased to hear from a messenger that the Three Purities had arrived. Although he had invited them, he'd never expected them to show up with their arrogance. He rushed to South Heaven Gate to greet the three.

"Haha, welcome, fellow Daoists," he said, smiling widely. The displeasure from Redcloud Ancestor's rejection was already fading.

Laozi didn't reply, Yuanshi made a noncommittal grunt, and Tongtian nodded in greeting. Di Jun's brows twitched, but he quickly relaxed them—at least they didn't attend Violet Manor's Immortal Conference.

He led the Three Purities through the layers of Thirty-Three Heavens and sat them close to the front, which they deserved based on their strength alone. They were the only intermediate Quasi-Saints in the Great Desolation.

Halfway through, Di Jun met Taiyi.

"Brother," Taiyi said. "Jieyin and Zhunti have arrived. I'll take fellow Daoists Three Purities to their positions."

Di Jun sent a look that screamed, "Are you sure you can do it?"

Taiyi frowned and ignored him. "Fellow Daoists, follow me."

Seeing Taiyi's firmness, Di Jun could only relent and return to South Heaven Gate to receive Jieyin and Zhunti personally.

Taiyi turned his back and gestured for the Three Purities to follow. Tongtian stepped forward, but Yuanshi mysteriously positioned her behind him while allowing Laozi to take the lead. Tongtian wanted to question Yuanshi's abrupt actions, but decided not to.

Yuanshi looked up to see Taiyi's displeased gaze. He smiled back. It was a soft smile that Yuanshi only showed his siblings, but it contained infinite provocation.

Taiyi took a deep breath and forced a smile. Once they were at the highest level, he took them inside Eminence Heaven Palace. He led them past Redcloud Ancestor and near the very front, to a level higher than Bai Ze and the rest of the demon sages.

Nuwa and Fuxi stood one level below the Heavenly Throne on its right, and Taiyi positioned the Three Purities at the same level on the left. On the fourth position from the Heavenly Throne, he said, "Fellow Daoist Laozi, please stand here."

Without waiting, he motioned toward the third position from the throne. "Fellow Daoist Yuanshi, please stand here."

Yuanshi didn't move. He stared at the first and second positions from the Heavenly Throne. Then, taking Tongtian by her shoulders, he moved her into the third position while he stood between them without waiting for Taiyi, still wearing that same smile.

Taiyi paused, but remained silent in the end. He stepped next to the left side of the throne and turned toward Yuanshi with a gentle smile.

Tongtian frowned, but not because of the strangeness of Yuanshi's actions. No, she was concerned with how hot it suddenly became. Despite being an immortal and congenital god, she could not help but pull at her collars.

* * *

When Di Jun greeted Jieyin and Zhunti, he sensed that Jieyin had entered the Intermediate Quasi-Saint Realm. In addition, Zhunti had also become a Quasi-Saint. Due to the distance to the West, none of the eastern major powers had felt their breakthroughs. Although both of them were inferior to the Three Purities, they shouldn't be underestimated.

He put on a smile and led the two western guests up the levels of Thirty-Three Heavens. That smile almost fell off when he entered Eminence Heaven Palace and saw the Three Purities standing one level lower than the Heavenly Throne.

Di Jun sent a questioning glance to Taiyi, but his brother was too busy having a stare-off with Yuanshi. Di Jun forced his smile back on as he placed Jieyin and Zhunti in front of Redcloud Ancestor and Zheng Yuanzi.

Zhunti frowned when he saw they were placed far below the Three Purities, but he said nothing after seeing his senior brother's calm expression.

After them, there was no one else Di Jun needed to greet personally, and the time of establishment neared.

Finally, when the pre-ordained time arrived, Di Jun walked in front of the Heavenly Throne and raised his arm. His eyes looked up and pierced the ceiling and into the very heavens.

"The Way of Heaven above, I, Di Jun, the ruler of the Demon Clan, see that the Great Desolation is disorderly and full of hardship. I will bear the burden of the Mandate of Heaven and unite them under one rule, bringing order and prosperity!"

Di Jun's voice echoed throughout the Great Desolation. The Way of Heaven had recognized his vow.

Golden clouds of merits ten thousand li long gathered above the Thirty-Three Heavens, their dazzling radiance almost blinding those present.

Di Jun closed his eyes and took a deep breath. When he opened them again, they were filled with unwavering determination. "From now on, I am the Heavenly Emperor Di Jun! We announce the establishment of the Heavenly Court!"

CHAPTER 22

Pangu Genesis Formation

Thirty percent of the golden clouds of merits descended onto Di Jun. Once he absorbed them, he yelled, "SEVER!"

A powerful pressure that reached 60,000 li was released. A golden-robed man flew out of Di Jun's three flowers, and he officially entered the Intermediate Quasi-Saint Realm.

All those present stared in shock. They hadn't realized they could use Karmic Merit to sever a Corpse and improve their cultivation. In reality, Karmic Merit could be used to upgrade an artifact, turn it into a meritorious artifact, or increase one's cultivation. Even just condensing it into a halo of merit could act as a deterrent against those who wanted to kill them.

Di Jun stored his Corpse back in his fiery clouds and flowers. He looked at the second level, where Taiyi, Nuwa, and Fuxi stood. His gaze lingered a moment on the Three Purities, but that was it.

"We confer upon Taiyi the position of Eastern Emperor of the Heavenly Court!"

As soon as Di Jun said those words, 10 percent of the golden clouds of merit descended onto Taiyi. He didn't use the merit to directly break through to the Intermediate Quasi-Saint Realm. Because he did not absorb the merit, they formed a halo behind him.

Di Jun didn't call attention to Taiyi's actions, turning toward Fuxi and Nuwa. "We confer upon Fuxi the position of Western Emperor of the Heavenly Court!"

Ten percent of the clouds of merit directly descended onto Fuxi, and he broke through into the Quasi-Saint Realm.

"I thank the Heavenly Emperor for your grace!"

After Fuxi stored his Corpse, Di Jun turned to Nuwa. His momentum had increased to the point that all those in the Great Unity Realm unconsciously kneeled in his presence.

"We confer upon Nuwa the position of Southern Emperor of the Heavenly Court!"

Nuwa absorbed ten percent of the golden clouds of merit. Her aura continuously approached the Intermediate Quasi-Saint Realm, but frustratingly, she never broke through.

Nuwa hid her disappointment and thanked Di Jun.

Di Jun turned his gaze on the Ten Demon Sages. All of them looked at the heavenly emperor with hints of expectation, and he did not disappoint. He officially appointed the demon sages as the Ten Generals of the Heavenly Court.

Ten percent of the golden clouds of merits were divided between them, and only Bai Ze directly broke through into the Quasi-Saint Realm. Although the other nine did not break through, their cultivation rose to the peak of the Great Firmament Realm and they were only a step away from becoming Quasi-Saints.

Di Jun continued to appoint officials until the end. The remaining clouds of merit descended onto the whole demon race, raising their strength by a minor stage. Overall, the Demon Clan's strength had risen to a new level.

"From now on, we the Heavenly Court will bear the Mandate of Heaven and rule the Great Desolation!"

The Demon Clan, now members of the Heavenly Court, kneeled

and cheered. Di Jun's aura washed over them, giving him the bearing of an emperor. Only a few guests at or near the Quasi-Saint Realm could resist kneeling from Di Jun's momentum.

Most of them had many more thoughts as they watched the splendorous scene. The Heavenly Court had utterly eclipsed the Titan Tribe and Violet Manor in power. Not only had Di Jun reached the Intermediate Quasi-Saint Realm, but they had gained two new Quasi-Saints, for a grand total of five!

Tongtian's perception of the Demon Clan's luck changed. Before, it seemed to be an amalgamation of every demon in existence, but now, the form changed into that of the sky. The sun, moon, and stars hung in that sky, shining brilliantly.

Suddenly, Tongtian smiled and glanced toward South Heaven Gate.

"DI JUN, YOU SMELLY CROW, WE DON'T ACKNOWLEDGE YOU OR HEAVEN, ONLY PANGU!"

Di Jun's smile froze, and terrifying coldness entered his eyes. He led the newly appointed demon emperors, ten generals, and the rest of the Demon Clan to South Heaven Gate, where he confronted an army of the Titan Tribe.

"Di Jiang, Our rule has been acknowledged by the Way of Heaven," Di Jun said. "Submit or die."

"Are you blind, you dumb bird? What heaven? We only revere Pangu!" Zhurong shouted.

"It's deaf, you blind idiot!" Gonggong said.

"Who're you calling blind, you coward!" Zhurong shouted.

The titans' argument didn't appease Di Jun at all. It only made him angrier. "You have the gall to argue in front of Us? Emperors, generals, and Our loyal soldiers: smite down these blasphemous barbarians and paint the land with their blood as an offering to the Way of Heaven!"

Di Jun charged at Di Jiang with the Celestial River Diagram in hand. Behind him, the Starry Sky appeared, and with a wave of his arms, comets shot out at Di Jiang.

The head of the titans snorted and waved his hands. The comets roaring toward him disappeared, and in the next moment, they shot back at Di Jun, smashing the Starry Sky behind him.

The heavenly emperor narrowed his eyes and increased the power of his attack. Instead of comets, the attack directly formed starlight shining down at his opponent.

Di Jiang repeated the same trick, but only some of the beams of starlight twisted, and none were sent back. The rest torched his body, burning his flesh.

"Di Jiang!" Jiuyin shouted as he joined the fight. Using his innate temporal abilities, he caused the starlight to lose energy and revert the injuries on Di Jiang's body.

Di Jun snorted and pressed the attack.

Di Jiang no longer tried to tank the attacks head-on. Using his innate spatial abilities, he weaved through the starlight and made himself and Jiuyin immaterial. Although they couldn't gain the upper hand, they tied down Di Jun.

On another battlefield, Taiyi eyed Zhurong. He didn't say anything and just charged forward with his flame-covered fist.

Zhurong sneered and used his innate ability to shroud his own fist in flames.

When the two fists clashed, a fiery explosion engulfed their surroundings. When the smoke cleared, Taiyi remained in place, but Zhurong had been forced back at least fifty steps with an expression of disbelief.

His most prized skill, his mastery over fire, had been bested? Zhurong roared, unwilling to admit defeat, and charged at Taiyi again with his whole body shrouded in flames.

"That idiot!" Gonggong said, running in to assist Zhurong. He pointed his hand at Taiyi and shot torrents of water.

Taiyi waved his hand. A wall of flame appeared to block it. The flame extinguished the water and created a massive fog. When the two titans rushed into the fog, Taiyi used his superior cultivation and abilities to suppress the two.

"Let me help!" Rushou, the Titan of Metal, said. His skin had turned into a silver that shone under the fiery lights of the sun and flames. Tianwu and Qiangliang, the Titans of Wind and Thunder, joined the siege against Taiyi.

Not even Taiyi dared to fight five titans head-on with his body alone. He retreated and summoned the Chaos Bell. The giant bell rang, dealing sonic damage to his foes. They froze for a moment, and Zhurong appeared the most affected.

Using this chance, Taiyi controlled the Chaos Bell to smash Zhurong.

Gonggong unleashed a piercing stream of water, Tianwu called forth a cyclone, Qiangliang unleashed a thunderous sonic boom, and Rushou hurled metal shards. The four elemental attacks slammed the Chaos Bell and stopped it in midair.

Taiyi frowned, tightening his control over the bell. However, the titans cooperated seamlessly. Where one would not be able to contend against the Chaos Bell, the others made up for it.

The titans had practiced numerous tactics after their unfortunate duel with Yuanshi in order to make up for their inability to use artifacts. They had grown in strength and coordination. Every single one of them reached the Peak Great Firmament Realm equivalent, so they were just able to contend with the early Quasi-Saint Taiyi and the Chaos Bell.

Fuxi turned his ire against Shebisi, the Titan of Storm. The Fuxi Qin appeared in his hands, and with a thrum of the strings, numerous lyrical blades manifested aimed at the titan.

Shebisi roared, and clouds exploded out of him. They rose above his head and called forth lightning, thunder, rain, and wind to instantly shatter the lyrical blades. The titan charged, bringing the storm with him.

Frowning, Fuxi played his qin faster. Strings erupted from the Fuxi Qin and formed a sonorous formation, amplifying the sound of his songs.

The storm and musical formation clashed. Thunder constantly disrupted the instrument's notes, but not for long. As lightning flew toward Fuxi, the sound of a pipa pierced the air, forcing the lightning to a halt. When the wind sliced at him, a flute whistled, calming the air around them. When rain splattered onto him, the beats of a drum repelled the droplets.

This was Fuxi's formation, Myriad Songbirth Formation!

While the war between song and storm continued, Nuwa locked onto Houtu and Xuanming, the only two female titans. She didn't have a top-grade cardinal spiritual artifact like Taiyi, but she'd reached the peak of the Early Quasi-Saint and had the confidence to handle two titans.

Her spiritual artifact, the Treasured Lotus Lantern, flickered and released a wave of light that surrounded them.

"Shall we?"

Houtu and Xuanming said nothing as they charged her in unison. They were a sight to behold; female titans were not any bit inferior to male titans in brute strength.

Xuanming formed raindrops around her and fired them at Nuwa. If Tongtian had seen the attack, she would have called it a mythological gatling gun. Houtu used her power of the land to summon spikes behind and below Nuwa.

Nuwa's Treasured Lotus Lantern flickered again and encased her in a green sphere, blocking the raindrops and spikes. She brought her hand in front of the lantern and a lotus of light formed above her palms.

She flicked the lotus at Xuanming. It seemed to float slowly toward the Titan of Rain, but it was actually incredibly fast.

Xuanming gathered the raindrops into one gigantic ball to shoot at the spectral flower, but it only shattered a few petals. Just as it was about to land on Xuanming, a stone slab erupted from the ground, blocking it. When the lotus lost the energy sustaining it, the stone slab crumbled, its integrity forever destroyed.

Houtu and Xuanming shared a look as they focused wholeheartedly on Nuwa. Nuwa didn't seem to care much as she focused on maintaining her green barrier of light.

Bai Ze saw there were still two titans left. "Go stall Jumang, I'll take Jizi."

The nine demon sages obeyed Bai Ze's orders, speeding toward the Titan of Wood. Bai Ze charged directly at the Titan of Lightning.

In the first clash between Bai Ze and Jizi, the demon general was knocked back with a pale face. Although he had reached the Quasi-Saint Realm, his flesh had not changed and was still at least two levels lower than that of a titan.

An apparition of a four-legged beast appeared behind Bai Zei. It had white fur, Bai Ze's face, nine eyes, and six horns on its head. This was Bai Ze's true form.

Under Bai Ze's control, the lightning bolts hurled from Jizi altered their course and struck the ground of Buzhou Mountain. Jizi snorted. He clad himself in lightning and charged at the demon sage.

Having learned his lesson, Bai Ze avoided physical confrontation with the Titan of Lightning, delaying him for as long as he could.

While their leaders fought, the giants of the Titan Tribes and the demons fought. The demons did not have as many high-end combatants as the Titan Tribe, but they were more numerous.

For every giant that fell, a hundred to a thousand demons died. As the battle raged on between the two forces, the peak of Buzhou Mountain was dyed red with blood, taking on a baleful air.

* * *

Di Jiang couldn't help but glance over at the bloodshed. The battle between the titans and the top echelon of Heavenly Court had produced no casualties so far, but the same couldn't be said for everywhere else.

Unlike the demons, who had a far higher reproduction rate, the Titan Tribe's natural reproduction was pitifully low, and they couldn't always rely on the blood pool within Pangu Temple.

"How dare you look away," Di Jun snarled as he launched 365 beams of starlight at Di Jiang and Jiuyin. Even with the combined efforts of the two, they suffered significant injuries. "Are you worried about the giants? You needn't, because your life will end here!"

Three flowers and fiery red clouds appeared behind Di Jun. Two of the flowers were occupied by Di Jun's two Corpses, but only one of them jumped out. He was clad in red battle armor with a spear in hand.

"Let me give you despair!" Di Jun said.

Upon seeing Di Jun reveal his Corpse, Taiyi increased the frequency of his attacks, bombarding the five titans and tilting the battle in his favor.

Nuwa didn't reveal her Corpse because she didn't have one. She had used the Law of Creation to temper her qi and enter the Quasi-Saint Realm.

Fuxi and Bai Ze didn't release their Corpses either. Since they'd used merit to advance and sever a Corpse, they needed time to stabilize the Corpses or risk losing them. Losing a Corpse would not only cause them to revert back to Golden Immortals of the Great Firmament, but if they could not re-cultivate, their path may be severed forever.

Di Jiang and Jiuyin shared a look. "Everyone return and regroup!"

The twelve titans immediately disengaged from their opponents, suffering minor injuries to do so. When they gathered together, Di Jun and his demon emperors and demon sages also stood as one and looked at the titans.

"If you surrender now, We can consider letting you live," Di Jun said.

Di Jiang snorted. "It's you who should be begging for your lives now."

"Pangu Genesis Formation, form!"

The twelve titans floated into the air in a pattern. Di Jun and the others wanted to stop it, but a mysterious, immense pressure froze them in place.

Blood-red energy leaked from the titans, encasing them in a humanoid shell. The shell gained flesh and blood before skin covered the entire body. A thick mane of hair grew from its enormous head and a bushy beard covered his face.

Even if they had never seen him before, all creatures instinctively knew him.

For he was Pangu.

Chapter 23

Starry Sky War Array

Tongtian, Yuanshi, and Laozi flew out of Thirty-Three Heavens through the South Heaven Gate to watch the battle. Several other invitees, including Redcloud Ancestor and Zhen Yuanzi, did the same.

The strength of the Demon Clan and Titan Tribes surprised the onlookers. Only the Three Purities could keep calm in the face of the power between these two overlord forces. However, even their faces changed when they saw the Pangu Genesis Formation.

Tongtian had already experienced Pangu's strength through the remnant memory of the Chaos Fiendgod of Time. She knew that the Pangu formed by the twelve titans paled in comparison to the genuine thing. The fake couldn't even capture one-hundredth of Pangu's charm.

But the Pangu Genesis still recreated an authentic chaos fiendgod.

The fake Pangu may have been a hundred times weaker than the real Pangu, but it was still an existence that crossed the threshold of a Golden Immortal of Primordial Origin. Sweat dripped down between Tongtian's brows just from being in its presence, and the fake Pangu wasn't even focused on them.

The false Pangu raised his hand above his head. "COME!"

The siblings all felt their bodies almost involuntarily fly toward the Pangu Genesis Formation, but they curbed that subconscious act and stabilized themselves.

"Bastard," Yuanshi cursed. The Pangu Genesis Formation wanted to summon them and recreate Pangu's spirit, but that would mean the death of the Three Purities. Even Laozi's indifferent face held a trace of hatred. Tongtian looked thoughtful as she continued to stare at the imposter.

Seeing that he couldn't summon the Three Purities, the fake Pangu frowned but still kept his hand raised. "COME!"

Taiyi frowned when he felt the Chaos Bell vibrate as if wanting to fly toward the false chaos fiendgod's hands. He grabbed the Chaos Bell and slapped it, causing it to ring loudly.

Light coalesced above the fake Pangu's hand, taking on a vague shape, but shattered into countless fragments before it could fully form. The fake's face soured with displeasure. He roared and unleashed a punch at the top echelon of the Demon Clan.

"Brother, wait!" Di Jun shouted when he saw Taiyi rush forward.

Taiyi smashed the Chaos Bell against the Pangu Genesis Formation. The fake Pangu's fist struck the bell, and the resulting tremor traveled over 100,000 li. Everyone within that distance heard a bell ring clamoring inside their ears, and those too weak fainted.

Taiyi spat out a mouthful of blood as he flew back, crashing into Buzhou Mountain. Blood started to leak from his nine orifices, and Di Jun rushed to his side.

"Are you alright?" he asked.

"I'm fine," Taiyi said, standing up and wiping the blood from his lips, his face still pale.

The rest of the Demon Clan fell silent at the absolute difference in power while the Titan Tribe cheered. Less needed to be said about the third-party observers.

Tongtian frowned as she watched the fake Pangu sluggishly walk toward South Heaven Gate. The power it displayed did not match its impressive aura. Rather than a Golden Immortal of Primordial Origin, it displayed power somewhere between a Quasi-Saint and a Saint.

"Scatter!" Di Jun shouted when he saw the Pangu Genesis Formation pull his fist back again.

The demons didn't need to be told twice, fleeing as far as possible. The second blow landed much faster, so a few were still caught in the shockwave and exploded. Most suffered major injuries, and a few died on impact. After a few more punches, the demons' casualties increased.

Di Jun could see that the Pangu Genesis Formation was growing stronger and stronger with each punch. No, the twelve titans controlling the Pangu Genesis Formation were growing more accustomed to its power.

"Form the Starry Sky War Array!" Di Jun shouted.

"Your Majesty, it isn't complete. We've only refined the formation flags for the 365 major stars!" Bai Ze shouted.

"We don't have any other choice. If this continues, we'll perish!" Di Jun said. He would have rathered expose their cards early and incomplete than face destruction.

"Whatever you're planning, do you think we'll let you?" Di Jiang's voice asked from the fake Pangu as he reached for Di Jun.

"Demons, protect us!" Di Jun shouted. Under his command, demons at and under the profound level began charging at the Pangu Genesis Formation without a care for their lives.

"Mere bugs!" the Pangu Genesis Formation shouted as he waved his hands, instantly killing all those rushing at him. But their sacrifice bought enough time.

Di Jun took the position of the Purple Majesty Star; Taiyi took his place at the Supreme Yang Star; Nuwa took the position of the Supreme Yin Star; Fuxi, the ten demon sages, and other demons of at least at the golden immortal level took their positions.

The Starry Sky appeared above Buzhou Mountain. Starlight shone from the 365 major stars and onto the demons correlating to them, forming a miniature Starry Sky.

The aura of the Starry Sky War Array trembled, sometimes blazing strong but other times flickering weakly. This was the result of only a third of the demons being Golden Immortals of the Great Firmament. The rest were split between Golden Immortals and Golden Immortals of the Great Unity, forming an imbalance.

"Haha, is this what you wanted to rely on to stop us?" The fake Pangu laughed as he unleashed two punches.

Di Jun snorted. He didn't have the spare concentration to speak nonsense with the titans. Under his control and with the cooperation of the other demons, the Starry Sky War Array expanded to engulf the Pangu Genesis Formation.

Luckily for them, they were at the peak of Buzhou Mountain, the place where the Starry Sky was closest to the land.

Each demon transformed into blazing stars that sped toward the fake Pangu. When the first star hit, the Pangu Genesis Formation halted for a moment before angrily slapping the star away.

Di Jun frowned when the demon controlling the star died, and the formation flag shattered, further destabilizing the Starry Sky War Array. Worse, that demon's sacrifice only amounted to a small scratch on the Pangu Genesis Formation.

Neither he nor the rest of the demons could shirk back in the face of death. If they faltered now, the Pangu Genesis Formation would be free to wreak havoc as it pleased.

Determined to die, Di Jun attacked the fake Pangu, smashing the Purple Majesty Star against the Pangu Genesis Formation. Taiyi, Fuxi, Nuwa, the ten demon sages, and the rest of the demons fought like crazy.

With each clash, more and more wounds appeared on the fake Pangu, but simultaneously, more and more demons perished. When a third of the demons forming the Starry Sky War Array died, the array collapsed.

Di Jun, Taiyi, Nuwa, Fuxi, Bai Ze, and the surviving demons all collapsed onto the ground. The weaker ones directly died from the backlash, while blood leaked profusely from the stronger demons' nine orifices.

Although Di Jun and the demon emperors had survived, three of the ten demon sages had perished during the confrontation.

"Hahaha, you stupid crow, time for you to die!" Zhurong's voice called out from the Pangu Genesis Formation.

The fake Pangu locked its hands together and raised them above its head. With a roar, it prepared to smash its fists down like a hammer, ending Di Jun's life. If he died, he would be the shortest-lived Heavenly Emperor, dying after not even one day.

Midway, the Pangu Genesis Formation froze. Cracks spread throughout its body where the stars had injured it. Like a porcelain statue, the cracks grew until a blood-red light spilled out of them. The Pangu Genesis Formation shattered, its skin falling off like broken pieces of glass, revealing the twelve titans encased in red light. The red light evaporated like smoke, and the titans fell to the ground, much like the demons had done earlier.

The titans didn't spit out blood as the demons had, but their aura drastically dropped. They barely had the strength of Golden Immortals of the Great Firmament at this stage.

Di Jiang glared at Di Jun and then glanced at the demons closing in on them. During the battle earlier, the Pangu Genesis Formation had only managed to wipe out a small portion of the demons before Di Jun formed the Starry Sky War Formation and blocked them.

If they forced it, they could probably kill Di Jun and his emperors, but by then, they would be swarmed by the demons. It remained to be seen how many of the twelve titans would survive.

"Retreat!" Di Jiang ordered.

"What? We have them on the ropes!" Zhurong protested, pointing to the bloodied demon emperors.

"Follow Di Jiang's orders! The losses would be too much even if we did kill them all," Gonggong said as he ran. "Unless you want your brothers and sisters to die just for that crow!"

Zhurong roared with fury. He glared one last time at Di Jun before following the rest of the titans to safety.

The Demon Clan watched the Titan Tribe's retreat. Di Jun didn't order the demons to attack either. The demons had been cowed by the Titan Tribe's Pangu Genesis Formation. He feared that he would lose the Demon Clan's trust if he ordered them to attack now. In addition, even if they eliminated the Titan Tribe, the loss would be too high and would only benefit the Ten Thousand Immortals Alliance.

Did Dong Wanggong think he couldn't spot him? Di Jun knew Dong Wanggong's thoughts. The mantis stalks the cicada, unaware of the oriole behind. Wanting to be the oriole? Dream on!

The invitees left by themselves without Di Jun needing to send them off. After the debacle with the Titan Tribe, how could Heavenly Court still have the spare thought to entertain them?

* * *

After the Titan Tribe returned to their headquarters at the base of Buzhou Mountain, all twelve titans entered Pangu Temple. They immediately used the blood pool to recuperate their losses suffered from using the Pangu Genesis Formation.

As Di Jiang had expected, the Pangu Genesis Formation had placed too much pressure on them. Even with flesh as strong as theirs, they could not bear the burden for long.

Still, it was not without gain. In using the Pangu Genesis Formation, Di Jiang had experienced the fleshly prowess of a true chaos fiendgod and found that the shackles limiting him had weakened.

The other titans had gained a similar feeling. Given enough time, they would be able to break into the Quasi-Saint Realm with strength, greatly boosting their powers. Once all twelve of them were Quasi-Saints, they could bear the power of the Pangu Genesis Formation better. Their control would improve, and they could utilize the formation's strength better, but the same weakness remained. If they could no longer bear the formation's pressure, they would receive a backlash and suffer for it yet again.

Once all the titans finished recuperating, Di Jiang asked for the causality report. He frowned when he heard that the Titan Tribe had lost over 30 percent of its members, but it was not all without gain.

"Kuafu, Chiyou, and Houyi have progressed nicely. If nurtured well, they might reach our level," their leader said. Although Kuafu, Chiyou, and Houyi had reached the equivalent of a Golden Immortal of the Great Firmament, the twelve titans were still more powerful at the same level. "Tianwu, Houtu, make sure to pay close attention to them."

The Titan Tribe was further split into twelve smaller tribes. Kuafu came from the Tianwu Tribe, while Chiyou and Houyi came from the Houtu Tribe.

"Now, let's move on to important business," Di Jiang continued. "Does anyone have a method to eliminate the Pangu Genesis Formation's backlash? At this rate, we might injure our foundation if we use it two or three more times."

All the titans' expressions turned grave.

"When the demons set up their array," Houtu said. "I noticed that each one carried a flag. Perhaps we can emulate them? Or at least have the flags bear part of the pressure to lessen the strain on us."

"That idea seems probable, but does anyone here know how to refine a formation flag?" Jiuyin asked.

The room fell silent. None of them had spirit, which was required to understand the law, but it also greatly added to refining artifacts. The most refining the Titan Tribe could do was shape materials.

"Forget it. Let's focus on the third matter," Di Jiang said. "What can we do about the Demon Clan, no, the Heavenly Court? I don't know what they did, but large amounts of merit descended. I don't know what use merit has, but I'm afraid it can increase the Heavenly Court's strength in the long run. What can we do to replicate their feat?"

"Hmpf, I say ignore it," Zhurong said. "I refuse to seek acknowledgement from the Way of Heaven! Merit comes from there. It's not worth anything to us at all."

"Stop being so stubborn," Gonggong chided. "We can't ignore the Way of Heaven no matter how much we dismiss it. It's a power that can damage us."

"What, are you afraid?"

"Yes," Gonggong answered bluntly. "The Heavenly Court already has five quasi-saints. Who is to say they won't have more in the future?

They also have that Starry Sky War Array. At a single glance, you can tell it's incomplete. As long as they have enough Quasi-Saints and they possess a formation and are willing to pay the price, they can defeat us."

"So we have to eliminate them as soon as possible. We should attack them right now."

Gonggong looked as if he was torn between smashing Zhurong's head into the ground and covering his face with his hand. He settled for turning away and ignoring the idiot.

"Let's form the Pangu Genesis Formation and kill as many demons as we can," Zhurong continued. He looked around, but none of the titans agreed with him. Angry, he snorted and shut up.

"How about we worship Father God?" Houtu suggested. "Father God incarnated into all things, the Way of Heaven should also be incarnated from Father God. Since the Heavenly Court rules the skies, why don't we rule the five regions?"

Di Jiang and the other titans' eyes lit up. They began discussing the exact details of the ceremony, but stopped when Houyi entered Pangu Temple.

"Honored Titans, the Three Purities appeared outside of the Titan Tribe, asking to see you."

Di Jiang frowned with worry. Why did the Three Purities come? To seek revenge?

Chapter 24

Nine-Revolution Arcane Art

Tongtian, Yuanshi, and Laozi waited outside of the Titan Tribe's temple, only turning their heads to look upon the twelve titans as they emerged. Tongtian narrowed her eyes when she sensed their aura, which had almost fully recovered.

"What do you want?" Zhurong brusquely asked.

Di Jiang frowned but didn't rebuke the Titan of Fire.

Tongtian smiled brightly as if Zhurong's rudeness made her happy. "We're here to help you."

Zhurong snorted, "What can you do for us? You're lucky the Demon Clan is around, or else we would target you!"

Tongtian's smile deepened. "The backlash from the Pangu Genesis Formation doesn't feel good, right?"

At the titan's silence, she continued, "We can help you refine twelve formation flags that can bear the pressure in your stead. In all of the Great Desolation, no one is more skilled at artificing than my Second Brother. After all, his inheritance came directly from Father God."

Many of the titans gritted their teeth. That fact shamed them because they considered themselves the orthodox lineage of Pangu.

"What is the price?" Di Jiang asked. He had to admit that there was no one more suitable than Jade Purity Yuanshi to refine the formation flags. Once he spoke, none of the titans went against his decision.

"Six drops of blood essence from each of you," Tongtian stated.

"Why don't you just directly kill us then!" Qiangliang roared. Anger colored his eyes as he glared at Tongtian, who continued to smile as if she hadn't felt it.

"Three drops are needed to refine the flags. The other three are payment for our services," she said. "You didn't think we were doing this out of the goodness of our hearts, did you?"

Di Jiang frowned. "That's too much. You only need two at most, and giving so many will weaken us. What if Heavenly Court attacks us? Are you saying you will protect us?"

Tongtian inwardly rolled her eyes. Outwardly, she said, "You don't have to worry about that. It will take more than 10,000 years for Heavenly Court to recuperate their losses, and by then, the Dao Ancestor's third sermon will be just around the corner. Di Jun would have to be an idiot to attack then. Not to mention the Violet Manor lurking around. I suppose I can lower it to five drops."

"Make it three," Di Jiang said. "For you to refine formation flags, you would need to learn the Pangu Genesis Formation. We can't give it for free."

"Are you joking?" Tongtian asked. "You and I both know that the Pangu Genesis Formation is useless to anyone else but you. Knowing it and not knowing it is no different."

"But you will be different. You will have our blood essence, and it's not impossible for you to make something of it," Di Jiang said. He gave Tongtian a pointed look. "Isn't that right, inheritor of formations? Three drops."

"Five drops," Tongtian said, not relenting.

"Then leave. If you can't accept three drops, then we don't have a deal."

Zhurong smiled viciously as he and the other titans brandished their abilities, and Tongtian's smile finally left her face.

Yuanshi stepped forward. "I told you, Third Sister, you shouldn't reason with these brutes. They can only understand strength."

Three flowers appeared behind Yuanshi, and his Corpse flew out. Laozi followed Yuanshi's lead. Tongtian sighed, and her white-robed Evil Corpse appeared.

The three revealed Corpses had the cultivation of the Early Quasi-Saint Realm. Coupled with the Three Purities, the twelve titans were facing off against six Quasi-Saints. And unlike the Heavenly Court, they had two more people at the Intermediate Quasi-Saint Realm.

"What's the meaning of this?" Di Jiang demanded.

"Are you blind? It's exactly what it looks like," Yuanshi said.

"Besides, aren't you the ones who showed hostility first? You can't blame us for retaliating," Tongtian said. "Not to mention, when you formed the Pangu Genesis Formation, you tried to absorb us. I'm sure you don't need me to say what would have happened if you'd succeeded, right?"

Di Jiang stayed silent as he stared at the six Quasi-Saints in front of him. With each passing second, the Three Purities' momentum continued to rise. They wouldn't have needed to be so fearful if they had been at their peak, but they had just recovered from the backlash of the Pangu Genesis Formation.

Finally, he sighed. "Alright, I agree, five drops. But the matter of trying to absorb you three will be put behind us. Deal?"

Yuanshi snorted and stored his Corpse. Tongtian followed suit and nodded.

"But we will only give three drops of blood essence each now. After you refine the formation flags, we can slowly exchange them," Di Jiang said.

Tongtian agreed in place of Yuanshi and Laozi. With the deal hammered out, the twelve titans returned to Pangu Temple. After squeezing out three drops of blood essence each, they exited and handed them to the Three Purities.

With the blood essences in hand, the Three Purities returned to Kunlun Mountain. Tongtian didn't plan on returning to Fangzhang Immortal Island for now. With how weakened Heavenly Court was at the moment, they couldn't destroy the alliance of 10,000 immortals, which meant that she couldn't grab the Kunlun Mirror amidst the turmoil.

Inside Three Purity Hall, the siblings counted their earnings, thirty-six drops of blood floating in front of them.

"I call them brutes, and they don't believe it," Yuanshi said, laughing with none of his usual sternness. "I only needed a single drop from each of them to refine the formation flags for them."

"It can't be blamed on them. They don't possess a spirit, so they can only estimate," Laozi said, but he was obviously in a good mood as he stroked his long white beard.

"Alright, alright," Tongtian said. "I just need three drops of Di Jiang's and Jiuyin's blood. Since they gave us three, I'll take two of each for now and take the last two after they hand over the rest. You can split the rest."

"I'm afraid not, Third Sister," Yuanshi said. "You're the one who came up with the idea, so you have to take more."

"No, no, I feel that you put in more work since you are the one refining the formation flags. If anything, you should take more."

"That's not right, you should take more."

Before Yuanshi and Tongtian could argue more, Laozi interjected. "We'll split it into three equal parts. We are all siblings, what's a few drops of blood between us?"

"But—" Tongtian wanted to continue, but Yuanshi interrupted her.

"That's right, we're siblings. Don't forget, we still owe you for the Ninth-Ranked White Lotuses of Purification," Yuanshi finished.

"Alright," Tongtian relented, but she had a smile that couldn't be wiped off her face. Aside from Di Jiang's and Jieyin's blood, she'd taken one drop each from Houtu, Rushou, Zhurong, Gonggong, and Jumang.

Now they'd just have to create a method to cultivate their flesh. After personally seeing the Pangu Genesis Formation and with the titans' blood essence, they advanced very quickly. Thus, the Nine-Revolution Arcane Art was created. Although you couldn't cultivate a body equal to a titan's, it could rival a giant's.

The 1st revolution correlated to the realm before Earth Immortal.

The 2nd revolution correlated to the Earth Immortal Realm.

The 3rd revolution correlated to the Sky Immortal Realm.

The 4th revolution correlated to the Profound Immortal Realm.

The 5th revolution correlated to the Golden Immortal Realm.

The 6th revolution correlated to the Great Unity Realm.

The 7th revolution correlated to the Great Firmament Realm.

The 8th revolution should correlate to the Quasi-Saint Realm.

The 9th revolution should correlate to the Primordial Origin Realm. At this level, the cultivator should attain a body akin to a chaos fiendgod's.

Of course, the last two were purely theoretical at this point. Not even the sixth and seventh revolutions had been fully created, only conceptualized.

Still, it was enough for now. The Nine-Revolution Arcane Art was only meant to be auxiliary; the priority was still cultivating the law.

Tongtian, Yuanshi, and Laozi returned to their respective halls. In Supreme Purity Hall, Tongtian took out a drop of Jiuyin's silver and and a drop of Di Jiang's gold blood essences.

She took out the Qiankun Cauldron borrowed from Yuanshi and dropped them inside. Tongtian began to merge the two drops' essences. It took her much longer than she expected, over a thousand years, but she was satisfied.

She saved the other rest for later and stared at that silver-gold drop of blood essence. She could feel the Law of Time emanating from within, but she could also feel the Law of Space entangled with it.

"Time is venerated; space is king. Then, what about spacetime?"

Tongtian opened her mouth and swallowed the drop of silver-gold blood essence. She began to circulate the Nine-Revolution Arcane Art.

First Revolution.

Second Revolution.

Third Revolution.

Fourth Revolution.

Fifth Revolution!

Tongtian smiled, but it wasn't the increase in her bodily strength that made her happy. She had incorporated the spacetime blood essence into her body, and although she didn't gain any innate abilities like the titans, her sense for the Law of Time increased, however slight it was.

In addition, she finally sensed the Law of Space that had eluded her for years. Once she mastered both of them, she would merge them into the Law of Spacetime.

Tongtian's smile took a self-deprecating manner. "I haven't even mastered the Law of Time yet or embarked on the Law of Space. Why am I getting ahead of myself?"

While she was busy cultivating the Nine-Revolution Arcane Art, Laozi had severed his second Corpse. After 3,000 years, Yuanshi also severed his second Corpse.

Tongtian left the Supreme Purity Hall to find Laozi. She wanted the Ninth-Ranked Red Lotus of Karma, and Laozi had focused on nurturing the red lotus first before nurturing the green lotus seeds. Once she received the Ninth-Ranked Red Lotus of Karma, Tongtian returned to Supreme Purity Hall to focus on reaching her optimum state. Once reached, she said, "SEVER!"

Three magnolia flowers appeared behind her above a silver river. On her right, a humanoid figure formed and flew into the Ninth-Rank Red Lotus of Karma.

The good thoughts she used to sever her Good Corpse were the emotions that came from being the orthodox lineage of Pangu. It was not wrong to take pride in one's lineage, but excessive pride would turn into arrogance.

For some, it might be their evil thoughts, but for Tongtian, it was her good thoughts.

A third pressure emanated from Kunlun Mountain again. It soon reached 30,000 li, then 60,000 li, and finally stopped at 90,000 li. By this point, the denizens of the Great Desolation were no longer surprised by the Three Purities' abnormal cultivation speed.

Back inside the Supreme Purity Hall, the Ninth-Rank Red Lotus of Karma released a red light and transformed. When the transformation was over, the lotus transformed into a man who looked like he could be Tongtian's brother.

The man wore red robes and had excessive beauty. It wasn't beauty that made him feminine, but a sort of handsomeness that transcended any form of description. Between his brows was an arrogance, open and unashamed.

Tongtian waved her hand and stored her Good Corpse, as there were only a few thousand years left before the Dao Ancestor's third sermon. Until then, Tongtian focused on comprehending the Laws of Time and Space.

* * *

Kong Xuan meditated under the Five Elements Tree. While under the connate spiritual root, his lips constantly moved as he gained insights into the five elements. Finally, he opened his eyes, and five colored lights emitted from his pupils before they dimmed.

After joining Violet Manor, Dong Wanggong had wanted to slice off a branch for Kong Xuan to refine into an innate spiritual artifact. He wanted to hook Kong Xuan in immediately after feeling the disparity between the Heavenly Court and Titan Tribe compared to Violet Manor. However, Kong Xuan stopped him, as he still needed to meditate under the complete Five Elements Tree.

Dong Wanggong had completely misunderstood Kong Xuan's thoughts, thinking that he was considering the overall future of Violet Manor. He'd given the phoenix's son two low-grade innate spiritual artifacts and one middle-grade innate spiritual artifact.

Kong Xuan snorted as he recalled this. Did Dong Wanggong really think his charisma was that impressive? Nothing more than a pawn for Hongjun's schemes. Still, Dong Wanggong had his uses.

Kong Xuan stood up and flew toward an essence-filled cave on Penglai Immortal Island. All in all, it actually surpassed his former residence near the Undying Volcano in the South. Once inside, he began to optimize his condition.

It was time to enter the Quasi-Saint Realm.

He reached his peak condition a hundred years later. Three flowers and five differently colored clouds appeared behind him. His qi separated into five balls of light, and each entered a cloud.

After some time, the balls of light emerged from the clouds; each had been stained by the cloud's color. They shifted and entered another cloud. When they came out, they had two colors. The process repeated until each ball glowed with five colors.

All five balls of light merged and entered Kong Xuan's body. His body released a five-colored aura, and along with it was tremendous pressure that eventually stopped at thirty thousand li.

Kong Xuan had finally entered the Quasi-Saint Realm.

CHAPTER 25

Hongjun's Third Sermon

As the deadline for Hongjun's third sermon neared, more and more followers of the Immortal Path began to cut their evil thoughts, good thoughts, or obsessions to enter the Quasi-Saint Realm.

In Fire Origin Cave, Redcloud Ancestor emitted a pressure that reached 30,000 li.

In Wuzhuang Temple of Longevity Mountain, Zhen Yuanzi successfully severed a Corpse and entered the Quasi-Saint Realm.

In the Darknoth Sea, inside Darknoth Palace, Kunpeng severed a Corpse and became a Quasi-Saint.

Near the Undying Volcano of the South, the Phoenix Clan felt a pressure that reached 30,000 li weighing them down. The elders frowned when they realized it was Jinchi, the Golden-Winged Great Roc, who had reached the Quasi-Saint Realm.

The Blood Sea trembled as terrifying turbulence originated in the center. Minghe sat atop his Twelfth-Ranked Red Lotus of Karma with the Yuanti and Abi Swords circling around him. A moment later, a figure with 70 percent similarity to Minghe appeared. His pure-white robes contrasted greatly against Minghe's blood-red ones.

None of these events escaped Heavenly Court's surveillance. With billions of demons under their flag, it was trivial for the Heavenly Court to dispatch a few demons to keep an eye on the Great Desolation—especially the territories of powerful gods like Redcloud Ancestor, Zhen Yuanzi, and Jinchi.

The only exception was Minghe, merely because he resided in the Blood Sea. Even Golden Immortals of the Great Firmament were liable to be stained by the bloody miasma rising from it. Only Minghe, who was born from it, was unaffected.

However, none of this mattered to Di Jun at the moment. His eyes narrowed as he glanced at the messenger kneeling below him. "Repeat what you just said."

The demon messenger shivered, but he dared not defy the Heavenly Emperor's orders. "Reporting to Your Majesty, the Violet Manor has sent out an emissary asking the Fox Clan to join them."

Although Di Jun had formed the Demon Clan and absorbed most of the remnants of the Hundred Clans—except for the Dragon Clan, Phoenix Clan, and Qilin Clan—there were still a few clans that did not throw their lot in with him. The Fox Clan was naturally among them.

"Dong Wanggong, do you really think We are afraid of you?" Di Jun muttered. "You should have obediently played your role as an island owner. Once the Dao Ancestor's third sermon is finished, your end will be near." He closed his eyes and calmed down. When he opened them, they were clear and unchanging. "Send an emissary to the Fox Clan. Tell them that they have until the end of the Dao Ancestor's third sermon to join the Heavenly Court."

"At once, Your Majesty." The demon messenger inwardly sighed with relief, finally able to escape from the heavy atmosphere of the throne hall.

Di Jun sighed. After the fateful clash with the Titan Tribe, more and more problems had been cropping up. "It's time to unify the rest of the remaining Hundred Clans."

* * *

The Fox Clan's patriarch smiled bitterly when he received Heavenly Court's messenger. After experiencing the horror of the Dragon-Phoenix Tribulation, he wanted to keep the Fox Clan out of the next tribulation. According to his experience, the protagonists of this one should be the Heavenly Court, Titan Tribe, and Violet Manor.

The Fox Clan had nearly perished during the Dragon-Phoenix Tribulation, but both the Heavenly Court and Violet Manor were forcing him to make a decision.

The fox patriarch hated the alliance of 10,000 immortals. If they hadn't sent someone, Heavenly Court would have been content to ignore them, and they would've passed the next tribulation safely.

As he sent away Heavenly Court's messenger, the patriarch summoned all of his clan's elders. They needed to make a decision soon.

* * *

In the chaotic boundary, the congenital gods gathered once more. At the head were the Three Purities. Each one possessed Late Quasi-Saint Realm cultivation bases, far above the rest. There was actually one less intermediate Quasi-Saint than advanced Quasi-Saints.

Perhaps Taiyi or Nuwa may have advanced to the Intermediate Quasi-Realm, but they'd had to take time to recuperate from the injuries they'd received in the battle with the Titan Tribe.

Tongtian spotted Jieyin and Zhunti. Of everyone present, she expected them to have reached the Intermediate Quasi-Saint Realm, not Di Jun. *Perhaps the West is too barren for them to get a decent innate spiritual artifact?*

She had accidentally stumbled onto the truth.

Aside from them, she spotted more than twenty Quasi-Saints, but it was hard to tell which one had stepped into the Quasi-Saint Realm by tempering their qi with the law.

Tongtian also spotted some new faces. Heavenly Court had lost quite a few demons in battle. Many of them had been guests of Violet Heaven Palace, so this opening allowed a few lucky congenital gods to come. She even spotted that annoying guy who loitered around Kunlun Mountain.

Soon, the doors to Violet Heaven Palace opened, and Haotian and Yaochi stepped out, still appearing as children. "The Master will begin his third sermon. Please enter."

The 3,000 guests filed into the main hall. Laozi, Yuanshi, Tongtian, Nuwa, Jieyin, and Zhunti entered first to take their positions of privilege. After them were the other Quasi-Saints: Di Jun, Taiyi, Redcloud Ancestor, Zhen Yuanzi, Kong Xuan, Jinchi, Minghe, and many more.

Notably, Dong Wanggong had attempted to enter the main hall above the others as head of the male immortals, but the collective glares from the Three Purities cowed him. So what if he was the head of male immortals christened by the Dao Ancestor? He was only an early Quasi-Saint, and the Three Purities were advanced Quasi-Saints.

Once everyone was seated, Haotian rang the Purple-Gold Bell. The clear chime echoed in the hall, and Hongjun appeared out of nothingness as if he had always sat on the cloud throne in front of them.

Tongtian looked closely at Hongjun. Before, he had given off a mystifying aura that she couldn't see through. Now, she couldn't sense him at all. Even if he hid his cultivation that far surpassed hers, Tongtian should have still been able to detect him.

It had nothing to do with the difference in realms but a lifeform's awareness of another life. Now, she couldn't sense that at all, as if Hongjun had become an inorganic mass with no emotions.

Tongtian couldn't ponder on such matters as Hongjun directly started to preach. Shimmering golden lotuses, soaring dragons, blazing phoenixes, roaring qilins, hundreds of blooming flowers, and many more spectacular phenomena occurred. It was as if the hall of Violet Heaven Palace had transformed into heaven and earth.

Hongjun's voice seemed to merge with the world, echoing directly into everyone's heads.

The Dao that can be spoken of is not the Eternal Dao.

The name that can be named is not the Eternal Name.

Nameless, is the origin of Heaven and Earth.

The named is the Mother of all things.

Thus, the constant void enables one to observe the true essence.

The eternal being enables one to see the outward manifestations.

These two come paired from the same origin.

But when the essence is manifested, it has a different name.

This exact origin is called the "Profound Mystery."

As profound the mystery as It can be, It is the Gate to the essence of all life.

The Dao can be infused into nature and put to use without being exhausted.

It is so deep and subtle, like an abyss that is the origin of all things.

It is complete and perfect as a wholeness that can

Round off all sharp edges;

Resolve confusion;

Harmonized with the glory;

Act in unity with the lowliness.

The Dao is so profound and yet invisible, It exists everywhere and anywhere.

I do not know whose creation It is, It existed before Heaven and Earth.

The spirit of the valley is immortal.

It is called the mystic nature.

The gate of the mystic nature is regarded as the root of the universe.

It is everlasting and cannot be consumed.

Heaven is everlasting, and earth is enduring.

The reason that they are everlasting is because they do not exist for themselves.

Hence, they are long-lived.

Thus, although the Saint puts himself last, he finds himself in the lead.

Although he is not self-concerned, he finds himself accomplished.

It is because he is not focused on self-interests and hence can fulfill his true nature.

Can one unite the body and the spirit as one and embrace the "Oneness" without departing from the Great Dao?

Can one achieve harmony with such gentleness by holding onto the true spirit within with the innocence of an infant?

Can one free oneself from worldly temptations and cleanse one's mind so that no faults shall occur?

Can a ruler love his people by governing with the Dao without personal intentions?

Can the mystic gate to all life essence be opened or closed without the virtue of the mysterious nature?

Can one gain the insight of nature and become a Saint without effort or action?

The Profound Mystery creates and nurtures all things without the desire to possess them.

It performs with all efforts without claiming credit.

It flourishes all beings without the intention to take control.
Such is the Way of Saints.

As Hongjun spoke, those too weak started to nod off as their consciousness drifted. If the first sermon was for all beings at the Great Firmament Realm and below, and the second sermon was for Quasi-Saints, then the third sermon was for the future Saints of Heaven.

Before 100 years had passed, more than 90 percent of the 3,000 guests had already fallen asleep. After 500 years, less than 1 percent were still awake. Even then, the Quasi-Saints struggled to comprehend the esoteric meaning behind Hongjun's words.

The Three Purities had it easier due to their Advanced Quasi-Saint Realm cultivation base, but even they struggled. What the Quasi-Saints could not understand, they forced themselves to memorize, even as their memories faded.

Jinchi and Kunpeng fell asleep at the two thousandth year.

Nuwa and Zhunti fell asleep at the two thousand and three hundredth year.

Kong Xuan fell asleep at the two thousand and five hundredth year.

Tongtian and Jieyin fell asleep on the two thousand and seven hundredth year.

Laozi fell asleep on the two thousand and nine hundredth year.

Yuanshi stayed awake throughout the whole sermon, but veins bulged on his head as he struggled to comprehend the profundities spoken by the Dao Ancestor.

Honjun's eyes flashed with surprise as he glanced at Yuanshi, but he quickly schooled his features. After he finished speaking, the myriad phenomena disappeared, and all 3,000 guests awakened.

They tried to recall Hongjun's sermon, but they could only remember vague recollections impressed on their minds. Some would discover that their future breakthroughs became easier, but the prime beneficiaries were the six in the front.

A hint of emotion returned to Hongjun's eyes as he scanned the numerous guests below. "After I became a Saint of Heaven, I held three sermons to educate all beings in Heaven and Earth. With my duties fulfilled, I will merge with the Way of Heaven and make up for its deficiencies."

Every single soul, no matter their true intentions, kneeled. "Please reconsider, Dao Ancestor!"

"Do not persuade me, I have already made up my mind," Hongjun said.

"The Dao Ancestor is benevolent!"

After he sat back down again, Di Jun let out a sigh of relief. He planned to deal with Violet Manor; with Hongjun occupied, he would have fewer scruples.

"Before I merge with the Way of Heaven, I will accept disciples to propagate my Immortal Path." Hongjun's looked upon the Three Purities. "Laozi, Yuanshi, Tongtian, are you willing to be my disciples?"

Without any hesitation, all three kowtowed. "Disciple greets Master!"

A smile appeared on Hongjun's emotionless face, and he turned to his next recruit. "Nuwa, you will have great merits in the future, and can also be my disciple."

"Disciple greets Master."

Behind Nuwa, Fuxi smiled, happy for his sister. On the other hand, Di Jun's brows trembled for a moment before smoothing.

Jieyin and Zhunti looked at Hongjun with bright eyes. After Nuwa, it was their turn next, right? However, Hongjun closed his eyes and went silent. The two started to fret.

With two loud thuds, Jieyin and Zhunti knocked their heads on the ground. "Please have mercy on us two brothers. The West is barren. We hope to bring prosperity to the West with your teachings!"

Hongjun sighed and looked at the two of them. "Although your merits are slightly lacking and are not of Pangu's orthodox lineage, you have great perseverance and pure hearts for the Great Dao. Would you two be willing to become my nominal disciples?"

Jieyin and Zhunti inwardly grumbled about Hongjun's unfairness. They also sat on the six prayer mats at the front, so why were they treated differently?

Still, they did not hesitate for a second and kowtowed. "Disciple greets Master."

Hongjun nodded. "The Heavens are heartless; Saints are not benevolent; all under Saints are ants!"

His words echoed in everyone's ears. All under Saints are ants? Didn't that include Quasi-Saints too? Each of them was a congenital god, a major power born in the Great Desolation. How could they be willing to be ants?

Hongjun ignored their inner thoughts and turned toward the six in front. "Under my Immortal Path, there should be seven Saints of Heaven."

Chapter 26

Grandmist Violet Qi

Jinchi's intestines turned green with regret. He could have also been one of the Dao Ancestor's disciples. Although the status was honorable, what he regretted more was what the position represented.

Under the Immortal Path, there should be seven Saints of Heaven. Including the Dao Ancestor, wouldn't that mean the six sitting in the front would become Saints of Heaven?

"Didn't I tell you that you would regret it?" Kong Xuan whispered.

Jinchi turned his gaze to his brother, his eyes full of regret. Unfortunately, there was no medicine for regret in this world.

Redcloud Ancestor was equally forlorn. What had possessed him to give up the seat to Zhunti? Wouldn't it have been good to continue sitting there and become a Saint of Heaven?

Kunpeng's eyes bore into Kong Xuan's back. If it hadn't been for Kong Xuan's attack back then, he would have gotten the fifth seat. He wouldn't have been like that idiot Jinchi and given it to Jieyin just because of the pressure from the other guests.

Hongjun didn't care about what 3,000 gods thought. He waved his hand, and three wisps of purple qi appeared in his palm. "Before I became a Saint of Heaven, I managed to grab eight Grandmist Violet Qis: the foundations of sainthood. I have already used one."

"The Three Purities are transformed from Pangu's spirit and bear Heaven-Opening Merit, they can become Saints of Heaven." Hongjun waved his hand, and three Grandmist Violet Qis flew in front of Laozi, Yuanshi, and Tongtian.

All three grabbed them and stored them under the envious gazes of everyone present.

Nuwa's emotions peaked when she saw Hongjun look at her. "Nuwa will have great merits in the future. You can also become a Saint of Heaven."

Nuwa couldn't keep her composure as she stored the Grandmist Violet Qi, ignorant of Di Jun's dark look.

Jieyin and Zhunti waited expectantly, but when they saw Hongjun stop talking, they started to fret again. They complained that the Dao Ancestor was biased, but they still begged for the Grandmist Violet Qi. "Master, please have mercy on us. When we become Saints, we promise that we will return the West to its previous prosperity."

Hongjun turned toward the two of them. "I hope you two can remember the oath you made today."

He waved his hand, and two strands of Grandmist Violet Qis appeared in front of Jieyin and Zhunti. The two western gods stored them, joy on their faces.

At this, none of the other gods could sit still anymore. The Dao Ancestor had eight strands total. He had used up one and bestowed six to his disciples. Shouldn't there be one more?

"Dao Ancestor, I am the Heavenly Emperor. Can I become a Saint of Heaven?" Di Jun asked.

Hongjun glanced at him and said, "The Saints are tasked with educating all creatures of heaven and earth. The Heavenly Emperor's duty is to rule heaven and earth. The Heavenly Emperor cannot be a Saint of Heaven."

Di Jun almost collapsed onto the ground. All under Saints are ants. Wouldn't that mean he, the Heavenly Emperor, was also an ant?

"Although the Heavenly Emperor cannot become a Saint, they are tasked with maintaining heaven and earth. At certain times, they can utilize the power of heaven and earth like a Saint."

"Dao Ancestor, as the head of male disciples, can I become a Saint of Heaven?" Dong Wanggong asked immediately.

The other gods all began to beg. They were afraid that the Dao Ancestor would really bestow the last Grandmist Violet Qi upon Dong Wanggong, forever severing their chance of sainthood.

Hongjun sighed and said, "The Great Dao is fifty; the Eye of Heaven is forty-nine; the last one escaped. If you can grasp that last one, you will attain hope."

He waved his hand. The last strand of Grandmist Violet Qi floated into the hall, swimming around. Everyone held their breaths, hoping that the Grandmist Violet Qi would choose them.

Kong Xuan's breath stilted when he sensed that the Grandmist Violet Qi showed signs of flying toward him! It may be a great fortune for others, but it was a disaster for him. He quickly hid his aura, and the Grandmist Violet Qi halted in its movement. After floating around a few more times, the Grandmist Violet Qi chose Redcloud Ancestor.

Redcloud Ancestor's face lit up with joy, blind to the envious looks of those around him. Laozi, Yuanshi, Tongtian, Nuwa, Jieyin, and Zhunti were the Dao Ancestor's disciples, but Redcloud Ancestor wasn't.

Didn't the Dao Ancestor say that as long as they grasped the last one, they would grab onto hope?

Once the last Grandmist Violet Qi had been distributed, Hongjun spoke once more, "Before I became a Saint of Heaven, I collected numerous treasures. Now they are useless to me, so I will distribute them."

Hongjun waved his hand, and a yin-yang diagram appeared in his hand. He turned to Laozi. "Laozi, as the head of the Three Purities and head disciple of the Immortal Path, I will bestow upon you the Taiji Diagram. It is a top-grade cardinal spiritual artifact formed from the handle of Pangu's Heaven-Opening Ax that can anchor your Karmic Luck."

Laozi reached out and grabbed the Taiji Diagram. His usual indifference disappeared as he lovingly caressed it. Not even when gaining the Grandmist Violet Qi did he have such a reaction. "Disciple thanks Master!"

Hongjun turned to Yuanshi as a banner carrying the color of chaos appeared in his hand. "Yuanshi, this is the Pangu Banner, a top-grade cardinal spiritual artifact. It integrates offense and defense into one and can also anchor your Karmic Luck."

Tongtian's eyes lit up, and she stared expectantly at her master. Sure enough, he did not fail her hopes as four seemingly plain swords appeared before him.

"After I defeated Rahu during the Dragon-Phoenix Tribulation, I attained these four Immortal Extermination Swords. They are not spiritual artifacts, but they have power exceeding a top-grade cardinal treasure. The Immortal Extermination Diagram was destroyed during the battle, but if you manage to restore and form the Immortal Extermination Sword Formation, four immortals at the same level need to unite in order to break it."

When everyone heard Hongjun's words, they sucked in a cold breath. After he merged with the Way of Heaven, there would be six guaranteed Saints and at most seven Saints. The Three Purities were united, so wouldn't it mean that Tongtian would be nearly impossible to defeat?

"This is the number-one killing formation in heaven and earth. It is too sharp and cannot anchor your Karmic Luck. You must remember not to deploy the Four Immortal Extermination Sword Formation lightly," Hongjun finished.

It was love at first sight. Tongtian accepted the four Immortal Extermination Swords and gently caressed the blades. She blinked when she realized that she had yet to thank the Dao Ancestor. "Disciple thanks Master."

Hongjun nodded and turned to Nuwa. "You are kind and do not like to fight, so I will bestow upon you two top-grade innate artifacts: the Mountain and River Diorama and the Red Hydrangea. The Mountain and River Diorama contains a Minor World within and can defend against all attacks from those weaker than you. The Red Hydrangea can instantly defeat those weaker than you, but its function does not end there.

"Heaven and earth will have three marriages: heaven, earth, and mortal. You will use this treasure to establish them and gain merit, thereby transforming the Red Hydrangea into a meritorious spiritual artifact no weaker than a cardinal spiritual artifact." Hongjun waved his hand, and both artifacts floated to their new owner.

Nuwa happily accepted them. Although she was unhappy that the Three Purities were given top-grade cardinal spiritual artifacts, the Red Hydrangea blew away any jealousy. "Disciple thanks Master."

Jieyin and Zhunti had a bad premonition once it was their turn. As they expected, the Dao Ancestor seemed to have forgotten them again. Helplessly, they could only thicken their skin and beg the him to bestow treasures.

Hongjun waved his hand, and four artifacts flew out to them. "I will give Jieyin the Twelfth-Ranked Golden Lotus of Merit to suppress your luck, as well as a high-grade innate spiritual artifact, the Vajra Pestle and Mortar. For Zhunti, I bequeath the top-grade innate spiritual artifact, the Plained-Colored Flag of West Clouds, and the high-grade innate spiritual artifact, the Eight-Treasure Merit Pond."

Jieyin and Zhunti thanked Hongjun profusely. All the treasures in the West couldn't hold a candle to these four spiritual artifacts.

Normally, they would have been overjoyed, but they couldn't ignore the preference given to the Three Purities and Nuwa. The four of them had received top-grade cardinal spiritual artifacts or something of similar value. But the only comparable artifact the Western gods had received was the Twelfth-Ranked Golden Lotus of Merit.

The thousands of overlooked gods couldn't care less about Jieyin and Zhunti's discontent. They kneeled, begged, pleaded, and cried for Hongjun to be compassionate and bestow treasures upon them too.

Hearing all the noise, Hongjun frowned. "Outside Violet Heaven Palace, I placed all my treasures in the Sealed Treasure Stone. If you have fate with them, you can try your luck after I merge with the Way of Heaven."

Everyone fell silent. They hated that Hongjun couldn't immediately merge with the Way of Heaven and let them leave.

He saw this but continued to speak without hurry. "Before I merge with the Way of Heaven, I will answer any questions you have."

"Asking Master, what is the Great Dao?" Laozi asked.

"The Great Dao cannot be spoken. It must be discovered by oneself. Others can guide you but can never teach you," Hongjun answered.

"Asking Master, why is Grandmist Violet Qi the foundation of sainthood?" Yuanshi asked.

Hongjun opened his mouth, but sudden coercion descended, causing everyone in Violet Heaven Palace to freeze. He was no longer Hongjun but the Way of Heaven. The Way of Heaven looked at Yuanshi and said, "The Grandmist Violet Qi is a fragment of the Way of Heaven. To become a Saint of Heaven, you will entrust a strand of your true soul to the Grandmist Violet Qi, entrust it to the Way of Heaven. As long as heaven and earth exist, Saints are eternal."

After he finished speaking, the coercion disappeared, and Hongjun returned to himself. He furrowed his brows before quickly smoothing them out.

Tongtian took note of this and couldn't help but frown. Entrust a strand of truesoul to the Grandmist Violet Qi. Wasn't this the same as placing a collar around herself for the Way of Heaven to control?

Tongtian did not speak out about these concerns and instead asked her question. "Asking Master, are there any worlds besides the Great Desolation?"

The coercion appeared again, and the Way of Heaven descended onto Hongjun once more. "The chaos is limitless. All things are possible. If the Great Desolation absorbs other worlds, its strength will improve, and so will the Saints' strength."

When the Way of Heaven disappeared, Tongtian couldn't help but quirk the corners of her lips upward. Wasn't this telling them to find other worlds for the Great Desolation to absorb?

No one else spoke as Hongjun gazed at them. He emitted a pressure that caused everyone to stay silent. Finally, the pressure lifted as he stared at Nuwa, waiting for her question.

"Asking Master, after Master merges with the Way of Heaven, is Master the Way of Heaven?"

Hongjun almost seemed to sigh in relief, but upon closer inspection, his facial expression did not change at all. This time, the Way of Heaven did not descend again. "After I merge with the Way of Heaven, Hongjun is the Way of Heaven, but the Way of Heaven is not Hongjun."

Nuwa frowned and nodded, seemingly understanding yet not understanding. Next was Jieyin.

"Asking Master, of the 3,000 laws, which one can achieve sainthood?" he asked.

"Any of the 3,000 laws can be used to achieve sainthood," Hongjun replied.

"After Master has merged with the Way of Heaven and we have something to report, how can we meet Master?" Zhunti asked.

"Unless a catastrophe that threatens heaven and earth occurs, I won't reveal myself under heaven and earth anymore," the master replied.

"Asking the Dao Ancestor, can I use the Way of Three Corpses to achieve the Primordial Origin Realm?" Taiyi asked.

The answer was simple. "No."

Hearing this, almost everyone's desire for Redcloud Ancestor's Grandmist Violet Qi increased as they subconsciously focused their attention on him.

"Asking the Dao Ancestor, if everything is destined, can nothing be changed?" Kong Xuan asked.

Hongjun gave Kong Xuan a deep look but still answered, "The small variables can be changed, but the general trend will remain unchanged."

After Kong Xuan's question, Hongjun answered a few more before preparing to merge with the Way of Heaven.

"High above the nine clouds, the truth floats free.

"Within heaven and earth, I shall enlighten all beings.

"Pangu, born of Taiji, formed the two rites and four cardinal directions.

"One way passes to three peers, two lights illuminate all seekers.

"The founder of the Immortal Path, one Qi transformed to Hongjun.

"Dao... MERGE!"

At first, nothing seemed to happen, but Hongjun became more and more indifferent. His sense of presence faded, and unless you concentrated, you would subconsciously ignore it. Simultaneously, the Way of Heaven was wholly exposed to them. It felt as if they were looking at all of heaven and earth at once.

These two contradictory images caused many of the 3,000 gods to become dizzy and even faint. Only those with great willpower and cultivation could persevere.

Tongtian watched all of heaven and earth. She saw how the world progressed, how six Saints came to being, how Houtu transformed herself to the Underworld to establish the cycle of Samsara, and how the Titan-Demon Tribulation began and ended. She watched the onset of the Conferred God Tribulation and how she was imprisoned in the end. She saw the Journey to the West and the Western Prominence Tribulation.

She saw all that and more. Tribulations came one after the other until the world was destroyed on the ninth tribulation: the Immeasurable Tribulation. But it didn't end there; she saw how the broken Great Desolation regathered and formed a primordial egg with a thirty-six-petaled lotus beneath it.

Pangu incarnates into all things; all things incarnate into Pangu!

CHAPTER 27

Sealed Treasure Stone

After Hongjun merged with the Way of Heaven inside Violet Heaven Palace, a thin silver film covered Tongtian's body. Due to her comprehending the Law of Time, her comprehension took much longer, but time flowed much faster for her. As a result, she awoke earlier than the others.

Tongtian saw her brothers were both in a state of enlightenment. She glanced around and saw it was the same for everyone else. With a wave of her hands, she covered Laozi and Yuanshi in silver bubbles. Not long after, her brothers opened their eyes. They saw the wading silver bubbles and turned to give her their thanks, but Tongtian held a finger to her lips. She motioned toward the other gods.

The three nodded and disappeared from the main hall of Violet Heaven Palace without disturbing anyone. Once outside, they saw the Sealed Treasure Stone. Hundreds of spiritual artifacts floated above, covered in seven-colored radiance.

Tongtian's Good and Evil Corpses appeared and helped her grab the treasures. Laozi's and Yuanshi's eyes lit up and they followed suit.

Inside the palace, Jieyin's eyes regain clarity. He paused and looked around. When he discovered the Three Purities missing, he murmured, "Not good."

He shook Zhunti and pulled him out of Violet Heaven Palace. His actions awakened Nuwa from her comprehension. Her brows furrowed, and she shook Fuxi awake.

Before she exited Violet Heaven Palace, Kong Xuan flew out while dragging his brother, Jinchi. This set off a chain reaction as Di Jun, Taiyi, Dong Wanggong, Xi Wangmu, and all the other guests quickly flew out.

Once outside, they saw the Three Purities madly grabbing treasures with their main bodies and Corpses. Spurred by a sense of urgency, they rushed to the hoard. Attaining treasures didn't just mean getting powerful tools but also the material needed to sever their three thoughts.

Most of the 3,000 gods didn't have a single innate spiritual artifact, much less a top-grade one like the Three Purities. The ones grabbing them with the most ferocity were Jieyin and Zhunti—not for themselves but for the whole West.

After retrieving a certain number, Tongtian discovered that she couldn't grab any more of the treasures from the Sealed Treasure Stone. Reluctantly, she retreated, but she was still happy as she counted her gains.

Most of the ninety spiritual artifacts were middle- or low-grade, but there were a few exceptions. Notable artifacts included the Twenty-Four Sea-Calming Pearls, Four Direction Pagoda, Sun-Moon Pearl, Chaos Hammer, and the top-grade innate Apricot Flag of Central Infinity. Tongtian felt most drawn to two artifacts broken from one.

One looked like a sword with a blade formed of thirteen spine segments, and the other was a whip with fifteen segments—the Kunwu Sword and Whip. Although the two were broken, Tongtian had the confidence to restore them.

Yuanshi's harvest wasn't bad either. He got the Soul-Felling Bell, Azure Lotus Flag of East Treasured Light, Yin-Yang Mirror, Jade Mirage Lamp, Godpiercing Saber, Fire-Wind Wheel, Male-Female Swords, Qiankun Ring, and many others.

Laozi now carried the Fire-Wind Prayer Mat, Eight Trigrams Cauldron, Eight Scenic Lantern, Shimmering Golden Rope, and the Seven Star Sword. He'd grabbed less artifacts than his siblings, but the overall quality was higher.

With treasure in hand, Tongtian had time to spy what everyone else had. She saw that Nuwa got the Demon Banner, which she would later merge with the immortal gourd to create the Demon-Summoning Banner. She saw Kong Xuan grab the Red Radiance Flag of South Transience.

Redcloud Ancestor was relatively unlucky as several gods purposely or inadvertently prevented him from grabbing any of the treasures, frustrating him to no end. His ever-present smile had turned into a frown.

When about half the treasures had been taken, they turned into streams of light and flew into the Great Desolation. They recalled the Dao Ancestor's words: if they had fate with the treasures, they could try their luck.

It seemed that the rest of the treasures didn't have fate with them, but how could they be willing to give up so easily?

The Great Dao is fifty; the Eye of Heaven is forty-nine; the last one escaped.

Without trying, how could they know that they weren't the one that escaped?

Only a few gods were still left hanging around the palace. Even Jieyin, Zhunti, Nuwa, Fuxi, and Di Jun left. Taiyi took one last glance at the Three Purities before departing. If looks could kill, Yuanshi would have killed him a hundred times.

Tongtian glanced at Violet Heaven Palace and watched Haotian and Yaochi close the gates for what may be eons. After hesitating for a moment, she bowed toward the person no longer sitting on the cloud throne.

Laozi and Yuanshi followed her lead. When the Three Purities straightened their backs, the only person left came forward.

"Daoist Tongtian, Daoist Yuanshi, Daoist Laozi," Minghe said.

"Daoist Minghe, is there something you need?" Tongtian asked.

"It's like this," Minghe said, beginning to explain his purpose. He had the white lotus from transacting with Tongtian, and he could nurture another red lotus with time, but he was missing the final lotus. It just so happened that Jieyin had gotten the Twelfth-Ranked Golden Lotus of Merit.

Just because Hongjun's Way of Three Corpses could only let the cultivator become a saint with the Grandmist Violet Qi, it didn't mean it was useless. On the contrary, it was beneficial. It increased their strength and allowed them to comprehend the laws more easily.

And wasn't there still a chance to grab a Grandmist Violet Qi?

"The way I see it, as long as we join forces, we can grab four lotus seeds from Daoist Jieyin," Minghe said. "Are you willing?"

"Join forces? If we wanted the golden lotus seed, we three are more than enough," Yuanshi said, poking a hole in Minghe's plans.

"I'm sorry, Daoist Minghe," Tongtian said. "We can't participate in your plans. At least on the surface, Jieyin and Zhunti are our junior brothers, and it wouldn't be just to force them to hand over the golden lotus seeds.

Who was he kidding? Offending Jieyin and Zhunti for a lotus seed they didn't need was not worth it at all.

"I see," Minghe said while forcing a smile. "I'm sorry for bothering fellow Daoists."

"Wait a moment," Tongtian called out as he turned to leave. "In my view, the West is barren, and Daoists Jieyin and Zhunti should not be averse to trading a few lotus seeds for treasure. But you should act quickly. If the two become Saints, it might be too late."

Minghe's eyes widened, and he cupped his fist. "Thank you, Daoist Tongtian. I hadn't realized such a method was feasible."

After he left, Yuanshi turned on his sister. "Why did you help him when there are no benefits?"

"There aren't any demerits either, so why not?" she returned.

With everything done, the Three Purities could finally fly back to the Great Desolation. Before they left, Tongtian turned to the Sealed Treasure Stone and stored it.

Inside Violet Heaven Palace, Haotian and Yaochi had retired to their rooms. Not even they could see Hongjun as they liked, but a figure suddenly appeared on the cloud throne again. Hongjun stared into the distance, looking right at Yuanshi, Tongtian, and Kong Xuan, who had returned to the Great Desolation.

"Variables?" he muttered.

Hongjun closed his eyes and vanished once more.

* * *

The Three Purities returned to Kunlun Mountain. In Three Purity Hall, they sat and discussed their future.

"Becoming a Saint grants one longevity equal to heaven and earth, but I don't want to be shackled," Tongtian said.

"Third Sister, your words are too extreme," Yuanshi chided. "Father God created heaven and earth. Becoming a Saint is akin to returning to his embrace."

"Father God did create us, but we are no longer part of him. We are us, not him."

Yuanshi frowned. "Third Sister has a point, but Father God has given us much, and we must help heaven and earth prosper."

It was Tongtian's turn to frown. After her epiphany from watching the Dao Ancestor merge with the Way of Heaven, she'd received some information about the general trend of heaven. The Great Desolation would undergo nine great tribulations.

The ninth tribulation was the last one, the Immeasurable Tribulation. Once the Great Desolation overcame it, it would become eternal and no longer undergo any more tribulations. On the flip side, it was more dangerous than all the previous combined, and there was a high chance of failure.

Heaven and earth would be destroyed after failing the Immeasurable Tribulation, and the destruction of heaven and earth would mean the death of all Saints. Tongtian didn't want to die. She would rather become a Golden Immortal of Primordial Origin.

The Dao Ancestor didn't explicitly say it, but Golden Immortals of Primordial Origin should be equal to chaos fiendgod, which meant they could survive in the chaos without the need for a world like the Great Desolation.

Tongtian faced Laozi. "What does Eldest Brother think?"

"We cannot escape the truth that we are transformed from the creator's spirit," he said. "And the Three Purities must become Saints. However, that doesn't mean there isn't a method to stay unfettered while becoming a Saint."

"Please enlighten me."

"Merge the Three Corpses into one and entrust the Grandmist Violet Qi to it. The Corpse becomes a Saint while we pursue becoming unfettered Golden Immortals of Primordial Origin."

"Is it possible?" Yuanshi asked. "Although the Corpses come from us, their foundation is a bit lacking."

"I do not know," Laozi admitted. "We can only take it one step at a time. Before worrying about whether or not a Corpse can become a Saint, we still need to find a way to become Golden Immortals of the Primordial Origin."

"I already have an idea," Tongtian said. "Hongjun's way is ultimately not my own, and I plan to take inspiration from the Way of Three Corpses. Instead of severing my thoughts, I will sever my past, present, and future from the River of Time and become unique; the one and only me."

"Third Sister comprehends the Law of Time, so this method is suitable for you." Laozi turned to Yuanshi. "What about Second Brother?"

"I still plan on becoming a Saint of Heaven," Yuanshi asserted. Neither Laozi nor Tongtian went against his decision, as they'd each have to decide their fate for themselves.

The Three Purities returned to their own halls and prepared to become Saints or Golden Immortals of Primordial Origin. Each waited for the green lotus seeds to become Ninth-Ranked Green Lotuses of Good Fortune.

* * *

Inside Eminence Heavenly Palace, Di Jun's expression turned ugly as he learned of what had happened during the Dao Ancestor's final sermon.

The Fox Clan, among many other remaining members of the Hundred Clans, had decided to join Heavenly Court. A few chose to join Violet Manor, but the alliance of ten thousand immortals wasn't satisfied.

Thus, Violet Manor, under the leadership of Shangxia Ancestor, attacked the clans that had refused to join them. They'd forced the clan members to become their mounts and seized the defeated's treasuries.

"Dong Wanggong, you really don't want to live anymore, do you?" Di Jun said through gritted teeth. In his eyes, Dong Wanggong had planned the assault beforehand to take advantage of the fact that the Heavenly Court was without a leader during the Dao Ancestor's sermon.

He discounted the idea that Violet Manor attacked without Dong Wanggong's knowledge. After all, Dong Wanggong and Xi Wangmu couldn't be that ignorant, could they?

Still, now was not the time for retaliation. Many demons had gained a lot of treasures from the Sealed Treasure Stone and now focused on entering the Quasi-Saint Realm. Di Jun didn't mind; they still hadn't refined all the formation flags for the Starry Sky War Array yet.

Even if Violet Manor added a few more Quasi-Saints, it would fall under the might of the Starry Sky War Array and the Ten Thousand Immortal Formation too!

During this time, a major event occurred to further upset Di Jun.

"Father God above, we are the Titan Tribe! We see that the land is full of disorder and disrespect for Father God. We will police and direct all creatures to the correct path!"

Di Jiang's voice echoed through the Great Desolation, even the Thirty-Three Heavens and Starry Sky. Immediately after, a massive number of golden clouds of merit, only slightly inferior to the one that appeared during the establishment of Heavenly Court, gathered above the Titan Tribe and descended.

* * *

Tongtian only made a note of the event. She wasn't part of the

Titan Tribe or Heavenly Court, so why should she care? Yuanshi was still refining the formation flags for the Pangu Genesis Formation, but she didn't want to wait anymore.

Who knew when Violet Manor would fall? After its brief period of glory, it fell to the bottom of all three forces again.

She only stayed so long to wait for the green lotus to mature. Once it did, she immediately flew toward the East Sea. As soon as she came within sight of the shores, she felt something call out to her.

Tongtian flew toward the origin of the sensation and discovered a spiritual mountain full of essence. She could see that an unfinished treasure was gestating.

Before she could smile, Tongtian saw three uninvited guests: Nuwa, Kong Xuan, and Jinchi.

Chapter 28

Kongtong Seal

Tongtian focused on Kong Xuan, his ever present shadow, Jinchi, and Nuwa. The two groups stared back at her and each other. Both parties had arrived to acquire the gestating spiritual artifact. No words needed to be said, but some things still must be acknowledged.

"Fellow Daoists, I feel that the treasure has some fate with me. How about giving me face and relinquishing it?" Nuwa asked.

Tongtian's lips twitched. Had that request been enough to move its listeners, the number of battles in the Great Desolation would have been reduced by half. Ever since the third sermon, numerous life and death battles had broken out over artifacts, and many of the 3,000 guests who had listened to the Dao Ancestor's sermon had perished.

But before Tongtian could speak, someone else did.

"Ridiculous," Kong Xuan interjected. "According to your words, since I feel that the treasure here has a connection with me, shouldn't you leave instead?"

Nuwa frowned, but she looked at Tongtian instead. "What does Senior Sister think?"

Throwing the ball to me and even playing the junior sister card? The edge of Tongtian's lip quirked upward. "I also feel that the treasure is destined for me."

At this, silence descended on the factions. If none of them wanted to give up, they could only fight for it.

Time passed slowly, and the spiritual light coming from the mountain grew brighter and brighter, signifying the near-birth of the spiritual artifact. Finally, a pillar burst from the mountain and into the sky.

Nuwa, Kong Xuan, and Jinchi took action at once. All three aimed at Tongtian.

Nuwa revealed her Intermediate Quasi-Saint Realm cultivation base. The Red Hydrangea appeared in her hand and smashed toward Tongtian.

Tongtian unsheathed the Qingping Sword, and with a metallic cling, the Red Hydrangea was repelled back to Nuwa. "Master said that it can defeat anyone weaker than you, but have you forgotten? I'm still stronger than you."

"That remains to be seen," Nuwa said as a diorama of mountains and rivers appeared behind her.

A faint glow enveloped the Qingping Sword, and Tongtian slashed toward Kong Xuan.

Kong Xuan grunted as five differently colored lights erupted from him. They became beams of light that shot out at the Supreme Purity, but her slash shredded the beams, forcing him to dodge.

Tongtian didn't pursue him as she charged toward the mountain. "Don't even think about it." She unleashed another slash, and a sword-shaped energy pursued Jinchi, who had flown toward the newly born treasure during the initial clash.

Jinchi waved his hand, and a saber that resembled a golden feather appeared in his grasp. Green qi covered the saber, and he slashed out. Unfortunately for him, it was far too weak. Tongtian's sword qi knocked his saber back and sent him crashing into the ground.

Before Tongtian could capitalize on the moment, five feather-like sabers that exuded qi corresponding to the five elements surrounded her. They shot out strings of light from their blades and connected with one another to cage her.

"Five Feathers Element Formation, rise!" Kong Xuan said.

"Using formations against me? Naive," Tongtian scoffed. She waved her hands and a thousand low-grade spiritual swords appeared.

"Myriad Sword Formation—Third-Level: Thousand Swords!"

The swords arranged themselves in three layers. The first and third layers rotated clockwise while the second layer rotated counterclockwise. Under the disruption of her Myriad Sword Formation, the Five Feathers Element Formation collapsed, unable to maintain itself.

Kong Xuan grunted as he summoned his five sabers back. Next, Nuwa's Mountain and River Diorama smashed down on the Supreme Purity.

Tongtian's Myriad Sword Formation became sluggish under the Mountain and River Diorama's crushing pressure. Furthermore, she could feel the diorama trying to absorb her into its world.

She snorted. She already knew the danger of falling into such a situation when the Qiankun Cauldron had sucked her in. She formed a seal with one hand, and the 10,000 swords gained a silvery glow around them. They rotated faster and repelled the Mountain and River Diorama.

During this time, Jinchi tried to grab the treasure again, but Nuwa sent the Red Hydrangea at him. Wind billowed around him, and he shifted out of the way, but the Red Hydrangea made a sharp turn and crashed into him.

Jinchi coughed a bloody mouthful as his face paled. He wasn't Tongtian, and the Red Hydrangea had slammed into him. As the Dao Ancestor once said, it can defeat anyone weaker than Nuwa instantly.

Jinchi fell weakly to the ground, and the Red Hydrangea smashed toward him again.

Upon seeing this, Kong Xuan charged to help Jinchi. He sent the white feather saber at the Red Hydrangea and managed to divert its trajectory. Once he appeared in front of Jinchi, he sent out the five feather sabers to circle around the Red Hydrangea and form a miniature formation.

Nuwa frowned when her connection to the Red Hydrangea grew blurry. She took out the Treasured Lotus Lantern, which shot out a light that struck the Five Feathers Element Formation, obstructing it and allowing the Red Hydrangea to escape.

During this time, she controlled the Mountain and River Diorama to fly for the spiritual light pillar on the mountain. Not wanting Nuwa to scoop away the treasure, Tongtian followed it with the Myriad Sword Formation around her.

A red flag appeared in Kong Xuan's hand, and he waved it. Mirage-like flames erupted and shot out at the Mountain and River Diorama and Tongtian. The Mountain and River Diorama paused, as did Tongtian's Myriad Sword Formation as it sliced through the flames.

"I also have a flag." Tongtian flipped her hand, revealing a yellow flag. Like the Red Radiance Flag of South Transience, the Apricot Flag of Central Infinity in Tongtian's palm was one of the top five flag artifacts.

Tongtian waved it, but nothing shot out like with the red flag. Jinchi suddenly felt the ground rumble, and under his gaze, the spiritual mountain started to move toward Tongtian.

Nuwa and Kong Xuan ceased fighting each other to attack Tongtian. The mirage-like flames honed in on her. The Mountain and River Diorama came crashing down from the other side. Just to be safe, Nuwa also shot the Red Hydrangea at her foe.

"It's still incomplete, but let me show you the power of the fourth level of the Myriad Sword Formation!" Tongtian shouted, waving her hand. An additional 9,000 swords of equal rank appeared and became the fourth layer of circling blades.

The Myriad Sword Formation's power quadrupled, instantly repelling the Mountain and River Diorama, Red Hydrangea, and Red Radiance Flag of South Transience.

Nuwa frowned. A figure flew out from her, bearing around 70-80 percent similarities to her. At this point, Jinchi had recovered, and his Corpse also flew out. With Kong Xuan's addition, Tongtian was surrounded by four Quasi-Saints.

"Senior Sister is much stronger than I thought," Nuwa admitted. "As expected of one of the Three Purities transformed from Pangu's spirit. But can you defeat all four of us?"

Tongtian smiled. "Junior Sister, you received the Red Hydrangea and the Mountain and River Diorama from Master, but have you forgotten what I received?"

Hearing this, her challengers' eyes narrowed. Nuwa said, "I don't believe you can recreate the Immortal Extermination Diagram in such a short amount of time."

"You're right, but I have two Corpses," Tongtian pointed out. "In addition, even if it's not complete, with an Advanced Quasi-Saint Realm cultivation base, it's more than enough to suppress you four."

After a tense silence, Nuwa sighed and retrieved her two artifacts. Before leaving, she said, "Then I'll congratulate Senior Sister for your gains."

Seeing Nuwa leave, Kong Xuan also stored his five feather sabers and Red Radiance Flag of South Transience. "I lost this time, but next time, I'll win."

Jinchi's Corpse returned to his body, and he followed after Kong

Xuan, but not before giving the Supreme Purity one last glare.

Tongtian shrugged and stored the Apricot Flag of Central Infinity and the 10,000 swords. She descended down the mountain, where the pillar of light erupted, and waved her hands.

A seal flew out of the ground and into her hand, the light disappearing the moment it did so. She sent her qi into it and began to refine it.

It doesn't have a grade, but it has forty-nine restrictions? Tongtian thought, confused. *It doesn't have much in the way of attack or defense either?*

She felt as if she'd fought a long hard battle, only to receive absolute crap as a reward. *Forget it, I'll return to Fangzhang Immortal Island first and slowly refine it. There's no way an artifact with forty-nine restriction is so weak, even if it is a no-grade.*

Tongtian flew into the East Sea and returned to Fangzhang Immortal Island, where she saw many more animals and plants flourishing. Although Fangzhang Immortal Island had been full of essence, the chaotic boundary was not suitable for life. Now that she'd moved it into the Great Desolation, it was thriving.

She returned to the core where she had refined a Supreme Purity Palace. It wasn't as good as Yuanshi's Three Purity Palace, but she had confidence in the formations around it.

Once inside, she spent the next 10,000 years refining the spiritual artifact. Only then did she learn of its name.

Kongtong Seal? The seal of human emperors? Tongtian realized with some shock. *I didn't expect it to be born so early. Does this mean Nuwa will create humanity soon?*

As she thought this, something resonated within Tongtian, and a vine appeared in her hand. This was the Immortal Gourd Vine she had taken nearly an eon ago. She wanted to refine it into a sword, but her intuition prevented it, as if it hadn't completed its purpose.

Is this also related to the creation of humanity? Tongtian wondered. *I'll have to pay attention to when Nuwa creates humanity. But why did I sense the Kongtong Seal? Nuwa should have felt fate with it because she will create humanity in the future, but why me and Kong Xuan?*

Tongtian crossed her arms. *Is it because I was a former human? No, that doesn't make sense. Otherwise, Kong Xuan wouldn't have felt it, too, assuming he wasn't lying. Is it because of the vine? But it didn't resonate with the Kongtong Seal until now.*

No matter, the Kongtong Seal is a good thing. Tongtian thought. With her increasing cultivation and understanding of the law, she realized the increasing importance of Karmic Luck. *With the Kongtong Seal, I can occupy a percentage of humanity's Karmic Luck.*

Karmic Luck came in many forms. For example, as descendants of Pangu, the Three Purities and the twelve titans were innately bestowed with luck. But Karmic Luck can also come from a force or race's prosperity. The more prosperous a race was, the greater the luck they had. Inversely, the more luck a race had, the greater their prosperity.

The Demon Clan became more prosperous after establishing the Heavenly Court and ruling over a portion of the Great Desolation. Thus their luck increased. With how abundant humanity would grow to be, their luck would have to be enormous.

Knowing this, the Kongtong Seal was even more important to Tongtian than the Twelfth-Ranked White Lotus of Purification. Still, it would only matter after humanity flourished.

She settled down and cultivated. During this time, she felt a resonance within Kunlun Mountain and knew that Laozi had severed his third Corpse. Now, she needed to wait for Laozi to merge his three Corpses together to see if they could become a Saint of Heaven.

Tongtian wasn't worried about her third Corpse; she already had a clue. If she guessed right, it should be related to humanity, and the day Nuwa created humanity would be the day she severed her Third Corpse.

For now, she needed to wait for a chance to grab the Kunlun Mirror. Her time would come 80,000 years later.

Chapter 29
Ten Thousand Immortals Formation

Inside Heavenly Court, Di Jun sat on the Nine-Dragon Throne and gazed at the assembled heavenly ministers and officials below him.

"Our subjects, the time has come to punish the alliance of 10,000 immortals, Violet Manor," he began. His words were neither rushed nor slow.

He glanced at Taiyi. During the nearly 100,000 years since the sermon, his brother had severed a Corpse and entered the Intermediate Quasi-Saint Realm. He turned to Fuxi and Nuwa. Fuxi had stabilized his cultivation and could enter the intermediate Quasi-Saint Realm at any time. Nuwa had entered the Intermediate Quasi-Saint Realm soon after returning from the Dao Ancestor's third sermon.

"The Dao Ancestor christened Dong Wanggong and Xi Wangmu the heads of male and female immortals, but they ignored the Dao Ancestor's words and selfishly harmed the creatures of the land. As the Heavenly Emperor, it is Our duty to punish him for his transgressions."

Di Jun glanced at the ten demon sages. Seven of the original demon sages had recently stepped into the Quasi-Saint Realm, leaving the remaining three at the peak of the Great Firmament Realm.

"Prime Minister Bai Ze," Di Jun summoned.

"Bai Zei is here, Your Majesty," Bai Ze said as he stepped forward.

"Report the composition of the Celestial Army."

"At once, Your Majesty." Bai Ze stood up and looked at all the officials in the hall. "The Celestial Army is composed of 379 Immortal Emperors, 1,211 Immortal Monarchs, and 4,634 Immortal Lords."

In the Heavenly Court, Golden Immortals of the Great Firmament were given the title of Immortal Emperors; Golden Immortals of the Great Unity were given the title of Immortal Monarch; and Golden Immortals were given the title of Immortal Lords.

"There are ten legions. The first legion is composed of 48,000 Profound Immortals; the second through tenth legions are composed of 4,000 Profound Immortals and 100 thousand Sky Immortals. The number of Earth Immortals is countless, Your Majesty," Bai Ze said as he finished his report and retreated to his position.

Di Jun nodded. "Our beloved subjects, with such a grand army, does the alliance of 10,000 immortals stand a chance?"

There was a resounding no.

"Should Violet Manor be acquitted of its crimes?"

Another resounding no.

"Then, as the Heavenly Emperor, I order the mobilization of the Celestial Army to destroy Violet Manor that has gone against the Dao Ancestor's decree. Eastern Emperor Taiyi."

"Subject-brother is here," Taiyi said as he stepped out.

"Take command of four demon sages, 365 Immortal Emperors, 500 Immortal Monarchs, 1,200 Immortal Lords, the first, second, and third legion. Destroy Violet Manor for their transgressions!"

"Subject-brother obeys the Heavenly Emperor's decree!" Taiyi said.

Under the sights of all the Demon Clan, Taiyi led the Celestial Army toward the East Sea. Their sheer numbers blotted out the sky.

Naturally, such a large movement couldn't be hidden from the major powers. Laozi and Yuanshi noticed it from Kunlun Mountain, as did Redcloud Ancestor who was visiting Zheng Yuanzi at Wuzhuang Temple. Minghe saw them from the Blood Sea, Jinchi looked up from his work near the Undying Volcano, and many others would not soon forget this legion.

The Titan Tribe made a note of it, but they didn't take action. It was not the time. Only nine of the twelve titans had broken through into the Quasi-Saint Realm.

Violet Manor's spies also reported the situation to Dong Wanggong and Xi Wangmu.

* * *

Inside the Violet Manor, Dong Wanggong sat at the head seat with Xi Wangmu on his left as his equal. Sitting in front of him, at a lower level, were seven early Quasi-Saints, including Kong Xuan and Shangxia Ancestor.

"Heavenly Court has determined that Violet Manor strayed from its original purpose and thus decided to eliminate us," Dong Wanggong began. "What does everyone make of this?"

"Preposterous! The Heavenly Court doesn't have the authority to rule Violet Manor! I suggest Fellow Daoist Dong Wanggong send a refutation of the slander and order Di Jun to cease at once," Shangxia Ancestor said, with most of the Quasi-Saints agreeing.

Dong Wanggong suppressed the irritation within him. He hadn't ordered Violet Manor to attack the remaining Hundred Clans to seize their treasury and take the survivors as mounts.

He had rebuked Shangxia Ancestor and the others, but by this time, Shangxia Ancestor had broken through to the Quasi-Saint Realm and refuted Dong Wanggong, claiming that they'd had no choice but to attack. If they hadn't seized the treasures, their strength would have continued to stagnate in the face of the Heavenly Court's increasing might.

The worst part was that the majority of the immortals sided with Shangxia Ancestor! He had bought them over by giving them treasures seized from the defeated clans. Even more presumptuous, he'd put himself in charge of distributing the spoils as he saw fit.

Dong Wanggong had tried to take control back, but he was helpless. As time passed, more and more Quasi-Saints appeared, but they stood behind Shangxia Ancestor. He had been pushed to the point where he doubted he could still retain his position if the Dao Ancestor hadn't publicly proclaimed him the head of male immortals.

Had it not been for Kong Xuan, Dong Wanggong did not doubt he would have been turned into a puppet. Or, if he cut out his second Corpse, he would have the strength to control Violet Manor.

Strength spoke loudest in the Greatest Desolation.

Now that Di Jun came knocking, Shangxia Ancestor wanted to hide behind him? In his dreams!

Dong Wanggong turned to the rest of the Quasi-Saints. "Anyone else?"

When his gaze connected with theirs, most of them averted their eyes. Under his pressuring stare, one of them finally spoke out. He was a mousy man sitting at the tail end.

"What if, what if we gave them some treasures? They should leave us alone then, right?"

Dong Wanggong sneered. How did he become a Quasit-Saint with that brain of his?

"Fool." Kong Xuan spoke up at this moment. "Heavenly Court doesn't care for such meager treasures. What they want is the dominance of heaven and earth. If we cave in, they might let us go this time, but their desire to end us won't disappear."

"What do you mean by this?" Shangxia Ancestor asked.

"I mean what I said—Heavenly Court doesn't want to destroy us because you attacked the Hundred Clans and seized their treasures. They are attacking us because we are an eyesore to their hegemony." Kong Xuan stood up and spread his arms. "Not just Heavenly Court, the Titan Tribe wants to destroy us too, because we are too powerful. Unless you decide to surrender to either of them, they'll never let us go."

"Daoist Kong Xuan, what do you suggest we do?" Dong Wanggong asked.

Kong Xuan turned to face the rest of the Quasi-Saints. "We fight. We fight and defeat Heavenly Court and the Titan Tribe. We will become the number one force in the Great Desolation, and no one will be able to oppose us. Not even the Three Purities."

At his words, the hall fell silent.

"Can we defeat them?" a voice asked.

Kong Xuan turned to the owner. "Then go surrender to them. But I'll tell you right now, the moment you do so, I'll cut you down."

Dong Wanggong closed his eyes. When he opened them, he saw the worry on Xi Wangmu's face. He placed his hand over hers and gave a comforting smile.

He let go and faced the Quasi-Saints present, an inextinguishable fighting intent in his eyes. "We prepare for war. Assemble all the immortals. We are going to show Heavenly Court the power of the Ten Thousand Immortals Formation!"

* * *

As the Celestial Army arrived, Tongtian also moved, but she saw an unexpected visitor. "Second Brother, why are you here?"

"You're going to fish in muddy waters when Heavenly Court and

Violet Manor fight, are you not?" Yuanshi asked, but it wasn't a question.

"Xi Wangmu's Kunlun Mirror holds great attraction for me, I must get it."

"Aren't you scared that the two will deal with you?"

"What's there to be afraid of? If they dare to attack me, I'll help the other side. Besides,"—Tongtian snapped her fingers, and the space around her split apart—""I'm confident that no one under heaven can hinder me."

"You already started mastering the Law of Space?"

"Just a bit," Tongtian said as she pinched an inch of air between her thumb and finger. "Nothing worth praising."

"No, it's amazing! As long as you master the Law of Space, not even a Saint will be able to stop you," Yuanshi praised. There was a tiny smile on his lips and gentle pride in his gaze.

Tongtian felt shy but also warm. "You're making fun of me. We've never faced off against a Saint, so that remains unknown. A-anyways, I'm going to spectate. What about you?"

"I'll come along, just in case," Yuanshi said, already following her. "I think the Five-Elements Tree should belong in better hands."

The two siblings shared a smirk.

They soon reached Penglai Immortal Island, but they didn't reveal themselves. Tongtian split the spatial layers and hid herself and Yuanshi between them. Within a month, Taiyi and the Celestial Army arrived.

"Dong Wanggong, Xi Wangmu, do you admit your crimes?" Taiyi's words echoed throughout the East Sea, and even the East Dragon Palace could hear it.

A moment of silence passed before Dong Wanggong's voice erupted out of Penglai Immortal Island. "Taiyi, does Di Jun not dare to show his face? As the head of male immortals christened by the Dao Ancestor, I pronounce Di Jun unworthy of his position! Immortals, form the Ten Thousand Immortals Formation!"

Ten thousand pillars formed of qi erupted at regularly spaced intervals across the island. They spread apart, expanding to ten times Penglai Immortal Island's size.

Taiyi felt the immensely powerful qi emanating from the Ten Thousand Immortals Formation and frowned. "Demons, form the Starry Sky War Array!"

The 365 Golden Immortals of the Great Firmament entered their position along with the 48,000 Profound Immortals. Taiyi sat at the position of the Purple Majesty Star.

The sky over them darkened as the Starry Sky appeared. Starlight shined down on the 48,365 demons forming the Starry Sky War Array.

It was a blinding white array against a miniature night sky illuminating the Ten Thousand Immortals Formation. In response, a net formed above the Ten Thousand Immortals Formation, blocking the falling starlight.

Seeing that the starlight couldn't damage the net faster than it could regenerate, Taiyi commanded the Starry Sky War Formation to descend. Because the array drew power from the stars above, he was sure they could outlast the Ten Thousand Immortals Formation, but he didn't want to draw out the battle.

The longer the battle went on, the greater the risk of the Titan Tribe attacking Heavenly Court while the army was away. Most of the Golden Immortals of the Great Firmament and almost all of the formation flags were with him, so Heavenly Court couldn't form another Starry Sky Formation.

Once inside, Taiyi saw a nondescript immortal of Violet Manor.

He rushed forward and attacked. The immortal flinched and defended, successfully repelling Taiyi's attack and surprising him.

Taiyi frowned and summoned the Chaos Bell. It rang loudly, causing a sonic attack. The immortal froze under the assault, allowing Taiyi to bash him.

The immortal screamed, but he discovered that he was only scratched and not heavily injured. He looked at his own body in shock and then at Taiyi. His surprise turned into gleeful confidence as he stared provokingly at Taiyi.

Taiyi wasn't the only one who discovered the abnormal defense. All the demons of Heavenly Court found that whatever opponent they faced couldn't be injured as easily. After a short clash, the Starry Sky War Formation ascended and separated from the Ten Thousand Immortals Formation.

Above and outside, Taiyi noticed that the overall energy of the Ten Thousand Immortals Formation had decreased, but it was only marginally. He frowned, scouring his mind for any method to overcome the formation.

The Starry Sky War Formation had several killer moves, but they were too costly. It would be great if they broke the Ten Thousand Immortals Formation, but if they couldn't, they might lose the battle.

Just as Taiyi was mulling over his choices, he turned around to see Tongtian and Yuanshi appear out of nowhere. Taiyi ordered Ji Meng, one of the Ten Demon Sages, to take temporary command while he met two of the Three Purities. "Daoist Tongtian... Daoist Yuanshi."

Yuanshi, as usual, was glaring at him, but Tongtian smiled at him. His throat went dry.

"Daoist Taiyi, it seems you're in quite the pickle. Do you want my help?" Tongtian asked, her smile widening.

Chapter 30

Fall of Violet Manor

Taiyi furrowed his brows. "What does Daoist Tongtian want in return?"

Tongtian wasn't part of the Heavenly Court, and she wouldn't help for no reason. He wasn't delusional; for her to offer aid, she must have an angle.

"I just want to save one person," Tongtian said.

Did she have a relationship with one of Violet Manor's immortals?

Whatever the reason, Taiyi agreed. It was not bad to exchange the life of one person for a swift end. However, there was a caveat. "As long as that person is not Dong Wanggong, you can save anyone you want."

A smile blossomed on Tongtian's face, causing Taiyi to become dazed. He came back to himself only after Yuanshi coughed into his fist, glaring harshly.

Taiyi glared back, but Tongtian saw none of this and continued on. "The Ten Thousand Immortals Formation is impressive. By utilizing the strength of 10,000 immortals, the formation can display power far greater than the limit of the Quasi-Saint Realm. However, the consumptions need to be sustained by the immortals within the formation and cannot be easily replenished."

Taiyi nodded. He knew this already.

"In addition, everyone inside will obtain great power surpassing most Quasi-Saints. I'm sure you have already experienced this fact yourself. But how can a powerful formation be without weakness? Since all the immortals inside share equal power, then they are only as strong as their weakest link.

"The formation is not perfect. Dong Wanggong must have only taught them the formation recently, and there are many weak points. As long as you kill two or three of the immortals and prevent them from sealing the gap, the Ten Thousand Immortals Formation will naturally collapse on itself," Tongtian concluded.

Taiyi furrowed his brows, but her words made sense. "Please enlighten me on the formation's weaknesses."

Tongtian pointed out several weak points. Unlike Heavenly Court, Violet Manor barely had enough Profound Immortals to form the Ten Thousand Immortals Formation. Naturally, there would be those who weren't as accomplished in utilizing the formation, forming weak points.

Taiyi nodded and returned to command the Starry Sky War Array. Despite his personal feelings, he wouldn't bet the Heavenly Court's future on Tongtian's words alone. He needed to test it out.

He commanded the Starry Sky War Array to descend again. Last time, they'd only managed to shave off a small percentage of the Ten Thousand Immortals Formation's energy before receiving several injuries on their side. This time, Taiyi targeted about a tenth of the weak points listed by Tongtian.

He also ordered the Celestial Army to target other random points to hide his probe. After a brief clash, the Starry Sky War Array ascended again. Under Taiyi's observation, he noticed that the Ten Thousand Immortals Formation did seem weaker despite the briefer clash between the two.

Ruthlessness flashed in Taiyi's eyes as he ordered, "Immortal Emperors, obey my, the Eastern Emperor's, command. Unleash the Ancient Annihilation Constellation!"

"Yes, Your Majesty!"

The 365 stars started to form into a specific pattern. A colossal humanoid with skin full of starlight emerged. He stood in the Starry Sky and held a bronze bell in his hand.

Dong Wanggong sensed an ominous premonition and clutched the Ten Thousand Immortals Book. He commanded the immortals to raise the defense of the Ten Thousand Immortals Formation to the absolute limit.

But Taiyi's next attack shocked him.

Not because of how powerful it was, but because of where he struck. Taiyi attacked five places, and those five places were the most significant weak points of the Ten Thousand Immortals Formation. Once the five immortals anchoring those points fell, the formation would follow.

"STOP HIM!!!"

The aura of the Ten Thousand Immortals Formation rose at a staggering rate, but it was too late. The Chaos Bell smashed into the formation, and Dong Wanggong sensed the death of one of the Profound Immortals. Following that, the flow of energy within the formation shrieked like a broken record.

The loss of a single Profound Immortal caused the Ten Thousand Immortals Formation to lose almost five percent of its power.

Taiyi raised the Chaos Bell and attacked again, with even more ferocity. Dong Wanggong wanted to intervene, but he was helpless. Two more Profound Immortals died, and the Ten Thousand Immortals Formation didn't just lose fifteen percent of its power, but twenty.

Only three of the 10,000 immortals had perished, but the formation was already teetering on the brink of destruction.

"Attack! Destroy the Starry Sky War Array, and kill Taiyi!" Dong Wanggong roared desperately. But he could already see it was too late, so before the Ten Thousand Immortals Formation shattered he wanted to make the Heavenly Court pay the price.

The white pillars encircled the Ancient Annihilation Constellation and attacked with reckless abandon, but it was too weakened to deal a fatal blow to Taiyi and the Celestial Army. The star colossus attacked again and destroyed another Profound Immortal. The Ten Thousand Immortals Formation's power dropped by another ten percent.

Dong Wanggong lashed out recklessly, but the final knife came from the most unexpected source. At least for him.

One of the nine foundational pillars, formed by a Quasi-Saint, lost its pure white and immortal-like aura. Shedding that skin, the pillar turned into a mixture of red, black, yellow, green, and white. It split into a separate formation, one that Tongtian recognized.

The Five Feathers Element Formation.

The mixture split into five differently colored feathers that swirled menacingly. At the center, Kong Xuan flew off into the distance, toward the Undying Mountain in the South.

"KONG XUAN!!!" Dong Wanggong roared. Not only did his departure cause the Ten Thousand Immortals Formation to fall apart, but Dong Wanggong felt his connection with the Five Elements Tree disappear. "If I live through this, I will hunt you down! Even into the chaos!"

"Haha, Dong Wanggong, you should worry about your life first!" Taiyi's voice echoed from the star colossus's lips. It didn't even bother to use the Chaos Bell anymore, smashing its empty palm down.

All the immortals under its path died; from Profound Immortals to Golden Immortals of the Great Firmament, none were spared. One of the fingers poked at the Shangxia Ancestor, who defended with all his might. Even so, he still spat out a mouthful of blood and was heavily injured.

"Wait, wait! I'm willing to surrender to Heavenly Court!" Shangxia Ancestor called out.

Droves of immortals and even Quasi-Saints followed his lead and surrendered.

"Your Majesty, Eastern Emperor, we were deceived by Dong Wanggong!"

"Yes, yes! We didn't mean to go against Heavenly Court, but Dong Wanggong forced us!"

"What head of male immortals? He's just a bandit! Your Majesty, please uphold justice and punish Dong Wanggong!"

Dong Wanggong's daoheart almost broke. He was the leader of Violet Manor, but nothing had gone his way. His only moment of glory was directly after the Dao Ancestor's second sermon, when he and Xi Wangmu had entered the Quasi-Saint Realm.

After that, Di Jun had established Heavenly Court, and the Demon Clan had immediately obtained five Quasi-Saints, becoming the number-one force in the Great Desolation. Dong Wanggong thought that at least they were still stronger than the Titan Tribe, but less than a day later, he discovered how laughable his thoughts had been.

The Titan Tribe possessed the Pangu Genesis Formation that could easily defeat Heavenly Court. Had it not been for some restriction, Heavenly Court might have perished. If Heavenly Court had perished, that would have meant Violet Manor was next—unless Dong Wanggong surrendered.

How could he be willing?

So, Dong Wanggong played the long game. He wanted to wait for Heavenly Court and Titan Tribe to deplete each other's strength. The moment both sides reached their weakest states, Violet Manor would strike.

Unfortunately, reality was cruel. Shangxia Ancestor led an impatient faction and attacked the remaining members of the Hundred Tribes for a short-term gain. Worse, Shangxia Ancestor showed signs of becoming the decision-maker.

He thought Kong Xuan had been his most loyal ally, but he was the one to deal the fatal blow at the critical moment, ruining any and all chances Dong Wanggong had of reversing the situation. Now, all those who should have stood behind him were condemning him.

Dong Wanggong felt a hand above his. He turned around to see Xi Wangmu smiling gently at him. He raised his other hand and covered hers.

"Have you said your last words?" Taiyi asked as he stared down at the head of male and female immortals from the Ancient Annihilation Constellation.

"Taiyi, I'll tell you right now, don't think you'll meet a good end either. I curse you; I curse you and Di Jun to a ruinous fate!"

Dong Wanggong took out the Nine-Dragon Cane, but he didn't attack Taiyi with it. Instead, he waved it, and a golden sphere covered Xi Wangmu and sent her away.

"You?!" Xi Wangmu cried out, but she didn't get a chance to finish. The golden energy of the sphere interacted with the silver mirror floating around her, activating it.

The Ancient Annihilating Constellation frowned and reached out to Xi Wangmu, who was shuttling through space.

"Your opponent is me!" Dong Wanggong said as he smashed the

star colossus's hand. His full-powered attack had actually shifted the hand's trajectory.

Taiyi frowned. Dong Wanggong was covered in a bright aura radiating pure yang energy. The power he displayed eclipsed that of an early Quasi-Saint and even showed signs of reaching the Peak Quasi-Saint Realm.

However, such an increase in strength had a price. Dong Wanggong was using his foundation, the first strand of Yang Qi in heaven and earth, to boost his strength. After this, whether he survived the battle or not, he would die. But Taiyi didn't look down on him; instead, he had a trace of respect in his eyes. Certainly more than Shangxia Ancestor and the rest of the cowardly immortals.

Three hundred and sixty-five stars shone brilliantly as the Ancient Annihilation Constellation dispersed, returning to its former form. Taiyi commanded the others, "Go, prevent anyone from escaping."

With the rest of the demons gone, Taiyi faced off against Dong Wanggong alone.

"Can you let her go?" Dong Wanggong quietly asked.

"I cannot," Taiyi succinctly said.

Dong Wanggong nodded and didn't say anything else; he knew it was useless. The best way to guarantee Xi Wangmu's safe passage was to incite chaos within the demons, and what better way than to kill their leader?

They exchanged countless moves, and it became apparent that Dong Wanggong held the upper hand, but Taiyi didn't fret. He just focused on defending using his Chaos Bell no matter how frenzied Dong Wanggong fought.

Finally, the two stopped. Dong Wanggong's body had turned translucent, able to disappear at any moment. He looked at Taiyi, then in the direction of Heavenly Court, and finally at the chaotic boundary where he had listened to the Dao Ancestor's sermon in Violet Heaven Palace.

"I'm unwilling, unwilling!"

With those words, Dong Wanggong turned into a wisp of golden light that soon dissipated, leaving behind his remaining treasure. Suddenly, space opened, and a hand reached out to grab the Nine-Dragon Cane.

Taiyi knew this was the Dao Ancestor's hand, so he didn't say anything and stored the rest of the treasures. Then, he glanced at the restrained remnants of Violet Manor.

"Eastern Emperor Taiyi is mighty," Shangxia Ancestor said at this moment. He, along with the other immortals, could not withstand the Starry Sky War Array without the Ten Thousand Immortals Formation.

A few Profound Immortals, Sky Immortals, and Earth Immortals escaped, but Taiyi didn't care. He had already trapped the strongest people of Violet Manor, including Xi Wangmu.

"Eastern Emperor, are we going to return to Heavenly Court now?" Shangxia Ancestor tentatively asked.

Taiyi nodded. "We are, but you aren't. A subordinate should follow their leader."

With Taiyi's words, the Celestial Army assaulted the remnant immortal with reckless abandon.

"Ahh, Taiyi, you bastard, this isn't what you promised!" Shangxia Ancestor shouted in his final moments.

"Didn't we already promise to join Heavenly Court?"

Taiyi sneered. "When have I ever promised you anything? The Heavenly Court doesn't need traitorous bastards like you."

The only one that didn't shout was Xi Wangmu. Her hatred-filled eyes glared at Taiyi, and she used her Kunlun Mirror to resist with all her might. Unfortunately, Taiyi wouldn't let her go, no matter how much he respected Dong Wanggong.

He didn't want to leave any hidden dangers, especially with the Titan Tribe eyeing them. But then a voice called out.

"Daoist Taiyi, did you forget our promise?"

Hearing the pleasant bell-like voice, Taiyi stopped. He turned to see Tongtian and Yuanshi watching in the distance. "How could I? Who do you want to save?"

Tongtian smiled and looked at Xi Wangmu, who froze.

"Impossible, anyone but her," Taiyi immediately balked.

Tongtian's smile disappeared. "I recall Daoist Taiyi said that I could save anyone but Dong Wanggong. Are you going back on your words, Eastern Emperor Taiyi?"

Taiyi frowned and hesitated. At this moment, Ji Meng spoke up. "You mustn't, Your Majesty!"

"Quiet!" Taiyi said, glaring. He turned to look at Xi Wangmu, who had turned remarkably docile. She had her head lowered and didn't dare to look at him. He stared as if to gaze through her deepest thoughts. "Alright."

Tongtian regained her smile. "Thank you, Daoist Taiyi."

Xi Wangmu didn't dare delay and flew to join Tongtian and Yuanshi. She had no guarantee that Taiyi wouldn't go back on his word.

"Thank you, fellow Daoists, for saving my life," Xi Wangmu said with cupped fists and a bow, seeming overly courteous.

Tongtian raised an eyebrow. She refused to believe that Xi Wangmu hadn't noticed her interaction with Taiyi before he'd started to strike the Ten Thousand Immortals Formation's weak points. She'd be surprised if Xi Wangmu were as grateful as she claimed, but Tongtian didn't care.

"I didn't save you for no reason," Tongtian said.

Xi Wangmu looked up, and her eyes connected with Tongtian's. "Please speak. If you want, I am even willing to be your servant."

This time, Tongtian really frowned. "Just hand over your Kunlun Mirror, I don't need you to serve me."

Xi Wangmu only hesitated for a moment before she handed the silver mirror over. "Daoist Tongtian, just a single innate spiritual artifact isn't enough to repay this lifesaving grace. Please let me become your follower."

"I said there is no need," Tongtian said, raising her guard.

She didn't bother paying attention to Xi Wangmu anymore and flew away with Yuanshi. Xi Wangmu chewed the bottom of her lips, and a flash of cruelty entered her eyes. She decisively followed after Tongtian and Yuanshi.

Tongtian continued to ignore her. She returned to Kunlun Mountain now that she had accomplished her goal, but Xi Wangmu followed her there too. Xi Wangmu couldn't enter Kunlun Mountain because of the arrays, so after a time, she settled down on a spiritual mountain west of Kunlun.

The essence wasn't as abundant as on Kunlun Mountain or Penglai Immortal Island, but it was still bountiful. Xi Wangmu even entertained a few guests, such as Burning Lamp Daoist, and taught him the method of Three Corpses.

Later, the mountain would become known as West Kunlun.

Chapter 31

Matchmaker

Tongtian sat in her Supreme Purity Hall with the Kunlun Mirror in her hand. Xi Wangmu had already erased the spiritual imprint in the innate spiritual artifact, allowing Tongtian to refine it without obstacle. Her mastery of the Law of Time and Law of Space only increased the refining speed.

The Kunlun Mirror had thirty-six restrictions, equal to a high-grade cardinal spiritual artifact. At the same grade, a cardinal spiritual artifact has more restrictions than an innate spiritual artifact, and similarly, an innate spiritual artifact has more restrictions than an acquired spiritual artifact.

Spiritual artifacts contained traces of the laws. It was for this reason that cardinal artifacts—treasures born during the creation of heaven and earth—were so sought after. They were imprinted with the purest laws.

Innate spiritual artifacts contained laws as well, but the laws imprinted were murky, hidden by the rules of heaven and earth. The user needed to decipher the truth of the laws. Acquired spiritual artifacts were even worse. The laws were imprinted into the artifact after it had been refined, and it was based on the artificer's own understanding of the law.

Contrary to Tongtian's expectations, it was not the Law of Spacetime that was imprinted into the Kunlun Mirror but the Law of Time and Law of Space separately.

Tongtian could only sigh and work on deciphering the laws contained within.

* * *

While Tongtian was focused on her latest treasure, Di Jun was worrying about other matters. Unlike the time he sent out the Celestial Army to destroy Violet Manor, Eminence Heaven Palace currently only held Di Jun, Taiyi, and seven of the ten demon sages.

"Tell Us, what issues have you discovered within the Starry Sky War Array?"

Ji Meng stepped forward and cupped his fists. "The Starry Sky War Formation has no major problems, but..."

"But?" Di Jun asked.

"There is no one suited to control the Supreme Yin Star."

When Ji Meng stepped back, Bai Ze stepped forward. "According to our calculation, if someone suited can control the Supreme Yin Star, the strength of the Starry Sky War Array will be increased by one tenth, but the overall combat ability will rise by at least three tenths."

Di Jun tapped the armrest of the Nine Dragon Throne. "In all the Great Desolation, no one is more suited than the lunar goddesses, Xihe and Changxi. Taiyi and We are born in the Supreme Yang Star, Xihe and Changxi are born in the Supreme Yin Star—a match made in heaven."

Bai Ze and the rest of the demon sages saluted Di Jun. "Congratulations on Your Majesties' marriages."

Di Jun waved his hand and quieted the celebratory words. "These matters still need to be considered. First of all, who would propose marriage. It's improper for Us or Taiyi to propose. Who should we send?"

"I believe Southern Emperor Wa would be suitable," Bai Ze said, stepping forward again. "The Dao Ancestor gave Emperor Wa the Red Hydrangea. It is destined to become a meritorious spiritual artifact after establishing the marriages of heaven, earth, and man. Your Majesty's marriage can be no other than the heavenly marriage."

Upon hearing Nuwa's name, Di Jun imperceptibly frowned. His thoughts invariably turned to the Grandmist Violet Qi. If Nuwa became a Saint of Heaven, then her prestige would instantly overshadow his, the Heavenly Emperor's. By that point, would it even matter if he was the Heavenly Emperor or not?

Di Jun had thought of taking Nuwa's Grandmist Violet Qi by force, but Nuwa herself was strong. In addition, Fuxi would side with her, and such an internal conflict would only benefit the Titan Tribe.

"We will put the matter of Our marriage for later," Di Jun said. "Heavenly Court is still missing the Northern Emperor. Do beloved officials have any suggestions?"

Shang Yang, a stag demon, stepped forward. "Answering Your Majesty, among the many demons of the Great Desolation, the ones with the highest cultivation are Kong Xuan, Jinchi, and Kunpeng. Kong Xuan was once part of Violet Manor and betrayed them at a critical time, so this official does not believe he is trustworthy. Jinchi does not stray from Kong Xuan, leaving only Kunpeng."

None of the three gods were simple. All three had reached the Quasi-Saint Realm already, so they likely wouldn't be tempted by Heavenly Court's innate spiritual artifacts. In addition, Di Jun still remembered how Kong Xuan had attacked Kunpeng in Violet Heaven Palace to secure a spot for Jinchi on one of the six prayer mats.

Too bad Jinchi was too useless and gave up the seat. Recalling his role, Di Jun smiled. Based on this incident, he believed Kong Xuan and Jinchi wouldn't join Heavenly Court easily.

Di Jun recalled Kunpeng's background. He was born in the Darknorth Sea. The sea wasn't as prosperous as the East and Central Regions, but it wasn't as barren as the West, just much harsher. In addition, Kunpeng created a force known as Darknorth Palace, becoming the overlord of his birthplace.

If Kunpeng joined the Heavenly Court, its strength would rise to another level.

Would such a person join so easily? Nevertheless, they still had to try.

"Dispatch one of the demon sages to Kunpeng," Di Jun said. "It's good if he agrees, and if he doesn't..." Di Jun left the rest unsaid, but everyone knew what he meant.

"What about the Ten Thousand Immortals Book?" a demon sage asked.

After seeing the power of the Ten Thousand Immortals Formation, Di Jun deeply desired it. Unlike Violet Manor, Heavenly Court had far more Profound Immortals and above. Even if they could only establish one Ten Thousand Immortals Formation, Heavenly Court's power would increase by at least 50 percent.

Taiyi shook his head. "After Dong Wanggong died, I took all except the Nine-Dragon Cane, but I didn't discover the Ten Thousand Immortals Book at all. Either Dong Wanggong destroyed it or it disappeared."

Di Jun sighed, but he didn't pursue the matter. After this, they continued to discuss the important matters for the future of Heavenly Court. Finally, the topic returned to the matter of marriage, and Di Jun summoned Nuwa.

"Fellow Daoist Di Jun," Nuwa said as she entered.

Di Jun inwardly frowned. After Nuwa had attained the Grandmist Violet Qi, she no longer addressed him as Your Majesty anymore, but he didn't show any dissatisfaction. "We are afraid We are going to have to trouble fellow Daoist Nuwa."

Nuwa raised an eyebrow. "What does Daoist Di Jun require of me?"

He glanced at Taiyi. Holding back his frown, he turned back to Nuwa. "It's a good thing for Daoist Nuwa. I believe it's time for Taiyi and We to marry. That is, to establish the heavenly marriage. We implore Nuwa to be a matchmaker."

Upon hearing this, Nuwa felt the Red Hydrangea react. Her eyes lit up, and she asked, "Who is Daoist Di Jun's target?"

"Solitary yang does not flourish; lone yin does not prosper. Taiyi and We are born of the Supreme Yang Star. Naturally, the only ones compatible with us are the two born of the Supreme Yin Star."

Nuwa recalled the two beautiful goddesses she had seen in Violet Heaven Palace. She could admit without vanity that she, Tongtian, Houtu, Xihe, and Changxi were each worthy enough to claim the title of the Great Desolation's number-one beauty.

"Leave it to me; I'll definitely persuade Xihe and Changxi," Nuwa said. "I assume Daoist Di Jun will seek Xihe's hand and Daoist Taiyi will seek Changxi's hand in marriage?"

Di Jun nodded. "I'll have to trouble fellow Daoist Nuwa."

Nuwa nodded and turned to leave, as she was also expectant of the results. However, to everyone's surprise, Taiyi spoke.

"Hold on a second."

"Daoist Taiyi, is there something wrong?" Nuwa turned around and asked.

Taiyi nodded. "Yes, there is one problem."

* * *

On the surface of the Supreme Yin Star, the moon of the Great Desolation, existed a solemn white palace. Next to it was the Lunar

Laurel Tree, a top-grade connate spiritual fruit with leaves formed of moonlight.

When Nuwa neared, she stopped at a certain distance. "Sister Xihe, Sister Changxi, am I not welcomed here?"

Not long after, the palace gates opened, and two goddesses walked out. One possessed an eternal yet ephemeral beauty, while the other resembled the lake's reflection of the moon—you could see it, but you could never touch it.

"How can that be? Please come, Sister Nuwa," Xihe said as she invited her guest to sit at the table and chairs under the laurel tree.

Xihe brewed some good tea she had obtained during her travels through the Great Desolation. After a few pleasantries, she asked Nuwa why she had come.

"It's like this," Nuwa began. "In the Great Desolation, there should be three marriages: heaven, earth, and man. Daoist Di Jun is born of the Supreme Yang Star and is the Heavenly Emperor, and Sister Xihe is born of the Supreme Yin Star. I've come today as a matchmaker. The marriage between you and Daoist Di Jun is the heavenly marriage of the Great Desolation, and the Way of Heaven will bestow great merits upon its completion. I don't know what Sister Xihe thinks of my proposal?"

When Xihe fell silent, Nuwa sipped her tea. She wasn't in a hurry. After all, she had already glimpsed something from the river of time. It could be said that the moment Di Jun and Xihe were born, their marriage was already destined.

Xihe closed her eyes and recalled the times she had seen Di Jun. They didn't cross paths much, only meeting during the Dao Ancestor's sermons, but Di Jun's appearance and aura were deeply imprinted into Xihe's mind.

Something inside Di Jun drew Xihe to him, and vice versa. Di Jun represented yang, and Xihe represented yin, and this attraction was innate. Even if Xihe fell deeply in love with another, her love for him could never exceed her natural attraction to Di Jun.

The only two who were a more excellent match were Dong Wanggong and Xi Wangmu. The two leaders of the fallen Violet Manor had been destined to become the Heavenly Emperor and Heavenly Empress, but they could not seize this chance.

"Please tell the Heavenly Emperor that I agree to his proposal," Xihe said.

Nuwa smiled. "Then I will leave Daoist Di Jun's betrothal gift here."

A fiery red gourd with a three-legged golden crow engraved on it appeared on the table. Even at this distance, Xihe and Changxi felt the intense heat radiating off of it, but instead of harming her, it nourished her naturally cold body.

"This is the top-grade Allcrow True Gourd: one of the seven gourds from one of the top ten connate spiritual roots, the Immortal Gourd Vine," Nuwa said.

Originally it had had the potential to become a high-grade cardinal spiritual artifact. Unfortunately, the Immortal Gourd Vine hadn't had enough nutrients to nurture this seventh gourd.

"Daoist Di Jun refined part of the Supreme Yang Star's quintessence into this gourd, and it will naturally produce an infinite amount of Solar Truefire as long as it can absorb the essence of heaven and earth. For Sister Xihe, it should be an invaluable treasure," Nuwa finished with a smile.

"Tell Di Jun I will wait for him on the marriage sedan," Xihei said. To refine part of the Supreme Yang Star's quintessence meant harming the foundation of the star. Even for Di Jun, it bore significant karma, so for him to gift this to her moved Xihe's heart.

"What about me? Did Eastern Emperor Taiyi say anything?" Changxi asked. Just as Xihe felt naturally attracted to Di Jun, Changxi also felt naturally attracted to Taiyi.

Nuwa made an awkward face. "This... Daoist Taiyi didn't mention anything, no. Only Daoist Di Jun asked me to come to be a matchmaker."

Hearing this, Changxi's expression fell. "I see. I'm sorry for bothering Sister Nuwa."

Nuwa felt apologetic, but she couldn't say anything. After a few more words, she left. She still had one last place to visit.

After Nuwa left, Changxi excused herself and returned to the palace in low spirits. Xihe sighed but didn't say anything in the end. She turned toward the Thirty-Three Heavens and then to Great Desolation, where the Titan Tribe was stationed.

"Perhaps it is better that Changxi won't be embroiled in this tribulation."

* * *

In Supreme Purity Hall, Tongtian fiddled with the Kunlun Mirror. She had already comprehended the partial Law of Time within, and it would only take a little more time to comprehend the Law of Space.

The Law of Space inside the artifact really wasn't much. It only allowed Tongtian to teleport great distances, making travel a bit more convenient. She still preferred the ability to hide between layers of space.

She had sped up time around her so that the process wouldn't take as long. Now that she was almost done, she considered what to do with the Kunlun Mirror.

Spiritual artifacts are useful because of the abilities contained within them, which can be used to increase the user's strength. However, the Kunlun Mirror was almost completely useless to Tongtian now, as she could replicate its effect using her own mastery. "Should I use it to merge with the connate gourd I got or just feed it to my Qingping Sword?"

While Tongtian was pondering, a guest appeared at Kunlun Mountain. The Three Purities gathered in Three Purity Hall inside Three Purity Palace and invited Nuwa in.

"A rare visitor, I wonder what Junior Sister has come for?" Laozi spoke first. He was the eldest and the strongest, having successfully cut off all three Corpses. Now, he just needed to merge them.

"It is a good thing," Nuwa said, but her smile was a bit stiff. "I've come in place of Daoist Taiyi."

Upon hearing that name, Yuanshi's face directly darkened. "What does that flat-feathered bastard want?"

At Yuanshi's reaction, Nuwa had an ominous premonition, but she still gritted her teeth. "Earlier, Daoist Di Jun asked me to become a matchmaker for him and Xihe."

"Oh? Are you here to invite us to the wedding?" Tongtian asked. Although the first marriage ceremony was exciting, she had already seen the Pangu Genesis Formation, so Heavenly Court didn't hold much interest to her.

Nuwa shook her head. "No, Daoist Taiyi wants to seek Senior Sister's hand in marriage."

Chapter 32

Heavenly Marriage

Yuanshi's face directly darkened. "A toad wanting to eat swan meat. Who does he think he is? Does he want me to pluck all his feathers and stew him?"

Although Laozi's expression didn't change, he didn't rebuke Yuanshi either. It could be seen that he silently agreed with Yuanshi.

Nuwa internally sighed at the Grand Purity and Jade Purity's adverse reactions, but as long as she could convince the Supreme Purity, then all would be well. There was a reason Di Jun had allowed her to deliver Taiyi's request. If Taiyi married Changxi, then it would be adding flowers to gold—pretty to look at but ultimately nothing substantial.

Marrying Tongtian, on the other hand, meant so much more. Tongtian was one of the destined Saints of Heaven, and unlike Nuwa and Fuxi, Di Jun had absolute trust in Taiyi. In addition, bringing Tongtian to their side meant adding all Three Purities to the Heavenly Court's forces.

Why wouldn't Di Jun agree?

Nuwa turned to Tongtian and almost flinched. Although Tongtian had a smile on her face and restrained her qi, Nuwa could feel the sword-like glint in her eyes and sharp aura surrounding her. Sweat formed on her brows, but she still forced a smile.

"Don't be so hasty to reject," Nuwa quickly said. "If you are willing to marry Daoist Taiyi, he is willing to give you this betrothal gift."

The siblings' expressions changed when a miniature bronze bell began floating in front of them. It was one of the three cardinal spiritual artifacts formed from one of the three pieces of Pangu's Heaven-Opening Ax, the Chaos Bell!

Laozi calmed himself. Although the Chaos Bell was powerful, he possessed the Taiji Diagram, so he didn't necessarily need it. Yuanshi possessed the Pangu Banner, so only Tongtian didn't have one of the three Heaven-Opening Treasures. He didn't know if she would agree under the allure of the Chaos Bell.

Yuanshi sternly addressed her. "Third Sister, don't be bewitched by the treasure. Second Brother will find a better treasure for you."

Tongtian, who had been dazed by the appearance of the Chaos Bell, turned and glared at Yuanshi darkly. "Shut up."

Yuanshi wilted. Why was Tongtian mad now? He was just looking out for her.

Tongtian faced Nuwa. "Junior Sister, please return. Even if Taiyi offers up the whole Heavenly Court, I will never agree to his proposal."

Seeing her steel-like determination, Nuwa could only sigh. She waved her hand to store the Chaos Bell before leaving. She should count her blessings; at least the Three Purities didn't directly attack and take the Chaos Bell as she had feared.

Perhaps this was because of their wariness of Heavenly Court. The Starry Sky War Array was not just a trophy on display, but a veritable contender for the top formation in the Great Desolation. Aside from the Ten Thousand Immortals Formation or the Pangu Genesis Formation, only Saints could fight back, and Saints had yet to appear in heaven and earth.

Tongtian returned to her Supreme Purity Hall to focus on comprehending the Law of Time and the Law of Space. Yuanshi stared at her back before sighing and returning to Jade Purity Hall.

A thousand years later, Yuanshi successfully severed his obsession and formed his Self Corpse.

* * *

Di Jun sighed for the umpteenth time. He watched his brother pace back and forth in the grand hall of Eminence Heaven Palace. Di Jun counted his lucky stars that it was only the two of them here, or the prestige of the two brothers might take a hit.

"You don't have to worry about the Chaos Bell," Di Jun said. "No matter how powerful the Three Purities are, they are not yet Saints. They still have to fear the power of the Heavenly Court."

Taiyi furrowed his brow but didn't say anything. His head snapped toward the entrance when he felt Nuwa's aura.

In a matter of moments, Nuwa stood in the hall with a smiling face, and Taiyi's heart soared. She nodded at Di Jun and said, "Congratulations to Daoist Di Jun for your heavenly marriage."

Taiyi waited for Nuwa's congratulation, but the corners of his lips that had been quirking upward fell again when Nuwa stopped speaking. She waved her hand, and the Chaos Bell returned to him. The meaning was obvious.

"My apologies, Daoist Tongtian…" Nuwa had to choose her next words carefully. "She has a sincere heart for the Great Dao and does not seek to entangle herself with unrelated matters."

Taiyi stood there frozen, staring at the bell. His hand finally grabbed the bronze treasure, and his knuckles whitened from his sheer grip on the artifact. Even though it was impossible, Di Jun and Nuwa feared he might destroy the cardinal spiritual artifact.

Di Jun sighed. He rose from his throne to pat his brother on the shoulder. "Don't worry about it too much. The Three Purities claim to be Pangu's orthodox lineage, so their arrogance can be imagined. We will show them their folly once we defeat the Titan Tribe, even if they are Saints. For now, let's choose another prospective wife for you."

Taiyi's back was to him, so Di Jun didn't see his face darken with each sentence he spoke. Taiyi pushed the well-meaning hand away and walked out of Eminence Heaven Palace, leaving behind a confused Di Jun.

Nuwa seemed to have guessed something from the look on Taiyi's face. When Di Jun turned his inquiring gaze on her, she only shook her head. "Daoist Di Jun, I can only advise you not to bring the matter of marriage up to your brother in the future. He has his own plans."

Di Jun nodded, still not understanding.

Nuwa didn't move to leave but instead waved her hand to reveal an orange-colored flag. "Daoist Di Jun, this is the Demon-Summoning Banner I refined by merging the immortal gourd I obtained with the Demon Banner. It's a high-grade cardinal spiritual artifact."

Di Jun looked at the flag that had floated in front of him, wondering why Nuwa had given it to him. Although a high-grade cardinal spiritual artifact was good, he didn't lack treasures as the Heavenly Emperor, and it wasn't worth much if he didn't practice the law contained within.

"Its offensive and defensive power are lacking," Nuwa informed him. "But it has two unique features. As long as a demon sends a strand of their truesoul into the Demon-Summoning Banner, their life and death will be under the user's control. Furthermore, if the demon perishes, they can revive as long as a strand of their truesoul remains in the Demon-Summoning Banner."

Di Jun's disinterested look turned covetous. He could not allow it to stay in any hand but his. He looked meaningfully at Nuwa and cupped his fists. "Then We will thank Daoist Nuwa for this gift."

Nuwa smiled and left.

She didn't pursue authority and didn't want to embroil herself in the politics of Heavenly Court. She was content to bear the name and quietly cultivate, but it seemed that Di Jun had begun to be wary of her and Fuxi after the Dao Ancestor's third sermon.

Nuwa hadn't noticed, but her brother did. After Fuxi had brought it to her attention, Nuwa had come to the conclusion that the Demon-Summoning Banner must not stay in her possession. Now, with the hot potato out of her hand, she returned to Southern Emperor Palace to cultivate in peace.

She wanted to focus on comprehending the Grandmist Violet Qi. She was already under heavy pressure from the Titan Tribe and their Pangu Genesis Formation, but after meeting with the Three Purities, she realized her inadequacies.

Compared to those three, she was too weak. She still hadn't forgotten how Jieyin had entered the Quasi-Saint Realm before the Dao Ancestor's second sermon. After attaining the treasures in the Sealed Treasure Stone, Nuwa estimated that Jieyin was at least at the Intermediate Quasi-Saint Realm or maybe even the Advanced Quasi-Saint Realm.

At this rate, she might become the weakest of the Dao Ancestor's six disciples. Nuwa had her own pride and wouldn't allow this, especially since Jieyin and Zhunti were only nominal disciples and got their status through shameless begging.

Nuwa tried to decipher the Grandmist Violet Qi, but there was no reaction. Helpless, she could only focus on severing her second Corpse.

Frustratingly, someone severed a Corpse ahead of her. Six hundred years later, Taiyi entered the Advanced Quasi-Saint Realm.

Pressed by a slight sense of urgency, she severed her evil thoughts 200 years later and successfully severed her second Corpse.

Now, Heavenly Court boasted two advanced Quasi-Saints.

While Nuwa and Taiyi were cultivating, Heavenly Court progressed in its own way. Since Nuwa had returned from the Supreme Yin Star and Kunlun Mountain, Heavenly Court had been preparing for the Heavenly Emperor's marriage.

They sent out numerous invitations to major powers; including Kunlun Mountain's Three Purities, Mount Sumeru's Jieyin and Zhunti, Darknorth Palace's Kunpeng, Firesource Grotto's Redcloud Ancestor, and Wuzhuang Temple's Zhen Yuanzi. The one major power they didn't invite was the Titan Tribe.

In Darknorth Palace, Kunpeng hesitantly decided to go after much time spent pondering. His Darknorth Palace didn't possess a powerful formation like Violet Manor, and offending Heavenly Court was not a wise decision.

Redcloud Ancestor, as usual, decided to attend with Zhen Yuanzi. They were born of different sources, but they were closer than real brothers.

"Senior Brother, what should we do?" Zhunti asked. Truthfully, he didn't want to go. Even if they went, how could matters of the East benefit the West?

"Di Jun is still the Heavenly Emperor after all, and we aren't yet Saints," Jieyin explained. "Even if we become Saints, the role of the Heavenly Emperor cannot be underestimated. When the Three Purities become Saints of Heaven, do you think they will obey the Heavenly Court? Will Di Jun be satisfied with the status quo? Heavenly Court will only have Nuwa as a Saint, but if they ally with us, they can contend with the Three Purities. Naturally, the West will benefit if Di Jun is smart."

Zhunti smiled. "I was too short-sighted. Senior Brother is wise."

Jieyin smiled compassionately and said, "Let us go. The West is still a distance away. It's better to arrive early than late."

The two disciple brothers became twin golden streaks of light across the sky. Upon their arrival, they were led to an area near South Heaven Gate. Only when the groom returned with the bride would the guests be seated.

Zhunti searched around but couldn't find the Three Purities. "Are they not here?"

Jieyin clapped his hands together. "If they aren't, all the better for us."

When the sun shone directly above the Thirty-Three Heavens, Di Jun appeared in front of everyone. He wore red wedding robes as he set off on his marriage sedan. Although it was nominally called a marriage sedan, it was a top-grade acquired spiritual artifact created specifically for Di Jun's wedding.

The sedan was composed of two parts: the Dragon Chariot and the Phoenix Carriage. The chariot, which was pulled by twelve dragon horses, was refined with the bones of dragons and had nine dragons sculpted on it. Its draconic aura enhanced Di Jun's majesty when he stood in it.

The carriage pulled by the chariot was refined using Waterlight Moon Jade, and had phoenixes engraved on it. If the chariot represented yang, the carriage represented yin.

Di Jun steered the marriage sedan to the Supreme Lunar Star. While watching it disappear into the distance, Zhunti couldn't hide his envious eyes. The materials were absolutely invaluable, but Heavenly Court used them for a mere marriage sedan. Seeing such extravagance only reminded Zhunti of how barren the West was.

Di Jun arrived at the Supreme Yin Star, and Xihe stepped onto the Phoenix Carriage. Like her husband-to-be, she wore festive red robes.

When Di Jun drove back to South Heaven Gate, all the guests watched curiously as Xihe stepped off. When they saw her face, they couldn't help but be enamored. Even if there was a goddess of beauty born right then, no one could surpass Xihe's radiance at that moment, be it in physical features or aura.

From then on, the phrase "A woman is most beautiful at her wedding" appeared in the Great Desolation.

The radiant couple led everyone to the second level of the Thirty-Three Heavens. The top layer was where Eminence Heaven Palace was located and where the Heavenly Emperor held court and lived. The second layer, Jade Lake Wonderland, belonged to the Heavenly Empress.

Di Jun and Xihe stood in front of the altar with their hands connected. Nuwa stood in front of them and summoned the Red Hydrangea above their heads.

"The Way of Heaven above, I feel that the yin and yang of the world are disorderly. I hereby establish the marriage as the representative of supreme yang and supreme yin. With the heavenly marriage established, yin and yang will no longer be in chaos and will henceforth reinforce each other!"

After Nuwa's prayer, golden clouds of merit appeared above Thirty-Three Heavens. The amount of merit was not as substantial as when Di Jun had established Heavenly Court, but it still caused all the gods present to look on in envy—especially Kunpeng.

The merit split into three parts. Di Jun and Xihe each received 40 percent of the total merits, while Nuwa's Red Hydrangea absorbed the last 20 percent.

"Sever!"

A woman with 70-percent similarities appeared next to Xihe as she successfully entered the Quasi-Saint Realm. She continued to absorb the merit and stabilized her cultivation at the Early Quasi-Saint Realm. Di Jun also severed a Corpse and successfully entered the Advanced Quasi-Saint Realm, attracting the envy of numerous guests.

They also thought of establishing a marriage, but they soon gave up. The reason Di Jun and Xihe gained so much merit was because of their identities as the Heavenly Emperor and Heavenly Empress. If they did it, it would only tie their luck and merit with another person for no reason.

Nuwa was also satisfied. She could feel the power of her Red Hydrangea increase by another level. She was already planning on finding the candidates for the earthly and mortal marriages.

Just as the atmosphere reached its peak, a familiar party-crasher arrived.

"Heavenly marriage, have you asked for our permission, you pair of flat-feathered crows?!"

Chapter 33

The Chaos Bell

An ugly expression immediately appeared on Di Jun's face. "Even if the heavens forgive you, I, Di Jun the Heavenly Emperor, will not! This is the second time you have dared to interrupt Heavenly Court's important ceremonies!"

He sent Xihe into the safety of Jade Lake Wonderland. Although she had also entered the Quasi-Saint Realm, her realm wasn't stable. Her strength would have been appreciated, but if she fell, then it would be a greater loss for the Starry Sky War Array.

Di Jun led the three demon emperors, ten demon sages, and ten legions of the Celestial Army to confront the Titan Tribe. Flying out of South Heaven Gate, he found the Titan Tribe standing belligerently in wait.

About an eon has passed since their last confrontation, and the Titan Tribe hadn't fully recovered from their losses. Luckily, the Demon Clan reproduced quickly, so their number had actually grown. On the surface, it seemed that Heavenly Court had the advantage.

But Di Jun frowned. He could see that the number of giants with the strength of Golden Immortals of the Great Firmaments had increased since last time. What was more worrying was that all twelve titans exuded the aura of a Quasi-Saint!

Including Xihe, Heavenly Court had six Quasi-Saints. However, they also had their Corpses. With Corpses, Heavenly Court could be said to have fifteen Quasi-Saints powerhouses, but the titans were still more physically powerful. Not to mention that they needed to use spiritual artifacts to compete with titans.

Nonetheless, Di Jun didn't show any weakness. "Di Jiang, last time, you could only flee with your tails behind your legs. This time, you won't be so lucky!"

"Big words from a burnt bird! You seemed to have forgotten you were the one beaten like a dog. This time, I'll make it your last moments!" Di Jiang shouted back, his killing intent skyrocketing.

Di Jiang didn't want Heavenly Court to have time to digest their merits. The Titan Tribe could not see the usefulness of merit, but he recognized its influence over time. The number of giants growing in strength increased and at a faster rate than before they had gained control of the land.

Di Jun split off his Good and Evil Corpses to face off against Di Jiang. Having already experienced the titan's power, Di Jun wanted to finish this as soon as possible.

Di Jiang immediately teamed up with Jiuyin. Although he was now a Quasi-Saint, he dared not face Di Jun alone.

Di Jun held the Celestial River Diagram in hand and formed the Starry Sky behind him. First, the Supreme Yang Star and the Supreme Yin Star shone brilliantly and shot out two beams. Then two beams entwined, creating an attack greater than the sum of its parts.

"Haha, Di Jun, do you only know this trick?" Di Jiang asked, laughing.

As the beams struck him, Di Jiang's body turned monochrome and dispersed into a gray fog. This smoky haze twisted space wherever it went and, moments later, reformed into Di Jiang.

Jiuyin was quick to display an equally impressive new ability. A silver light encased his form and he blurred. He shifted away, and the beam struck where he had stood just a second ago.

When the twelve titans had reached the Quasi-Saint Realm, their innate abilities had upgraded, allowing them to transform their bodies into their elements. Even if a giant were to reach the Quasi-Saint Realm, they would never be able to achieve the same feats.

Di Jun snarled, but he didn't let up his attacks. Beams of starlight shone from the 365 major stars and arrows of starlight rained down from the 48,000 minor stars.

While Di Jun battled Di Jiang and Jiuyin, Fuxi confronted Shebisi again. These matchups weren't a coincidence. Both sides wanted a rematch so they could settle once and for all who was superior.

The Fuxi Qin appeared in Fuxi's hands, and the apparitions of numerous other instruments, including a pipa, flute, and many more, appeared around him. Each one released a note that bypassed Shebisi's hard exterior and harmed his soft internal organs.

Shebisi frowned. Although Fuxi had not entered the Intermediate Quasi-Saint Realm, his power had at least doubled. Without delay, he transformed into a storm, raining down thunder, water, and wind.

Fuxi could dispel his clouds, repel his lightning, and shatter the rain; but as long as the thunderstorm remained, Shebisi could continuously supplement his energy and repair his injuries, allowing his strength to increase with time.

Western Emperor Xi frowned. As soon as he attempted to disperse the thunderstorm, Shebisi increased his offensive, forcing Fuxi to deal with him.

Fuxi grew concerned as Shebisi went all out and didn't conserve any energy, unlike last time, when he'd had to defend. If this continued, he would be pushed into a corner. He sighed, and his Corpse came to help deal with the titan.

Upon seeing the Corpse, Shebisi focused all his attack on it. If it perished, Fuxi would likely regress to the Great Firmament Realm, making it much harder to re-enter the Quasi-Saint Realm.

While her brother battled the storm titan; Nuwa faced off against Houtu, Xuanming, and Qiangliang.

Nuwa frowned. She could sense that Houtu had already entered the Intermediate Quasi-Saint Realm. She was the only one of the twelve titans to do so.

Xuanming attacked first. Tens of thousands of raindrops emerged and shot out at Nuwa.

"Just the same trick," Nuwa said as she held her Treasured Lotus Lantern. Lotus-shaped energy flew out to block the raindrops and shot toward the Titan of Rain.

Unlike the last time, when the lotus shattered the raindrops, they turned into water vapor and condensed into a mist. The deeper the lotuses flew into the mist, the smaller they became as their energy was drained.

Houtu took this chance to attack, and spikes erupted underneath Nuwa. Nuwa frowned. Her Treasured Lotus Lantern formed a green-colored barrier to block it. To prevent any more such attacks, she decided to take to the skies.

Qiangliang appeared immediately above her. The Titan of Thunder let out a devastating roar that sent ripples through the air and caused Nuwa to pale.

Houtu and Xuanming took this chance to attack with the strongest move they could unleash as swiftly as they could. Qiangliang clasped his fists together and smashed them down, seeming to blur from the sheer vibration contained within.

Just as the three-pronged assault was about to connect with Nuwa, mountains and rivers grew from her body. She herself disappeared into the Mountain and River Diorama as the three attacks slammed into the spiritual artifact. It shook violently, but held strong.

A red blur shot out of the Mountain and River Diorama and slammed into Qiangliang's chest, knocking him back. His aura reduced by half, and his strength dramatically decreased. Just as the Red Hydrangea moved to hit Qiangliang again, earth and rain merged to knock the flower back.

The diorama flew forward, smashing toward the three titans and revealing Nuwa standing in her original place.

Houtu raised the earth, Xuanming shot gatling rain at it, but the Mountain and River Diorama absorbed the earth and rain as nourishment. In response, soil and rock emerged from the land and clung to the Titan of Earth.

Moments later, a colossal humanoid emerged. Its height reached over a hundred li, and it raised its fist above its head before bringing it down.

Nuwa grunted as the Mountain and River Diorama caved slightly from the punch. She supplied it with more qi, bolstering it against Houtu's oppressive might. While resisting Houtu, Nuwa resumed attacking Qiangliang with the Red Hydrangea.

She knew the difficult nature of sound-based attacks thanks to her brother, so she wanted to get rid of Qiangliang first. Although Houtu's strength increased, her speed had taken a hit, so it was the perfect chance.

Xuanming moved her body into the Red Hydrangea's path. Her body expanded, growing only slightly smaller than Houtu's form. She had transformed into a mixture of water vapor and rain, and the only part not transformed were her eyes.

When the Red Hydrangea entered Xuanming's body, she shrunk by half, but the Red Hydrangea was trapped.

Nuwa frowned. A woman with 70 percent similarities to her appeared holding the Treasured Lotus Lantern. It was her Good Corpse. While she entangled Houtu with the Mountain and River Diorama, her Good Corpse took aim at Xuanming.

By the time her Good Corpse retrieved the Red Hydrangea, Qiangliang had already recovered to join Houtu and Xuanming. Their battle raged on.

Still, the most intense battle was between Taiyi and Zhurong, Gonggong, Rushou, Jizi, and Tianwu.

"Take my punch!" Zhurong yelled as he transformed into the incarnation of fire.

Taiyi snorted, entirely fearless of fire attacks. The apparition of a three-legged golden crow appeared behind Taiyi as he rushed forward.

When Zhurong unleashed his flaming fist, Taiyi didn't directly take it. Instead, he shifted to the side and placed his palm on Zhurong's arm, and the Solar Truefire cultivated from the core of the Supreme Yang Star began devouring Zhurong's flames.

Zhurong recoiled and ripped his own arm off. As his separated arm fell to the ground, Taiyi's Solar Truefire devoured it and flew back to its master.

"Haha, and you call yourself the Titan of Fire?" Gonggong mocked Zhurong, who had regrown his flaming arm, still in his fiery state. "Watch me!"

Gonggong transformed into an incarnation of water and smashed his fist toward Taiyi. Water extinguished fire, so Gonggong held an inherent advantage. But when Taiyi unleashed the Solar Truefire, Gonggong also recoiled and repeated Zhurong's action. The only difference was that the Solar Truefire lost some of its mass after evaporating Gonggong's water.

Zhurong sneered. "Are you the Titan of Water? Why did you lose to fire?"

Gonggong glared at him but said nothing.

Rushou sighed as his skin turned to steel. "Enough bickering. Let's kill him together."

As the master of metal, Rushou knew that Taiyi curbed him because of his mastery over fire. Fire melted metal, and unless his strength exceeded Taiyi's, Rushou saw no chance at victory, but that didn't mean he would give up. In addition, he wasn't alone.

Tianwu—the Titan of Wind—and Jizi—the Titan of Lightning—joined their three comrades in battle. Even for Taiyi, five Quasi-Saint titans were a bit much. In the previous battle, Taiyi had held the advantage in realm. Now, they were more evenly matched.

Taiyi waved his hands, and the Chaos Bell appeared. It expanded rapidly and smashed down, trapping Jizi within it. The bell's gong echoed throughout the whole battlefield, causing everyone to glance over.

They froze.

The Chaos Bell still had the same shape, but Taiyi had altered its surface. On one side, there was an engraving of a handsome man in his twenties. He wore noble robes and had a three-legged crow behind him.

The watchers would not have thought much if it was just this. Although engraving your image onto your artifact was a bit tasteless, they couldn't dictate what others did to their own artifacts.

It was the engraving on the other side that stunned onlookers.

Etched into the other side was a woman wearing billowing robes. Her hair fluttered, and she held an unsheathed sword, giving her a valiant air. It was Supreme Purity Tongtian.

* * *

From the West, Zhunti couldn't help but furrow his brows. "Senior Brother, did the Three Purities ally with Heavenly Court?"

Jieyin also furrowed his brows, thinking deeply of the implication. "I do not know. But it can be seen that Daoist Taiyi and Daoist Tongtian's relationship is more complex than we thought."

All the other guests, heavenly officials, and Titan Tribe members couldn't help but speculate about the relationship between Heavenly Court and the Three Purities—especially that of Tongtian and Taiyi.

* * *

"I'm going to kill him," Tongtian said as she picked up her Qingping Sword and flew out of Three Purity Palace.

Although the Three Purities hadn't attended Di Jun's wedding, he was still the Heavenly Emperor acknowledged by the Way of Heaven, so they paid attention. They had already had an inkling of the Titan Tribe's plan when they'd asked Yuanshi to speed up his refining of the formation flags.

What they didn't expect was the gall of Taiyi. His marriage proposal failed, so he brazenly engraved Tongtian and himself on the Chaos Bell. Not only was this an insult to Pangu, but it shamed them too.

"Third Sister, calm down!" Laozi said. He grabbed Tongtian's arm but was dragged along with her. He had focused on merging his three Corpses and didn't cultivate the Nine-Revolution Arcane Art to the same extent as Tongtian, so her brute strength surpassed his.

Laozi turned to Yuashi for help, only to see him gearing up with the Qiankun Cauldron and Three-Treasured Jade Scepter in his arms. "Second Brother, what are you doing?!"

Yuanshi sneered. "Since Taiyi dares to humiliate Third Sister like this, I'm going to end the Heavenly Court! I knew I should have plucked his feathers when I had the chance."

Laozi felt his wrinkles deepen in the belligerent air around his two siblings. "Can't you two tell? The next tribulation is coming up, and the two protagonists are Heavenly Court and the Titan Tribe. If we muddy the water, we'll be dragged in! It's better to focus on understanding Grandmist Violet Qi or ascending to the Primordial Origin Realm."

His words brought clarity back to Tongtian's eyes. She snorted. "I'll let him live a bit longer, but once I get the Chaos Bell, I'll definitely restore its former appearance. And if he is still alive, I'll pluck his feathers myself!"

"Third Sister, do you want me to refine an artifact to cook him?" Yuanshi offered, glaring in Taiyi's direction. "We'll slice him into a thousand pieces and feed it to the demons."

Tongtian recoiled from Yuanshi's vivid description. "You don't need to go that far."

Laozi sighed. As time passed, the secrets of heaven became more and more blurred, but he could still deduce that the war between Heavenly Court and Titan Tribe would erupt soon. Once it did, then the tribulation would begin.

Chapter 34

Hongjun Descends

Bai Ze's face twitched when he saw what Taiyi had done to the Chaos Bell. It might benefit the Heavenly Court in the short-term by letting others think that they had a relationship with the Three Purities, but this would sow enmity with them.

Disregarding the Titan Tribe, the Three Purities might also attack Heavenly Court in the future. Although Bai Ze didn't think the two would ally with each other, an additional enemy might be the straw that broke the camel's back.

He wanted to split Taiyi's head open and see exactly what the Eastern Emperor was thinking.

Bai Ze hid his dissatisfaction and focused on the enemy—Jumang and an army of giants. He wasn't Fuxi, he couldn't face off against a titan alone.

The Titan of Wood had transformed into a giant tree, even taller than Houtu. Green particles drifted down from its branches and leaves, healing any injuries the giants incurred while draining the vitality of any demons they touched.

Bai Ze and the rest of the demon sages directed the Celestial Army against the giant army. Like before, more demons died for every giant killed, but most of them were weak in the Earth or Sky Immortal Realm. Given enough time, the demons could recuperate their loss.

He adopted the cruel tactic of using cannon fodder to drain the attention and energy of the giants and commanding the stronger Golden Immortals and above to deal the killing blows. With his tactical prowess, the giants started to fall despite Jumang's aid.

Jumang was just one titan, how could he heal a whole army? If he continued, Heavenly Court might as well just give up then and there.

Of course, Bai Ze was cautious. He kept the demons needed to form the Starry Sky War Array in the safest location or in reserve.

Di Jiang had noticed, but he was helpless. Members of the Titan Tribe were not suited to battlefield tactics. They could work together, but they weren't suited for large tactical formations. They preferred to use brute force and charge forward like berserkers.

He needed to raise morale, and the best method was to kill the enemies' leaders.

Di Jiang glared at Di Jun. With the Celestial River Diagram in hand, he was too difficult to kill quickly, even with Jiuyin's aid. Alone, he would already be dead.

His eyes turned to regard the other battlefield. Taiyi's momentum was too strong. Even against five titans, he still had the upper hand. Nuwa appeared unthreatened by his forces. She didn't aim for a quick victory just to delay time and increase Heavenly Court's advantage. Bai Ze was too far, so that only left one target.

Di Jiang and Jiuyin shared a look.

When the Heavenly Emperor unleashed his next attack, Jiuyin slipped in front of Di Jiang. He activated his temporal abilities to the max, and the starlight slowed to a crawl—not just the starlight, but Di Jun as well. However, Di Jun had experienced this technique once and had already shielded himself.

Unfortunately, the titans' target wasn't their leader. Di Jiang merged with space, and when he reappeared, he was behind Fuxi.

Fuxi couldn't react in time. If Di Jiang's fist landed, he would certainly be fatally wounded or killed instantly. The titan gritted his teeth and slapped the Fuxi Qin, but to his surprise, Fuxi had switched places with his Corpse.

Di Jiang still brought his fist down, destroying the Corpse.

Fuxi coughed up a mouthful of blood as his face paled. His aura weakened and hovered between the Quasi-Saint and Great Firmament Realms.

Di Jiang and Shebisi pincered Fuxi, intending to kill him. Fuxi defended, but it was obvious that he'd be dead within five breaths. Still, five breaths were long enough for Nuwa to suck Fuxi into her Mountain and River Diorama.

She gritted her teeth as Houtu took this chance to land an attack on her, but she also used the force to widen the distance between them. Di Jun and Taiyi appeared next to her, and the twelve titans also regrouped.

"How is Daoist Fuxi?" Di Jun asked.

Nuwa had an ugly expression on her face, and she shook her head. "He won't be able to fight, and it remains unknown whether or not he can stay in the Quasi-Saint Realm."

Di Jun appeared saddened as he retrieved a jade bottle for Nuwa. "This contains Threelight Divinewater. Give it to Daoist Fuxi."

Nuwa inspected the jade bottle and saw that it contained over a hundred drops of Threelight Divinewater, shocking her. This was probably all the Threelight Divinewater in the entire Heavenly Court. All of her previous resentment over Fuxi's injuries turned to gratitude.

Di Jun pretended not to notice the change in her emotions and stared at the twelve titans on the other side. Their feud had long stained Buzhou Mountain red with blood, and this battle would only prove even deadlier than their last one.

"Form the Starry Sky War Array!" Di Jun ordered.

As the demons formed the array, Di Jiang hesitated. He saw the engravings on Taiyi's Chaos Bell and couldn't help but suspect the Three Purities. Although they had agreed to put the past behind them, it was only a verbal agreement.

What if they conspired with Heavenly Court to exterminate the titans?

His thoughts were interrupted by a lunar star floating out of South Heaven Gate; it was Xihe. Di Jun had suspected that the Titan Tribe might make trouble again, so he had already taught Xihe the Starry Sky War Array, and now, it was put into use.

Di Jun took the place of the Purple Majesty Star, Taiyi the Supreme Yang Star, and Xihe the Supreme Yin Star. With the three core stars of the Starry Sky War Array in place, the pressure it exuded magnified.

No longer did it waver with instability. In fact, its strength had vastly increased since Taiyi had used it against Violet Manor. It was helped by the fact that the array had been formed at the peak of Buzhou Mountain, the location closest to the Starry Sky.

Di Jiang no longer hesitated. "Form the Pangu Genesis Formation!"

Di Jun was well-prepared, but so was Di Jiang. When the Heavenly Court announced Di Jun's marriage, Di Jiang was already urging Yuanshi to finish the formation flags. Now, each of the twelve titans held a formation flag infused with their blood. The twelve flags were dubbed the Titanomachy Formation Flags by Yuanshi after he and Tongtian finished them.

All twelve titans floated in the air, encased in a blood-red light. Organs, muscle, and skin materialized one after the other, forming a muscled man wearing a loincloth and sporting untamed hair.

The false Pangu opened his eyes. An enormous pressure spread out, causing the giants and weaker demons to prostrate themselves. He raised his hand above his head and said, "Come!"

Although the Pangu Genesis Formation did not attempt to summon the Three Purities, it released a call to the Heaven-Opening Treasures in order to make up for its lack of weapons.

In Kunlun Mountain, both Laozi and Yuanshi frowned when they felt the resonance from the Taiji Diagram and Pangu Banner. They snorted and suppressed it. Within the Starry Sky War Array, Taiyi did the same.

The illusion of an ax appeared in the false Pangu's hand since he couldn't summon the three Heaven-Opening Treasures. Although incorporeal, it still emitted the aura of a top-grade cardinal spiritual treasure.

The Pangu Genesis Formation brought down the illusory Heaven-Opening Ax. Heaven and earth seemed to have returned to chaos, and the illusory ax cleaved it in half, separating it once more.

Pangu Heaven-Opening First Art - Chaos Splitter

Not even the Starry Sky War Array could block the ax. The false Pangu had advanced at least three levels since its last use, so its cleave heavily injured all the demons in its way instantly.

It was not that the overall power of the Pangu Genesis Formation rose, but the twelve titans' control of the formation had reached near-perfection. Inside the formation, Di Jiang sighed in relief when nothing went awry. It seemed that the Three Purities hadn't sabotaged the Titanomachy Formation Flags.

The Pangu Genesis Formation raised the weapon above its head again, gathering power to unleash the second ax strike.

Di Jun felt the terror of all the demons within the Starry Sky War Array. It reached the point that the array began to collapse in on itself from sheer fear. Only Taiyi remained composed.

As the controller of the Starry Sky War Array, the Heavenly Emperor forcibly stabilized it from collapsing in on itself. "Attack! Do you think you'll survive if the array breaks? It'll only make our deaths faster!"

Under Di Jun's command, the demons switched to a do-or-die mentality and furiously attacked the Pangu Genesis Formation. Di Jun unleashed the Ancient Annihilation Constellation, and a colossus composed of stars appeared with Di Jun's face.

The Chaos Bell materialized in the star colossus's hand as he approached the Pangu Genesis Formation that was still gathering power.

"Bai Ze, what are you doing? Attack!" Di Jun shouted at the frozen demons as he smashed the Chaos Bell on the false Pangu, the bell ringing as it struck.

The Pangu Genesis Formation barely took half a step back. It didn't even appear injured, and continued to gather power for the second strike.

While the Ancient Annihilation Constellation attacked the Pangu Genesis Formation, Bai Ze commanded the demons to attack the giants. The equilibrium brought by Jumang's contribution was lost instantly as the demons started to overwhelm the giants. Only the giants near the peak of the Great Firmament Realm such as Kuafu, Chiyou, and Houyi, survived the waves and waves of desperate demons.

"Die, Di Jun!" Di Jiang's voice echoed from the false Pangu as it brought its ax down a second time.

Pangu Heaven-Opening Second Art - Open Heaven

The ax bisected the Ancient Annihilation Constellation, destroying it. When it finished its arc, the Starry Star War Array scattered, and all the demons within crashed into the ground, killing a third of them instantly.

Di Jun glared hatefully at Di Jiang's face on the Pangu Genesis Formation. Di Jiang didn't bother to unleash the third of the Pangu Heaven-Opening Art and just brought it down.

Before he could, coercion that affected even the Pangu Genesis Formation descended. Accompanying it was the mysterious song that lifted the spirits of anyone who heard it; a melody of golden lotuses, phoenix cries, and dragon roars.

Hongjun had descended.

"From henceforth, the Demon Clan shall rule the skies, and the Titan Tribe shall rule the land. For ten eons, neither side shall war with the other. This is my, Hongjun's, decree!"

Hongjun's words spread throughout the Great Desolation. All the demons and giants knelt in reverence. Di Jun and the other demons cried out in ecstasy. Was Hongjun secretly supporting them?

"Hongjun, we respect you as the Dao Ancestor, but don't think you can order us as you like!" Di Jiang and the other titans roared from within the Pangu Genesis Formation.

As long as they killed Di Jun and the other demon emperors—especially Nuwa, who was fated to become a Saint of Heaven—no one would be able to stop the Titan Tribe's supremacy.

"I'll give you one move. If you can injure me even the slightest bit, you can do as you like," Hongjun said.

After a second of hesitation, Di Jiang agreed. He'd originally been confident about taking down Hongjun with the Pangu Genesis Formation, but now that he faced the Dao Ancestor in person, his arrogance withered.

In addition, Di Jun's efforts weren't in vain. He sensed that the Pangu Genesis Formation wouldn't last much longer. The false Pangu raised its ax once more and prepared to unleash the third ax art.

Pangu Heaven-Opening Third Art - Dividing Earth

All of Buzhou Mountain shook under the might of the ax strike. Every living being in the vicinity felt their spirits and flesh splitting, even the giants who only possessed truesouls.

In the face of this horrifying strike, Hongjun remained unfazed. He reached out with his hands and lightly tapped the ax head. Cracks splintered through the illusory metal, and the weapon shattered a moment later.

The Pangu Genesis Formation followed suit as all the twelve titans crashed to the ground, much like the demons. Hongjun's figure turned translucent as he started to disappear. "Remember my decree. Demons shall remain in the sky, and the Titan Tribe shall remain on the land. For ten eons, war is forbidden!"

With an ashen face, Di Jiang led the giants back to their head-quarters while Di Jun led the demons back to the Thirty-Three Heavens.

Back in Pangu Temple, the twelve titans sat together again. They didn't need much time to heal this time since the Titanomachy Formation Flag had born most of the burden.

"Hongjun's power exceeded my imagination," Di Jiang said, frowning. "I don't think we could defeat him even if all of us possessed peak Quasi-Saint strength.

Anger and stubbornness colored the other titans' faces, but they stayed silent. Even their trump card, the Pangu Genesis Formation, seemed flimsy in the face of the Dao Ancestor's horrifying power.

"We should consider how to deal with Hongjun after we defeat Heavenly Court," Jiuyin said. "Our biggest enemy is the demons. Everything else can be considered later."

Di Jiang nodded. "Jiuyin is right. What we need right now is to restore the Titanomachy Formation Flags. We must strengthen them as much as possible."

Each titan took out a flag. Every single one had a slight rip on it. Their expressions darkened. The only ones who could help them were Yuanshi and Tongtian, but asking would require them to fork over more blood essence.

"Luckily, we've already settled our grievances," Di Jiang said. "We shouldn't need to pay a higher price to restore and strengthen them."

"Once we all reach the Peak Quasi-Saint Realm in power, I want to see how those beasts can resist us," Zhurong said, and for once, Gonggong didn't counter him.

"What I'm worried about is that Nuwa will become a Saint of Heaven during these ten eons," Houtu said, causing all the titans to frown again.

"Hongjun said that the foundation for sainthood is the Grandmist Violet Qi," Di Jiang said. "As long as we grab it, we can try to decipher it so one of us can become a Saint.

"But whose can we take?" Rushou asked. "If we make attempts on the Grandmist Violet Qis in the Three Purities' hand, they may join Heavenly Court in dealing with us."

"Before we worry about them retaliating, we have to consider Hongjun's response," Shebisi said. "We can't discount him taking action to save Nuwa."

"There is one person we can deal with," Xuanming said. "Unlike the Three Purities, Nuwa, Jieyin, and Zhunti; he isn't Hongjun's disciple either."

All the titans shared a look, and a look of understanding dawned on their faces.

"Redcloud Ancestor."

Chapter 35
Heaven-Opening Sword Art

Di Jun sat on the Nine Dragon Throne with a grave expression. He asked Nuwa, "How is Daoist Fuxi?"

Nuwa smiled slightly. "Thanks to Daoist Di Jun's aid, my brother barely managed to keep his Quasi-Saint Realm cultivation base. He just needs another innate spiritual artifact to progress again."

Di Jun nodded. "That's good. Once he recovers, I'll send some suitable artifacts to him."

As the Heavenly Emperor, he had wanted to suppress Nuwa and Fuxi's influence to bolster his prestige, but after seeing the Pangu Genesis Formation's increased power, he could no longer care about such matters.

"Have you felt anything from the Grandmist Violet Qi?" Di Jun asked. He was uncertain if he wanted Nuwa to become a Saint, but at this point, only a Saint could deal with the Pangu Genesis Formation.

Nuwa shook her head. "For so long, I haven't sensed any changes. My intuition tells me the time hasn't arrived yet."

Di Jun nodded. "It seems that we cannot rely on the Grandmist Violet Qi. We can only strengthen the development of the Demon Clan. If we can gather 48,000 Golden Immortals, then I believe the Starry Sky War Array can compete with the Pangu Genesis Formation."

After discussing a few more matters with Nuwa, she left, and he was left with Taiyi.

"Even if Nuwa is a Saint, we can't rely on her," Di Jun said. "She is an outsider, after all. Who knows what thoughts she will have once she achieves sainthood."

"Brother, you mean?"

He nodded. "You should become a Saint of Heaven. I'm the Heavenly Emperor, so I can't become a Saint, but you can."

Taiyi frowned. "But we can't take Nuwa's Grandmist Violet Qi. It'll cause the subjects' hearts to chill."

"Who said anything about taking Nuwa's Grandmist Violet Qi?" Di Jun asked. "Isn't there one ripe for the taking?"

"You mean Redcloud Ancestor's?" Seeing Di Jun nod, Taiyi fell into contemplation. Finally, he agreed.

Di Jun smiled. "I knew I could count on you. Focus wholeheartedly on increasing your strength and wait for a chance. We probably aren't the only ones eyeing Redcloud Ancestor's Grandmist Violet Qi."

Taiyi nodded and left. Once he was alone, Di Jun took out the Demon-Summoning Banner. He planned on having every demon aside from the demon emperors and sages place a strand of their truesoul into it.

This way, they would no longer suffer a repeat incident of the Starry Sky Way Array's destruction. Furthermore, it would strengthen his control over Heavenly Court, and Nuwa wouldn't be able to make any waves even if she achieved sainthood.

Once Di Jun announced the order for every member of the Demon Clan to place a stand of their truesoul into the Demon-Summoning Banner, almost everyone willingly complied. In their eyes, there was no difference if they did or did not.

After experiencing the horror of the Pangu Genesis Formation a second time, they wanted a method to save their lives if they perished in the war ten eons from now on. It was another safety net. Plus, the Heavenly Emperor said they could retrieve their strand of truesoul if they entered the Quasi-Saint Realm.

The only ones to show resistance were some of the Golden Immortals and above. They didn't like placing their lives in the hands of others, but under Di Jun's heavy-handed methods and peer pressure, they conformed.

* * *

"Strange," Laozi muttered as he pinched his fingers to calculate the secrets of heaven. "The tribulation should have begun, yet it is now showing signs of stopping? Did the Dao Ancestor delay the tribulation for some reason?"

"Maybe the tribulation should not have arrived now," Yuanshi said. "The Dao Ancestor merged with the Way of Heaven, and his action is equivalent to the Way of Heaven's will."

Laozi nodded. He could only accept such an explanation for now. With the battle now over, Yuanshi and Laozi entered Three Purity Palace.

Yuanshi stopped and looked at Tongtian. "What's wrong, Third Sister?"

Tongtian took back her gaze and entered the palace. "It's nothing."

The three of them sat in Three Purity Hall and discussed the recent battle before moving on to other matters.

"Third Sister, both Eldest Brother and I have severed our third Corpses. Do you know when you will?"

"If I'm not wrong, it should be some time in the future when Nuwa achieves sainthood," Tongtian said, much to her brothers' confusion, but she didn't take it to heart. "What about you two? Both of you have severed your three Corpses; any progress on the fusion?"

"It's thanks to Third Sister's advice," Yuanshi said with a smile. "The moment I severed my Self Corpse, I could already sense the connection between myself and them. I've already started the merging process, and all I need is time."

"The Way of Three Corpses is meant to merge with the original body," Laozi started. "But I don't want to achieve sainthood with my original body, so I'm trying to create a new method to just merge the Three Corpses together."

"It looks like I'll be the slowest out of the three of us," Tongtian said with a sigh.

She recalled when she had first transformed. With the aid of the Chaos Clock shard, Tongtian had embarked on comprehending the Law of Time and stepped into the Quasi-Saint Realm ahead of her brothers, but her lead had disappeared.

"You don't have to lament," Yuanshi comforted. "With Third Sister's talent, you won't fall too far behind us."

Tongtian smiled and waved her hand. "I meant nothing by it."

After all, Tongtian still had memories as a human. Having become the Supreme Purity, she was still very satisfied. In her eyes, it would be strange to continually be ahead of both brothers, but that didn't mean she would give up.

Her stagnant progress was only temporary. She was using it to increase her foundation, so when she stepped into the Primordial Origin Realm, she would ascend to heaven in one step.

"Alright, I'm going to enter secluded cultivation," Tongtian announced. "The Pangu Genesis Formation's three ax strikes have given me much inspiration, and I feel like I can create a supreme sword art."

"Then we'll await Third Sister's accomplishment," Yuanshi said as

Tongtian returned to her Supreme Purity Hall. He and Laozi continued to discuss and debate the way.

When Tongtian sat down in a lotus position, she closed her eyes and recalled the three strikes of the Heaven-Opening Ax Art the Pangu Genesis Formation had displayed.

Compared to the seven strikes unleashed by Pangu in Tongtian's memories, they didn't contain even a hundredth of the charm of the authentic Pangu's strikes. This only confirmed her suspicions.

Pangu wasn't in the Primordial Origin Realm or the chaos fiend-god equivalent. Pangu should be at the very peak of the Primordial Origin Realm or at the realm above it.

Tongtian rid herself of unnecessary thoughts. She still couldn't comprehend the esoteric mysteries behind Pangu's strikes, but she could understand the one unleashed by the false Pangu. By using the false Pangu's ax strikes as a comparison, she could deduce some of the profundities behind Pangu's power.

She fused her understanding of the first strike of Pangu's Heaven-Opening Art with her understanding of swordsmanship and the Laws of Time and Space. When she finally finished, she smiled.

She created her own swordplay inspired by Pangu's Heaven Opening Art, the Heaven-Opening Sword Art. Although it only had one strike, Tongtian was confident that no single Quasi-Saint could withstand it.

What's more, during her meditation, she found a point of fusion between the Law of Time and the Law of Space, creating an embryonic understanding of the Law of Spacetime.

Tongtian pinched her hand to calculate how much time had passed, and her eyebrows almost reached her hairline when she discovered she had been cultivating for 90,000 years.

Once again, Tongtian felt the worthlessness of time. She exited

Supreme Purity Hall to find Three Purity Hall empty. Both her brothers were in their own halls quietly cultivating, so she didn't disturb them.

She felt someone wandering outside Kunlun Mountain and couldn't help but frown. *Is it that annoying guy, Burning Lamp, again?*

Tongtian didn't trust Burning Lamp Daoist. At the end of the Investiture of the Gods, he betrayed Yuanshi and joined Buddhism to become Dipankara, the Lamp-Bearing Buddha.

To Tongtian's surprise, it wasn't Burning-Lamp Daoist but an unknown demon loitering around. With her curiosity peaked, her figure disappeared from Three Purity Hall to pop up in front of the demon.

It was a female fox demon. She wore a pristine white dress and possessed alluring features, but she hadn't perfectly hidden her nature, for two white fox ears sprouted atop her head.

"What's a Golden Immortal like you doing here?" Tongtian asked from above the fox demon.

The Golden Immortal in question started, but she quickly regained her composure and kneeled to Tongtian. "This little demon is Meihu, an envoy from Heavenly Court."

Tongtian had originally thought that the fox demon had wanted to become a follower of the Three Purities to protect herself and remove herself from the Titan-Demon War, but it seemed she was wrong. "What does Heavenly Court want with us?"

"Answering the Supreme Purity, this little demon was sent to deliver gifts." After she finished speaking, Meihu revealed at least a hundred chests filled with valuable materials.

"Huh?" Tongtian asked. "Does Heavenly Court want us to ally with them?"

Meihu shook her head. "No, these are gifts from the Eastern Emperor."

Tongtian's expression immediately darkened. She waved her arm, sending the fox demon flying back 1,000 li along with the hundred chests. She wanted those valuable materials, but that didn't mean she could be bought.

With a snort, Tongtian returned to Three Purity Palace.

For the next 1,000 years, several more demon envoys appeared outside of Kunlun Mountain, but Tongtian refused to see them. Even when Yuanshi took action and killed a few, they still showed up, so they gave up and sealed Kunlun Mountain to prevent anyone from approaching.

Burning-Lamp Daoist, who had always wanted to apprentice under one of the Three Purities, hated Heavenly Court to the core, but he was too weak and could only swallow this grudge silently.

On West Kunlun, Xi Wangmu, who had retired from interfering in the Great Desolation, allowed the demon envoy to rest in her territory, acting as a bridge between them and the Three Purities. However, she couldn't see the Three Purities either. When the major powers saw this, some said that Xi Wangmu feared the Heavenly Court and surrendered to them. Others said that she wanted to serve the Three Purities and thus tried to manage their external relationships.

In Yin-Yang Palace on West Kunlun, Xi Wangmu sent the demon envoy to rest with a smile. When they left, her smile disappeared, and a deep hatred emerged from her eyes. She glanced at Kunlun Mountain but quickly averted her eyes. Instead, she gazed toward the Supreme Yang Star and Supreme Yin Star, and no one knew what she was thinking.

* * *

Close to the Undying Volcano near the South, Kong Xuan sat beneath the Five Elements Tree. Red, black, yellow, green, and white auras emerged and intermixed around him.

When he opened his eyes, he waved his arm, and the Five Elements Tree behind him trembled and split into seven pieces: five branches, one trunk, and roots. His five feather-shaped sabers came forth and each merged with the branch correlating to the same element.

The trunk transformed into a fan handle while the five branches transformed the fan itself, forming a five-colored feathered fan. One of the top ten connate spiritual roots, the Five Elements Tree, disappeared, but a high-grade cardinal spiritual artifact, the Five Elements Fan, was born.

The grade of the spiritual artifact was a bit lacking, but it would suffice for now. It had the potential to become a top-grade cardinal spiritual artifact; all it lacked was an opportunity.

Kong Xuan waved the Five Elements Fan, and five colored lights emerged. He tested the Five Feather Formation, Five Line Formation, Five Elements Formation, and other techniques that relied on the five elements.

He nodded with satisfaction.

"The Dao Ancestor created the Way of Three Corpses, but I wish to achieve the Primordial Origin Realm, so I will create my way, " Kong Xuan said. "I cultivate the Law of Five Elements, so I will call it the Way of Five Elements."

Kong Xuan closed his eyes. After over 10,000 years, he opened them and said, "Sever!!"

A yellow light emerged from Kong Xuan's body and transformed into a yellow-robed Kong Xuan. "Meet the Main Body."

Since the Dao Ancestor had severed emotions to achieve enlightenment, Kong Xuan severed the five elements. Each Corpse severed would cultivate the element it had come from.

Once Kong Xuan severed all five Corpses and they reached their limit in their comprehension of the law, he would reintegrate them with himself, becoming complete. Once he became complete, he would achieve Primordial Origin and become a Golden Immortal of the Primordial Origin.

The price was Kong Xuan's ability to use the five elements he had been born with, and he'd already lost the ability to conjure earth light. That's why he'd refined the Five Elements Tree into the Five Elements Fan to replace his innate ability.

In truth, the best replacements would be the top five flags: the Apricot Flag of Central Infinity, the Red Radiance Flag of South Transience, the Azure Lotus Flag of East Treasured Light, the Plain-Colored Flag of West Clouds, and the Black Domination Flag of North Profound Origin.

Unfortunately, Tongtian held the Apricot Flag of Central Infinity, Yuanshi held the Azure Lotus Flag of East Treasured Light, and Zhunti held the Plain-Colored Flag of West Clouds.

Chapter 36

Kunpeng Creates Demon Script

Tongtian left Kunlun Mountain. She couldn't stand the meandering demons outside her door. The demon envoys came bearing gifts, so she couldn't declare war on the Heavenly Court. Plus, that would form karma between them, maybe even dragging the Three Purities into the tribulation between the Titan Tribe and Heavenly Court.

If they had been on Earth, Tongtian would have long ago ordered a restraining order against Taiyi, but unfortunately, this was the Great Desolation. But she could still run away, couldn't she?

When she did so, Burning-Lamp Daoist frowned and looked in the direction Tongtian had flown off to. He couldn't sense her, but he felt an intuition that something related to him was that way. After a moment of hesitation, Burning-Lamp Daoist shook his head and continued to camp outside Kunlun Mountain.

* * *

In Darknorth Palace within the Darknorth Sea of the North, Kunpeng stared at the 2,999 tablets lying on the ground in front of him. His eyes were bloodshot as if he hadn't slept in centuries.

In his hand was the three-thousandth tablet. He used his fingers to carve the last stroke of the word. It was a language unrecognizable to the Great Desolation's sole writing system, Dao Script. Kunpeng's hand trembled, and the three-thousandth tablet fell onto the ground with a clack.

After seeing Di Jun use merit to cut two Corpses, once during the establishment of Heavenly Court and once during the heavenly marriage, Kunpeng had brainstormed ideas to gain merit and cut his second Corpse.

After reviewing the three times merits had descended, Kunpeng discovered that merit was awarded for contribution to heaven and earth. Di Jun establishing Heavenly Court brought order, as did the Titan Tribe ruling the land. Heavenly marriage also brought order, creating a trend for others in the Great Desolation to follow.

He didn't have anything that could contribute to the Great Desolation, at least not yet. Bringing order made the sky and land prosperous, but what about heavenly marriage? It was for the lifeforms to follow, so benefiting all life would bring merit.

And which race had the most members? Demons.

After Di Jun had brought the remnant lifeform and Hundred Clan together, 99 percent of life had become part of the Demon Clan. Kunpeng himself was no exception.

To increase the Demon Clan's prosperity, he created the Demon Script.

When Pangu formed heaven and earth, he had also created Dao Script as the language most of the congenital gods used to write. Even the signs on Violet Heaven Palace and Three Purity Mountain bore this writing. However, Dao Script was too esoteric, and only Golden Immortals and above could understand it.

Demons at the Profound Immortal Realm and below made up most of the Demon Clan's population, but they couldn't use it. If he created Demon Script, wouldn't it benefit the Demon Clan?

After thousands of years, Kunpeng finally created the last words of his new script. Tribulation clouds gathered above him, but he wasn't afraid. On the contrary, he grew excited.

"The Way of Heaven above, I, Kunpeng, see that the Demon Clan is without its own words, so I created the 3,000 words of the Demon Script to represent all things under heaven to benefit the Demon Clan!"

Tribulation lightning descended, aimed not at Kunpeng but at the 3,000 tablets in front of him. Without Kunpeng's input, every last tablet floated into the air.

The tribulation struck the tablets, shattering them, but the words persisted. They hovered in the air, formed from light, and continued to withstand the heavenly tribulation. With each lightning bolt they endured, their light glowed brighter, and so did the wisdom behind them.

Numerous major powers and forces directed their attention to the huge movement caused by Kunpeng, including Heavenly Court. Logically speaking, as the leader of the Demon Clan and Heavenly Court, it should have been Di Jun, the demon emperors, the ten demon sages, or a member of Heavenly Court who created Demon Script. But it was Kunpeng, an unrelated demon, who succeeded.

In total, 3,000 bolts of tribulation lightning descended. After the final strike, the tribulation cloud dispersed, and merits descended.

Kunpeng restrained his excitement as he watched 60 percent of the Karmic Merit merge with the Demon Script. Ten percent fell onto all the demons in the Great Desolation, and the last 30 percent fell on Kunpeng, allowing him to sever his second Corpse and become an Intermediate Quasi-Saint.

He waved his hand, and the Three Thousand Demon Script floated above his palm. The text had become a top-grade acquired meritorious spiritual artifact which would gain more merit with each demon who used it. The artifact didn't have any powerful offensive or defensive methods, but it could anchor his luck.

After creating the Demon Script, Kunpeng now sensed the existence of the Demon Clan's Karmic Luck and felt it increase by at least 10 percent. As long as he held the Three Thousand Demon Script in his hand, he would enjoy 5 percent of the Demon Clan's luck!

* * *

In Eminence Heaven Palace, Di Jun frowned. He more than anyone hoped Kunpeng's Demon Script would fail to survive the Heavenly Tribulation. This way, although the subsequent heavenly tribulation would become more difficult, he could allow someone from Heavenly Court to create the Demon Script.

With the recognition of the Demon Script by the Way of Heaven, Kunpeng's prestige among the Demon Clan would invariably rise. It wasn't enough to threaten his position as the Heavenly Emperor, but it would divide the Demon Clan in two.

Di Jun narrowed his eyes. He had planned to either recruit or kill Kunpeng if he rejected his offer, but now, he couldn't order Kunpeng's death. If he killed Kunpeng, his reputation would plummet among the Demon Clan. He might even receive a backlash because of the former's contribution.

He immediately recalled the demon envoys that he had prepared for Kunpeng. Di Jun replaced them with one of the demon sages and increased their number by tenfold. When they left, Di Jun silently tapped the armrest of the Nine Dragon Throne. "Kunpeng, I hope you choose wisely and don't force me, or else..."

Di Jun's eyes drifted to the Demon-Summoning Banner by his side.

* * *

After the Demon Script passed the Heavenly Tribulation, Tongtian decided to travel north to the Darknorth Sea. She had already visited Buzhou Mountain and much of the East, but she hadn't traveled to the North, West, or South yet.

Tongtian had some interest in the West, but not in its current state. Specifically, she was interested in the West during the time of Journey in the West, when Buddhism had been created and reached its height. Well, that interest stemmed more from Sun Wukong, the Great Sage Equal to Heavens, than anything really Buddha-related.

For now, Jieyin and Zhunti hadn't created Buddhism.

The North and South held equal attraction for Tongtian. Kunpeng just so happened to create Demon Script, tipping the scales. If she had traveled south, her path would have intersected with Kong Xuan's and raised her guard against him.

Tongtian turned into a silver streak of light as she traveled north. The farther north she went, the colder it got. When she arrived at the Darknorth Sea, snow fell perpetually. Tongtian had never visited the arctic or Antarctica, but she knew that the temperature could never compare to the Great Desolation's North.

If a regular human, no matter what he wore, were to travel here, he would certainly die of frostbite.

Yet, the black sea never froze, not even on the surface. Tongtian hovered near the surface and scooped up some water, which instantly encased her hand in a layer of ice as she pulled it up.

"No wonder the North is the second-most barren region after the West without anyone's self-destruction. Just this Frostnorth Truewater is enough to kill many Profound Immortals and lifeforms not suited to this environment," Tongtian muttered.

Frostnorth Truewater originated from the Onesource Masswater in the core of the Darknorth Sea. Even a single drop of Onesource Masswater was enough to crush a Sky Immortal to death.

Tongtian had another understanding of Kunpeng's strength. Before he had gained the ability to transform into a great roc, he was a massive kun fish, and he lived in the core of Darknorth Sea. This meant that Kunpeng's fleshly body was likely inferior only to a titan's.

She frowned when she discovered numerous Golden Immortals circling her.

"Hand over your treasures if you know what's good for you," the apparent leader said. He smiled confidently with even a trace of ridicule as he stared at Tongtian's ice-encased hand.

Tongtian sighed and flicked her hand, shattering the ice. She formed a sword finger and poked the air in front of her. The Golden Immortals hadn't reacted to her breaking the ice, but several sword lights shot out from her fingertip. By the time they realized something was wrong, it was already too late as they died with holes in their head.

This wasn't the first time rogue immortals had tried to rob her, and as usual, she killed them. Tongtian felt nothing as she watched their corpses fall into the sea and sink to the bottom. Their lives were the same as blades of grass to her.

Would the past me be horrified by the current me? Tongtian briefly thought, but she shook her head and wandered in a random direction.

After 300 years, Tongtian discovered a giant island, the first one in millions of li. It had little to no vegetation and a giant point atop, likely an underwater mountain that had surfaced.

She had been flying nonstop for thousands of years. Tongtain thought it would be a good place to rest, so she flew down, looking for a cave to make her temporary home. To her surprise, she discovered that the land and mountain were made of some sort of green-black material.

Thinking that it might be a good material to refine a sword arti-fact with, Tongtian tried to carve a chunk out, but to her surprise, her sword qi only left a shallow mark. Now, more sure than ever that she had discovered a treasure, Tongtian unsheathed her Qingping sword and carved it into the unknown material.

Moments later, trembling erupted underneath her feet. The seawater receded, revealing more land. When the ground rose halfway to the clouds, a furious roar echoed. "Who is it? Who dares to awaken this turtle?!"

Tongtian's eyes widened as she stared into the sky to see a giant turtle head. So large was it that Tongtian's whole body didn't even measure to the turtle's pupil.

"Was it you?"

Despite being in the Advanced Quasi-Saint Realm, Tongtian found herself gulping when confronted with the massive turtle. Judging by the size of its head, it should be around 100,000 li in size.

How could such a creature exist?

Seeing Tongtian not answer, the turtle opened its jaw and breathed out. It was just a simple breath, but it easily reached the force of a peak Golden Immortal of the Great Firmament.

Tongtian was blown off into the distance. The blast made her regain her bearings. "Please wait a second! I thought it was just a simple mountain formed from unique materials, so I wanted to carve some out. I didn't realize it was your shell, I apologize!"

She held her breath as the giant turtle's eyes focused on her. Just as she thought the turtle would continue to attack, he said, "Okay, as long as you don't do it again."

That's it? Tongtian thought. Although she wanted to resolve their conflict, she had never expected to do it so easily. "Excuse me, but who are you? Someone of your power should not be unknown."

The turtle opened its mouth and yawned, causing the surrounding 10,000 li to ripple from that single action. "I don't like going out, so it's normal you don't know about me. Oh, that fish that turned into that little bird knows of me, but after seeing me once, he fled."

Fish that turned into a little bird, that should be Kunpeng, right? Tongtian thought.

"I'm Xuangui. What about you?" the giant turtle asked.

Thunder rang in Tongtian's head. *Xuangui, the Profound Turtle whose legs became the four pillars supporting the sky after Buzhou Mountain shattered?*

"I'm Supreme Purity Tongtian," she answered.

"Oh, Supreme Purity Tongtian? That's a nice name," Xuangui said, nodding his head. "I apologize if you're someone famous. But, like I said, I like to stay here, so I don't know much about the rest of the world."

"That makes sense. If you don't mind me asking, how'd you reach the Peak Quasi-Saint Realm? I don't recall you attending the Dao Ancestor's sermons."

She hadn't noticed when Xuangui had been asleep, but once he was awake, she could feel the strong vitality and aura rolling off of it. She doubted she could defeat it even if she reached the same realm. Not even the addition of her two brothers would change the outcome. They wouldn't lose, but they wouldn't win either.

Xuangui shrugged, sending waves crashing. "I didn't do anything. I just slept and became like this. You went to the Dao Ancestor's sermon?"

Seeing the interest in Xuangui's eyes, Tongtian nodded.

"Then you must know why I can't transform. I've longed to transform and change my shape, but I never could. Would you be so kind as to enlighten me as to why I can't?"

"Most creatures undergo a heavenly tribulation and transform after reaching a certain level. I don't know why you can't."

"Oh, I see," Xuangui said with a sigh.

Perhaps it's because he's the future pillar separating heaven and earth? But that wouldn't make sense. Why would the Way of Heaven know that Buzhou Mountain would be destroyed? Tongtian thought. *That's impossible, right?*

Ignoring the discomfort in her heart, Tongtian said, "Do you want me to relay what the Dao Ancestor said during his sermon? Maybe you can discover a method."

"Really?" Xuangui asked.

Tongtian nodded and sat in a lotus position in front of Xuangui, who settled down in a comfortable position to listen. She began to speak, and although she couldn't replicate the phenomenon of golden lotuses blooming, Phoenix's cries, and Dragon's roar, her words still carried a unique charm that immersed anyone who listened.

When she finished 9,000 years later, the aura on Xuangui had converged, no longer rolling off uncontrollably like before. But he still couldn't transform.

Xuangui sighed. "Thank you for your help."

Tongtian shook her head. "It's nothing. I didn't help you transform in the end."

"No, you still helped me. I don't have anything to help you, but I do have a connate spiritual root if you don't disdain it."

"How can I? If I'd helped you transform, I could take it with peace of mind, but since I didn't, I shouldn't."

"Your sermon was helpful to me. Although I still can't transform, it brought me many benefits," Xuangui insisted. "You should take it, it's not useful to me. And if you don't, I plan to destroy it."

"Why? Connate spiritual roots are rare things. Why would you destroy it?"

"You'll know why when you see it."

Her curiosity peaked, Tongtian followed Xuangui's instructions and flew to the mountain's peak—or rather, the peak of the turtle's shell. There, she saw a tree with a bronze trunk and iron-colored leaves whose roots dug into the shell.

"It's really annoying," Xuangui said. "If you hadn't come, I would have tried to destroy it by now. However, I don't have anything else, and it should be a good gift. What do you think?"

"Then I'll thank Daoist Xuangui," Tongtian said, her eyes never leaving the tree. She'd never expected to discover one of the top ten spiritual roots growing atop the Profound Turtle's shell.

Allheaven Jianmu was the tree's name. It had no other features except for its strong vitality, exceptional height, and sturdiness when it matured. When it reached maturity, it would be likened to other World Trees like Yggdrasil or Ashvattha.

However, Tongtian didn't plan on putting it on display. She wanted to refine it into a sword once it reached maturity. It might even become a top-grade cardinal spiritual treasure if it was lucky, and no one ever thought they had too many treasures.

After Tongtian plucked the Allheaven Jianmu tree, she stayed with Xuangui for a bit longer. She pointed out some problems in his cultivation and guided him, becoming his mentor of sorts.

During this time, she discovered that the Profound Turtle was mild-mannered and kind. Although he would retaliate lethally if someone attacked him, he wouldn't go looking for trouble. Xuangui was practically a pacifist in the Great Desolation.

One day, Tongtian frowned and stared toward the East. She flipped her hand, and the Immortal Gourd Vine appeared in her grasp. She could feel it being drawn to something in the East. "Sorry, Daoist Xuangui, I'll need to leave now."

CHAPTER 37

Birth of Humanity

Inside Southern Emperor Palace on the fourth level of Thirty-Three Heaven, Nuwa sighed.

"What's wrong?" Fuxi asked. He had healed from his injuries and was preparing to sever his Corpse again.

"I've been comprehending the Grandmist Violet Qi all this time, but I still haven't discovered anything," Nuwa said.

Fuxi frowned. "Maybe your chance hasn't come yet. There's no rush."

"Do you really believe that? You've seen how powerful the Pangu Genesis Formation was. Even the Starry Sky War Array at its peak could not match it."

Fuxi stayed silent. As the creator of the Starry Sky War Array, he knew how powerful it was, which was why he was even more horrified by the Pangu Genesis Formation.

"If I do not become a Saint before the time set by the Dao Ancestor," Nuwa said. "The Demon Clan will be doomed. And, we'll be forced to run away like losers for the rest of our lives—if we don't die during battle, that is."

A tense silence descended between them. Suddenly, Nuwa stood up. "I'm going out."

"Out? You mean into the Great Desolation?" Fuxi asked. He moved forward to stop his sister. "You can't. Didn't the Dao Ancestor say that demons should remain in the sky?"

"The Dao Ancestor said that the two sides should not war, and the Demon Clan should rule the sky while the Titan Tribe rule the lands. He said nothing about walking the lands," Nuwa calmly replied. Seeing the concern on her brother's face, she sighed. "You don't have to worry about me. I'm already in the Advanced Quasi-Saint Realm. If the Titan Tribe wants to do anything to me, can't I escape?"

"But," Fuxi started, still not willing to let Nuwa encounter any danger.

"You've always protected me since I was born. I became the Dao Ancestor's disciple and gained the chance to achieve sainthood thanks to you," Nuwa said, her eyes softening. "This time, let me protect you. Too many of us will die if I don't become a Saint."

Fuxi sighed, stepping out of her way upon seeing the determination in her eyes.

Nuwa revealed a smile more beautiful than a blooming flower. "Don't worry, I'll succeed."

When Nuwa left Heavenly Court, only a few people knew. Di Jun only glanced in her direction before returning to his cultivation. Kunpeng had rejected Heavenly Court's invitation and even started recruiting demons in the North

Kunpeng may not have had aspirations of dominating heaven and earth, but it was clear as day that he refused to serve anyone. His only choice was to achieve this freedom by force. All he needed was a chance.

* * *

When Nuwa stepped out of South Heaven Gate and into the Great Desolation, Buzhou Mountain was no longer under her feet.

During the last two battles between Heavenly Court and the Titan Tribe, Buzhou Mountain had been leveled twice. Now, it was half its height, and the peak no longer connected to the Thirty-Three Heavens.

Seeing the weakened mountain, Nuwa sighed. She had once called it her home before the Titan Tribe forced her out, sowing enmity and causing her to join the Demon Clan. Seeing its current barren state, a dismal mood overtook her.

No longer did essence fill every nook and cranny. The spiritual herbs and plants that once inhabited the land had gone extinct, leaving weeds and grass in their place. Treasures once filled the caverns, but they had all been plundered; nothing remained.

All that was left were the vestiges of its once-grand reputation as the number-one mountain of the Great Desolation.

Slowly, Nuwa walked down the mountain, step by step. After the coercion had disappeared, numerous animals had made the mountain their home, filling it up with another kind of vitality. These animals were later heaven lifeforms, and unlike nascent heaven lifeforms like congenital gods, they weren't born mature or with any knowledge.

Later heaven lifeforms didn't even open up their spirituality yet; only when they become Earth Immortals would they open up their spirituality and gain sentience. Until then, they were mere beasts that relied on instinct.

Nuwa stretched out her hand, and a sparrow landed atop it. Using her other hand, she gently stroked the sparrow's head. It preened under her caress. She pulled back and let the sparrow fly away, smiling.

Years later, the sparrow would achieve the rank of Earth Immortal and gain spirituality thanks to Nuwa's grace.

Step by step, Nuwa slowly reached the bottom of the mountain. She took care not to alert any of the nearby giants as she flew off into the distance. Nuwa didn't purposely cultivate; she just toured the regions of the Great Desolation. Even so, her cultivation progressed gradually until she was a hair's breadth away from severing her Third Corpse. All she needed was an epiphany.

During her travels, she felt an aversion to the creatures living on the land. Nearly two eons had passed since the Dao Ancestor had separated Heavenly Court and the Titan Tribe. Now, the Demon Clan of Thirty-Three Heaven could be said to be a totally different species from the demons that remained on land.

Most of the demons of the land ascended from later heaven lifeforms, and they kept many habits from when they were mere animals. They only knew how to take without giving anything back to the world, depleting the essence of heaven and earth.

The Titan Tribe was no different.

They acted like a force of destruction, killing and feasting on any animals they caught. Giants needed an enormous amount of food not just to stay alive but to strengthen themselves, and absorbing essence took too long.

This practice brought about the extinctions of many species. The loss wasn't limited to one area alone, but entire swathes of land. When they hunted everything they could, they simply moved on to the next region. Now, the territory near the Titan Tribe was completely devoid of life.

Nuwa also saw that the Titan Tribe had shown signs of splitting into twelve separate tribes based on their titan leader. The distance would reduce the rate of overfeeding, but it didn't solve the problem at its core.

She continued to travel, hoping to find a peaceful race that didn't ruin the land they lived on. Nuwa visited a number of locations and races, but none of them fit her requirements.

"It'd be great if there were a race that could bring fortune instead of misfortune," Nuwa said. Her eyes widened as she felt the Grandmist Violet Qi in her thrum.

"Race? Is my chance for sainthood related to a peaceful race?" Nuwa muttered. She felt more confident in this plan when the Grandmist Violet Qi vibrated even more. "But I haven't found any race like that during my travels. No, if it was something that could just be found, someone else would have done so by now."

Nuwa seemed to have realized something as her eyes lit up. "Yes, it should be something only I can do. I practice the Law of Creation. I can create a new race, something I haven't done yet."

The Grandmist Violet Qi's resonance increased. Emboldened, Nuwa immediately went to work. Currently, she was walking on a vast plain, so her first thought was to create a creature suitable to live there.

Nuwa grabbed a handful of dirt, mixed it with water, and began to form a four-legged beast. When she finished, it had dark fur, a horse-like head, two curved horns, and hooved feet. She then breathed life into it, but it died not long after it started moving, confusing her.

"Why didn't I succeed?" Nuwa asked herself. After over a hundred years of standing still, she finally found the answer. Although she wanted the new race to be of the later heaven stage, she couldn't use ordinary materials.

She immediately thought of the Ninesky Blessdirt she had obtained from Tongtian. She pulled it out and began to craft the creature again. After 1,000 years, she breathed life into it, and a new race was born.

Thanks to being the first of its race created by Nuwa, it was already at the Sky Immortal Realm. "I shall name you Cattle, and all others after you shall be known as cattle."

The newly named Cattle bowed. "Thank you, Empress Nuwa."

Nuwa nodded, satisfied. It had a mild and gentle temperament, but she hadn't succeeded. She furrowed her brows, wondering why it failed. Perhaps it wasn't the new race that the Way of Heaven wanted.

She traveled the Great Desolation once more and created two more races: pigs and chickens. Pigs were omnivorous and weren't picky about their food, while chickens liked to roam around and eat poisonous insects that harmed vegetation.

Still, Nuwa had yet to achieve sainthood. Her travels eventually led her back to Buzhou Mountain.

Nuwa sighed. "Why haven't I succeeded? All three are peaceful and won't bring harm."

She stared at the three creatures she had created, who lowered their heads in reverence and shame for their uselessness. Finally, after days of observation, she noticed the problem. "Although Cattle is strong, his horns are not sharp enough. Pig can eat a lot, but it cannot defend itself. Chicken has a sharp beak and talons, but they are too dull, and it is too small. Even if a creature is peaceful, how can it propagate if it cannot defend itself?"

Nuwa had another headache. She needed to create a peaceful creature, and it needed to be able to defend itself. But if she sharpened their claws or fangs too much, wouldn't it turn into a predator, the exact opposite of a peaceful race?

She sighed and shifted her gaze, which landed on Buzhou Mountain. "Buzhou Mountain? Pangu's spine."

Nuwa's eyes brightened with inspiration. What race was more suited to the Great Desolation than one modeled after Pangu? All creatures in heaven and earth were born from Pangu, and his form was the most perfect for cultivating. Hence every lifeform chose a humanoid form after transforming—even the giants born after the titans had humanoid body shapes.

She grabbed a handful of Ninesky Blessdirt to form them again. This time, she took 1,000 years to shape the new race. When she was done, she breathed life into it, but contrary to expectations, her creation crumbled into dust.

Nuwa tried several more times, even imbuing the Ninesky Blessdirt with her blood, but nothing she tried worked. She could feel it. Once she created this new race, she would achieve sainthood.

As time passed and her failures increased, Nuwa grew increasingly impatient.

"Is something troubling, fellow Daoist?"

Nuwa frowned, facing the newcomer. She hadn't sensed Kong Xuan appearing next to her at all. Upon closer inspection, she sensed that he had become one with the land, thus hindering her perception of him.

"Why is Daoist Kong Xuan here?" Nuwa asked. Although Kong Xuan had betrayed Violet Manor in the end, he had once been Heavenly Court's enemy. Not to mention, she had fought with Kong Xuan and Tongtian over a spiritual artifact before, although both of them had eventually lost.

Kong Xuan pretended not to notice Nuwa's wariness toward him. "Fellow Daoist seems to be troubled by something. Although I do not claim omnipotence, I still consider myself knowledgeable. Perhaps I can help solve your troubles."

Nuwa hesitated. Although she didn't trust Kong Xuan, the allure of sainthood was too much. Before she spoke, she felt a familiar aura and gazed into the distance.

Not long later, Tongtian arrived. Nuwa felt something in the Supreme Purity's possession that attracted her. "Senior Sister."

*　*　*

On the way to Buzhou Mountain, Tongtian suddenly paused as she heard a familiar voice.

"Little friend has a predestined fate with my West."

Tongtian stopped just in time to see Zhunti capture a Profound Immortal Realm demon. With a satisfied face, the incarnated Boddhi Tree turned around and froze, seeing Tongtian staring at him with a smile.

Zhunti's awkward smile disappeared, and he clapped his hands together as if he hadn't just kidnapped an immortal. "Greetings, Senior Sister."

"Greetings to you as well, Junior Brother," Tongtian said. "I know the West is barren and that Junior Brothers are working hard to revitalize the West. I can turn a blind eye to most things, but don't go too far, understand?"

Zhunti continued to smile. "I don't understand what Senior Sister is saying. I'm simply ferrying those with predestined fate. Their opportunities lie in the West and not the East. I am helping them."

Tongtian rolled her eyes. She almost believed Zhunti because of the sincere smile on his face. The East was prosperous, and the West was barren. Not even Heavenly Court and the Titan Tribe cared for it. Who would want to go at this juncture?

"Forget it, I don't want to argue with you. You know in your heart what you can and cannot do," Tongtian said as she flew off, leaving Zhunti still standing there.

Zhunti sighed in relief when she left. "Senior Brother is right; Daoist Tongtian is the mildest of the Three Purities. If it were Yuanshi, he would have attacked me, and Laozi would have forced me to go back empty-handed."

Tongtian continued to fly all the way to Buzhou Mountain, where she found Nuwa. To her surprise, Kong Xuan had also appeared.

"Junior Sister," Tongtian said after Nuwa greeted her.

"I have a question I hope Senior Sister can solve for me," Nuwa said.

Tongtian saw Kong Xuan's expression sour, but she didn't care. "If it is within my abilities, naturally, I will."

"It's like this," Nuwa started to explain that she wanted to create a peaceful race, but for some reason, she always failed.

Tongtian made a strange expression. *Humans, peaceful? That's got to be the biggest joke I've ever heard.*

Tongtian did not betray her true thoughts. She had already discovered the reason why after Nuwa spoke about her troubles, because her Grandmist Violet Qi vibrated and resonated with one of Tongtian's possessions.

With a flip of her hand, Threelight Divinewater appeared in her palm. "Since Junior Sister used Ninesky Blessdirt to form the body, the water cannot be ordinary. All things are split into yin and yang, bringing balance. The Ninesky Blessoil is yang, and the Threelight Divinewater is yin."

Upon receiving the Threelight Divinewater, Nuwa smiled joyfully. "Thank you, Senior Sister."

She mixed the Ninesky Blessoil and the Threelight Divinewater to create a mud mixture that glowed seven different colors. With her experience, Nuwa only took a hundred years to form the first creature.

The second took even less time. Unlike the first, the second had two lumps on her chest and nothing dangling from her crotch: a female. Like Tongtian said, all things were split yin and yang, and thus her new race should be half male and half female.

After creating several thousand of them, Nuwa grew tired. She could feel her spirit becoming fatigued, but she knew she hadn't created enough yet. By chance, she caught sight of the Immortal Gourd Vine in Tongtian's hand.

"Senior Sister, may I borrow that for a moment?" Nuwa asked.

Tongtian didn't say anything, letting the Immortal Gourd Vine fly into Nuwa's hand. Nuwa took it and dipped it into the mud mixture. She flung it, and drops of mud fell down, turning to the same race as the handcrafted ones, but a few had disfigurements.

When Nuwa created 129,600 members of the new race, she smiled in satisfaction. "I shall call you Humanity."

"Humanity?" the first human created by Nuwa asked. Then, he spoke again. "Humans, we are humans! Humans!"

"Humanity, Humans!" all 129,600 humans shouted, causing the world to resonate.

Boundless merits descended from the sky. An immortal song entered every lifeform's ears, the sky and earth roared, the sun and moon faded, and the world turned upside down. The only things that could be heard were the cries of the newly born humans and the boundless merit descending.

Seventy percent of the merit directly merged into Nuwa's body; 10 percent flew into the Immortal Gourd Vine, turning it into a meritorious spiritual artifact; 10 percent dispersed among the newly created humans; and the last 10 percent fell onto Tongtian for her contribution, much to Kong Xuan's envy.

Nuwa directly absorbed all the merit bestowed upon her. Once she did so, the Grandmist Violet Qi merged with her truesoul, and Nuwa could feel herself breaking the limit of the Quasi-Saint Realm. Her body rose into the air, and a holy light radiated off of her.

It was a soft and gentle light, but it illuminated all of heaven and earth. Every creature knelt under her coercion. Just like when Hongjun had achieved sainthood, numerous phenomena occurred, dazzling all creatures.

Nuwa had become a Saint of Heaven.

Chapter 38

Severing Her Obsession

In Eminence Heavenly Palace, Di Jun's expression darkened as he felt the infinite coercion spreading from Nuwa. It was a good thing for the Demon Clan to have a Saint, and he didn't need to worry about becoming a puppet emperor with the Demon-Summoning Banner in hand.

However, what if Nuwa took back the Demon-Summoning Banner by force?

A Saint couldn't be the Heavenly Emperor, but Nuwa had a brother. What if she wanted to install him as the Heavenly Emperor?

Di Jun gritted his teeth and resisted the coercion. When he thought he couldn't resist anymore, the Nine Dragon Throne shrouded him in an imperial light that protected him, further supporting his resistance.

How could the Emperor of Heaven kneel to anyone, even a Saint?

On the third level of heaven inside Taiyi's palace, the advanced Quasi-Saint struggled not to kneel under the coercion. He gained a deeper understanding of what it meant that all under Saints were ants.

Taiyi roared as he used everything he had to refuse to kneel. The Chaos Bell appeared above Taiyi's head and rang, alleviating some of the pressure he felt.

Finally, he managed to hold himself up but still bowed under the coercion.

In the Darknorth Sea, Kunpeng grunted and used all his strength, but he still fell to his knees under Nuwa's coercion.

In complete contrast, Xuangui only slightly lowered his head. If he'd really wanted to, he could have forcibly ignored the pressure, but he didn't see the point, so he lowered his head.

In the Blood Sea, Minghe's eyes flashed with envy as he was forced to his knees. He silently swore that he would attain the same power in the future.

In the main hall of Wuzhuang Temple on Longevity Mountain, Zhen Yuanzi and Redcloud Ancestor both kneeled. Zhen Yuanzi sighed at the Saint's might, as just her birth created such a stir.

Next to him, endless desire spilled out of Redcloud Ancestor's eyes. He also had a strand of Grandmist Violet Qi, but he couldn't decipher it at all. Should he also leave and wander the Great Desolation?

Laozi's and Yuanshi's expressions darkened as they felt Nuwa's coercion. They didn't expect that out of the seven people who had received Grandmist Violet Qi, it would be Nuwa who achieved sainthood first.

As the Taiji Diagram appeared behind Laozi, he understood that he had delayed his ascendancy to Sainthood because he wanted to let his three Corpses merge and become a Saint of Heaven. Still, he had never once believed that anyone, including his siblings, would surpass him.

Yuanshi also used his Pangu Banner to resist kneeling. Of the Three Purities, he held the greatest pride, bordering on arrogance. So, to see someone achieve sainthood and not be among the Three Purities damaged it. He vowed to be next.

On Mount Sumeru in the West, Jieyin and Zhunti both did their best to resist Nuwa's coercion. Like Taiyi, they managed to stay standing but still bowed, with Zhunti bowing lower.

Zhunti couldn't help but sigh and wonder when they would be able to achieve sainthood.

In the South, Jinchi unwillingly knelt down. After all these years, he still hadn't severed his second Corpse. While on his knees, he wondered how his brother fared. Surely he wouldn't kneel, right?

At the epicenter, the coercion surpassed all other locations. Blood spilled out of Kong Xuan's nine orifices as he fought against the Saint's coercion. With one last unwilling roar, Kong Xuan fell onto one knee.

Tongtian also resisted, but it was a subconscious action stemming from her pride as one of the Three Purities. Most of her focus was on realizing her obsession. To outsiders, her eyes seemed dim.

So that's it, Tongtian thought. When she saw humanity's birth, she realized that she didn't hold much obsession with them—or rather, her past as a human.

Her memories as a human had become sidelined while her identity as Tongtian took center stage. Her times as a human influenced her, but deep down, she no longer considered herself one of them. Eons of time had broken that connection.

If humanity wasn't her obsession, then what was?

The answer was herself—or more specifically, her identity as the Supreme Purity.

Because she accepted this identity at the core of her being, she also feared the original Supreme Purity's ending in the Investiture of the Gods. Near the end, four Saints besieged her, or rather, him.

The four Saints who united against her were her brothers and the two western Saints. Worse, not only was the Supreme Purity defeated, but the Dao Ancestor locked him in Violet Heaven Palace after the battle.

That fate was why Tongtian worked so hard to deepen the relationship between the Three Purities. When she had discovered the Twelfth-Ranked White Lotus of Purification, she made sure to share the Ninth-Ranked White Lotuses of Purification with her brothers, making them feel like they owed her.

Her efforts bore fruit. Rather than acting as individuals, they acted as one unit. However, it was unknown how long this would continue. The Three Purities would split up after the creation of their individual forces.

Well, so what?

Tongtian still didn't want to come into conflict with her brothers, but she would no longer fear it. If they blocked her way and forced her into confinement, forget her two brothers, she'd even cut down Hongjun!

One sword to seek the Great Dao.

"Sever!"

A silver river appeared behind Tongtian, and on the third flower, a humanoid figure appeared. It jumped and merged with the Ninth-Ranked Green Lotus of Good Fortune and transformed into her third Corpse. Tongtian's cultivation, which had stagnated for over an eon, progressed, and she entered the Peak Quasi-Saint Realm. Coupled with her willpower and noble identity, Tongtian only bowed slightly under Nuwa's coercion.

When Nuwa saw this, she knew that surely none of the Three Purities were simple. Once she became a Saint, she understood why the Dao Ancestor said that all under Saints were ants, but Saints also had restrictions.

As the coercion disappeared, Nuwa glanced at the newly created humans with turmoil in her eyes. When she became a Saint of Heaven, she peered into the secrets of heaven and discovered that the Way of Heaven didn't want the Demon Clan or the Titan Tribe to win. No, the Way of Heaven wanted her fledgling humanity to become the final winners, the new masters of the Great Desolation.

Nuwa felt the urge to destroy this young race, but she couldn't bear to do it. Humanity was akin to her own children. In the end, she sighed and decided to go with the flow. If she helped the Demon Clan, the Grandmist Violet Qi fused with her truesoul would stop her.

Once the coercion disappeared and humans regained their voices, they knelt even lower and addressed Nuwa as Mother Nuwa.

"Daoist Tongtian," Nuwa said. "Since I have achieved sainthood, I will no longer live in the Great Desolation. I will open up a grotto in the chaotic boundary in a thousand years. If you are interested, you can come and listen to my sermon." Her voice didn't just spread to Tongtian, but a similar message echoed throughout the Great Desolation. Afterward, she returned the Immortal Gourd Vine.

"I'll definitely come." Tongtian said, accepting the Immortal Gourd Vine back and not minding the change in Nuwa's address. "How can I miss the chance to listen to the sermon of a Saint?"

Nuwa nodded and ascended to the sky. Along the way, she chanced upon a qingluan. She waved her hand and captured the divine bird. "From now on, your name will be Caiyun, and you will be my mount."

Caiyun couldn't be happier. "Thank you, Mother Nuwa."

The qingluan had made her way to Buzhou Mountain after the coercion had disappeared, hoping for a stroke of fortune. True, a divine bird like her had been reduced to a mount, but she was satisfied. Many other beasts were willing to become a Saint's mount.

Riding on Caiyun's back, Nuwa disappeared into the distance.

* * *

With Nuwa gone, Tongtian took this time to observe her Obsession Corpse. His features were handsome. Though not at the level of her Good Corpse, his features surpassed her Evil Corpse. All in all, he looked like a mixture of the two wearing cyan robes.

"From now on, you will be called Lingbao," Tongtian said.

Lingbao smiled and cupped his fist. "Lingbao greets Main Body."

She rolled her eyes and stored her Obsession Corpse in one of the three flowers with the rest of her Corpses. Then, she turned to face the 129,600 humans.

Their small size struck a chord in her. Before, Tongtian had always thought she was average in height, at least compared to a human, but only now did she realize she was wrong. Humans only stood at around one-twentieth her height—barely the length of her finger.

Seeing the lost look in their eyes, Tongtian wanted to help. Even if she no longer considered herself human, she had been in another life. But before she could intervene, she looked up and felt the Grandmist Violet Qi cautioning her against it.

Tongtian frowned. Why was the Way of Heaven warning her? She couldn't discover the reason, so she turned to leave. Kong Xuan seemed to have wanted to do something but suddenly stopped with an ugly expression, making her feel better.

Just as she turned to leave, a voice called out. "Please wait!"

Tongtian and Kong Xuan stopped and turned around. One of Nuwa's handcrafted humans had walked up in all his naked glory and kneeled down. "Revered Immortal, please accept me as your disciple!"

Before Tongtian could speak, Kong Xuan spoke. "Since you want to apprentice under me, then I will accept you."

Tongtian threw an annoyed glare at the damn peacock. Maybe Yuanshi had been right when he'd called them flat-feathered beasts. Contrary to her expectations, the human didn't get up and looked toward her.

Kong Xuan's expression darkened while Tongtian's brightened. It must have been because Nuwa had spoken to her instead of Kong Xuan. She schooled her expression and tried to appear more dignified.

"It's not that I cannot accept you as a disciple, but you must pass my test first," Tongtian said. "Do not worry, I won't make it too hard since you are a newly born later heaven lifeform, but I will test your willpower and ingenuity."

The human was elated. "Thank you, Revered Immortal!"

"Don't thank me so soon." She pointed at a location higher up on Buzhou Mountain. "If you can climb up there, I will accept you as my disciple."

Without waiting for the human to react, Tongtian flew to the location she'd pointed at. She arrived in an instant, but it would take the human decades.

She wasn't worried that the human would die of old age on the journey. Unlike the hundred-year life expectancy of later generations, Nuwa had endowed the first generation of humanity with superior vitality. Coupled with the waning, yet still abundant essence remaining on Buzhou Mountain, living for a few thousand years would be no problem at all.

As Kong Xuan left, he glared angrily at the human, who shrunk back. When he looked at the rest of the humans, they all huddled together with fearful looks. Seeing none of them step forward, Kong

Xuan hated iron for not becoming steel and left after waving his sleeve.

On the mountain, Tongtian waited for her prospective disciple. With a wave of her hand, she carved a deep cave into the rock. Once she stepped inside, darkness shrouded her. Tongtian moved her hands a few times, and sword light shot out from her fingers.

In the next moment, the darkness disappeared as a vast sky appeared in the cave, and an endless prairie filled the ground. Tongtian had recreated the sky and land using a formation. If a Golden Immortal of the Great Unity had created such a grotto, they would have had to spare massive amounts of energy and resources.

Lastly, she built a temple with Allheaven' written in Dao Script above the entrance in the center of the grotto. She walked inside and sat atop her Twelfth-Ranked White Lotus of Purification above the raised platform, waiting for the human.

CHAPTER 39

Later Heaven Method

Tongtian first focused on comprehending the Law of Time and the Law of Space. Her comprehension ability had more than doubled, and all her previous uncertainties and doubts disappeared. Still, she had made far more progress in the Law of Time than the Law of Space. Naturally, her progress in fusing the two laws was abysmal.

A few decades later, Tongtian opened her eyes and peered into the distance. Her eyes pierced the temple doors, the grotto, and all the way through Buzhou Mountain. There, separated from the rest of humanity, she saw the human who wanted to become her apprentice.

He now wore clothing made of leaves and some fur. Tongtian continued to observe him as he climbed the mountain. During the day, he scaled trees and avoided all the fierce beasts that could easily kill him. At night, he hid in a shelter.

The human primarily ate whatever fruits or berries he could find. The only rare instance he could eat meat was when he discovered an animal weaker than himself. After killing it, he would roast it over a fire before consuming its flesh.

Tongtian nodded. Although his actions seemed ordinary, one couldn't forget that humanity had just been born, and they had no knowledge or inherited memories to rely on. They were just like babies with adult bodies. For the human to develop clothing, create fire, and seek shelter was praiseworthy enough.

She estimated that he would arrive in a hundred years or so, so she had to prepare. The cultivation method bestowed by the Dao Ancestor began at the Earth Immortal Realm; there was no cultivation method for later heaven lifeforms. So, she'd have to create her own.

Tongtian closed her eyes and recalled Nuwa handcrafting humanity. Because she had been present, she knew humans had 129,600 acupoints and numerous meridians. The more she understood human physiology, the more she sighed.

Although humanity was born weak, they were modeled after Pangu. As such, their forms were perfect for cultivation. As long as they opened all of their acupoints, they could eventually possess talent equal to a congenital god—but that would take a miracle.

Perhaps because of this innate talent, the Way of Heaven had imposed a restriction on every human. The more acupoints they opened up, the harder the later ones would be to open.

"No, I'm thinking about it the wrong way," Tongtian said. "What does the human body have to do with my Supreme Purity Scripture? The Immortal Path places more emphasis on spirit and comprehending the law. There's no need to completely unleash the potential of the body—as long as they can absorb essence, that would be enough. Opening more acupoints will increase potential but it is not a prerequisite."

To begin, the cultivator needed to sense the essence of heaven and earth and condense it within the body. So, the first realm would be called the Essence Condensation Realm.

For the next step, the cultivator would use the absorbed essence to open their acupoints. The more acupoints opened, the more essence the cultivator could absorb. The number of acupoints determined their potential, and thus, she named the second realm the Foundation Establishment Realm.

After the Foundation Establishment Realm, the cultivator would link their acupoints using their meridians. The human body had Twelve Standard Meridians and Eight Extraordinary Meridians. The meridians and acupoints would transform into a formation within the body and aid the flow of essence within. Like the Foundation Establishment Realm, the number of meridians determined potential, and the realm was henceforth known as the Inner Formation Realm.

Once in the Inner Formation Realm, the body would be strengthened as a side effect. The cultivator would increase the flow and efficiency of their essence; directing it to their forehead, center chest, and lower abdomen; opening their three dantians. When all three dantians were opened, the formation would strengthen, and the realm would be called the Dantian-Opening Realm.

Up to this point, the cultivator was adapting and changing their body. Now, it was time to upgrade the spirit by using essence to nourish and strengthen it. In this realm, the cultivator's spirit would transform three times, forming three stages. First, they would open up their Sea of Consciousness to reach the Spirit Condensation Stage. In the second stage—the Spirit Creation Stage—they would concentrate their soul and spirit in the Sea of Consciousness and transform them into a corporeal form residing therein. Finally, they would expel all impurities and distill them into a Nascent Spirit at the Spirit Purification Stage. All three stages together should be known as the Primal Spirit Realm.

Finally, the last stage before immortal ascension. The cultivator would process all the essence in their body using their acupoints and meridians into their dantian. Each stage of refinement would bear the risk of cultivation deviation and must be treated with the utmost care.

After each successful refinement, the essence in their dantian would strengthen until it reached the limit upon the ninth time—but they'd still need to repeat the process for the two other dantian. Hence, this realm was named the Essence-Refining Realm.

The last realm came to be known as the Heaven Ascension Realm. Merging all three nine-refinement essences in the dantian, reverse nascent, and later heaven would open the gates to immortality—making a nascent heaven lifeform!

Although there were still some kinks to smooth out, Tongtian smiled with satisfaction. *If Eldest Brother had created this method, he would have called the Inner Formation Realm the Core Formation Realm, right?*

Tongtian no longer pondered and peered out of her grotto. She pinched her fingers and calculated what had happened to humanity while she was creating a method suitable for them to cultivate.

After the human who wanted to be her apprentice had left, the humans handcrafted by Nuwa had led the other humans to survive on Buzhou Mountain. They ate fruits and berries, roots and barks, but they eventually learned to hunt. Although casualties were high, so was their reproduction rate. After a hundred years, the population nearly doubled, even with all the deaths.

In addition, Tongtian could sense Cattle, Pig, and Chicken secretly protecting humanity. Although they couldn't fend off Golden Immortals, they could still fight other Sky Immortals and weaker creatures.

Tongtian's eyes sharpened when she saw a bolt of lightning strike dead wood, lighting it on fire. The first human created by Nuwa saw this and tried all methods to replicate this, eventually learning how to make fire.

He taught this to his people, reducing their casualties by using the fire to cook and fend off beasts. Karmic Merit directly descended onto him, promoting him to the Golden Immortal Realm. His name was Suiren, and he became acknowledged as the revered Fire Ancestor of Humanity.

Unlike the Immortal Path, people who directly use merit to promote themselves were known as Merit Immortals, and they cultivated the Merit Path. After embarking on this path, they could only gain strength by gathering merit.

Tongtian didn't observe much longer, as her future disciple finally arrived.

When the human arrived at the cave, he gulped in fear but still courageously entered the darkness. Once inside, his eyes widened in shock as he saw the vast sky and grasslands. He couldn't help but wonder if he had stepped into a different dimension; that would explain why he saw such a scene inside a cave.

His eyes quickly caught sight of the temple at the center, clearly an abnormality on the flat grassland. Excitement coursed through him as he ran to it at full speed, but the joy did not last long. No matter how fast or how long he ran, he got no closer.

The human's expression turned serious as he slowed. He no longer ran like a sprinter but like a marathon runner. The sun never set in this strange world, so the human continued to run until sweat poured off his back and drenched his entire body. Days turned to months, and months turned to years. Still, the human never stopped running. He drifted between consciousness and unconsciousness as the light dimmed in his eyes. Even so, his legs kept moving, even if all he could do was drag his feet.

Finally, his perseverance bore fruit, and he stepped onto one of the jade steps leading into the temple. He couldn't react in time and fell onto his face, losing consciousness.

When he came to, the human discovered he was lying in the temple with a new set of cyan robes. He patted the robes, marveling at the difference in texture and comfort compared to the leaves and fur he had once covered himself with.

Sensing a powerful gaze on him, he looked up to see Tongtian staring down at him. He bowed three times and kowtowed nine times to show his respect. "Disciple greets Master."

Tongtian chuckled. "Since you have passed my test, I will accept you as my nominal disciple. Once you reach the Golden Immortal Realm, you can become my personal disciple."

The disciple frowned. "Master, what's the Golden Immortal Realm?"

"That is still too soon for you to worry about," Tongtian said. "Do you have a name?"

"Wutian," he said, repeating the name on his lips a few times as if he was unaccustomed to saying it. His eyes brightened. "Yes, my name is Wutian!"

Tongtian watched as if something had changed within the human—Wutian. His aura converged, and he seemed like a completely different person. He was like a sharp blade, very much to her taste.

She went to press her finger to Wutian's forehead, but the difference in size made it seem like she was going to squish his head like a bug. Wutian had to consciously stop himself from taking a step back. When her finger touched his forehead, Wutian entered a daze as a tide of information entered his mind. It was the Supreme Purity Scripture Later Heaven Method.

Wutian couldn't digest all the information at once, so Tongtian only imprinted the instructions for the first three realms into his mind.

When the human awakened, he kneeled once more in excitement. "Thank you, Master!"

Tongtian waved her hand. "Alright, go ahead and practice the method."

Wutian nodded, but after a moment, he showed hesitation. "Master, can I teach it to the others?"

Just as Tongtian was about to say yes, she frowned. She felt the Way of Heaven warning her again. So she could only accept people who came her way, and she couldn't be proactive? She sighed. "You cannot. Only those of my Supreme Purity Lineage can learn this method. Of course, if you derive a new method from mine, you are free to teach whoever you want."

Wutian was a little disappointed, but he quickly accepted Tongtian's words. After hesitating once more, he asked, "Can I ask Master's name?"

Tongtian blinked. Thinking back, she hadn't explained her identity, had she?

"Listen well," she said. "I, your master, am one of the Three Purities, the orthodox descendant of Pangu. I am Supreme Purity Tongtian!"

Wutian trembled as if he had received the shock of his life. Tongtian could even hear him muttering. The words were unintelligible, so even she couldn't decipher them. At her level, she could actually glean the thoughts of a mortal like Wutian easily, but she didn't care to. What information could Wutian have?

Tongtian closed her eyes and began to refine the cultivation method she had created. When Wutian returned to his senses, he looked up to see his master sitting in a lotus position with a sword resting on her legs. If she hadn't moved earlier, he would have thought she was a very life-like statue.

Wutian sat down and began to sense the essence around him. Not even a minute later, he sensed the essence of heaven and earth. He made a strange face. Was he actually a genius for being able to sense it so quickly?

He moved on to the next step: absorbing the essence into his body. A day later, he stood up with incomparable excitement. "Master, Master, I mastered the Essence Condensation Realm!"

Tongtian opened her eyes and scanned him. The corner of her lips twitched. "Stupid boy. Try to sense the essence in your body again."

Wutian furrowed his brows but did as Tongtian said. His eyes widened. "Why is the essence leaking out?"

"Because you haven't mastered it yet. You haven't opened any of your acupoints. How can you store the essence? Only when you naturally draw in essence without any conscious effort will you reach mastery of the Essence Condensation Realm." Tongtian closed her eyes and ignored the human.

Wutian's face flushed, but he quickly calmed down. He copied Tongtian's position and attempted to reach mastery. A week later, his body would unconsciously absorb the essence of heaven and earth around him, surprising Tongtian. According to her estimation, it should have taken him a month, even if Nuwa had handcrafted him.

Tongtian allowed Wutian to move on to the next step of condensing essence and using it to open his acupoints.

While Wutian was busy cultivating, humanity grew. After Suiren, a woman named Zhengyi created clothes to protect humanity and also received merit from the Way of Heaven. After her, a man named Youchao built the first shelter and taught others how to, and once again, the merits descended. These three became the three ancestors of humanity.

The Way of Heaven's generosity toward humanity inevitably

caught the attention of numerous major powers. A few wanted to see what was so special about humanity, but aside from having spirituality since birth, they were found to be unexceptional. Because Nuwa had created them, no one dared to be too overbearing, especially after discovering that Tongtian was also staying on Buzhou Mountain.

Even the Titan Tribe had investigated humanity, but soon lost interest after not discovering anything too unique. Since humanity posed no threat, they didn't want to fight with Nuwa over it, so they didn't touch the humans.

The only ones daring enough to attack them were beasts and the later generations of demons disconnected from the Demon Clan of Heavenly Court. However, they could still fend them off with the protection of Suiren, Zhengyi, Youchao, Cattle, Pig, and Chicken.

When humanity had existed for almost a thousand years, Tongtian opened her eyes. It was time to listen to Nuwa's sermon. She gazed at Wutian. He had entered the Foundation Establishment Realm within the first year but stayed there for centuries to open as many acupoints as possible.

"Wutian," Tongtian called out.

"Yes, Master?"

"I will be leaving for a while. You've been cultivating without rest for nearly a thousand years. You should return to your people; your roots lie in humanity. It's best not to divide yourself too long."

"Understood," Wutian said, looking into the direction he'd come from. He had been separated from humanity for over 90 percent of his life.

As he set off, Tongtian's figure disappeared from Allheaven Temple.

CHAPTER 40

Wa Outer Heaven

Ever since the Dao Ancestor's third sermon, Tongtian hadn't left the Great Desolation. Now, she entered the chaotic boundary once more to listen to Nuwa's sermon. Along the way, she reunited with her brothers.

"Congratulations to Third Sister for cutting off your last Corpse," Yuanshi said. Laozi also gave a rare smile on his increasingly indifferent face.

"Do you two feel uncomfortable because Nuwa became a Saint before you?" Tongtian asked. Laozi and Yuanshi stayed silent, but Tongtian got her answer. "You don't need to worry about it too much. Nuwa used Karmic Merit to become a Saint. I'm sure any one of us could accomplish the same feat if we used the Heaven-Opening Merit in us, but I wouldn't recommend it."

Karmic Merit had many uses, but it wasn't Karmic Luck. However, Heaven-Opening Merit was different due to its meaning. It also accrued luck for the possessor, so using it was short-sighted.

"I don't know if there is a difference between merging three Corpses or merit, but generally, relying on external forces is inferior," Tongtian said, easing her brothers' wounded pride.

"I'm ashamed to need to be reminded by Third Sister," Laozi said. "It seems that my daoheart is not strong enough."

"No worries," Tongtian said. "I was present near Nuwa when she became consecrated, and I could tell that she was lacking in comparison to the Dao Ancestor. Of course, she is still a Saint, so we can't underestimate her. The longer we take, the further the distance will widen, so we can't be too complacent."

"Third Sister's words are correct," Yuanshi said. "I feel like I will be able to merge all three Corpses soon, so I should be able to achieve sainthood within an eon."

Laozi looked at Yuanshi, apparently hearing this for the first time.

Tongtian cupped her fist. "Then I will congratulate Second Brother ahead of time. It seems that Eldest Brother and I have some catching up to do."

Yuanshi smiled, feeling gratified. Tongtian was the first to enter the Quasi-Saint Realm, and Laozi severed three Corpses first. Now, he could finally take a step ahead of his two siblings. Although he was the second-born, he did not feel inferior to Laozi at all.

The Three Purities found Nuwa's Immortal Grotto in the chaotic boundary. She had taken the chaos energy and opened up a minor world. Nuwa had created a paradisiacal land by transforming chaos into yin and yang and shaping them into the five elements.

Inside this world, the Three Purities saw a palace with the words Wa Palace written in Dao Script above the gate. They flew in along with the other attendees.

Inside, Nuwa smiled at them. "Fellow Daoists, please take a seat."

The Three Purities sat on seats on the same level as Nuwa. They ignored the fact that Fuxi sat on the same level as them next to Nuwa, while all the other guests sat at a lower level—including Di Jun and Taiyi.

Upon seeing Taiyi, Tongtian's gaze sharpened as her aura converged into a single sharp edge, as if ready to attack at any moment.

Instead of retreating or apologizing, Taiyi smiled at her, igniting the sparks between them even more.

The guests began to murmur and theorize about the exact nature of the relationship between Tongtian and Taiyi. They quickly stopped when Yuanshi's aura shrouded over them. In the silence, the Jade Purity directed his ill intent at Taiyi, who only looked at Tongtian, ignoring everything else.

Before the scene could dissolve, Nuwa distracted them by greeting Jieyin and Zhunti, who arrived late as usual. Like the Three Purities, Nuwa placed them at the same level as herself. There were now nearly 3,000 guests, so Nuwa sealed off Wa Palace.

"Thank you, everyone, for coming to my Wa Outer Heaven," Nuwa said. "Since I have achieved sainthood, I will educate anyone with the fate to come here as my master did. Allow me to explain my Way of Good Fortune."

As Nuwa spoke, the world resonated with her words, and numerous phenomena occurred. Green clouds emerged from the floor, making everyone feel as if they were sitting on clouds high in the sky.

Tongtian tapped her forefinger on the sheath of her Qingping Sword as she ruminated on the Law of Creation Nuwa had mastered. She had fought Nuwa before and gained a glimpse of it. Comparing her past comprehension and her current level, the difference was akin to heaven and earth. It was as if Nuwa once only knew how to do simple multiplication, but she had suddenly mastered trigonometry.

Tongtian continued to comprehend the Law of Creation and use it as a reference for the Law of Time and Law of Space. Although the laws were different, every single one of them could lead to the Great Dao.

When 1,000 years passed, Nuwa stopped speaking, and the myriad phenomena stopped. Slowly, everyone begrudgingly awakened from their comprehensions. Still, they got up and thanked Nuwa.

With her sermon done, Nuwa excused the listeners. Aside from the Three Purities and the two from the West who said a few words before leaving, the rest quickly filed out. Only Fuxi, Di Jun, and Taiyi were left inside.

"Daoist Nuwa," Di Jun began. He froze when Nuwa cast a glance at him, feeling as if all of heaven was crushing down on him. But the feeling quickly disappeared, as if it was a mere illusion. He gritted his teeth and continued, "About the Titan Tribe..."

"Unless the Titan Tribe forces the Demon Clan to the point of no return, I will not strike," Nuwa said definitively.

"Sister," Fuxi said, frowning.

"You don't need to say anymore," Nuwa said. "It's not that I don't want to act, but I can't."

Fuxi couldn't help but ask, "Is it because you became Saint?"

Nuwa stayed silent.

"As long as Daoist Nuwa is able to take a shot against the Pangu Genesis Formation at the critical time, then I am confident we can defeat the Titan Tribe," Di Jun said.

Nuwa closed her eyes and said nothing. When she opened them, she stared at her brother and then sighed. "Daoist Di Jun, from now on, I'll be living in Wa Outer Heaven and won't show up in the Great Desolation unless something important happens. I'll have to ask you to take care of my brother in my stead."

A hint of excitement flashed through Di Jun's eyes. "Don't worry. Daoist Fuxi is one of the four demon emperors, how can I not take care of him?"

"Then I'll thank Daoist Di Jun ahead of time," Nuwa said.

"I won't bother Daoist Nuwa anymore," Di Jun said. He turned to leave, but Taiyi didn't budge from his spot. "Taiyi?"

"I want to see a Saint's power," Taiyi said. "I want to see the difference between a Saint and a Quasi-Saint."

"Brother!" Di Jun grabbed Taiyi's shoulder and gave Nuwa an apologetic look. "Please don't take his words to heart. You've known him for years. He's just like this."

Taiyi removed Di Jun's hand from his shoulder and stared into Nuwa's eyes. "Just one move. That's all I ask for."

Seeing the steel-like determination in Taiyi's eyes, Nuwa nodded. "Alright."

"Daoist Taiyi, prepare yourself," she warned. She didn't make any extravagant techniques. No dragon roars or phoenix cries rang out. All she did was point at Taiyi with her finger.

Taiyi felt all the hairs on his body stiffen and stand on end. The world disappeared, and only the finger and he remained. The fingertip approached him slowly, but Taiyi couldn't move at all. He roared and managed to summon the Chaos Bell to block it in the nick of time.

Not a moment later, the finger lightly tapped the Chaos Bell. A thunderous ring echoed in Wa Palace. Taiyi crashed into the wall, coughing up blood.

Di Jun's eyes widened. Nuwa clearly hadn't done anything special, yet his brother—an advanced Quasi-Saint—was sent flying without being able to put up any resistance. No wonder the Dao Ancestor said all under Saints were ants.

Taiyi stood up with some difficulty. Although his injuries appeared severe, it was nothing that time couldn't fix, and his foundation had not been damaged at all. "Thank you."

Nuwa pointed at Taiyi again, and a green glow covered him. To his surprise, he discovered that all his injuries had been healed in an instant. Not only were Saints mighty, but they possessed mysterious means as well.

Di Jun and Taiyi left, as Nuwa wanted to talk to Fuxi alone.

"Brother, if possible, can you extricate yourself from the Demon Clan?"

"Is the Demon Clan doomed?" Fuxi asked, immediately thinking of the reason.

Nuwa shook her head. "Not necessarily, but the war with the Titan Tribe will be perilous. The chances of Di Jun and Taiyi surviving aren't high either."

Fuxi smiled. "How can I shirk away at the slightest hint of danger? We received many benefits from joining Heavenly Court. How can I abandon them like this? Speak no more, I won't leave."

Nuwa sighed. She silently vowed to pay attention to Fuxi and prevent him from dying, even if she had to suffer punishment from the Way of Heaven.

* * *

"Eldest Brother, did you gain any inspiration for fusing your three Corpses after the sermon?" Tongtian asked.

"Third Sister did as well?" Laozi returned.

Tongtian smiled. "Just some inspiration, nothing solid."

Laozi nodded.

After returning to the Great Desolation, halfway to Kunlun Mountain, Tongtian split off. "When Nuwa created humanity, I accepted a nominal disciple. It's been a thousand years, I should see how he is doing."

Laozi felt the Grandmist Violet Qi in his possession resonate, but it was only for a fleeting moment. His eyes turned as he made a decision. "You actually accepted a disciple. I wonder how his roots are."

Tongtian scratched her cheeks. "He's very weak, not even an immortal. How about you wait until he's at least an Earth Immortal?"

"Nonsense," Yuanshi said. "Since Third Sister accepted a disciple, the first of the Three Purities lineage, we should take a look."

Tongtian eventually agreed. She didn't really have anything to hide, so she brought them to Allheaven Temple on Buzhou Mountain. There, Tongtian sent a message to Wutian for him to see her.

While she was gone, Wutian had returned to the rest of humanity. Due to his cultivation, he stood out and was immediately noticed by Suiren, Zhengyi, and Youchao. They summoned Wutian and asked him why he was so strong, and he answered truthfully.

All three ancestors' eyes lit up at his report. Although they had solved the issues of food, safety, and shelter, they could not strengthen humanity, and many still fell to ferocious beasts. They asked Wutian if he was able to teach them the method, but he said that it could only be taught to his master's disciples.

The three ancestors were disappointed but did not blame him. Wutian still had a method to strengthen the able men and women of the tribe. He created weapons, and merits descended.

Tongtian had already warned him about the danger of reliance on merit, so Wutian didn't absorb the merit to increase his cultivation, instead forming a Halo of Merit behind him. The introduction of weapons instantly increased the overall strength of humanity severalfold.

The weapons were formed from bones, stones, or other sharp objects attached to sticks. Wutian wasn't pleased with the end product, but this was the best he could do right now, as he couldn't manipulate and forge bronze or iron.

Wutian didn't rest on his laurels. While he continued to open his acupoints, he also created a set of simple martial arts to teach his fellow humans. The martial arts didn't instantly increase their strength like weapons, but they provided long-term benefits. By practicing them, humans could unlock the acupoints in their bodies without using essence or a cultivation method. Because of this, more merits descended down on Wutian, but he still didn't absorb them.

Humanity came to respect Wutian's contribution to the race and to revere him as humanity's fourth ancestor: the Martial Ancestor.

During this time, Wutian occasionally returned to Allheaven Palace, but Tongtian was never there. When he suddenly heard Tongtian's message, his eyes lit up.

He told the three ancestors, "Eldest Brother, Second Sister, Third Brother, my master has summoned me. I have to leave now."

Suiren nodded. "Go, don't make her wait too long."

Wutian smiled and left the cave they'd made him. He had already reached the Inner Formation Realm, so he could reach the grotto much faster this time. He entered Allheaven Temple and froze as he saw two unfamiliar men with his master.

Still, that shock only lasted for a second. He cupped his fist together and greeted them respectfully. "Disciple greets Master, and greets seniors."

Wutian wanted to say more but felt a dangerous sensation coming toward him. He snapped his head up to see a handsome middle-aged man wearing black robes glaring daggers at him.

CHAPTER 41
Martial Arts

Tongtian slapped Yuanshi's shoulder. "What are you trying to do? You're literally going to kill him with that stare!"

"Third Sister, although it's astounding that he has spirituality before reaching the Earth Immortal Realm, his origin is too shallow," Yuanshi said. "Second Brother will find a better disciple for you."

Tongtian glared at Yuanshi. "He's the disciple I accepted. No matter what his qualifications are, it's my choice. So, shut it."

Yuanshi pursed his lips. Aside from glaring daggers at Wutian, he said nothing more.

Tongtian coughed into her hands and then motioned to Laozi and Yuanshi. "This is your eldest Uncle-Master, Grand Purity Laozi. This one is your second Uncle-Master, Jade Purity Yuanshi."

Wutian cupped his fists and saluted them. "Junior greets two Uncle-Masters."

Yuanshi's complexion softened a bit, and he nodded.

Laozi reached into his robes and pulled out a jade-white pill. "Since this is our first meeting and you called me Uncle-Master, this will be my meeting gift. This is a Spirit Purification Pill. Once ingested, your spirit will be cleaned, and your mind will become clear, speeding up your ability to sense the essence of heaven and earth."

"Thank you, Eldest Uncle-Master," Wutian said as he grabbed the pill floating in front of him, trying not to swallow it immediately. He looked up and tried to avoid making eye contact with Yuanshi.

Yuanshi snorted but still waved his hand. A jade slip appeared and floated in front of Wutian. "This talisman contains a barrier that can block even one strike from a Quasi-Saint. With how weak and annoying you are, no doubt you'll get yourself killed. This can extend your life by a bit."

Wutian allowed Yuanshi's disparaging words to enter one ear and go out the other. He quickly stored it and said, "Thank you, Second Uncle-Master."

Yuanshi turned to Tongtian. "With this, you can have peace of mind now, right? Hurry and return to Kunlun Mountain."

Tongtian rolled her eyes. "If you want to go back so quickly, return. I'll wait until my disciple is at least an Earth Immortal."

Laozi and Yuanshi left not long after, leaving Tongtian and Wutian alone.

The Supreme Purity sat back on her Twelfth-Ranked White Lotus of Purification and smiled. "Tell me what you've been doing all these years while I was gone."

"Yes," Wutian said as he sat down. He recounted all that had happened and how he had created a set of martial arts to help humanity increase their combat power.

"You've done well," Tongtian said. "Remember, Karmic Merit is useful, but you must not overly rely on it."

"Disciple understands; disciple wants to become an Earth Immortal through his own strength."

"As long as you understand. Right, aside from the clothes and the Supreme Purity Scripture Later Heaven Method, I haven't bestowed anything upon you. Speak. What kind of weapon do you want?"

"A spear," Wutian said without any hesitation.

Tongtian nodded. She waved her hand, and a stone spear rose from the floor. She held it in her hand. The spear appeared like a toothpick between her fingers. She engraved dozens of formations on the spear while gathering essence into it, turning it into an acquired spiritual artifact.

With the spear artifact refined, Tongtian floated it to her disciple, who eagerly took hold of it. It was a head taller than him, and the tip exuded a fierce sharpness. He swung it a few times, and the air split from his movements.

Tongtian laughed. "Are you satisfied?"

Wutian nodded without hiding his elation.

"You know, I could have given you a better artifact. Are you disappointed?" Tongtian suddenly asked.

Wutian shook his head. "No, I'm very satisfied. I know that I'm currently too weak now, and having something too precious will be far beyond my ability to possess."

Tongtian nodded. "Good, at least you aren't stupid." Her eyes scanned Wutian, making him feel like she could sense everything about him. "Not bad. You actually opened up more than 100,000 acupoints and linked the Twelve Standard Meridians and Eight Extraordinary Meridians. Not bad at all. I'll pass on the instructions for the next realm."

Like before, Tongtian poked Wutian's forehead, delivering the method to enter the Dantian-Opening Realm. This time, it took less time for Wutian to digest the information.

"Take the Spirit Purification Pill, it'll be a great aid for you to open the upper dantian."

"Disciple will retreat now," Wutian said as he left the main hall and went into the side room.

There, he sat on his cot in a lotus position like Tongtian. After entering his optimal state, Wutian swallowed the Spirit Purification Pill. As soon it passed through his throat, it dissolved and evaporated entirely.

Then, he felt as if he had been doused in an ocean of ice-cold water. It wasn't an unpleasant sensation. Rather, it was delightful, as if an unknown burning sensation inside of him had finally cooled.

The sensation lasted an indeterminable amount of time, and when it was over, many complexities that had once puzzled him had become much simpler. Even the essence of heaven and earth was easier to absorb.

Wutian sighed with soul-deep relief. As expected of one of Laozi's pills. He closed his eyes and focused on entering the next realm. Within a month, he opened up a dantian and entered the Dantian-Opening Realm.

The human body contained dantians in the head, chest, and abdomen that could be opened. The upper dantian was the smallest, the middle dantian was in between, and the lower dantian was the largest.

The three dantians could be opened in any order, but opening the middle first made it easier to open the upper or lower dantians. The lower dantian could hold the largest amount of essence, increasing the cultivator's power the most. However, the upper dantian cleared the thoughts and made it easier to sense the dantian in the body.

Thanks to the Spirit Purification Pill, Wutian had opened the upper dantian first. Once he opened it, his mind became even clearer and his thoughts came faster. He took this chance to sense the location of his other two dantians. While he couldn't open them now, sensing their location allowed him to prepare for the future.

Wutian would need to absorb more essence to prepare for the next step, so he focused on creating more martial arts and perfecting his current techniques. In his room, Wutian mimicked the forms of various animals and tried to replicate their strength using the human body. Midway, he stopped as he heard his master summon him.

"Master," Wutian said as he bowed.

"I noticed that your martial arts primarily strengthen the body and not the spirit," Tongtian said. "The Immortal Path places more importance on the spirit, and I originally did not want to teach you any body-strengthening methods, but it seems that your heart cannot calm down and forget your fellow humans."

"Master, I am a member of humanity. I cannot selfishly only think of myself." Wutian's tone obviously leaked his intention to continue creating martial arts, diverting his focus.

Tongtian nodded. "Since you have made your decision, I, your master, won't stop you. Your uncle-masters and I created a body-strengthening method years ago, and I will impart it to you now. However, that is on the condition that you do not slacken on your spiritual cultivation. Do you understand?"

Wutian nodded eagerly. "Disciple agrees!"

"The technique is called the Nine-Revolution Arcane Art. You are too weak, so I will only impart the first revolution to you. You cannot practice the technique until you become an Earth Immortal, but you can use it as a reference." Tongtian tapped his forehead again.

Wutian's eyes glazed over. Unlike before, it lasted for over a year, but when his eyes regained their clarity, they were unprecedentedly bright. Wutian excused himself and returned to his room to remedy the deficiencies in his martial arts.

Before, martial arts had only strengthened the body a bit, since its primary purpose was to increase combat power. After Wutian received the first revolution of the Nine-Revolution Arcane Art, he wanted to make martial arts strengthen the human body too.

Tongtian didn't mind. In fact, she secretly encouraged it even if she didn't show it. After she had returned from Wa Outer Heaven, she'd noticed that her merits had increased ever so slightly.

After seeing Wutian, she realized it was due to the fact that he had used her Supreme Purity Scripture Later Heaven Method as the basis for martial arts. If she contributed even more, wouldn't she receive more merit and maybe even part of humanity's luck?

The Way of Heaven wouldn't persecute her for her actions, right? After all, she had only taught Wutian and forbade him from directly teaching the Nine-Revolution Arcane Art.

After this, she wouldn't pay much attention to the creation of martial arts anymore. It was not like she could directly get involved. If Wutian asked her to enlighten him, she would, but if she tried to advise him, the Way of Heaven would warn and maybe even punish her.

Tongtian focused on merging her three Corpses. In the main hall of Allheaven Temple, she sat on her Twelfth-Ranked White Lotus of Purification while her Obsession Corpse, Lingbao, sat in front of her. To his left and right sat her Evil and Good Corpses, Shangnan and Shangxin.

All three of them radiated the aura of Quasi-Saints, but her Obsession Corpse's was the strongest. As the most recent Corpse, and one she severed when she was at the Advanced Quasi-Saint Realm, Lingbao had an Advanced Quasi-Saint Realm cultivation base.

Shangnan, her Evil Corpse, had also reached the Advanced Quasi-Saint Realm, but Shangxin only had an Intermediate Quasi-Saint Realm cultivation base. Unlike her, they couldn't sever a Corpse to raise their cultivation, so Tongtian could only use the power of the law to temper their qi until they advanced.

Before merging, Tongtian wanted to have all three Corpses at the

Peak Quasi-Saint Realm. This way, their foundation would be incomparably firm and increase the chance of becoming a Saint of Heaven.

Tongtian was transformed from Pangu's spirit that split into three pure qis. With that as her source, her origin was exceptional—the peak of the Great Desolation—and the only ones who could rival her were Laozi and Yuanshi. But her Corpses were a different story.

The three Corpses were severed from her thoughts. Even if they merged, the merged Corpse's origin would be lacking, and Tongtian didn't know if it would be enough to become one with the Grandmist Violet Qi.

While Tongtian cultivated, Wutian descended back to humanity and taught them his newly created martial arts. Unlike the martial arts he created the first time, these ones not only increased the body's strength but also slightly increased one's lifespan.

Soon, the majority of humans began to learn martial arts, drastically increasing their overall strength. With the increase in strength came a decrease in death. With the decrease in death, the living space declined, and they naturally had to expand their territory.

As they expanded their territory, the number of deaths naturally increased, but their numbers rose faster than they lessened, and their overall strength increased to a whole new level. Their population of 129,600 increased to over a million in just 10,000 years.

As another 10,000 years passed, Wutian successfully became an Earth Immortal. As promised, Tongtian imparted the Earth Immortal, Sky Immortal, and Profound Immortal portions of the Supreme Purity Scripture to him.

She also crafted an acquired spiritual spear using the leaves and a broken branch of the Allheaven Jianmu Tree for him. It appeared plain and simple, but it was comparable to innate spiritual artifacts in durability. In addition, unless Wutian actually used it, no one would realize its value.

After ensuring that Wutian had the ability to protect himself in her absence, Tongtian left Buzhou Mountain and returned to Kunlun Mountain. Her spirits rose as the faint homesickness faded.

The first thing she did was enter Three Purity Palace. It wasn't Laozi or Yuanshi who she saw first, but Laozi's Good Corpse, Taishang Laojun, sitting on Laozi's prayer mat. Tongtian noticed something strange as she studied him. Suddenly she smiled.

Tongtian visited Grand Purity Hall, where Laozi was refining pills using the Eight Trigrams Cauldron. Her smile widened as she said, "Congratulations to Eldest Brother for merging all three Corpses."

Chapter 42

The Shura Race

Laozi turned to his sister, a hint of emotion crossing his indifferent face. He waved his hand, freezing the fire burning under the Eight Trigrams Cauldron. Even the medicinal fragrance faded.

"It's nothing much," Laozi said. "You might have guessed it already, but even if I gave the Grandmist Violet Qi to my Corpse, it could not become consecrated."

Tongtian's smile disappeared, and her expression became serious. "Is it because the foundation is too lacking?"

"Perhaps," Laozi said. "Corpses are ultimately incomplete beings, even if merged. Unless we can find a way to make up for their deficiencies, a Corpse cannot become a Saint."

"Do we really have to shackle ourselves to the Way of Heaven?" Tongtian frowned. "How about asking Nuwa if she has a method?"

Laozi deliberated for a moment before shaking his head. "Even if she did, she would likely be unwilling to see us become Saints of Heaven with our Corpses and achieve the Primordial Origin Realm with our bodies."

She sighed. It was not like she didn't understand why Nuwa would refuse to tell them. The Three Purities were already one of the strongest groups in the Great Desolation. If all three became Saints and had two more at the same level, wouldn't heaven and earth become theirs in all but name?

Nuwa didn't know that the Three Purities would split because of conflicting views, at least according to the original myths.

"How is your progress?" Laozi asked.

"So far, so good," Tongtian said. "I found a way to merge them, but I plan on waiting for all three to reach the Peak Quasi-Saint Realm before beginning."

"Take these," Laozi said. He waved his hand, and a jade bottle full of pills flew in front of Tongtian. "These are my recent creations, Nine-Yang Arcane Pills. Ingesting one will allow a later heaven life-form to become a Golden Immortal of the Great Firmament."

"I can't take this," Tongtian said, pushing the bottle back. "The preciousness of these pills is worth too much. Rather than wasting these, I just need some more time."

"Take it, Third Sister. I concocted them to repay you. I still owe you for the white and red lotuses." Seeing her hesitation, he said, "If you don't take it, I will feel indebted to you, obstructing my way."

Tongtian sighed. "Alright then, I'll accept."

She excused herself to Supreme Purity Hall. Yuanshi had locked himself in Jade Purity Hall because he had reached a critical juncture during the fusion of his three Corpses with himself.

Tongtian checked the bottle and discovered thirty-three Nine-Yang Arcane Pills inside. In addition, there were over a hundred Six-Yang Arcane Pills and three hundred Three-Yang Arcane Pills. If she gave a hundred to humanity, they would instantly become an undeniable force in the Great Desolation.

Tongtian had her Good Corpse, Shangxin, swallow a Three-Yang Arcane Pill. His qi increased to a point where it would have taken her a hundred years to reach. A hundred years sounded short, considering that it took other beings tens of thousands or maybe a million years to reach the Golden Immortal Realm. Besides, Shangxin already had the cultivation base of a Quasi-Saint, so this was absolutely an enormous amount of time saved.

While Tongtian raised the cultivation of her three Corpses, the Great Desolation underwent numerous changes. Chief among them was the expansion of the human population.

Despite their weak individual strength, one quality that outstripped other races was their reproduction speed. The million-member population expanded into a hundred million, and they began to spread everywhere in the East.

They would even encroach into the South as time passed. The West had enough land but was too barren for the growing population of humanity. Although hot, the South had plenty of plants and animals for them to gather and hunt, but they suffered high casualties due to the number of dangerous beasts and other natural disasters. The North was just too cold for the humans to survive. Few plant life and animals lived there, and they hadn't learned how to fish.

Humanity's overall strength increased, but their concentrated power decreased since they could not contact each other over long distances. Each separate settlement lived the best they could, struggling to survive with no real improvement to their way of life.

On Buzhou Mountain, more and more demons had appeared. They weren't the Demon Clan of Thirty-Three Heavens, or the Heavenly Demon Clan, but the new generation born on the land. The Earthly Demon Clan's numbers soared, and so did their overall strength. The four ancestors of humanity and the three animals could fend them off, but each clash resulted in too many deaths.

As a result, the four ancestors of humanity moved the core from

Buzhou Mountain to near the East Sea. Some of the humans stayed and took refuge in the Titan Tribe.

This intermingling of giants and humans eventually led to the birth of half-giants. Although they were born weaker than giants, they grew stronger by cultivating the Strength Path. Additionally, they had spirits, which allowed access to the use of spiritual artifacts.

The twelve titans silently acquiesced to this trend. They had previously considered destroying humanity, but after discovering how weak they were, they didn't want to give Nuwa an excuse to take action against them for something that could not threaten them.

On the other hand, humanity's actions displeased Heavenly Court. They thought that since Nuwa had created humanity, they should be the Demon Clan's ally, yet they actually turned traitor and joined the Titan Tribe.

Heavenly Court took no overt action since the Dao Ancestor had already said they should rule the skies and not tread on land for ten eons. Secretly, several demons descended and gathered the demons native to the land to target the humans closest to the Titan Tribe.

Not only did this cull the number of humans, but it also cemented humanity's current reliance on the Titan Tribe. The human populations near Buzhou Mountain shortened the distance between themselves and the Titan Tribes. They merged with many titan branch tribes, but most preferred the Houtu Tribe since the others treated them like servants in all but name.

While the newest race of the Great Desolation drew everyone's eyes, another new race was about to be born in the Blood Sea.

* * *

An island floated in the core of the Blood Sea. Unlike the miasma-filled air around most of the sea, the core exuded a gentle red light filled with vitality. Anyone who cultivated the Strength Path here would receive twice the gains with half the effort.

At the center of the island was a palace made of scarlet stone, like dried blood. Inside Crimsonsap Palace's main hall sat Minghe on his Twelfth-Ranked Red Lotus of Karma. In front of him floated two figures, one wearing white and untainted by the bloody aura, and the other wearing red, seemingly formed out of the bloody aura.

There was a third object floating in front of him: a golden lotus. It was the Ninth-Ranked Golden Lotus of Merit that he had traded from Zhunti at a high price. Raising it didn't take much from Minghe since the Ninth-Ranked Golden Lotus of Merit primarily fed on merit.

The Blood Sea gathered all the blood and broken souls suffering grievances in the Great Desolation. It was why the miasma was so strong. The Blood Sea continuously received merit from the Way of Heaven for being the garbage dump of the Great Desolation and preventing the baleful air from contaminating the rest of the world.

Still, the harvest was not enough for Minghe to use. He had entered a bottleneck for his third Corpse, so he wanted to gather a massive amount of merit to sever his Obsession Corpse.

Since he had witnessed Nuwa becoming a Saint of Heaven by creating a new race, he wanted to replicate her feat. Minghe stored his two Corpses and flew out of the palace, carrying the Ninth-Ranked Golden Lotus of Merit in his hands.

Minghe exited the gates of Crimsonsap Palace, which was shaped like the mouth of a furious fiend. Outside, floating in front of the island, were over 100,000 copies of Minghe.

The four in front exuded the aura of Golden Immortals of the Great Firmament; four hundred exuded the aura of Golden Immortals of the Great Unity; four thousand exuded the aura of Golden Immortals; while the rest ranged from Profound Immortals to Earth Immortals.

These copies were Minghe's bloodgod incarnations. As the master of the Blood Sea, he could use the sea as he liked, including forming thousands of incarnations of himself. As long as the Blood Sea persisted, he would forever be eternal. No one could kill him. He doubted even a Saint of Heaven like Nuwa could accomplish this feat.

Of course, he wasn't so brash as to test this theory out.

Minghe raised his hand into the sky. A pillar of broken souls pierced the clouds, catching the attention of numerous major powers. The broken souls screamed in rage, agony, and torment, but Minghe ignored their pitiful cries and merged them into his bloodgods.

He stuffed several—sometimes even hundreds—into a single one, significantly altering their forms. Every one of them grew two or three pairs of arms and two or three heads, each displaying a different expression. Half of them changed into females with alluring features, while the males had wrathful and fierce appearances.

Each showed a belligerent expression, as if they couldn't wait to pounce on each other and rip them to shreds, but they all obediently kneeled to Minghe. "We greet the Ancestor!"

Minghe nodded. "From now on, you shall be known as the Shura Race!"

As soon as Minghe spoke those words, clouds of merit descended from the skies. Eighty percent of the merit was absorbed by Minghe, and the newly created shura race absorbed the rest.

"Sever!"

Using the merits, Minghe successfully formed his Obsession Corpse, but he wasn't happy. He'd received less than a tenth of the merits Nuwa had when she'd created her new race.

"I created more shura than she did humans, and all of them are stronger than any current human—even the four most powerful ones combined," Minghe muttered. "So why did I get so little merit? Is it because Nuwa is destined to become a Saint, so that's why the Way of Heaven was so generous?"

Minghe glared at the skies. After a while, he snorted and glanced at the four shuras with the cultivation base at the Great Firmament Realm. "Your names shall be Bali, Kharakantha, Vemincitrin, and Sakra. You four shall be the Shura Kings who rule over the shura in my stead."

The four Shura Kings obeyed and accepted their positions. Unknown to Minghe, when he named the fourth Shura King, Sakra's eyes flashed with a mysterious light that quickly disappeared.

"To help you rule over them and defend my Blood Sea, I will bestow this high-grade innate spiritual artifact," Minghe said as a war drum floated between the four of them. He waved his sleeve and turned around, entering Crimsonsap Palace once more.

The four Shura Kings glanced at each other and immediately began to fight for the spiritual artifact. While Bali, Kharakantha, and Vemincitrin were busy fighting one another, Sakra retreated a fair distance away.

Sakra gathered lightning in his hand and shot it at his fellow Shura Kings. They screamed in pain, but it wasn't enough to defeat them once and for all. All three glared at Sakra and ganged up on him without any semblance of teamwork. When the chance presented itself, they would turn on each other without a second thought.

Sakra's eyes weren't shrouded in bloodlust. With cold logic in his heart, he incapacitated his fellow Shura Kings one by one. He became the winner and accepted the war drum as his prize. "You shall be called Alambara."

* * *

On Kunlun Mountain, Tongtian glanced in the Blood Sea's directions. "Shuras? One of the six races dominating the Six Paths of Reincarnation?"

In Buddhism, all life could be born into six kinds of creatures depending on the karma they accumulated while they lived: the Heaven Realm, Human Realm, Shura Realm, Animal Realm, Hungry Ghost Realm, and Hell Realm.

She recalled that Buddhism especially loved converting evil creatures like shuras into enlightened beings. If she created an avatar and sent it into reincarnation to be reborn as a shura, wouldn't she have a way to sneak into Buddhism?

Tongtian laughed. Reincarnation hadn't been created yet. The dead souls still lingered in the Great Desolation or gravitated to the Blood Sea. Buddhism itself was yet to be created, but that didn't mean she couldn't prepare ahead of time.

While Tongtian was plotting, she felt a powerful coercion emanate from Kunlun Mountain.

"Second Brother has achieved Sainthood?"

Chapter 43

Heavenly Venerable of Primordial Beginning

All living beings felt the coercion emanating from Three Purity Palace. Compared to when Nuwa had been consecrated, it was vastly stronger, forcing all beings to kneel as a show of reverence to the new Saint of Heaven. The only exceptions were Tongtian and Laozi, who Yuanshi deliberately weakened his coercion on. For everyone else, he strengthened it, forcing them to kneel faster.

In Heavenly Court, Taiyi gritted his teeth as he glared hatefully in the direction of Kunlun Mountain. He swore he would become a Saint of Heaven or Golden Immortal of Primordial Origin no matter the cost.

As Yuanshi's coercion spread, purple qi arrived from the east. The fragrance of ten thousand flowers flooded heaven and earth as dragons roared, phoenixes chirped, and the majestic song of immortals played in everyone's ears. Even the sun and moon dimmed as if ashamed of being in the Saint's presence.

"I am Jade Purity Yuanshi, the Heavenly Venerable of Primordial Beginning!" Yuanshi's voice echoed throughout the Great Desolation. "In 3,000 years, I will open my doors and accept disciples. Those with talent, luck, and deep origins can come to test if they have fate with me!"

As soon as he finished speaking, the coercion receded.

Then, the excitement came. Every congenital god, demon, and even mortals like the humans grew excited. They may not have understood what a Saint of Heaven represented or have lived long enough to remember Nuwa's consecration, but becoming a disciple of someone so powerful was a once-in-a-lifetime opportunity.

A figure walked out of Peachsource Grotto of Jiuxian Mountain. His eyes contained infinite light and determination as he flew toward Kunlun Mountain.

A red-robed figure exited Cloudsky Grotto of Taihua Mountain and flew in the same direction.

In Goldawn Grotto of Jadespring Mountain, a figure sitting in a lotus position opened his eyes. He turned toward where the coercion had emanated from and, after a moment of hesitation, flew out.

A golden dragon soared out of Magu Grotto of Erxian Mountain. His body radiated draconic pressure and forced all the gods and demons flying to Kunlun Mountain to avoid him.

A white-robed god sitting in Goldlight Grotto of Qianyuan Mountain came out and followed in that same path.

For the next 1,000 years, Kunlun Mountain seemed to have become the center of the Great Desolation as all beings congregated there. Even if they did not fit the requirement of having talent, luck, and sufficient foundations, what if they happened to get lucky?

Before the potential disciples arrived, Tongtian left Supreme Purity Hall and entered Three Purity Hall, where she saw Yuanshi sitting. From a single glance, he appeared as if he was the origin of all things, and all things were birthed from him. The transcendent aura he radiated far surpassed Nuwa's.

Yuanshi turned his gaze on Tongtian, and she froze. She felt as if any secret she had was instantly seen through by Yuanshi, much to her extreme discomfort. For an instant, the sensation Yuanshi gave off reminded her of when the Dao Ancestor looked at her after the Way of Heaven had descended upon him. But just as quick as it came, that feeling disappeared, and Tongtian almost thought it was her imagination.

"Third Sister, I'm impressive, aren't I?" Yuanshi asked with a smug smile.

Tongtian's eyes twitched. She walked to her sitting brother and kicked him in the shin.

There was a loud sound akin to a metal ball hitting a metal wall, but neither Tongtian nor Yuanshi changed their faces. Before his consecration, she'd had the strongest body, having cultivated the Nine-Revolution Arcane Art the furthest. But Yuanshi was a Saint now. Even if his flesh had been weak, only people on the same level as him could have made use of that flaw.

They just stared at each other, neither breaking the awkward silence. Thankfully, before this could go on too long, Laozi entered.

"What are you two doing?"

"Nothing, I was just congratulating Second Brother on his consecration," Tongtian said as she sat down on her designated prayer mat.

Laozi saw Yuanshi's lips twitch, but he said nothing. Instead, he also sat down. "Congratulations to Second Brother for becoming a Saint."

Yuanshi nodded. "I've gained new insight into my Way of Primordial Beginning. Let's discuss our ways again."

Tongtian and Laozi nodded. Objectively, it was closer to Yuanshi guiding them, but he could still benefit from listening to Tongtian's understanding of the Law of Time and the Law of Space and Laozi's understanding of the Law of Infinity. Still, Tongtian and Laozi got the most out of their discussion.

When Yuanshi finished explaining his Way of Primordial Beginning, Laozi became even more unfathomable, and his eyes held everything and nothing within. Tongtian's aura turned ethereal. Although she was in front of you, you would feel like she was infinitely far, akin to the moon's reflection in the water.

"Thank you, Second Brother," both of them said.

"No problem. Aren't we siblings?" Yuanshi asked, repeatings Tongtian's words from eons ago. "Since I have become a Saint, the secrets of heaven have become clearer to me. I can answer any questions you have, such as if your Corpse can achieve sainthood."

"Then explain," Tongtian said, glaring. "Stop whetting our appetites."

"Your Corpses can become Saints," Yuanshi immediately answered. He wanted to pause for a moment, but upon seeing his sister's increasingly lethal glare, he quickly continued. "However, the source, the foundation of your Corpse, is lacking. Thus you have to make it with Karmic Merit. As long as you gather enough merit, your Corpses can achieve sainthood."

"Do we need to create a race like Nuwa?" Laozi asked.

Yuanshi shook his head. "Nuwa and Minghe received merit because the races they created benefit heaven and earth. If you arbitrarily create a race and they bring harm to the world, you will be affected due to the karma they sow."

"I've observed the shura race. All they know is how to kill and slaughter. How can they benefit the world?" Laozi asked.

"They are born from the Blood Sea and the broken souls full of resentment. The more of them are born, the less resentment fills heaven and earth. And when they die, their resentment will disappear."

"And humanity?"

Yuanshi shook his head. "They bear a fate greater than the shuras, so I cannot say. I can reveal some secrets of heaven, but others, you must learn for yourself and never divulge."

Hearing this, Laozi frowned and pinched his fingers. The Grand Purity tried to calculate the exact benefits brought about by humans, but he immediately stopped because he sensed that he would receive backlash if he continued.

"Brother, have you sensed the Immeasura—" Tongtian stopped as she sensed the Way of Heaven's warning.

Yuanshi shook his head. "Third Sister, it is not time to reveal this secret."

Tongtian nodded. Contrary to her expectation, Yuanshi did not seem panicked by the Immeasurable Tribulation. If you failed the Immeasurable Tribulation, then everything would be over, especially for Saints of Heaven who shared prosperity and longevity with heaven and earth. Yet, Yuanshi seemed to hold no regrets.

The Jade Purity pointed toward the East. "Eldest Brother, your chance lies near the East Sea."

Laozi turned thoughtful at this declaration. A moment later, a white-robed Daoist holding a staff emerged from him. It was his Good Corpse, Taishang Laojun. The Corpse flew to the direction he'd been pointed in.

Yuanshi turned to Tongtian. "Third Sister's opportunity hasn't arrived yet."

Her brows furrowed as she recalled The Dao Ancestor's words.

"The reason that they are everlasting is because they do not exist for themselves.

Hence, they are long-lived.

Thus, although the Saint puts himself last, he finds himself in the lead.

Although he is not self-concerned, he finds himself accomplished.

It is because he is not focused on self-interests and hence can fulfill his true nature."

Saints should not be concerned with self-interests nor hold power. Despite this, they still must hold a high position. Tongtian's mind spun as she recalled a particular bit of information. Laozi was the founder of the Human Teachings, Yuanshi was the sect master of the Enlightenment Sect, and she was the sect master of the Interception Sect.

Saints of Heaven were teachers and masters. They taught others and guided them to benefit heaven and earth. Tongtian's eyelashes flickered. The Immortal Path focused on the detachment of oneself and absorbing the essence of heaven and earth for one's benefit. Was that really compatible with a Saint's role?

"I understand," Tongtian said. Then she stood up and retreated to Supreme Purity Hall.

Laozi's eyes flashed, wondering if Tongtian understood what her chance was. He felt a sense of urgency. Yuanshi had already achieved sainthood before him, and he didn't want to be the last of his siblings to do so.

Yuanshi just stared at Tongtian's retreating figure. After a while, he also returned to Jade Purity Hall. He had just entered the Primordial Origin Realm, so he needed to understand his new realm and consolidate all his gains.

In Supreme Purity Hall, Tongtian murmured to herself. "Do I really need to establish the Interception Sect?"

She wasn't opposed to establishing the Interception Sect, but the battle between sects was the main reason why she would clash with Yuanshi, Laozi, Jieyin, and Zhunti. Tongtian didn't fear them, but she did not feel much motivation to set up the Interception Sect. Hell, she didn't have much interest in teaching others in general, much less the sheer number of disciples the Tongtian of myths had.

She remembered Duobao, Jinling, Wudang, Guiling, Zhao Gongming, Yunxiao, Bixiao, Qiongxiao, and countless others. It was one of the reasons why Supreme Purity had been able to form the Ten Thousand Immortals Formation and face off against the four Saints with his Immortal Extermination Sword Formation.

Tongtian placed a hand across her chest. For some reason, it panged. She shook her head and discarded the mysterious pain.

Does that mean the Ten Thousand Immortals Book should eventually fall into my hands? Tongtian wondered. She was still quite interested in one of the most powerful formations in the Great Desolation.

Still, that didn't mean she wanted to establish the Interception Sect. *What other actions can I take to gain immense merit? Form the Sixth Paths of Reincarnation? Forget it, I don't have the qualifications.*

Tongtian tapped her fingers on the Qingping Sword's scabbard. *Creating a race is out of the question. Even if I create a race that fits with one of the six realms of reincarnation, it might not guarantee enough merit. If I used my original self to do it, it would be more than enough since I also have Heaven-Opening Merit, but I don't want to resort to that.*

She had a bit of a collector's mindset. The rarer something was, the less she was willing to part with it, and Heaven-Opening Merit was definitely one of the rarest things in existence. Not to mention that it gave her a percentage of the world's Karmic Luck without her having to do anything.

Unless something calamitous happens to the Great Desolation, I doubt I can gain enough merits to achieve sainthood. Tongtian's finger froze as her eyelashes flickered. *According to myth, Gonggong destroyed Buzhou Mountain, the pillar of heaven, causing heaven and earth to crash into each other. Nuwa used five-colored stones to mend it and separate heaven and earth. One chunk of the five-colored stone disappeared and turned into Sun Wukong, but that's not the point.*

If I can prepare a new pillar of heaven to prevent heaven and earth from collapsing on each other, would I get enough merit?

The more Tongtian thought about it, the more she felt certain that this was the perfect choice. She wasn't thinking about killing Xuangui ahead of time and using his legs as pillars. No, she had something much better.

A bronze-barked tree with iron-colored leaves appeared in front of Tongtian. The Allheaven Jianmu Tree had a sturdy trunk, branches, and roots. As long as it was properly nurtured, it could become a pillar that supported heaven and earth, like Yggdrasil or other world trees.

After staring at it for a while, Tongtian gritted her teeth and summoned a jade bottle in her hand. The topper flew off, and a stream of water containing three different kinds of shining light melted into the connate spiritual root. After the Allheaven Jianmu Tree absorbed half of all the Threelight Divinewater Tongtian she had, its vitality heightened dramatically despite not growing in size.

Lingbao, her Obsession Corpse, emerged from her body and grabbed the connate spiritual root. The rest of her Corpses also appeared. All three had reached the Peak Quasi-Saint Realm, and it was time to merge them.

* * *

In Wuzhuang Temple on Longevity Mountain, Redcloud Ancestor sighed. He flipped his hand, and the Grandmist Violet Qi appeared in his palm.

He had only successfully severed one Corpse, and was stuck in the Early Quasi-Saint Realm. He needed to calm down and succeed in cutting off his second Corpse, but his heart was restless.

He glanced toward the closed door Zhen Yuanzi had retreated behind to sever his second Corpse. Redcloud Ancestor's eyes hardened, and he stood up. He wanted to walk the earth and find a chance for enlightenment.

Who knew, perhaps something would be waiting for him.

Chapter 44

Redcloud Ancestor's Tribulation

In the Houtu Tribe, Houyi's eyes clouded over for a moment. His eyes regained clarity when Chiyou slapped his shoulder. "What's wrong?"

"It's nothing," Houyi said, but he couldn't help but furrow his brows. For a moment, he felt as if he had learned something, but that feeling disappeared as soon as it came.

Houyi shook his head. He shouldn't get distracted. He and Chiyou looked back to see Houtu walking toward them. She wasn't in her titan form but shapeshifted into a more average size with one head, two arms, and two legs.

"Are you two ready?"

"Yes," Houyi and Chiyou answered.

They followed Houtu as she left the territory of her tribe and returned to the origin of the Titan Tribe, the valley containing the Pangu Temple. There, all twelve titans had gathered in Pangu Temple for the first time in a long while.

Di Jiang spoke first. "Yuanshi has become a Saint."

At this, all assembled became gloomy. The titans and Three Purities both claimed to be the orthodox lineage of Pangu. When one side became far stronger than the other, their claim was strengthened.

Not only that, but this meant there were two forces that could surpass them even if they formed the Pangu Genesis Formation. For titans who had the ambition to rule over heaven and earth, how could they accept someone towering over them?

"What if we invited Yuanshi to fight against Nuwa?" Gonggong suggested.

"Are you stupid?" Zhurong yelled. "Wouldn't this be admitting that we are inferior to the Three Purities? No way! I'll be the first to object."

Gonggong frowned. "Stop being so stubborn. If we invite Yuanshi, we can curb Nuwa. And if they can kill each other, even better."

"Hmpf, the Titan Tribe doesn't need an outsider's help. We would shame our identity as Pangu's orthodox lineage!"

Although none of the titans dismissed Gonggong's suggestion, they didn't refute Zhurong's words either. Even if they knew that Gonggong's suggestion was the best way, they still rejected the idea with all their heart. They were the descendants of Pangu. How could they stoop so low as to rely on an external force for victory?

"Enough," Di Jiang said as it seemed that Zhurong and Gonggong would begin to fight again. "Even if we ask Yuanshi, he might not necessarily agree, even if we pay a high price. For him, it might not be best for any force to rule the Great Desolation. It's best if a Saint can appear from one of us twelve."

"We follow the Strength Path because we have no spirit. Can we become Saints of Heaven?" Houtu asked.

"Hongjun never said we couldn't," Di Jiang said. "We should at least try. We just need the Grandmist Violet Qi. Even if we can't, it'll be good to prevent the birth of one more Saint."

"You are talking about Redcloud Ancestor?" Jiuyin asked.

Di Jiang nodded. "Among the people who received the Grandmist Violet Qi, he's the only one who is not Hongjun's disciple. We don't know if Hongjun would step in to protect his disciple, but judging from how he indirectly protected Nuwa, it's very likely. Thus, our greatest chance is striking against Redcloud Ancestor."

The twelve titans looked at one another and unanimously agreed before moving on to the next item on the agenda.

"During this time, the demons have reproduced immensely. It's a good thing for us since we can have a constant supply of food, but if so many demons are born in the land, what about in Thirty-Three Heavens?"

"With Thirty-Three Heavens' abundant essence, the demons born there should be stronger and more numerous," Shebisi said.

Di Jiang nodded. "We need to increase our numbers too. Reality has already proven that giants and humans can birth half-breeds. They aren't as strong as true giants, but they can dramatically increase our strength and population. We should integrate as many humans as possible before the time limit set by Hongjun is up."

"Could this be Nuwa's trap?" Jiuyin asked.

"Even if it is, do you have any suggestions to increase the population in a short amount of time?" At Di Jiang's question, Jiuyin fell silent. "I'm not saying we should trust humans. Execute them if you see them do anything suspicious. We just need their reproductive ability. Treat them as livestock if you wish."

"Wouldn't that be too much?" Houtu asked. "They still give birth to the demigiants. If we indiscriminately kill them, wouldn't it breed resentment from the demigiants? They are half human after all."

The twelve titans looked at one another and laughed. "They are just weak bugs. Why do you care for them so much?"

"Little Sister," Di Jiang chided. "You're just too kind. Who cares about them? Between the humans and us, naturally, the giants will be more inclined toward us. You worry too much."

Houtu bit back her words and sighed, faltering against their arrogance.

"We'll move on to the next issue," Di Jiang said. "During this period of peace, four giants have reached the Peak Great Firmament Realm in strength. We should teach the method to break through to the Quasi-Saint Realm in preparation. Any objections?"

Hearing none, Di Jiang ordered the four giants to enter. They were Houyi and Chiyou from the Houtu Tribe; Kuafu from the Tianwu Tribe; and the newest addition, Xingtian from Rushou Tribe.

* * *

Almost every creature had started migrating toward Kunlun Mountain in hopes of becoming one of Yuanshi's apprentices, forming an unnaturally peaceful state. In this time, Redcloud Ancestor traveled far across the Great Desolation. He even mingled with a few humans around the world who remembered him in tales told for generations.

He had just crossed the border between the East and the North when he suddenly felt a sense of crisis. Without hesitation, he summoned the Qiankun Map, and a painting of the world appeared above him just in time to block a golden spear.

"Daoist Jinchi?" Redcloud Ancestor guessed.

The Golden-Winged Great Roc snorted and waved his sleeve as he brandished the golden spear in hand. "Redcloud, hand over the Grandmist Violet Qi and you can leave with your life!"

The number-one nice guy in the Great Desolation, Redcloud Ancestor, finally snarled in anger. "My Grandmist Violet Qi was given to me by the Dao Ancestor. What does it have to do with you?"

Jinchi snorted. "If it hadn't been for you, Zhunti wouldn't have pushed me off my seat. Your actions caused me to lose my chance to become a Saint. It's only natural that you repay this cause!"

"Why don't you go look for Jieyin and Zhunti to settle the grievances? I'm sure they would compensate you," Redcloud Ancestor said as he dodged Jinchi's spear strike.

"Are you acting or really that dumb?" Jinchi asked. "If Jieyin and Zhunti were really reasonable, would they have stolen my seat? And even if they do compensate me, can it compare to being a Saint?"

Redcloud Ancestor stayed silent as he used the Qiankun Map to block Jinchi's attack once more.

"Hahaha, you know it yourself that it's impossible. Since you caused me to lose my chance at Sainthood, fork over the Grandmist Violet Qi or die!"

Redcloud Ancestor grunted and blocked Jinchi's attack again. "Once I become a Saint, I'll help you become a Saint. Believe me!"

Jinchi sneered. A green glow covered his body as he split into two identical copies. One charged at Redcloud Ancestor from the front, forcing him to block, while the other appeared behind him, spear poised to impale him.

As the golden spear burst out of Redcloud Ancestor's chest, his figure turned red and dispersed into clouds. The clouds drifted far away and reformed into Redcloud Ancestor. He clutched his chest where the spear had pierced him with a pale face.

Jinchi snorted as both his copies floated next to each other, brandishing his spears. On each speartip, wind gathered and created a whirlwind. The two copies pincered Redcloud Ancestor again, one from the front and one from the back.

"You forced me!" Redcloud Ancestor expanded the Qiankun Map and overlaid the painting with reality, causing the two copies of Jinchi to halt. He took this chance to distance himself and remove a red gourd from his waist.

He uncorked the red gourd, and silver shards exploded out of the opening, raining down on both Jinchis and causing one to dissipate into green wind while the other's face paled. Although not a hair was out of place on Jinchi's head, he clutched his head and groaned.

"What did you do?!" he roared.

"This is the Nine-Nine Soulscatter Gourd," Redcloud Ancestor said. "Anyone who is hit by it will have their spirit and soul damaged. Daoist Jinchi, if you leave now, I can pretend none of this happened!"

Jinchi growled as he removed his hand and grabbed the spear's shaft. "Do you think I'll give up so easily? All under Saints are ants, and I'm not willing to be an ant!"

"Good words. Unfortunately, you are too useless!"

Both men's expressions changed when they heard a third person's voice. They turned to see another congenital god flying toward them, followed by several others. About a dozen of these congenital gods exuded the auras of Quasi-Saints, while over a hundred Golden Immortals of the Great Firmaments eyed Redcloud Ancestor with desire.

"Taichu Ancestor?" Redcloud Ancestor asked, stunned. He remembered him; they had been bosom friends. Not as close as he and Zheng Yuanzi, but they had faced life and death together. "Why?"

Taichu Ancestor glanced at his old friend coldly. "Don't blame me, I also don't want to become an ant. If you hand over the Grandmist Violet Qi, I can guarantee your life and compensate you."

Redcloud Ancestor laughed. So that was the case. They wanted the Grandmist Violet Qi in his possession, and for it, they would forget their camaraderie built over eons. A steely glint entered his eyes. He yelled, "If you want it, you'll have to kill me!"

Taichu Ancestor didn't hesitate and drew a flying sword. Under his manipulation, it shot out at Redcloud Ancestor. He wasn't the only one, as all the other Quasi-Saints also attacked with their own methods.

Redcloud Ancestor condensed the Qiankun Map in front of him as a shield to block all the attacks, but the spiritual artifact couldn't hold. It crashed into him and sent him flying back. The blood he spat out matched the red of his eyes as he glared at his assailants.

"Since you want to stop me from achieving Sainthood, don't blame me for being ruthless!"

Red clouds manifested around him, permeating the air. Jinchi frowned and immediately used the Law of Wind he had partially comprehended to blow away the red clouds near him, but it was no use.

"Red Cloud Formation, rise!"

Instantly, a massive corrosive cloud encased everyone. Most of the Quasi-Saints snorted and covered their bodies in qi, and the Golden Immortals of Great Firmament struggled to do the same. Rather than an offensive formation, the Red Cloud Formation was closer to a defensive and trapping formation, but that would soon change.

In the center of the formation, Redcloud Ancestor stimulated the Nine-Nine Soulscatter Gourd. Silver shards shot out into the air before raining down back into the Red Cloud Formation, dyeing the shards red.

"Nine-Nine Cloudscattering Formation, activate!" Redcloud Ancestor shouted.

Those within the formation felt a sudden burst of dizziness. Jinchi, who was most familiar with the sensation, covered himself in a whirlwind that scattered the red clouds and shards. Everyone else suffered as their spirits began splitting under the assault of the formation, and the Golden Immortals of the Great Firmament dropped like flies. Their bodies were intact, but their spirits and souls had been destroyed.

Redcloud Ancestor continued his attack on the Quasi-Saints inside, increasing the intensity. He wanted to deal with them as fast as possible. His qi was dwindling, and even the Nine-Nine Scoulscatter Gourd weakened under the constant pressure.

Formations were more mobile than arrays, but they had a critical weakness that arrays did not possess. Formations drew energy from the caster and their components, not the environment, weakening them and shortening their duration.

Redcloud Ancestor frowned as he calculated that his formation would not be enough to kill all the Quasi-Saints before it disappeared. A hint of ruthlessness flashed in his eyes.

Shielded in his whirlwind, Jinchi sensed the soul aspect of the formation weakening. His eyes brightened as he saw the formation itself falling apart. Soon, the clouds dissipated, revealing Redcloud Ancestor panting midair as he glared venomously at Jinchi and the six surviving Quasi-Saints.

Jinchi snorted and charged at him. Taichu Ancestor and the other Quasi-Saints cursed as they followed after the Golden-Winged Great Roc.

Redcloud Ancestor tried to dodge the spear thrusts, and he did, but only the first few times. The sixth strike pierced his chest, but to Jinchi's confusion, Redcloud Ancestor grabbed the spear shaft and flashed an ominous smile.

He glanced at the approaching Quasi-Saint and asked, "Jinchi, aren't you wondering why my Qiankun Map isn't here?"

As soon as Jinchi heard this, he realized something was wrong. He tried to retreat, but Redcloud Ancestor's grip prevented him from fleeing.

"Jinchi! You and everyone who covets my Grandmist Violet Qi will die!"

A bright red light erupted from Redcloud Ancestor's chest, and a massive explosion engulfed Jinchi and the six Quasi-Saints who had also sensed something wrong but were too close to make a break for it.

* * *

Over 10,000 li away, Redcloud Ancestor crashed into the earth as he felt his Corpse self-detonate. He grabbed his chest as his aura plummeted and his cultivation base threatened to drop to the Great Firmament Realm.

He gasped for breath as he tried to stabilize his realm. The moment his cultivation seemed to stabilize, Redcloud Ancestor flew off. He needed to return to Longevity Mountain and recuperate. Firesource Grotto wasn't safe enough, and if Zhen Yuanzi also coveted the Grandmist Violet Qi, then he could only accept his fate.

But before Redcloud Ancestor could make it far, a green-robed figure stopped him. He had gloomy eyes, a hooked nose, and a sharp chin.

"Daoist Kunpeng," Redcloud Ancestor said through gritted teeth.

"Redcloud, hand over the Grandmist Violet Qi." .

"Even you want it, huh?" Redcloud Ancestor asked, defeat leaking from every word.

From afar, a sea of blood appeared on the horizon as Minghe arrived. "Not just him, but me. No one is willing to be an ant."

Facing Kunpeng and Minghe, Redcloud Ancestor almost went crazy. He had already detonated his Corpse, yet he still couldn't escape calamity. His eyes blazed as he enacted his last-ditch attempt. A strand of purple qi appeared in his hand. "You both want it, but who should I hand it to?"

Both Kunpeng and Minghe didn't bother responding and attacked Redcloud Ancestor. They had never thought of letting him live in the first place. However, before either could reach him, five lights corresponding to the five elements struck them, forcing them to defend.

"WHO?!" Kunpeng yelled as he looked toward the source of the attack.

Standing in the air was a blue-robed man holding a five-colored fan in his hand. Behind him, a gold-robed man made a sorry sight with burns and dried blood all over him.

"Kong Xuan, Jinchi," Redcloud Ancestor greeted dully.

Kunpeng glared hatefully at Kong Xuan. If Kong Xuan hadn't used underhanded means to allow Jinchi to sit on the fifth prayer mat, that seat would have been his! He wouldn't have given it up like that idiot, either.

While the three sides entered a stalemate with the Grandmist Violet Qi as the prize, to Redcloud Ancestor's horror, a fourth party entered the fray.

"Hey, this is quite the exciting lineup. Why don't you allow me to join?"

Redcloud Ancestor turned his head to the newcomer. His voice had become devoid of any hope as he identified the newcomer. "Daoist Tongtian."

CHAPTER 45

Black Lotus of Destruction

Upon Tongtian's arrival, Minghe, Kunpeng, and Jinchi glanced at each other with the intent to team up. Only Kong Xuan ignored her and continued staring at Redcloud Ancestor impassively.

"Daoist Tongtian, why are you here?" Minghe tentatively asked. "You already have one strand of Grandmist Violet Qi, you don't need two."

Tongtian nodded. "You're right."

Minghe inwardly sighed in relief, but her next words made him realize he had relaxed too soon.

"But I owe Daoist Redcloud a debt," Tongtian said. "He once saved my life, isn't it only natural I should save his?"

"Is it enough for you to go against all of us?" Kungpeng asked. There was a sharp glint in his eyes as his aura rose.

Tongtian smiled, but it did not reach her eyes. Her aura exploded out of her, so sharp that everyone in the vicinity felt the sting of phantom blades flying past them. "Are you, an intermediate Quasi-Saint, threatening me, a peak Quasi-Saint?"

Kunpeng stayed silent, but Minghe brazenly answered, "Then I can only offend Daoist Tongtian."

The bloody sea behind Minghe rose and rushed forward like a

tsunami, intent on drowning Tongtian and Redcloud Ancestor. Kunpeng, Jinchi, and Kong Xuan flew back to avoid the blood wave.

Tongtian flew in front of Redcloud Ancestor, blocking him with her body. She didn't draw her Qingping Sword. Instead, she formed a sword finger and slashed down.

A crescent-shaped sword light shot forward, splitting heaven and earth. When the sword light met the tsunami, it parted like the red sea.

Minghe frowned as he tried to merge the blood sea back together, but to his shock, the area from Tongtian to Redcloud had disappeared from within the two halves of the blood sea. He still felt that the blood sea was connected and had never been split, but that was impossible.

Seeing an opportunity, Kunpeng's eyes shone as he charged toward Redcloud Ancestor. When he moved, his body teleported past Redcloud Ancestor and crashed into the ground. He frowned, flew back into the air, and saw Tongtian's impish smile.

He scowled. A massive phantom depicting a giant, scaled kun fish appeared behind him. The thousand-li fish opened its mouth and began swallowing everything in front of it. The kun fish sucked up all of the surrounding dirt, rocks, trees, air, blood, essence, and even qi.

The Law of Devouring? Tongtian thought as her robes billowed from the suction. The spatial barrier dissipated as the qi maintaining it faded, and she saw Redcloud Ancestor's face pale even more as qi left his body.

Tongtian unleashed another sword light. The attack pierced the phantom kun fish, shattering it to pieces. Kunpeng looked like something inside him shattered along with it. She wanted to take this chance to get rid of him, but she had to move out of the way as the blood sea rushed toward her.

As Tongtian battled the combined might of Minghe and Kunpeng, Jinchi couldn't help but worry. His figure turned into a green-gold blur and hurtled toward Redcloud Ancestor, but before it could reach the injured god, a sword light repelled him.

Holding back the blood threatening to spill out of his mouth, Jinchi glanced at his brother anxiously.

Kong Xuan spared him a glance and sneered. "Now you know regret?"

"Yes, yes!" Jinchi said. "I've known regret since the third sermon. Brother, please grab the Grandmist Violet Qi for me."

"Aren't you afraid of me grabbing it for myself?"

Jinchi froze. The thought had never occurred to him. Although Kong Xuan was his older brother, Jinchi had treated him akin to how a human child treated their father. "If Brother keeps it, it's better than giving it to outsiders!"

Kong Xuan nodded in satisfaction. "Now's not the time. If we take action now, we'd only exhaust ourselves." He glanced at an empty area. "In addition, there's more than us waiting for a chance."

* * *

Tongtian's forefinger slashed horizontally, beheading Minghe. His body turned red and dissolved into a pile of blood that merged with the rest of the blood sea.

She turned around to see over a hundred copies of Minghe surrounding her. Only ten had the strength of a Golden Immortal of Great Firmament, while the rest only had the strength of a Golden Immortal of the Great Unity.

Suddenly, a figure charged out of the blood sea beneath her. It was Minghe, sitting atop the Twelfth-Ranked Red Lotus of Karma with the Yuanti and Abi Swords circling him.

A sword with vine etchings on its blade and green hilt appeared in Tongtian's hand. She used the top-grade innate spiritual artifact, the

Seven-Gourd Sword, to repel Minghe; sending him flying into the distance.

Kunpeng suddenly appeared behind her with his fingers transforming into talons aimed at her back. The front half of the Seven-Gourd Sword became fiery hot, while the back half became chilling cold. Tongtian turned around and slashed the sword into Kunpeng's claws, also repelling him and leaving his hand in tatters.

Tongtian appeared in front of Redcloud Ancestor again and smiled playfully at her foes. "Do you have any other tricks you want to pull out?"

After a moment of silence, the blood sea surged and transformed into even more bloodgod incarnations of Minghe. "Taste my Blood God Formation!"

The bloodgods took on a red glow that connected each of them, and a massive formation shrouded the entire area. Within the formation, Tongtian felt her blood quite literally boil. She looked at her hand to see it turning a shade of red like a cooked lobster, but instead of panicking, she smiled.

She formed a barrier around Redcloud Ancestor to prevent the formation from affecting him. Then, ten bloodgods charged at Tongtian, but she deflected them all. She raised an eyebrow when she felt that each one of them had displayed power equal to an early Quasi-Saint.

While Tongtian fended off the bloodgods rushing them, the essence she'd formed from merging Di Jiang's and Jiuyin's blood essences circulated, integrating with her body. Her bodily strength increased from an early Quasi-Saint's to an intermediate Quasi-Saint's.

When she felt that the silver-gold blood essence of spacetime could no longer improve her body, the Seven-Gourd Sword disappeared in her hand, and a white gourd appeared. Tongtian uncorked it, and a white liquid poured out.

The liquid metal qi split into over a hundred branching lines and formed a giant formation. The lines eviscerated any bloodgod incarnation in their way, and from within the Blood God Formation, silver-white light radiated out.

Tongtian hadn't refined the white gourd into the Immortal Beheading Flying Blade, but a formation artifact. As long as the essence within the gourd did not run out, it could form the Immortal Beheading Formation without its master using any of her qi.

With a thunderous explosion, the Blood God Formation collapsed back into the blood sea. This time, the sea lost much of its vibrancy as most of it soaked into the ground.

Minghe stared at Tongtian in disbelief as he retreated. He couldn't believe that she could destroy his formation so quickly. Unbeknownst to him, he had chosen to use his formation on the wrong Purity. It would not have fared so horribly if it had been used on Laozi or Yuanshi before his consecration.

Tongtian looked up as a giant shadow shrouded her. A giant peng bird was swooping down on her with its talons aimed at Redcloud Ancestor behind her. The Immortal Beheading Formation formed several layers of protection, but they shattered like glass under Kunpeng's assault, managing only to slow him down.

She allowed the white gourd to float near her as the Seven-Gourd Sword appeared in her hand. The blade took on a haunting silver glow, much like the silver shards from Redcloud Ancestor's Nine-Nine Soulscatter Gourd.

Kunpeng's talons clashed against the Seven-Gourd Sword, and Tongtian found herself taking a few steps back in the air, surprised by the strength of Kunpeng's body. After that brief clash, Kunpeng immediately flew away before the Immortal Beheading Formation could trap him. He shivered as he stared at Tongtian's sword. His soul had trembled at the moment of the clash, and he knew ten more would irreparably mar his soul.

Seeing both Minghe and Kungpeng cowed by her strength, Tongtian swung her attention to Kong Xuan and Jinchi. Jinchi was still in the early Quasi-Saint Realm, but Kong Xuan had wordlessly reached the Advanced Quasi-Saint Realm.

"Aren't you going to join?" she goaded. "You might actually stand a chance at grabbing Daoist Redcloud's Grandmist Violet Qi if you do."

The corner of Redcloud Ancestor's eyes twitched uncontrollably. It was fine if Tongtian played around, but his life and future were on the line. However, since he was so injured and could only rely on Tongtian, he had no rights to speak of.

"Before we fight, how about a trade?" Kong Xuan asked, shocking everyone present, including Tongtian.

Wondering what game the peacock was playing, she replied, "Oh, and what are the terms?"

A nine-petaled black lotus appeared in Kong Xuan's hand. "This Ninth-Ranked Black Lotus of Destruction for your Apricot Flag of Central Infinity."

Tongtian narrowed her eyes. "I can refine that into a high-grade innate spiritual artifact at most, and you want to trade that for a complete high-grade innate spiritual artifact? Do you think I'm stupid?"

"You're right," he admitted, nodding. The nine-petaled black lotus disappeared, and in its place was the Twelfth-Ranked Black Lotus of Destruction! However, it had numerous cracks on it, and the spiritual light around it flickered. "What about this Twelfth-Ranked Black Lotus of Destruction? It's damaged, but if you managed to fix it, it's not impossible to restore it to the power of a top-grade cardinal spiritual artifact."

Kunpeng and Minghe had to stop themselves from reaching for the artifact. They had their eyes on the prize: the Grandmist Violet Qi. Even if the Twelfth-Ranked Black Lotus of Destruction was amazing, was it more important than the chance to become a Saint?

Jinchi looked at Kong Xuan in surprise. His brother had given him the Ninth-Ranked Black Lotus of Destruction to sever his first Corpse. He had wanted to use it again to sever his second and third Corpses, but Kong Xuan had stopped him, saying there would be something better.

"Alright," Tongtian said as a yellow flag appeared in front of her.

The Apricot Flag of Central Infinity flew toward Kong Xuan, and the Twelfth-Ranked Black Lotus of Destruction flew toward Tongtian. No one moved, and time seemed to still as the two treasures passed each other.

Everyone seemed to have released a sigh of relief when they reached their new owners' hands unimpeded. The moment Tongtian touched the Twelfth-Ranked Black Lotus of Destruction, her eyes dimmed.

Kong Xuan stored the Apricot Flag of Central Affinity and waved his fan. The lines of light correlating to the five elements burst out and attacked the Immortal Beheading Formation, forming a mysterious pattern. Although the Immortal Beheading Formation did not need Tongtian's control to operate, it could not reach its full potential without her.

In seconds, it started to crack, and Redcloud Ancestor looked at Tongtian in worry. He said her name like a plea.

Tongtian's eyes regained their brightness as cold sweat coated her back. She quickly stored the Twelfth-Ranked Black Lotus of Destruction and Seven-Gourd Sword. She grabbed the Immortal Beheading Formation Gourd and sucked all the metal essence back in.

With her mastery of formations, she had discerned that Kong Xuan's Five Elements Line Formation was a level above her Immortal Beheading Formation. It may have been inferior in terms of offense, but it was too perfect.

The Immortal Beheading Formation relied on the Law of Metal Tongtian comprehended while studying the sword, but Kong Xuan's Five Elements Line Formation had all five elements instead of just metal. Besides, the five elements together were far greater than the sum of their parts.

Tongtian waved her hand, and 10,000 swords appeared. "Arise, Myriad Sword Formation!"

Under her control, they formed four layers of circling blades. The first layer had ten swords, the second layer had ninety, the third layer had 900, and the fourth layer had 9,000.

When the Myriad Sword Formation and Five Elements Line Formation clashed, the surrounding space was destroyed. It even seemed to collapse in on itself where the two met.

"Amazing," Tongtian said. "If I wasn't at the Peak Quasi-Saint Realm, I'd have no guarantee of suppressing your formation. If you claim number two in formation mastery, only I would exceed you."

Kong Xuan said nothing as he waved his fan and increased the power of his formation, but so did Tongtian. The clash between the two formations maintained output only a peak Quasi-Saint could unleash for an instant.

As the battle raged on, Kong Xuan frowned. Ultimately, he was still at the Advanced Quasi-Saint Realm. Tongtian was at the peak of the Quasi-Saint Realm, meaning that her qi reserves surpassed his. His eyes hardened as a plain black spear appeared in his hand.

He controlled his Five Elements Line Formation to overlap with Tongtian's, causing both formations to come to a halt as he thrust his spearhead at Tongtian.

Tongtian's eyes turned serious as she felt the endless murderous aura rolling off the spear. She grabbed the handle of her Qingping Sword, but before Kong Xuan could reach her, he retreated as a bronze bell passed where he had been.

Both Tongtian and Kong Xuan turned to face the intervener.

"Eastern Emperor Taiyi."

CHAPTER 46

New and Old Enmities

The Chaos Bell flew to rest behind Taiyi. He glanced quickly at Kong Xuan before turning his attention to Redcloud Ancestor.

"Even Heavenly Court wants my Grandmist Violet Qi?" Redcloud Ancestor helplessly asked.

"Daoist Redcloud, did you forget how you came into possession of that gourd?" Taiyi demanded. "We asked you to become one of the four demon emperors, but you rejected us. Now, it's time to pay back your debt."

Redcloud Ancestor opened his mouth but shut it. He knew that it was useless. Heavenly Court had just found a reason so that they could steal his Grandmist Violet Qi in a righteous manner.

"That's good and all, but that is not your decision whether you can take Redcloud's Grandmist Violet Qi or not," Tongtian said, blocking Taiyi's line of sight.

"Daoist Tongtian, this has nothing to do with you. Leave; I don't want to hurt you," Taiyi said.

Tongtian laughed. It was a beautiful laughter like bell chimes, but anyone who heard would feel a chill in their hearts. The Qingping Sword left its sheathe with an audible sharpness.

"Die."

Tongtian thrust the Qingping Sword forward. The space in front of her twisted and shattered, and she moved like she'd teleported in front of Taiyi. Taiyi felt as if an invisible force was pulling his body toward the sword tip, and there was nothing he could do to escape.

Gong!

The Qingping Sword struck the Chaos Bell, shattering the surrounding space like a popped bubble and sending the Chaos Bell crashing into Taiyi. After being sent over a li away, he managed to stabilize himself, but a trail of blood leaked down his lips.

In a burst of flames, Taiyi flew back toward Tongtian. Unwillingness and a sense of loss lingered in his eyes, but those emotions quickly disappeared.

Tongtian just rested the Qingping Sword over her shoulder and scanned her surroundings. More and more gods were appearing due to the commotion caused by the constant battles, and she even recognized an old acquaintance—Qiankun Ancestor.

"You leave me no choice," Taiyi said as he sent the Chaos Bell crashing toward her.

It acted as a signal for everyone to attack. Kong Xuan and Jinchi charged forward with spears in hand. Minghe sent his Yuanti and Abi Swords flying out at Tongtian, and Kunpeng unleashed a piercing shriek in his true form and dove talons-first.

Tongtian brandished her sword as she focused on the Chaos Bell. Despite how easily she had sent Taiyi flying earlier, that attack had used all her qi and understanding of the Law of Space, yet it resulted in Taiyi leaking only a little blood.

She could use the Law of Time, but trump cards only worked because no one knew about them.

However, as the Chaos Bell neared her, Tongtian sighed and lost interest. Her sword pierced a path to the black spear in Kong Xuan's hand.

Sword tip met spear head, and the world lost color for an instant. Both were sent flying back into the distance, Kong Xuan more so than Tongtian.

Kunpeng's eyes lit up with glee as his claws inched closer to Redcloud Ancestor. Red clouds emerged and formed a barrier, which Kunpeng easily destroyed. Suddenly, warning bells went off in his head as he turned to see the Chaos Bell crashing into him. He didn't have time to dodge and was sent flying with heavy injuries.

Jinchi was the next to arrive, his gold spear directed at Redcloud Ancestor. Redcloud Ancestor gritted his teeth as the spear pierced his shoulder. His body transformed into red clouds and flew away but was blocked by a wall of blood.

The red clouds reformed into Redcloud Ancestor, clutching his bleeding shoulder. Hatred spewed forth as he glared at Minghe. Then, Tongtian appeared in front of her ally out of thin air, swinging her sword.

Sword light erupted, vaporizing 80 percent of Minghe's blood sea. Tongtian didn't press the attack but instead observed her surroundings. Taiyi was still flying in the sky; Kong Xuan had returned; Kunpeng, Minghe, and Jinchi had returned to their original positions; and many factionless immortals were being drawn toward the commotion.

"Haha, such an exciting battle, and you didn't invite us?"

Tongtian sighed and turned toward the source of the sound, where she saw six of the twelve titans. Zhurong had spoken first, but Di Jiang led the group. Alongside them were Jumang, Xuanming, Qiangliang, and Shebisi.

"Tongtian, hand over Redcloud, or don't blame us for being impolite," Di Jiang ordered.

"Geez, you really burned the bridge after all the partnership we had," Tongtian joked. "Well, I can see that I'm unwanted. Redcloud and I will leave now."

Di Jiang felt the spatial fluctuations and stretched his hands to stop Tongtian, activating his ability in the process. "Stop her!"

Unfortunately for him, a titan's ability was more short-ranged and relied on the body, so he could do nothing as he watched Tongtian grab Redcloud Ancestor and disappear. The air swallowed their bodies, akin to them disappearing under waves of water.

When they left, the atmosphere turned sullen and tense. Di Jiang gritted his teeth and glared hatefully at where Tongtian had been. He focused his eyes on Taiyi, not bothering to mask his killing intent.

Taiyi glared back, his expression equally as ugly. The demons that had been hiding appeared one after the other behind Taiyi. He had brought half of the Ten Demon Sages, equalizing the force between him and the titans.

Kunpeng took this chance to escape into the distance, likely to chase after Tongtian or heal his injuries. Taiyi glanced at him but did not give chase.

Minghe also flew off with his treasures and blood sea. Kong Xuan and Jinchi did the same, as did all the spectators hoping to get lucky during the clash between Tongtian and Redcloud against everyone else. This left only the members of Heavenly Court and the Titan Tribe.

Just as it seemed the third battle between Heavenly Court and the Titan Tribe would erupt, Di Jiang raised his arm and motioned the titans to return.

"But," Zhurong started to object, but Di Jiang cut him off.

"If we start the third battle, then Hongjun might directly kill us."

"I'm not afraid of the Dao Ancestor. If he wants to fight, let's fight!"

"Stupid! Even after we get the new Titanomachy Flags from Yuanshi, it still isn't enough to fight Hongjun. He can take the third ax strike without any effort, so we'd only lose. I don't fear losing, but if we are all killed, what about the tribe?"

Confounded by Di Jiang's logic, Zhurong gritted his teeth and grumbled but did not argue. He quietly followed after the rest of the titans, but not before giving Taiyi one last provocative glare.

Taiyi only snorted and ordered the demon clan to retreat. Before returning to Thirty-Three Heaven, Taiyi glanced toward where Kunpeng had fled.

* * *

While Minghe was flying back to the Blood Sea to replenish the blood he'd lost battling Tongtian, a green-gold wind sped ahead of him. It stopped right in front of him to reveal Kong Xuan and Jinchi.

Minghe furrowed his brows. "What are Daoists Kong Xuan and Jinchi blocking my way for?"

"It's nothing," Kong Xuan said. "I traded my Twelfth-Ranked Black Lotus of Destruction to Daoist Tongtian, so I need a replacement."

Minghe's expression immediately turned sullen. He wordlessly used the remaining blood sea that he carried with him to transform into bloodgod incarnations and set up the Blood God Formation.

Kong Xuan snorted. "If you still had the whole sea of blood you began with, I might have had some trouble, but you don't."

He waved the Five Elements Fan in his hand, and five rays of light shot out, mingling together to form the Five Elements Line Formation. It trapped Minghe's formation within and used the five elements to deconstruct the Blood God Formation like a millstone.

Within the Blood God Formation, Minghe struggled like crazy. With each passing second, his formation weakened as the blood rapidly evaporated under Kong Xuan's Five Elements Line Formation. Finally, the formation could not be sustained any longer and completely collapsed.

He glared at Kong Xuan and Jinchi as he resisted the Five Elements Line Formation using the Twelfth-Ranked Red Lotus of Karma. "Kong Xuan, I won't forgive you!"

"Say all you want, but your end is still the same," Kong Xuan said. His attack was weak enough that Minghe could resist, but it would drain his qi reserves rapidly. After all, his goal was to take the red lotus, not destroy it.

"Haha, don't you know? I am eternal as long as the Blood Sea does not dry!" Minghe shouted. "Do you really want me to scheme against you from now on?"

"I already attacked, do you think I don't know that you would seek revenge even if I let you go?" Kong Xuan asked. "Furthermore, you're weaker than me. Without your Twelfth-Ranked Red Lotus of Karma and Yuanti and Abi Swords, you are nothing to me!"

"If I can't have it, no one can!"

Kong Xuan's eyes turned ruthless as he appeared in front of Minghe. A black spear materialized in his hand and pierced through the Twelfth-Ranked Red Lotus of Karma's defenses straight through Minghe's head. Minghe's body dissolved into blood and fell onto the ground, soaking into the dirt.

The Twelfth-Ranked Red Lotus of Karma's light flickered, obviously damaged by Kong Xuan's attack. It and the Yuanti and Abi Swords tried to fly to the Blood Sea, but Kong Xuan captured them. He gave the swords to Jinchi and started to refine the lotus.

"Once I nurture the Twelfth-Ranked Red Lotus of Karma back to its peak condition, I'll give you red lotus seed to cut off your second Corpse," Kong Xuan said.

"Thank you, brother," Jinchi happily replied as he followed him back to the South.

Far away in the Blood Sea, a figure emerged. It was Minghe!

He had an ugly expression as he glared in the direction of his killer. "Kong Xuan, Jinchi, this isn't over! Not by a long shot!"

Minghe flew back to Crimsonsap Palace. Inside, he saw his three Corpses. He could reform his original body anytime, but his Corpses were another story, so he always left them in the safety of the Blood Sea. He sat down and began to raise the bloodgod incarnation he had taken over to his previous power.

* * *

Kunpeng grunted as he suppressed the injury threatening to burst in his body. After fleeing a certain distance, he transformed back into a humanoid form. His eyes flashed with hatred as he recalled how Taiyi had sneak attacked him. It was as if he had been Taiyi's target all along!

He paused when he saw a figure wearing a yellow robe embroidered with nine dragons, each with nine claws on each hand, blocking his path. "Daoist Di Jun, why are you here?"

Di Jun smiled, but it had no warmth. "Don't you already know? You rejected Heavenly Court's invitation and established a demon clan in the North. Aren't you splitting the Demon Clan's power and affecting our ability to fight the Titan Tribe?"

"Why would the Darknorth Demon Clan fight the Titan Tribe? This is the Heavenly Court's duty; we have nothing to do with the battle," Kunpeng said. He tried to flee, but Di Jun blocked him again.

"Defeating the Titan Tribe is the duty of all demons, including you." An orange banner appeared in Di Jun's hand. "Now, you have two options, either place a strand of your truesoul into the Demon-Summoning Banner or die."

"Di Jun!" Kunpeng roared. "Aren't you afraid of people calling you a tyrant, forcing others to place their truesouls into the Demon-Summoning Banner and holding their lives in your hand?"

Di Jun smiled. "Since you've chosen death, don't blame Us. And you don't need to worry about tarnishing Our reputation. With how injured you are, it wouldn't be a surprise if you got ambushed by some sinister rogue, dying in the process."

Kunpeng roared as 3,000 characters wrapped around him. It was the Three Thousand Demon Script. Not only did it have a stalwart defense, but it was most effective against other demons!

Di Jun snorted. "It may merely suppress others, but have you forgotten who We are? We are Di Jun, the Heavenly Emperor, and ruler of all demons!"

The Three Thousand Demon Script quivered and cowered in front of the Heavenly Emperor's presence. Kunpeng wanted to cry; his trump card had turned out to be useless. Still, he didn't give up, attempting to flee once more.

"You think We will let you escape?!" Di Jun roared as he used the Celestial River Diagram to smash Kunpeng into the ground. Blood continuously leaked from his mouth as his new and old injuries from Taiyi erupted simultaneously.

"Wait, wait!" Kunpeng begged as the Heavenly Emperor neared. "I'm willing to serve you!"

Di Jun waved the Demon-Summoning Banner, and Kunpeng hesitated. Seeing the increased killing intent in Di Jun's eyes, he could only place a strand of his truesoul into the Demon-Summoning Banner with a bitter smile. He'd have a chance of revival if he died, but at a heavy cost. There was no free lunch in the world, and Kunpeng couldn't trust Di Jun to revive him if he were to die.

"If you only knew when to surrender, it would have never come to this," Di Jun said. He ordered Kunpeng to take him to Darknorth Palace and subjugate the Darknorth Demon Clan.

During this process, the hatred in Kunpeng's eyes increased as he watched Di Jun take everything that was once his.

One day, one day, he would get his revenge!

Chapter 47

The Twelve Golden Immortals

Over 10,000 li away from the battle, Tongtian and Redcloud Ancestor reappeared. Tongtian released a breath as she felt the consumption of her qi. Teleporting herself while carrying Redcloud Ancestor required ten times more qi than when she was by herself.

"Daoist Redcloud, how are... you?" Tongtian turned around to ask and stopped.

Redcloud Ancestor was floating in the air with his eyes closed. His aura, which almost dropped to the same level as a Golden Immortal of the Great Firmament, suddenly stabilized and even showed signs of returning to its peak—no, not returning but surpassing.

Redcloud Ancestor snapped his eyes open and shouted.

"Sever!"

"SEVER!!"

"SEVER!!!"

Redcloud Ancestor's words echoed over 10,000 li as his aura shot up, soon reaching 60,000 li. Simultaneously, a figure emerged out of his body bearing the exact same features as Redcloud Ancestor, except without a trace of emotion on his face.

"Wuqing greets the main body," Redcloud Ancestor's Obsession Corpse said as he saluted.

"That's good and all, but quickly store him right now," Tongtian said, face palming. "Congratulations on severing your Corpse and improving your cultivation, but you just attracted everyone. We're going to have to run again."

Redcloud Ancestor smiled sheepishly as he quickly stored his Obsession Corpse. Once again, he and Tongtian teleported away before anyone could reach them.

When they reappeared, Tongtian asked, "Where do you plan on going? Do you want to come to Kunlun Mountain?"

He shook his head. "Daoist Tongtian has already saved my life, it's more than enough. I don't want to impose on you any more than this."

"If you are sure," Tongtian said as she disappeared. She still had to visit another acquaintance she'd met at the same time as Redcloud Ancestor.

Alone once more, he sighed. He felt as if the mist blocking his view had been lifted, and he could see a clear path to sainthood. Even the Grandmist Violet Qi felt more intimate.

The only problem was that he risked falling into the Early Quasi-Saint Realm again. He had to recondense his Evil Corpse as soon as possible.

Redcloud Ancestor drifted to the sky and turned into white clouds. His abode, the Firesource Grotto, was no longer safe. He couldn't defend against the throngs of people looking for the Grandmist Violet Qi with it.

This also left out Longevity Mountain. He didn't want to burden Tongtian and the remaining Three Purities on Kunlun Mountain, much less his bosom friend. Even if the Ginseng Fruit Tree could hasten his recovery, Redcloud Ancestor did not want to put Zhen Yuanzi in danger.

Out of everyone, the one with the greatest opportunity to kill him and take his Grandmist Violet Qi was Zhen Yuanzi, yet he never had.

* * *

Qiankun Ancestor soared away disappointed. He had hoped that Tongtian would fall under the siege, but she'd escaped. Although the former fiendgod still couldn't remember that the Qiankun Cauldron had once belonged to him, unexplained hatred burned within him. If he had had the strength to kill Tongtian, he would have done so long ago.

But now, it seemed impossible. With a Saint of Heaven as her brother, who would dare kill her? Defeat her, yes, but kill her? You'd have to have a death wish.

His expression changed when he saw Tongtian appear in front of him.

"We meet again, Qiankun Ancestor." Tongtian smiled brightly, and it was a smile that terrified the former chaos fiendgod to no end. She didn't bother with useless pleasantries, promptly attacking with her sword finger.

He quickly brought out the Qiankun Ruler and slashed forward, clashing against Tongtian's finger. The Qiankun Ruler couldn't break through the sword light shrouding Tongtian's finger, and his whole arm was flung backwards, numb from the force.

As her forefinger flashed at him, Qiankun Ancestor felt his body chill as the fear of death overtook his mind. He used all his abilities to dodge or block approaching death. However, the Law of Qiankun evaded him; he couldn't teleport or even form a barrier as his control over the space around him slipped from his grasp.

The Law of Space was superior to the Law of Qiankun, not to mention Tongtian's mastery of the Law of Space was greater than

Qiankun Ancestor's mastery of the Law of Qiankun. She locked the space, preventing him from escaping.

"Wai—" Qiankun Ancestor never had a chance to finish as Tongtian's finger pierced his head. The light in his eyes faded with the destruction of his soul.

Tongtian took the Qiankun Ruler and whatever other treasures he had stored on him. She watched in dull silence as his body fell to the ground like a meteorite and created a crater. She had expected a grand chase or at least a longer fight, but it ended rather anticlimactically. With a sigh, her figure disappeared into space.

When she neared Kunlun Mountain, she saw a massive crowd outside. With so many people, it only naturally made sense that conflict would start. In such a situation, the empty gaps of space around a few people made them stand out more.

Tongtian's return went unnoticed. The vast majority of them were under the Golden Immortal Realm, and she was a peak Quasi-Saint. Even a Golden Immortal of the Great Firmament couldn't have detected her flying into Kunlun Mountain.

When she entered Three Purity Hall, she saw her brothers already present and waiting. She sat down on her designated prayer mat and greeted them.

"I'm surprised that Eldest Brother isn't in Grand Purity Hall cultivating or concocting pills," Tongtian said.

"How can I miss seeing the first inheritors of the Jade Purity lineage?" Laozi asked.

Tongtian nodded in agreement.

She closed her eyes and waited. There were only a few years left until the end of the 3,000-year time limit, and during this time, neither of her brothers had questioned her disappearance.

When she opened her eyes again, the armistice was up, and it was time for Yuanshi to accept some disciples. Yuanshi waved his hands and opened a hole in the array guarding Kunlun Mountain.

Starting from Three Purity Palace, jade steps formed one by one and descended onto the base of the mountain where Yuanshi had opened the hole.

"All those who can traverse all 3,000 steps within the time limit have the qualifications to become my disciple."

Hearing this, Tongtian couldn't help but tease him. "Qualifications, huh? Not fate?"

"To climb my Jade Enlightenment Steps, they must possess talent, luck, and perseverance. But just because they qualify, why do I have to accept them as disciples?" Yuanshi asked.

Tongtian nodded. Yuanshi was an exalted Saint of Heaven. As long as he asked, 99.9 percent of all life would kneel and accept becoming his disciple.

"Are you interested in accepting a disciple?" Yuanshi asked. "As long as Third Sister asks, I can give anyone who passes my test to you."

Tongtian looked upon the Jade Enlightenment Steps, her eyes piercing through the illusion and mysticism surrounding them. The only one she had an interest in was the immortal wearing gold robes. His true form was that of a yellow dragon, and she really wanted him as a mount, not a disciple.

"Forget it," Tongtian said. "I already have a disciple. I'll give him some more time to grow before accepting more. Won't it be embarrassing if his junior brother surpasses him too much in strength?"

Yuanshi snorted but said nothing. His eyes returned to the cultivators attempting to pass his test. While he was testing them, he was also evaluating their characters.

As the time limit neared, thirteen cultivators successfully passed Yuanshi's Jade Enlightenment Steps. They were:

Guang Chengzi from Peachsource Grotto of Jiuxian Mountain.

Chi Jingzi from Cloudsky Grotto of Taihua Mountain.

Daoist Huanglong from Magu Grotto of Erxian Mountain.

Ju Liusun from Cloudsoar Grotto of Jialong Mountain.

Daoist Taiyi from Goldlight Grotto of Qianyuan Mountain.

Mystic Master Lingbao from Yangsource Grotto of Kongtong Mountain.

Broadart Venerable Manjushri from Skymist Grotto of Wulong Mountain.

Daoist Samantabhadra from Whitecrane Grotto of Jiugong Mountain.

Daoist Cihang from Luojia Grotto of Peach Mountain.

Daoist Yuding from Goldawn Grotto of Jadespring Mountain.

Venerable Daoheart of Jaderoof Grotto of Jinting Mountain.

Virtuous Monarch Qingxu from Violetyang Grotto of Qingfeng Mountain.

The thirteenth was Burning Lamp Daoist, the god who had loitered around Kunlun Mountain ever since the Three Purities had entered the Quasi-Saint Realm. Due to the fall of Violet Manor and the shortage of 3,000 guests, he had gotten the chance to listen to the Dao Ancestor's third sermon, but because of his low realm, he could not gain much from it.

Yuanshi didn't stare at Burning Lamp Daoist. No, he stared at the seventh person who passed his test, Mystic Master Lingbao. The god sweated under Yuanshi's gaze, wondering if he had done something wrong.

"Change it," Yuanshi suddenly said.

"Huh?" Mystic Master Lingbao said.

"Your name is displeasing. Change it immediately," Yuanshi repeated.

Mystic Master Lingbao wanted to ask how it was displeasing. He had been using it since he had transformed, but facing Yuanshi's increasingly threatening look, he surrendered. "Y-y-yes, I'll be called... called Baoling from now on!"

Yuanshi paused and considered it for a moment before nodding. "You can be one of my personal disciples."

Although he had been forced to change his name for unknown reasons, excitement coursed through Mystic Master Baoling after Yuanshi accepted him as a disciple.

Off at the side, the edge of Tongtian's lips twitched. She couldn't help but think that the innocent Mystic Master Baoling had been forced to change his name because of her. In fact, it was exactly as she thought.

After accepting Mystic Master Baoling as his disciple, Yuanshi went ahead and accepted the rest of the first twelve people who passed his test as direct disciples. These twelve would later become the famed Twelve Golden Immortals.

When Yuanshi looked at him, he hesitated. "Burning Lamp Daoist is a fellow guest of Violetheaven Palace. Why must a Golden Immortal of the Great Firmament like you demean yourself to become my disciple?"

Burning Lamp Daoist directly kneeled. "I wholeheartedly seek the Great Dao. For it, there is no demeaning act, only sincerity. I beg Heavenly Venerable to accept me as your disciple."

Yuanshi hesitated a moment but acquiesced in the end. He had seen Burning Lamp Daoist's perseverance. Even before Yuanshi had decided to accept disciples, he'd waited outside for eons, hoping for a chance.

"I cannot accept you as a true disciple. How about this? You can become the vice sect master of the sect I will establish in the future and will share my burden."

"I thank Heavenly Venerable for your grace," Burning Lamp Daoist said.

After accepting the thirteen people in front of him, Yuanshi expelled all the other test-takers out of Kunlun Mountain and sealed the barrier once more. Those expelled were disappointed and tried to re-enter only to discover it was impossible.

One demon suddenly spat on the ground. "A'pei! Do you think you're all that special just because you've become a Saint? Once I find a better master and gain enough strength, I'll make you regret this!"

Many cultivators near him quickly distanced themselves from the demon that cursed Yuanshi, but a few nodded in agreement. When the demon tried to curse again, he discovered that he couldn't move at all. Not just him, but the others who had nodded in agreement or showed similar sentiments also froze.

The onlookers watched in horror as the frozen people disintegrated until nothing was left, not even their clothes or treasures. Everyone else quickly retreated as far as possible as they stared at Kunlun Mountain in horror.

Because of Yuanshi's awe-inspiring display of power, almost everyone left, not wanting to draw his ire. A few persevering people stayed and waited, hoping for Yuanshi or any of the Three Purities to take them as disciples.

"Third Sister, are you interested in accepting a few disciples?" Yuanshi asked.

Stunned by the sudden question, Tongtian looked his way, but she quickly rejected the question. Right now, she only wanted to focus on cultivating. Accepting a disciple could wait until after her Corpse became a Saint of Heaven. She only had one disciple, and she let him have free rein.

Yuanshi didn't force it and brought his new disciples to Jade Purity Hall. There, he taught all of them the Jade Purity Scripture cultivation method. After they learned it, he began to preach to them much as the Dao Ancestor had during the first sermon.

* * *

Far away from Kunlun Mountain and everything that had transpired, Lingbao, Tongtian's Corpse, tunneled to the center of Buzhou Mountain.

After many years of effort, Lingbao finally reached the spiritual vein under Buzhou Mountain, where he saw signs of how prosperous it had once been. He quickly deduced that the spiritual vein should have at least been ten times greater. Lingbao searched until he found where the essence had shifted to. The place with the most potent vein would be the new center of the Great Desolation and where he would plant the Allheaven Jianmu Tree.

Over another 100,000 years of tunneling even deeper under the land, Lingbao finally discovered it. Perhaps to prevent its decline, the new center of the Great Desolation was hidden deep underground.

Lingbao sat in a lotus position above the spiritual vein, waiting for a chance. He took out the Allheaven Jianmu Tree and nurtured it slowly with the vein's essence so as to not harm it. In addition, he used the Karmic Merit he'd gained from becoming Wutian's master to nurture the connate spiritual root. Compared to the snail's pace of progress with the essence of heaven and earth, merit had more effect.

Lingbao requested to use the Heaven-Opening Merit to cultivate the Allheaven Jianmu Tree, but Tongtian vehemently denied his request, so he could only continue slowly nurturing it, hoping Wutian would earn more merits for him.

Chapter 48

Achieving Primordial Origin

At the new headquarters of humanity near the East Sea, Wutian walked through the rows of students practicing their horse stance.

After witnessing the temple at the center of the training ground Wutian had built, Youchao had commented, "If I hadn't constructed the first shelter, the merit would have gone to you." There was no envy in his words, only admiration. Even if Wutian took his place as the third human ancestor, Youchao would have no bitterness because it would mean greater prosperity for humanity.

At this time, negative emotions such as envy, greed, and other desires had not appeared in humanity. They all had to work together to survive in this hazardous world. When did they have the time to scheme and betray one another?

"How can that be? If you hadn't constructed the first building, I would have never been able to think of this," Wutian had said.

As the holy ground of humanity and where all the most remarkable talents gathered, all of them cultivated the martial arts created by Wutian. They could all be considered half-disciples of his. When he was done inspecting his students, Wutian returned to the temple at the center. In the main hall, a statue of Nuwa stood at the center. Three figures were kneeling before it: Suiren, Zhengyi, and Youchao.

When Wutian entered, they stood up and greeted him with a smile. "It's been a burden. We became immortals by merits and don't understand martial arts well, so we can only rely on you, Fourth Brother."

"What are you saying? As the Martial Ancestor of humanity, this is my duty." Wutian sighed. "Although I managed to create martial arts and extend their lifespans, I still haven't created a method for them to reach immortality."

Suiren also sighed. "Aside from those of us who made significant contributions and became merit immortals, only Fourth Brother managed to become immortal by your own strength and improvement. The rest have slowly died after all these years, and the lifespan of each succeeding generation has decreased."

Youchao walked forward, clad in furs, and slapped Wutian's shoulders. "We can only improve by gaining merit. We still have to rely on Fourth Brother."

"But we can't just rely on Fourth Brother," Zhengyi said. "Thanks to Fourth Brother's words, I managed to gain inspiration, and I can improve the clothes-making process. It isn't just me; didn't Eldest Brother and Third Brother get inspiration?"

Suiren and Youchao laughed.

After talking for a bit, Wutian also knelt in front of Nuwa's statue and offered incense in her honor. After standing up, he stared at the statue's face, or rather, where it would have been. Despite being only a statue carved by humans, the face was hidden behind mist upon completion.

"Fourth Brother, should we build a statue for your master too?" Suiren asked tentatively. "If she hadn't accepted you as a disciple, our race would have never gained martial arts."

Wutian considered it for a moment but eventually shook his

head. "No need. Mother Nuwa created us. That's why we enshrined her. Master has given me grace but did not directly benefit the human race. I cannot ask you to enshrine a statue of her just because of me."

Suiren, Zhengyi, and Youchao nodded, accepting Wutian's words. Honestly, they didn't wish to enshrine her either, but they still considered Wutian's feelings. They had improved humanity's survival rate, but Wutian was directly responsible for increasing their strength, and strength equaled status.

"Eldest Brother, Second Sister, and Third Brother," Wutian said. "I'm going to visit the settlements of humanity. I'll try to impart some martial arts for those who had forgotten."

"What about the ones here?" Youchao asked.

"There's no need. There's already a master just shy of an Earth Immortal in power, he can instruct them. Truthfully, I've reached a bottleneck in my cultivation. I'm hoping this journey can help me break through."

Suiren, Zhengyi, and Youchao nodded. Despite Wutian being only in the Profound Immortal Realm, his strength and experience in battle had already surpassed theirs.

Wutian left the headquarters of humanity without alerting anyone else, his departure went unnoticed.

He first traveled west, where his race had migrated from. During his journey, he took on the guise of an old master using the auxiliary ability of the Nine-Revolution Arcane Art. While in his guise, he imparted his martial arts to whatever human settlement he encountered during his journey.

While teaching a young child with martial potential, Wutian felt a stare on his back. He felt no ill intent, but even if a snake stared at a frog with no malice, the frog would still feel uncomfortable.

Wutian looked up to see an old man with long white hair and a beard wearing white Daoist robes. Although the face was a bit different, he could still see that the Daoist had around 75 percent similarities to Laozi.

He approached him and bowed. "Junior greets Uncle-Master."

Taishang Laojun waved his hand. "No need. I'm just here to look around. Ignore me."

Although he said that, how could Wutian really ignore Taishang Laojun? After this, Wutian followed behind Taishang Laojun as he observed humanity. Sometimes, he acted like a follower. Other times, he acted like a teaching assistant or a servant, supporting Taishang Laojun.

Wutian's actions pleased Taishang Laojun, and he didn't mind giving Tongtian's disciples a few pointers. Although he didn't step into the Golden Immortal Realm, Wutian's accumulation increased. Now, all he needed was a chance or epiphany.

Their journey eventually led them back to near the East Sea. Unlike before, Laozi ascended Shouyang Mountain and sat at the peak for thousands of years.

During this time, the essence of heaven and earth gathered on the mountain. As a result, the surrounding humans gathered to cultivate. Wutian used his authority as the Martial Ancestor to seal off the mountain to prevent anyone from disturbing Taishang Laojun's cultivation.

Still, more and more humans gathered as if sensing something. As the years passed, brilliant lights of black and gold radiated from the peak of Shouyang Mountain, and Taishang Laojun's voice spread throughout the Great Desolation.

"I am Taishang Laojun, the Heavenly Venerable of Virtuous Way! In 3,000 years, I will achieve sainthood. During this time, I will preach the way to all those who have fate!"

As promised, he immediately began to preach. As he spoke, the essence of heaven and earth around Shouyang Mountain rose in density. With each passing year, the song of the Way of Inaction further permeated the surrounding land.

Although a few major powers wondered why Grand Purity Laozi addressed himself as Taishang Laojun, they paid it little mind and quickly made their way to him to listen. When they arrived, they saw a mass of humans hanging on his every word.

The major powers attempted to blast them away to get a better spot, but the moment they took action, an invisible force expelled them 100,000 li away. After making an example of them, the newcomers did not dare make a ruckus and calmed down to listen.

Wutian remained on Shouyang Mountain, guarding Taishang Laojun. As such, he was the closest person to the budding Saint and thus benefited the most. The barrier separating him from achieving the Golden Immortal Realm shattered, and Wutian could've become a Golden Immortal at any moment. Still, it was his other gains from listening to Taishang Laojun's sermon that made him most happy.

He had finally created the Earth Immortal Realm for his martial arts.

During his sermon, Taishang Laojun also modified the Grand Purity Scripture into a simpler method that Later Heaven lifeforms like humans could cultivate to become Earth Immortals.

Tongtian had based her method on formations, and Taishang Laojun had based his method on alchemy. So, instead of creating a formation within the body after the Foundation Establishment Realm, practitioners of the Grand Purity Scripture would form a golden core within their bodies.

When the 3,000 years ended, Taishang Laojun stopped speaking, much to Wutian and everyone else's dismay. Endless clouds of merit appeared and descended onto him, which he absorbed.

"Today, I establish the Human Way and anchor its luck with the Taiji Diagram! The Way of Humanity is to strive for self-improvement!"

Then, immense coercion descended. Numerous phenomena like when Nuwa and Yuanshi had become Saints occurred again. It didn't reach the same level as Yuanshi, but it equaled Nuwa's coercion when she was consecrated.

The Great Desolation welcomed its fourth Saint of Heaven.

* * *

In Wa Outer Palace, Nuwa's expression turned unsightly. When Taishang Laojun established the Human Way, he also took a portion of humanity's luck that belonged to her. Her eyes pierced through the chaotic boundary and into the Great Desolation.

Nuwa furrowed her brows when she saw Taishang Laojun. She pinched her fingers, trying to calculate the secrets of heaven, but was blocked by Yuanshi. She frowned and discovered that she could not pass through Yuanshi's interference at all.

"Just what are you hiding?"

* * *

While everyone had their attention drawn to Shouyang Mountain due to Taishang Laojun's consecration, Tongtian and Yuanshi felt another pressure. It didn't resemble a Saint's coercion and instead reflected the might of infinity.

Tongtian looked to Grand Purity Hall. "The moment Eldest Brother's Corpse became a Saint, he achieved the Primordial Origin Realm?"

The pressure of a Golden Immortal of Primordial Origin disappeared much sooner than a Saint's coercion. If the birth of a Saint resembled a national holiday, then the birth of a Golden Immortal of Primordial Origin was like an individual's birthday.

Thanks to the pressure that had emanated from Laozi, the Saint's coercion was repelled from Kunlun Mountain, and Tongtian didn't need to bow. She left Supreme Purity Hall and entered Three Purity Hall, where Laozi and Yuanshi joined her.

"Congratulations to Eldest Brother for achieving Primordial Origin and sainthood," Tongtian said, followed by Yuanshi's salutations.

"It's nothing, I had not expected to achieve the Primordial Origin the moment my Corpse achieved sainthood," Laozi said. Seeing Tongtian's questioning look, he continued, "The moment you achieve sainthood, all 3,000 laws that form the foundation of the Great Desolation will appear before you. You grasp one and instantly understand the complete law."

Yuanshi nodded. "I took the Law of Chaos."

"And I took the Law of Infinity," Laozi said. "Since Second Brother and I took the Laws of Chaos and Infinity, no one else can achieve sainthood or the Primordial Origin with these laws in the Great Desolation anymore."

"So it's like that," Tongtian muttered.

"Has Third Sister decided what law to master yet?" Yuanshi asked, much to her confusion. "Your chance to achieve sainthood has arrived."

Hearing this, Tongtian felt the Grandmist Violet Qi with Lingbao tremble with excitement as if its moment had come. When Taishang Laojun's consecration ended, she seemed to have understood something.

Yuanshi didn't wait and directly addressed the world. His words echoed throughout the Great Desolation. "I, Jade Purity Yuanshi, the

Heavenly Venerable of Primordial Beginning, establish the Enlightenment Sect and use the Pangu Banner to anchor the sect's luck! I seek to enlighten those who seek the Great Dao, to clarify the truth, explain the myriad miracles, and illuminate the past and future. All living beings shall know good and evil, distinguish good and bad, seek advantages and avoid disadvantages, and seek the path of detachment!"

Karmic Merit descended onto Yuanshi again, and the signs of him achieving sainthood arrived again. His actions didn't just surprise the major powers of the Great Desolation but also his siblings.

You could actually become consecrated twice?!

In addition to the consecration, Yuanshi clearly felt a portion of the Great Desolation's luck split off and settle onto him. Instantly, his comprehension furthered and his cultivation advanced.

With the creation of the Enlightenment Sect, the Twelve Golden Immortals also felt the 3,000 laws become clear and their cultivation speed rise. Although they couldn't take advantage of it now, it would greatly increase their speed once they entered the Great Firmament Realm.

When Yuanshi finished his second consecration, he looked at Tongtian. "Third Sister, what are you waiting for?"

The Grandmist Violet Qi increased the frequency of its vibration as if nudging Tongtian's Obsession Corpse to quickly form a sect too. But Lingbao gritted his teeth and kept his mouth shut, unwilling to utter a word.

Back in Kunlun Mountain, Tongtian also forced herself not to speak. An invisible force kept pushing her to form a sect, but she fought against it. Her body trembled and veins bulged on her forehead.

Finally, the Grandmist Violet Qi in Lingbao slowly stopped vibrating, and the invisible force coercing her receded. Tongtian felt a sense of loss, as if something that had once belonged to her had been taken away.

"Third Sister," Yuanshi said with a frown.

"You don't need to say any more, I don't want to become a Saint of Heaven by establishing a sect," Tongtian said. Her eyes became sharp, and a sword-like aura converged around her. "I have my own path! The things I don't want to do, no one can force me to!"

* * *

Within the core space of the Great Desolation, unreachable by time or space, Hongjun frowned. He opened his eyes, pierced through the boundary of the Realm of Heaven, and looked at Tongtian.

"A variable has appeared."

Chapter 49

One Day Five Saints

On Mount Sumeru, Zhunti glanced toward the East, where Taishang Laojun had been consecrated, and Yuanshi had achieved sainthood twice. He felt the Grandmist Violet Qi within his body vibrate and gained insight into how to achieve sainthood.

A Saint's job was not to rule but to guide others, and no other region needed more guidance than the West. As long as he set up his own teachings, then endless merits would descend, and he would become Saint of Heaven.

However, Zhunti had always considered himself Jieyin's younger brother. How could the junior brother set up a sect and ask his older brother to join?

Zhunti turned to Jieyin, who was sitting on the Twelfth-Ranked Golden Lotus of Merit like a statue, as if the successive consecration of two Saints had not occurred. He knew Jieyin was at a critical time in his cultivation, and he was torn between interrupting and staying quiet.

As the Grandmist Violet Qi increased the intensity of its vibration and Zhunti's anxiety increased, Jieyin suddenly opened his eyes, which contained infinite karma. A coercion unique to Saints emanated from him.

"Senior Brother!" Zhunti cheered.

"Junior Brother, we should set up a teaching and bring salvation to all life in the West," Jieyin said. He had merged his three Corpses into himself and grasped the Law of Karma. As such, he understood cause and effect.

The Dao Ancestor took the two of them as his disciples to repay the karma he owed to the West. When he and Zhunti had begged three times, it was nothing more than the Dao Ancestor's ploy to decrease the karma owed. Now that Jieyin and Zhunti had decided to form a sect, then the effect would be further decreased. He also owed the Dao Ancestor karma after accepting the Grandmist Violet Qi.

Zhunti nodded.

Jieyin began first, and his coercion increased with each word spoken. "I, Jieyin, feel that the living beings of heaven and earth are embroiled in bitterness."

"I, Zhunti, will guide all life to kindness, a life of bliss and without suffering," the younger brother said.

In unison, they declared, "Together, we establish the Liberation Sect and anchor its luck with the Twelfth-Ranked Golden Lotus of Merit!"

Endless clouds of merit descended onto Mount Sumeru. Jieyin had already merged his Corpses, so his aura continually increased. Achieving sainthood was only a matter of time, but Zhunti looked bitter. His aura had risen, but he knew didn't have enough merit.

"Why?" Zhunti asked. "When Laozi established the Human Way, he was able to achieve sainthood in an instant. Even Yuanshi could do it. Why is it that when we do it, our merits are lacking? The Way of Heaven is biased!"

The Three Purities were formed from the spirit of Pangu. Thus, they were loved by the Way of Heaven. Even if they lacked merit, they only needed to supplement the deficiency with the Heaven-Opening Merit.

Zhunti faced Jieyin. "Senior Brother, what should I do?"

He could feel the Grandmist Violet Qi rampaging, waiting to merge with his soul. If he could not achieve sainthood in this instant, he felt he would not have another chance for eons.

Jieyin stayed silent and then sighed. "Junior Brother, our origins are lacking. If I hadn't established a sect, I would not have been able to achieve sainthood even though I merged three Corpses. Since you lack merit and cannot merge your three Corpses, you can only borrow merit from the Way of Heaven."

"Borrow?" Zhunti asked with furrowed brows.

"Yes, make forty-eight oaths to exchange future merits now," Jieyin said. "The only problem is that you will be even more shackled by the Way of Heaven."

Zhunti gave a bitter smile. "I can only worry about oaths if I become a Saint. If I don't become a Saint now, I don't know when I can.

"If I should achieve the Great Dao, yet there are hell beings, hungry ghosts, or animals in my land, may I not attain perfect awakening!

"If I should attain the Great Dao, yet humans and heavenly beings in my land remain stagnated in the three lower realms at the end of their lives, may I not attain perfect awakening!

"If I should attain the Great Dao, yet humans and heavenly beings in my land are not all the color of genuine gold, may I not attain perfect awakening!

"If I should attain the Great Dao, yet humans and heavenly beings in my land differ in appearance and vary in beauty, may I not attain perfect awakening!

"If I should attain the Great Dao, yet humans and heavenly beings in my land are unaware of their past lives and don't know events of at least the past hundreds of thousands of millions of eons, may I not attain perfect awakening!

"If I should attain the Great Dao..."

Zhunti made oath after oath until he'd reached forty-eight. Upon the final oath, the endless merits descended. There was more than enough for Zhunti to achieve sainthood, yet he was torn between bliss and bitterness.

Powerful coercion emanated from Zhunti's body, alerting all beings of the Great Desolation to the birth of the sixth Saint of Heaven. Golden light emanated from Mount Sumeru, illuminating all the West. Any living beings touched by the light were consumed with endless yearning and desire for the source of that light and involuntarily migrated toward Mount Sumeru.

The golden light continued to travel past the western boundaries toward the East. When it reached Buzhou Mountain, two snorts could be heard as the golden light was shattered.

On Mount Sumeru, Jieyin and Zhunti discussed the situation with heavy consideration. The younger Saint said, "Beneath the Dao Ancestor, Yuanshi should be the most powerful Saint of Heaven."

"Like me, he should have become a Saint by merging his Three Corpses," Jieyin said. "Not to mention the Way of Heaven consecrated him twice. It's unknown what stage he has reached in the Primordial Origin Realm."

"Now that four Saints have appeared, why hasn't Tongtian become a Saint? No matter if she knows or not, as long as she establishes a sect, she should immediately achieve sainthood."

"Unless something went wrong?" Zhunti asked with a smile. That was good. With how powerful Yuanshi was, the East and West had barely achieved a balance between the four Saints.

"I feel it is not so simple," Jieyin said. "The only way Tongtian would not want to achieve sainthood is if she wanted something else."

"You mean to say that Tongtian wants to achieve the Primordial Origin Realm with strength?" Zhunti asked.

"Can there be any other reason?" Jieyin asked, causing Zhunti to mutter to himself.

Whatever these two thought, the coercion disappeared after their consecration ended.

Jieyin frowned as he looked at Zhunti. With his mastery of karma, he could see a line going from Zhunti to the East. "Junior Brother, Saints are untouched by karma, but that does not mean we cannot pay attention to it. The ones to bear the cause and effect are the ones nearest us."

"I know," Zhunti said, his resentment clear. "I owe Daoist Redcloud karma, but what can I do to repay him for giving up a seat and allowing me to get a strand of Grandmist Violet Qi?"

"Then?"

"As long as he dies, the karma will end," Zhunti concluded. "Even if Tongtian intervenes again, I don't believe she can block a Saint's method as a Quasi-Saint."

Time passed as they plotted Redcloud Ancestor's demise. The various living beings of the Great Desolation settled down to hold excited discussions about what had happened.

Four consecrations in one day!

They had thought the Saints would appear slowly, one after the other like Yuanshi after Nuwa. Who knew that four would appear in one day? They looked toward Kunlun Mountain, wondering if the third Purity would also achieve sainthood, but its inhabitants remained silent.

Suddenly, the day's fifth coercion appeared, but it did not originate from Kunlun Mountain, nor was the speaker a woman.

"I, Redcloud, establish the Interception Sect!

"The Great Dao is fifty, the Eye of Heaven is forty-nine, and hope is one! Under my sect, all living beings can reverse their fate and intercept the ray of hope. All life in the Great Desolation can achieve the Great Dao!"

After Redcloud Ancestor spoke those words, his aura increased, but it still lacked the final step. When the coercion started to weaken, Redcloud Ancestor swore thirty-six oaths to the Way of Heaven, finally gathering enough merit to complete his consecration.

"Those with a predestined relationship with me can come to my Firesource Grotto to become my disciples!" The newest Saint announced.

* * *

In Three Purity Hall, Tongtian's expression darkened. A portion of the Karmic Luck she had originally occupied flowed out from her. Although she couldn't sense her own luck—as it was normally illusionary—this time, the effect was too large. The Twelfth-Ranked White Lotus of Purification shivered as Tongtian controlled it to anchor her luck and prevent it from seeping out while she mulled things over.

I didn't expect that Redcloud would set up the Interception Sect instead of me. The general trend is the establishment of the Interception Sect, and the variable is who would become its founder. Since I didn't establish the Interception Sect, part of my luck was transferred to Redcloud. But that's fine, when my Allheaven Jianmu Tree becomes the pillar sepa-

rating heaven and earth, my luck will return and even grow without the danger of being besieged by four Saints.

Tongtian felt slightly apologetic to Redcloud for taking her place, but after a moment, she shook her head. Redcloud Ancestor was supposed to die when Kunpeng and Heavenly Court besieged him, but due to her intervention, he had survived. Since she'd saved him, it was only part of cause and effect that he would take her place.

* * *

When his coercion disappeared, Redcloud Ancestor released a burst of booming laughter. After laughing for five minutes straight, he calmed down and glanced toward Heavenly Court. "Hmpf, you're lucky that you are the protagonists of this tribulation. Otherwise, I'd personally clean you up."

He flew down from the mass of clouds he had been hiding in to return to the land.

Redcloud Ancestor had restored his Good Corpse, but he hadn't cut off his evil thoughts to form his Evil Corpse yet. While cultivating, he had sensed Taishang Laojun's consecration; followed by Yuanshi's, Jieyin's, and Zhunti's. The Grandmist Violet Qi, which had been silent, had suddenly started throbbing like crazy, allowing him to achieve sainthood.

Despite the thirty-six oaths he'd made, Redcloud Ancestor still smiled happily. The first place he went to wasn't Firesource Cave but Longevity Mountain. He hadn't tasted Zhen Yuanzi's Ginseng Fruit for a long time, and he almost couldn't restrain his gluttony.

Redcloud Ancestor spent a few years at Wuzhuang Temple, feasting on Ginseng Fruits. In fact, he ate so much that Zhen Yuazi angrily chased him away and forbade him from visiting for at least an eon.

On the way back to Firesource Grotto, Redcloud Ancestor stopped and saw a demon.

"Saint, please accept me as your disciple!" the demon begged. He was a golden rat with an eye for treasure.

Redcloud Ancestor pinched his fingers and discovered that the rat in front of him had a relationship with himself. "Alright, I will accept you as my first disciple."

"Duobao thanks Master!" Duobao said. He reached into his sleeve and pulled out a book. "I came across this when I was searching for treasure eons ago, and I think Master should have it."

Redcloud Ancestor accepted the book, and his lips curled into a smile when he read the title. "Haha, I never expected the Ten Thousand Immortals Book to fall into my hands. Not bad, not bad."

He continued onward, taking Daoist Duobao back to Firesource Grotto with him. When he arrived, Redcloud Ancestor found a swarm of demons and congenital gods roaming outside.

Redcloud Ancestor didn't waste any time setting up a formation he had learned from the Ten Thousand Immortals Book. Only those who could pass his formation would be accepted as disciples.

Unlike Yuanshi, Redcloud Ancestor accepted thousands of disciples. He separated them into two ranks, inner and outer disciples. Of the thousands that passed, the only four that became direct disciples were Daoist Duobao, Sacred Mother Jinling, Sacred Mother Wudang, and Sacred Mother Guiling.

Chapter 50

Houyi Shoots Nine Suns

After the era of Saints arrived, Kunlun Mountain, Mount Sumeru, and Firesource Grotto became holy grounds that all cultivators yearned for, and the Great Desolation entered a state of peace.

An eon later, Heavenly Court celebrated the birth of Di Jun and Xihe's children. Despite being born on the Supreme Yin Star, Xihe was a golden crow. She bore ten children, each one a golden crow at the Profound Immortal Realm.

Di Jun invited all major powers to attend the celebration of his sons' birth, but aside from Nuwa, none of the Saints of Heaven came. The Heavenly Emperor's expression darkened for a moment, but it disappeared as quickly as it appeared.

He could understand why Redcloud Ancestor didn't come, considering Heavenly Court had tried to snatch his Grandmist Violet Qi. What puzzled Di Jun was that Redcloud Ancestor hadn't sought revenge at all, as if he had forgotten this enmity.

Still, Di Jun couldn't help but grow angry that Tongtian didn't appear. Out of the people who had received the Grandmist Violet Qi, she was only only one not consecrated. He had briefly considered taking her qi away, but quickly abandoned the idea.

Ignoring Tongtian's own strength, she had two Saints of Heaven for brothers. If Di Jun dared to touch her, not even Nuwa would be able to protect him or Heavenly Court.

After the grand celebration, peace and quiet did not return to Thirty-Three Heavens.

As golden crows, Di Jun's ten sons were born with Solar Truefire within them. Even Golden Immortals of the Great Firmament could be killed by them if they weren't careful.

Due to their low cultivation base, the ten golden crows could not control the Solar Truefire within and killed many demons in Heavenly Court by accident. As the Heavenly Emperor's sons, no one dared to be harsh with them. They ran amok even more, even purposely killing the demons that tried to rein them in.

"Before our war with the Titan Tribe, all the demons will be killed by you rascals first!" Di Jun shouted in rage as he slammed his palm on the Nine Dragon Throne.

His sons cowered as they saw their father's fury. They quickly hid behind their mother.

"Husband, don't be too harsh with them," Xihe said. "They're just children."

"Before they are children, they are the heavenly princes," Di Jun said, but his tone noticeably softened. "As the heavenly princes, they are killing their own subjects. How can the Demon Clan accept that they were killed by their own rulers and not the Titan Tribe?"

"It's not our fault," Di Jun's eldest son, Di Hong, griped. "Who told them to get in our way? They know we can't control the Solar Truefire in our bodies."

Di Jun leveled a glare at Di Hong, who shrank behind his mother. "Get in your way? They wouldn't have gotten in your way if you had stayed in your Ten Sun Palace and cultivated diligently!"

"But it's so boring!" Luya, the youngest prince, protested. He also hid behind Xihe when Di Jun directed his glare at him.

"That's it," Di Jun said. "Until you reach the Golden Immortal Realm and learn to control the Solar Truefire, you will be trapped on Penglai Immortal Island!"

Since the fall of Violet Mansion, Penglai Immortal Island had fallen into Heavenly Court's control. They had also tried to search for Yingzhou Immortal Island to no avail. Fangzhang Immortal Island was of course still under Tongtian's ownership, and they didn't dare offend the Three Purities at this point in time.

Di Jun's decision immediately elicited his sons' displeasure and vehement refutations. However, he was firm in his decision and sent the Demon Preceptor to escort them to Penglai Immortal Island.

"Husband," Xihe said as she watched Kunpeng escort her sons away.

"If you are worried about whether Kunpeng will take any malicious actions against them, you shouldn't be," Di Jun said. "As long as a strand of his truesoul resides in the Demon-Summoning Banner, he won't dare to rebel."

"It's not that, but is it perhaps too harsh to send them to Penglai Immortal Island?" Xihe asked.

Di Jun sighed as he stepped off his throne and hugged Xihe from behind, resting his chin on the nape of her neck. "It's also for their own good. Discontent has been brewing within the Demon Clan because of their actions. I can protect them now, but can I protect them for the rest of their lives?

"In addition, they don't know how high the heavens are. Even if I am the Heavenly Emperor, I'm not powerful enough to go against the Saints. Their time on Penglai Immortal Island will temper their brashness. The Fusang Tree there can also increase their cultivation speed."

Xihe nodded, accepting Di Jun's decision despite the reluctance in her heart.

* * *

"Kunpeng, Kunpeng, tell us about the Titan Tribe," the golden crows asked as the Demon Preceptor escorted them out of Thirty-Three Heavens.

After Di Jun had conquered Kunpeng and the Darknorth Demon Clan, he'd named Kunpeng the teacher of all demons for his contribution in creating Demon Script. Demon Preceptor sounded nice on paper, but it gave Kunpeng no power at all.

Kunpeng had expected Di Jun to give him the title of Northern Demon Emperor. Di Jun's act only amplified Kunpeng's desire to break free of the Heavenly Emperor's control. However, as a strand of his truesoul was still in the Demon-Summoning Banner, he could only bide his time.

"The Titan Tribe is truly terrifying," Kunpeng said with a sigh. "Many brave demons fell to them during the first two battles. They even almost made it into Heavenly Court!"

"Hmpf, so what?" Di Hong asked. "I know Father can easily take care of them if he gets serious."

"Yeah, yeah!" Luya added. "We don't even need Father, we can take care of them ourselves!"

"Your Highnesses, you mustn't!" Kunpeng said as he showed a fearful expression. "The Titan Tribe likes to eat demons the most. If you get captured by them, you'll be gobbled up. Even your bones will be eaten, and His Majesty will become sad."

The ten golden crows became fearful for a split second before their pride surged. They sneered. "Eaten? We'll burn them to a crisp!"

"Tell us more about the Titan Tribe," they demanded. When

Kunpeng hesitated, the princes urged him. "Just tell us already, that's an order! You got it?!"

Kunpeng finally relented with a helpless expression, teaching them basic information about the Titan Tribe, but mostly how terrible the giants were to demons, igniting their racial pride.

Not long after, Kunpeng arrived on Penglai Immortal Island. After settling them in, he activated the barrier array. Not only did it prevent invasions by Quasi-Saints, but it also trapped the ten golden crows.

When Kunpeng left, he had a sneer on his face. "Stupid brats that don't know how high the heavens are."

After flying for a while, a figure split from Kunpeng's body and flew in the direction of Kunlun Mountain. Kunpeng himself returned to Thirty-Three Heavens.

* * *

The golden crows spent the subsequent three eons trapped on Penglai Immortal Island. Even when they didn't consciously cultivate, the Fusang Tree and the constant rays from the sun made them stronger year by year.

One day, while the ten brothers were loitering around the island, they suddenly turned to see a mousy woman sneaking around. Di Jun had recalled all demons to prevent the princes' Solar Truefire from killing any more of them, so she must have been an intruder. After exchanging glances, the ten brothers flapped their wings and surrounded the newcomer. As they had not entered the Golden Immortal Realm, they still hadn't gained the ability to transform.

"Who are you? How'd you get in?" Di Hong questioned.

Trapped in the encirclement, the mousy woman shrunk back and cowered. "Please, don't hurt me! I only entered because I wanted to find shelter. I'll leave immediately!"

"Hmpf, do you think we are so easy to deceive? Only strong people like Kunpeng or Father can enter Penglai Immortal Island's barrier," Luya said.

The mousy woman opened her eyes wide in shock. "If this is Penglai Immortal Island, then you are the ten demon princes?"

"Of course," one of the golden crows said, puffing his chest in pride.

"This little one greets Your Highnesses!" the mousy woman said as she quickly kneeled.

Di Hong frowned. "Hurry up and tell us how you entered."

"How?" the woman repeated. "I was just running away and wanted to hide somewhere. I didn't feel any barriers at all when entering."

When the ten demon princes heard this, their eyes lit up in excitement. They had long grown tired of confinement. "Show us!"

Withering under their stifling presence, the woman quickly complied and led them to where she had entered. Di Hong and his brothers shouted in joy upon discovering that there was indeed a hole leading out of the formation.

As the ten golden crows flew out, Luya suddenly stopped, turned around, and asked, "You're a demon too, right? Why were you running?"

The mousy woman showed a bitter smile. "The giants wanted to kill me and eat me. I'm just a weak demon, what can I do against the Titan Tribe? Every day, the giants come to devour us lesser demons. They even keep some of us like livestock!"

"Those damn barbarians!" Di Hong shouted. "Come, Brothers, let's teach those dumb giants a lesson."

Following Di Hong's lead, the rest of the golden crows flew toward the land from the East Sea.

The mousy woman left at Penglai Immortal Island snorted and shapeshifted into a beautiful but cold immortal. Her eyes reflected endless hatred. "Di Jun, did you really think that just because you controlled Penglai Immortal Island, you knew everything? Hmpf, since you killed Dong Wanggong, I will make you lose everything you care for. Let's start with these ten mongrels."

* * *

As Di Hong and his brothers flew in the direction of the Titan Tribes, they unleashed the power of Solar Truefire from their bodies. It didn't only look like ten additional suns had appeared in the sky, it felt like it too.

Wherever the golden crows passed, the land dried up, the water evaporated, vegetation withered, mountains turned into erupting volcanoes, and forests burst into flames. Along their way, countless living beings died—both demons and humans. As they searched for the Titan Tribe, the demon princes brought devastation and damage to the Great Desolation.

The ten brothers finally reached the Tianwu Tribe and used their Solar Truefire to burn whatever targets they could find. The majority of the giants were still at the Profound Immortal level, and the few giants at the Golden Immortal level were burnt to a crisp.

Just as the boys were excitedly massacring whatever giants they could find, a flying ax struck one of the brothers.

"Sixth Brother!" Di Hong cried.

"I'm okay!" the sixth golden crow said. Although he tried to appear strong, he couldn't hide the weakness in his voice.

"Who is it? Who dares attack us?!" Di Hong shouted as flames burst from his body.

"I!" Kuafu shouted as he ran toward the golden crows. He brandished the offending ax, and his body grew to over 1,000 zhang in size, dwarfing the crows. "Since you dare incinerate the Tianwu Tribe, pay for your actions with your life!"

"Ha, the Titan Tribe is destined to fall to my Demon Clan. So what if we kill a few ahead of time?" Di Hong returned as he and his brothers charged at Kuafu, intending to burn him alive.

Kuafu sneered and swung his weapon, nearly striking the golden crows. But even if he didn't directly hit them, all ten brothers suffered damage from the razor-sharp wind brought about by the swing.

"Ah, not good. He's too strong, flee!" Di Hong and his brothers finally felt the terror of death. Without a word, they quickly turned tail and ran.

"Want to leave? Not with your life!" Kuafu shouted, giving chase.

He chased them for ten days but could never catch them. Despite reaching the Peak Great Firmament Realm in power, Kuafu didn't have any long-range attacks, so he could only continue chasing and uselessly swinging his ax. During this time, the golden crows discovered this and used guerilla tactics to keep Kuafu busy.

Although he was far more powerful than the demon princes, Kuafu was alone, and the power of the Solar Truefire gradually wore him down. He wanted to rest, but the golden crows would attack him if he did. He wanted to sip the water of the river, but they would evaporate all the water.

Kuafu slowly weakened, but he never gave up chasing Di Jun's sole heirs. Even as he tired, his ax swings never wavered, never weakened. His vision grew blurry, but he never lost sight of the crows.

Finally, he stopped moving and stood still. All life had perished from his body. Even the powerful lifeforce of a giant could not withstand the continuous assault of Solar Truefire. Kuafu had been slowly roasted to death.

"Haha," Di Hong and his brothers laughed happily. They covered their bodies in flaming spheres, becoming more like suns as they rammed into Kuafu's body, leaving only ash.

"That'll teach you the power of the ten demon princes!" Luya shouted as he celebrated with his brothers.

Just as the golden crows were immersed in their festivities, a heart-broken roar echoed throughout the area. "Kuafu!"

Di Hong, Luya, and the rest of the golden crows turned around to see another giant wearing fur and carrying a bow. They shared a look and sped toward him, intent on incinerating him.

Tears trailed down Houyi's face as he saw the demon princes flying toward him. He released an earth-shattering roar as his aura exploded outwards. The tears evaporated from his face as he pulled out an arrow and notched it on the bow.

His first arrow blurred toward the incoming golden crows. It was like a black dot, but it was so fast it turned into a seemingly impossibly long streak. Before Di Hong and the others knew what happened, one sun vanished from the sky.

"Second Brother!" Di Hong shouted. He roared at Houyi, "You bastard, how could you! Pay with your life!"

Wrath clouding their judgments, they continued to charge. Houyi pulled two more arrows and let them loose. Only then did the golden crows awaken from their mad state. They grieved for the death of their fourth and seventh brothers, but they knew they had to flee.

"Want to escape now? Too late!" Houyi said as he continued to fire arrow after arrow at the golden princes.

The major powers who had noticed the commotion couldn't help but sigh in amazement. "I heard that the Titan Tribe had an amazing archer, but I never believed it until now."

"What powerful arrows! Only those in the Early Quasi-Saint Realm and above could take them, and he still hasn't entered the

Quasi-Saint Realm. How powerful will his arrows be when he enters the Quasi-Saint Realm?"

Houyi didn't know that all the major powers of the Great Desolation were paying attention to him now. Even if he'd known, he wouldn't have cared. All he cared about was taking revenge for Kuafu.

As he notched his ninth arrow, he aimed for the smallest sun, the one formed by Luya. He let loose and the arrow streaked toward its target. Before it could reach the boy, Di Hong slammed into Luya, forcing him out of the way to take the arrow in his place.

"Eldest Brother!" Luya shouted mournfully.

Di Hong tried to tell Luya to escape but couldn't form the words. The moment the arrow had struck, he'd lost all strength and died not a second later. Tears streamed down Luya's face, but he still ran. He swore that he would get revenge in the future.

Houyi notched the tenth arrow, but before he could fire, he was forced to dodge the gigantic bronze bell that struck where he had been standing.

"Houyi, how dare you kill my nephews?!" Taiyi roared angrily.

Chapter 51

Mindforce

In Eminence Heaven Palace, Di Jun's expression sank. From the Throne of Heaven, he detected that the Karmic Luck and Merit of Heavenly Court were drastically plummeting for some reason. "Go check to see if anything significant is happening in the Great Desolation. And if any demons are causing chaos without orders, kill them!"

The only reason he could think of for the luck or merit of Heavenly Court to weaken was if a demon was wreaking havoc in the Great Desolation or harming the vitality of the Demon Clan. The first person Di Jun thought of was Kunpeng, but he quickly dismissed the idea. Kunpeng was standing in line and showed no suspicious reaction.

A demon official sent to discover the reason quickly returned. He kneeled and said, "Reporting to Your Majesty, ten suns have appeared in the land below!"

Another demon also rushed in and kneeled. "Your Majesty, it's the princes. They are laying waste to the land below and are rushing toward the Titan Tribe!"

"What?!" Di Jun shot up, losing his composure.

All the demons present exclaimed in surprise.

Di Jun quickly looked at Taiyi. "Eastern Emperor, go and fetch those bastards back!"

"Yes!" Taiyi said, cupping his fist before turning into a streak of red light rushing out of Thirty-Three Heavens.

Di Jun wasn't done yet. "Prepare two legions, descend into the land, and dispatch someone to Penglai Immortal Island. I want to see who dares to scheme against Our children!"

"Yes!" The demon officials accepted the Heavenly Emperor's orders and mobilized with the utmost efficiency.

* * *

From the crater where it had crashed, the Chaos Bell dislodged itself and returned to Taiyi. High in the sky, he slowly flew in front of the last golden crow.

"Uncle," Luya cried out bitterly. "Eldest Brother and the others…"

Taiyi nodded. "I know. Don't worry, the Titan Tribe will pay for their transgressions. Now step back."

Luya obediently flew a distance away but remained close enough to rush to Taiyi if anyone attacked him. With Luya safe, the Eastern Emperor turned his attention back to Houyi. He didn't waste any useless words and directly rushed toward Houyi. Fire shrouded his body like armor.

Despite his physical prowess, Houyi was blown back by Taiyi's tackle. He gritted his teeth and punched back, but all he got was a scorched fist for his troubles. He knew when he was outmatched, and tried to flee.

Taiyi intercepted Houyi's attempted retreat, pummeling him with the Chaos Bell. Its bronze hue burned a fiery red as it melted the giant's skin. The air around Houyi evaporated, and even space burned from the devastating heat Taiyi had imbued into the Chaos Bell.

Unlike his nephews, Taiyi perfectly controlled the range, preventing unnecessary damage to the Great Desolation.

Houyi's skin turned black from the char. He even spat out a mouthful of blood that soon evaporated from the heat. Just as the Chaos Bell hurtled toward him a second time, a turbulent tornado smashed into the Chaos Bell and altered its trajectory.

Taiyi turned to see Tianwu closing in. "Damn bird, did you forget Hongjun's order?!"

He sneered. "Since he dared kill nine of my nephews, he must pay the price!"

"Those damn birds deserved to die!" Tianwu shouted. "Ravaging the land and even assaulting my Tianwu Tribe—if Houyi didn't kill them, I would!"

"Good, good! Then you die too!"

Taiyi smashed the Chaos Bell toward Tianwu. Even if Tianwu had reached the Intermediate Quasi-Saint Realm, Taiyi had also grown stronger—as evidenced by how he'd infused Solar Truefire into the Chaos Bell.

Tianwu grunted as the Chaos Bell crashed into him, burning him as it sent him flying several li.

Taiyi scoffed. "You needed five titans to fight me before. What can you do just by yourself?"

Deciding to ignore Tianwu for the moment, he rushed Houyi. Even without the Chaos Bell, he was more than enough to kill the giant. It would just take a bit longer, that's all.

Giants were not beings that accepted defeat so easily. Using the chance Tianwu had bought him, Houyi retreated a distance and notched another arrow. "Go!"

Houyi's words seemed to travel with the arrow as it soared at the

Eastern Emperor. Taiyi grunted and shifted his flight pattern, but the arrow actually curved as if it had a mind of its own!

Taiyi slapped the arrow away just as it was about to reach him. Defying all expectations, the arrow pierced his palm, and from the point of injury, a mysterious energy seeped into his body. Neither his qi nor the Solar Truefire could slow it down, and it only disappeared when the energy reached his shoulder.

The Eastern Emperor's killing intent toward Houyi grew stronger. He didn't know what type of technique it was, but he could not let this threat grow anymore. Taiyi appeared in front of Houyi, and a burning sword in his hand.

Houyi raised his bow and blocked the burning sword, but he was forced onto his knees under the demon's might. The sword was slowly incinerating his body, and it would only be a matter of time before it sliced through the bow and eviscerated him.

Taiyi increased his strength, his body burning with sparking flames. Just when it seemed that Houyi could no longer resist, his eyes lost all emotion. His aura suddenly surged, breaking through the limit of the Great Firmament Realm.

Upon discovering this, Taiyi pushed his body and qi to the limit, trying to kill Houyi before he fully ascended. But to his shock, he discovered that Houyi was slowly pushing him back.

With a grunt, Taiyi retreated several steps as Houyi repelled him. It seemed that his ascension was inevitable.

"Haha, our Titan Tribe has finally produced another Quasi-Saint master!" a voice from the distance shouted. Moments later, the Titan of Thunder appeared. "Taiyi, today is your death date!"

Taiyi snorted. "With just you three?"

"Not three, but seven!" Di Jiang said as he and several other titans appeared. "Not even you can defeat all seven of us at the same time."

"He can't alone, but what about with Us?" Di Jun's voice boomed from above. Behind him were two legions of the Celestial Army.

"Haha, still no," Di Jiang said, chuckling. "It seems that the war between us will begin before the time limit is up."

"War? No, this is punishment for your blasphemous actions! We will have you accompany Our sons in their death!" Di Jun's eyes focused on Houyi, wanting to rip him to shreds at that very instant.

Just as it seemed that the war between the Titan Tribe and Demon Clan would begin prematurely, a mighty coercion descended in a 100,000-li radius.

The two leaders snapped their heads toward the source with the same thought in their minds. *Hongjun/Dao Ancestor?!*

It was not an old Daoist that appeared, but a black-robed, middle-aged man. Jade Purity Yuanshi glanced at both sides, his eyes pausing on Houyi for the briefest of moments. His stare froze Di Jiang and Di Jun from the sheer pressure despite him not taking any action yet.

"Have you forgotten the Dao Ancestor's orders? War shall not occur until the time limit is up! Return to Thirty-Three Heavens."

"Yuanshi!" Di Jun shouted. "They killed Our sons!"

Yuanshi just glanced at him. "Instead of worrying over your sons' deaths, you should worry about how much they decreased your Karmic Luck. Return! I won't repeat myself!"

Di Jun gritted his teeth, but under absolute power, he could only comply. He glared daggers at the titans and Houyi one last time before leading the Celestial Army back to Thirty-Three Heavens.

Taiyi didn't look at the titans or Houyi but gave one unwilling glance at Yuanshi before following his brother.

Yuanshi paid them no attention as his figure disappeared. *All under Saints are ants.* After he became a Saint of Heaven, he stopped caring about those unrelated to him—especially those targeting his sister.

When Yuanshi left, the titans were conflicted. They had once been equal to the Three Purities, but now, the two groups were on completely different levels. Even if they defeated the Demon Clan, the Saints would always hover above them unless they could have one themselves.

Di Jiang shook his head and tried to rid himself of unnecessary thoughts. He, along with the other titans, surrounded Houyi. After slapping Houyi's shoulders, he said, "Not bad. We finally have another Quasi-Saint."

Houyi seemed to have awakened from a daze. He stared at his hands in disbelief, still burnt from Taiyi's assault. "I've entered the Quasi-Saint Realm?"

"Yes," Tianwu said with a smile. Even with the deaths of his tribe members, the gains exceeded the losses. "But what should we call him now? Giant doesn't seem to fit anymore, and he's not a titan."

"Does it matter?" Qiangliang asked. "If he's not a titan, let's call him a gigant—a great giant."

"Houtu, what's wrong?" Jumang asked, seeing Houtu wasn't reveling in the celebration. His words alerted the others to the Titan of Earth's silence.

Houtu shook her head. "It's nothing. I just feel saddened by the number of deaths."

"Don't worry, we'll get revenge on the demons for the murder of our tribesmen," Di Jiang said. The other titans roared their agreement.

Houtu opened her mouth to say it wasn't just the giants' death that concerned her, but the look on her siblings' faces stopped her. She glanced at the scorched land and sighed.

* * *

Back in Eminence Heaven Palace, Di Jun cradled Xihe in his arms as she sobbed into his chest.

"My sons, my sons!" Xihe cried out, her words muffled in her husband's robes.

"Don't worry, We will make the Titan Tribe pay," Di Jun said as endless hatred filled his eyes.

"When will that be?" Xihe asked, removing herself from Di Jun's embrace to glare at him. "I want him to pay, and I want him to pay now. If you can't get revenge for our sons, then I will."

Di Jun watched her leave for the Supreme Yin Star. He sighed and slumped onto the Nine Dragon Throne. Days later, he looked up and saw Taiyi walking in. "Is it done?"

Taiyi nodded. "Yes, Nuwa agreed to take in Luya." After some hesitation, he asked, "Brother, how are you feeling?"

"How are We feeling? We will recover," Di Jun said, a hint of frostiness in his words. "How much has the Demon Clan grown in these years? What will Our forces look like in a few eons?"

Taiyi sighed. "We will have over a thousand Golden Immortals of Golden Firmament and barely over 50,000 Golden Immortals. The Starry Sky War Array should be able to reach its peak."

Di Jun nodded. "Anything else? Did you discover any weaknesses of the Titan Tribe?"

Taiyi shook his head.

"Keep searching. We need something to gain an advantage over the Titan Tribe."

* * *

Tongtian opened her eyes and exited Supreme Purity Hall. There, she saw the recently returned Yuanshi. "That wasn't like you."

"What wasn't?"

"Intervening between the Titan Tribe and Demon Clan. Would it not be in your best interest for both sides to fall as soon as possible?" Tongtian asked. She also looked forward to the grand war between both forces because it meant the time of her consecration was near.

"I have my plans," Yuanshi said avoidantly. "What other questions do you have?"

"What technique did Houyi use? No matter how powerful a Golden Immortal of the Great Firmament is, he shouldn't have been able to injure Taiyi to that extent," Tongtian said as she recalled the scene. Many of the major powers who had witnessed the battle were likewise puzzled.

"It's mindforce," Yuanshi said. Before Tongtian could ask, he elaborated, "It's a technique realized by imbuing your attack with your thoughts. Of course, it's not that simple, as the amount of will and heart needed directly excludes those with weak daohearts. Mindforce also exhausts the mind much faster than qi or essence."

"You sound as if you know the technique."

"Of course, I created it from Hongjun's Way of Three Corpses."

"Then why would Houyi know it?" Tongtian asked suspiciously.

"Who knows, perhaps he had chanced upon an epiphany. Want to learn?"

Tongtian knew her second brother had avoided her query, but she still nodded. She didn't care about the relationship between him and Houyi. Everyone had their own secrets. After gaining the Daoheart Scripture from Yuanshi, Tongtian returned to Supreme Purity Hall.

When she left, Yuanshi gazed upwards. His eyes pierced through the roof and zeroed in on the Supreme Yin Star of the Starry Sky. "Don't let me down."

CHAPTER 52

Earthly Marriage

Life seemingly returned to normal after the Ten Sun Catastrophe, but both the Titan Tribe and Demon Clan knew it was only the calm before the storm. Before old grievances could be settled, new ones were made. Such was the nature of war.

However, that was a worry for the future. When Houyi returned to the Houtu Tribe, the whole tribe celebrated his advancement.

"A toast for Houyi!" Chiyou said, raising a cup of wine made from naturally fermented fruits that the giants had discovered. There weren't many of them, so it was only brought out on special occasions.

Houyi drank cup after cup. He probably drank nearly half of all the wine saved up by the Houtu Tribe, but none of the giants cared. To them, the gigant instantly became the most respected warrior after Houtu.

When the celebration was over, Chiyou pulled Houyi aside. "My brother, how did you break into the Quasi-Saint Realm?"

Although Chiyou was happy for him, he was also envious. He had reached the Golden Immortal of the Great Firmament level first, but he had been stuck at the final step.

"I don't know," Houyi said. "Without realizing it, I had suddenly broken through. Perhaps it was because I was facing a crisis of life or death. If I didn't break through, I would have died."

Chiyou nodded. He wanted to engage in battle and replicate Houyi's feat, but there were too few opponents for him. And the Titan Tribe would never allow two giants to engage in a fatal battle just for the chance of one of them becoming a gigant.

When Chiyou left, Houyi sighed. There was something he hadn't told Chiyou or even Houtu. The truth was that he couldn't recall what had happened when Taiyi had attacked him and when he broke through to the Quasi-Saint Realm. It was as if he had suddenly fallen asleep and discovered that he had accomplished several incredible feats while sleepwalking.

Even if he told the truth, Houyi doubted that anyone would believe it. Besides, a voice in the back of his mind told him not to, and Houyi trusted his instincts.

After the banquet, he returned to his regular routine. Well, that wasn't exactly true. He still hunted and cultivated normally, but instead of focusing on his physical prowess, he trained his mind.

After shooting down nine golden crows and injuring Taiyi, he had received an epiphany. *Where my heart goes, the arrow follows.* It was an incredible technique that strengthened the power of his arrows through concentration, but it required a strong daoheart. Overuse would result in mental fatigue and even deep sleep, if not a soul injury.

He hadn't yet given it a name. Before shooting the golden crows, the technique was still in its conceptual stages, untested. "Let's call it mindforce," he mumbled to himself.

Houyi paused, wondering why the name seemed so familiar. He shook his head, ridding it of the déjà vu he felt.

The next day, Houyi took his bow and left the Houtu Tribe to hunt. With his increased strength, he easily took down a beast the size of a mountain and carried it home. On the way back, he paused in his steps when he noticed an unconscious woman.

She was tiny, a fraction of his height. A human.

The woman's eyelashes flickered as she opened her eyes. She slowly sat up and blinked her eyes to get rid of her hazy sight. Then she noticed Houyi.

She screamed.

Houyi gently laid his hunted game down and tried to reassure the woman, but his massive height had obviously scared her. Left with no other choice, he shrank until he was only a head taller than her.

The woman, who had hidden behind a giant rock, peeked out to stare at the miniaturized gigant. When she saw Houyi looking straight at her, she quickly hid behind the rock again but discovered that he had somehow appeared in front of her. Her face flushed upon seeing Houyi's handsome face, and she quickly looked down.

Houyi also froze as he saw the woman's beauty. Unlike the coarse skin of the humans he knew of, the woman had tender, white skin like a newborn's. She wore white robes instead of clothing made of fur or leaves, which only accentuated her features.

"What's your name?" Houyi asked before he could stop himself.

The woman stayed silent, and just as Houyi thought she couldn't or wouldn't speak, she suddenly said, "Chang'e, my name is Chang'e."

Houyi brought Chang'e back to the tribe with him. Because she couldn't live in his normal home, Houyi built a smaller, human-sized one. While in the tribe, he mainly used a human form since Chang'e was scared by his giant size.

A century passed in a flash. Compared to Houyi's eons of life, these hundred years couldn't even make up a tenth of a percent of his life, but he treasured the memories of these hundred years the most.

During that century, Houyi had moved from the core of the Houtu Tribe to the periphery where most of the human and demi-giant tribespeople lived. He once questioned why his fellow giants would stoop so low to live with humans, but he finally understood after meeting Chang'e.

While living with her, Houyi recalled the time when Di Jun had married Xihe and the grand celebration they'd held. He would know; he'd crashed the wedding with the Titan Tribe, after all. Houyi wanted to marry Chang'e, so he sought out Houtu. Since Nuwa had presided over Di Jun's and Xihe's marriage, then Houtu would preside over theirs.

Recalling the merits that had descended when Nuwa established the heavenly marriage, Houtu agreed. When she had prepared the ceremony and started the establishment of the earthly marriage, she had received a warning from the Way of Heaven, causing her to halt. Even if she had forcibly gone through with it, they would have received Karmic Sin instead of Karmic Luck.

Houtu hadn't only wanted to preside over Houyi and Chang'e's marriage for their happiness but also to increase the overall luck of the Titan Tribe. She'd have to take care in this establishment, as forcing it would only worsen their Karmic Luck.

The Titan of Earth summoned her siblings to determine how she should proceed. After several rounds of debate, they decided to send a messenger asking Nuwa for an audience. If she accepted, then Houtu would go to Wa Outer Heaven to discuss the terms for her establishing the earthly marriage. To prevent Nuwa from taking advantage of this meeting, the other titans would wait outside Wa Outer Heaven, ready to form the Pangu Genesis Formation at any time.

Houtu didn't think it was likely that Nuwa would accept, but she still sent a messenger. To her surprise, Nuwa actually agreed.

The twelve titans made their way to the chaotic boundary. When they reached Wa Outer Heaven, Houtu entered while the rest waited outside as they planned. Upon entering, a child-like artifact spirit greeted the Titan of Earth.

"Welcome, Lady Houtu," the child said. "I am Spirit Pearl, and Mother Nuwa is waiting inside Wa Palace."

"I've troubled you," Houtu said as she followed Spirit Pearl, showing none of a titan's usual ferocity. After all, she was a guest in Nuwa's home base and she came with a request, not to pick fights.

"Welcome," Nuwa said. She did not rise to greet Houtu, merely waving her toward the seat a level lower than her, showing her feelings on the status between the two.

Even when her host hid her true strength, Houtu's intuition told her that Nuwa could kill her with a finger. So, she didn't object and obediently sat down. "I've come to Daoist Nuwa with a request."

"Oh? And what is that request?" Nuwa asked leisurely.

Houtu took a breath and explained, "I heard that Daoist Nuwa holds a treasure known as the Red Hydrangea. With it, you can establish three marriages: heavenly, earthly, and mortal. I've come here for the earthly marriage. Houyi and Chang'e qualify for the earthly marriage."

Nuwa nodded. "Those two do indeed qualify."

A smile blossomed on Houtu's face. Her previous words had only been a guess, and Nuwa had confirmed her suspicions. But Nuwa's next sentence made that smile disappear.

"But why should I?"

"Daoist Nuwa is joking," Houtu said. "The earthly marriage is predetermined by the Way of Heaven. How can you joke about such matters?"

"I never thought I would hear a titan speak about the Way of Heaven. Don't you fellows only respect Pangu?" Nuwa asked, ignoring Houtu's increasingly ugly expression. "Leave. I am a demon. Do you think I would preside over Houyi's marriage after he killed nine demon princes? More importantly, why should I help the culprits that chased my brother and me away from our home and killed his Corpse?"

"Daoist Nuwa, no, Mother Nuwa. Everything can be negotiated. I believe we can work out a deal as long as the price is right," Houtu began. As a titan, she didn't like to beat around the bush. She knew nothing she said could erase what had already happened, so she directly asked what price the titans had to pay.

Nuwa closed her eyes for a brief moment as if to consider Houtu's words. After opening them, she said, "Tell me the inner workings of the Pangu Genesis Formation, and I'll agree."

"Impossible." Houtu rejected it without a second thought. The titans had agreed to tell the Three Purities in order to improve the Titanomachy Flags and because the two groups had no reason to fight, at least for now. The demons, on the other hand, were a different story. "Change the condition. What about materials? The Titan Tribe has collected a vast amount of them during our rule over the lands."

The two haggled over the price for years before finally settling on the Titan Tribe giving Nuwa five percent of all the materials they collected over the years as payment. They also grabbed numerous artifacts, but they didn't want to give them to the Demon Clan, even if they couldn't use them. It would be better to waste the Demon Clan's time and have them refine spiritual artifacts themselves.

It took over a thousand years before the Titan Tribe delivered the agreed-upon materials to Nuwa. They could have sent it to Thirty-Three Heavens and avoided the hassle, but the one they made a deal with was Nuwa and not Heavenly Court. Why would they deliver materials to their sworn enemies?

Let Nuwa deliver them if she wanted to give them to the Demon Clan.

With the payment received, Nuwa flew to the Houtu Tribe. All twelve titans also arrived, less to watch the ceremony and more to monitor Nuwa in case she tried anything.

Nuwa looked at Houyi without emotion. Strictly speaking, she didn't really hate Houyi. It was Di Jun's sons who had died and not hers, after all. When she glanced at Chang'e, an indiscernible look flashed across her eye for the briefest of moments.

"The Way of Heaven above, after the heavenly marriage is the earthly marriage. With Houyi representing yang and Chang'e representing yin, I hereby establish the earthly marriage!"

As with Di Jun and Xihe's marriage, clouds of merit descended onto the Houtu Tribe. Nuwa's Red Hydrangea absorbed 20 percent of the merits, while Houyi and Chang'e split the rest of the merits between themselves.

Houyi absorbed the merit and increased his strength, but his brows couldn't help but furrow in worry when Chang'e still remained an ordinary mortal despite absorbing 40 percent of the merit.

He glanced at Nuwa, wondering if she had interfered, but Nuwa directly stored the Red Hydrangea and left, disdaining to explain. Houyi turned to Houtu for help, but she also shook her head. All twelve titans and giants present had seen Chang'e absorb the merit. They couldn't very well accuse Nuwa of playing tricks with the evidence present.

Houyi began to worry. He knew that humans had short lifespans. Unless they cultivated to become Golden Immortals, they would die of old age. Unfortunately, Chang'e had no talent regarding cultivation, whether it be Laozi's Grand Purity Scripture Later Heaven Method or Wutian's martial arts.

Houyi wracked his brains trying to find a method to turn Chang'e immortal. His search eventually led him to Kunlun Mountain. He had heard Grand Purity Laozi was the most skilled alchemist in the Great Desolation, so he came seeking an elixir of immortality.

Laozi rejected him, but Houyi would not give up. He kneeled outside Kunlun Mountain for a hundred years but Laozi still refused.

At this time, a woman appeared in front of Houyi and asked, "Why have you been kneeling here for so long?"

Houyi looked at the woman. She exuded a feminine beauty only rivaled by Chang'e. "You are?"

"I am Xi Wangmu," Xi Wangmu said, pointing at the mountain west of Kunlun Mountain. "I usually reside on West Kunlun. When I have nothing to do, I take a stroll."

Houyi nodded and explained his purpose.

Upon hearing this, Xi Wangmu sank into thought. "I have an elixir of immortality. It can make any human who drinks it unaging, but it will not increase their cultivation. If you don't disdain it, I can offer it to you."

Houyi profusely thanked her and quickly returned to the Houtu Tribe after accepting. He had not seen Chang'e for over a hundred years, but it was a small price to pay for the eternity they would spend together. He gave Chang'e the elixir, but the moment she drank it, an invisible force pulled her into the sky.

Houyi chased after her, but Chang'e was pulled onto the Supreme Yin Star and locked within Coldlight Palace. When he stepped onto the Supreme Yin Star, the Quasi-Saint Changxi greeted him.

"Give her back!" Houyi screamed as he notched his arrow, preparing to kill the goddess.

Changxi raised her hand, motioning for Houyi to stop. "Don't worry, Chang'e isn't in any danger, but I cannot guarantee her life if you kill me. The moment you kill me, she will die too."

Houyi hesitated. He wanted to dismiss her words, but she seemed extremely confident. Plus, for the owner of the Supreme Yin Star, killing a powerless mortal like Chang'e was as simple as waving her hand.

"Did you think that you could live happily after killing my sister's sons?" Changxi asked.

"Don't speak in riddles, return Chang'e to me. Or don't blame me for beating a woman!" Houyi said.

"It's not impossible to release her from my Coldlight Palace." Changxi pointed to the Lunar Laurel Tree. "As long as you cut that tree down without harming the source of the Supreme Yin Star, I'll release Chang'e."

"So easy?" Houyi asked. He walked up to the laurel tree and grabbed the ax attached to his waist. He started to hack away at the trunk, but he discovered that as soon as his ax head left, the cut quickly healed.

"It's not so easy. The Lunar Laurel Tree is connected to the source of the Supreme Yin Star. Whatever damage the tree receives, it will be immediately healed," Changxi said.

"You tricked me!" Houyi roared as he raised his ax against her.

"Do you not care about Chang'e anymore?"

Houyi stopped his ax.

Changxi continued, "I did not trick you. As long as you can cut it down, I'll fulfill my promise. If you do not chop it down, I guess I can only send Chang'e to her death."

Houyi growled but returned to hacking away at the Lunar Laurel Tree. He used all the strength of his Quasi-Saint Realm body, but he could only leave a shallow mark on the trunk that quickly healed. He continued to chop at it. He put all he had into each and every strike until he felt that he had no power in his body, but the results were the same.

Days went by, followed by months, years, decades, centuries, and eventually millenia passed him by. Houyi continued to chop at the laurel tree with a single-minded obsession. His eyes grew dull as if he had lost all reason, becoming a machine that could only swing the ax.

Houyi no longer existed. Only a woodcutter stood in his place.

Changxi watched from afar as the woodcutter continued to chop the Lunar Laurel Tree with a sigh. A figure appeared beside her, and Changxi greeted her, "Sister."

Xihe stared at the mindless Houyi with hatred. She sneered. "This punishment is too cheap for him. When the ten eons are up, you should stay on the Supreme Yin Star. Do not join the war." With those words said, Xihe turned and left.

Changxi sighed. She almost couldn't recognize her sister anymore. A moment later, another woman walked next to Changxi. Surprisingly, it was Chang'e!

Chang'e's face was a mirror copy of Changxi's. A moment later, Chang'e merged with Changxi. She turned to leave, never noticing that beneath Houyi's feeble ax strikes, his strength gradually rose.

Chapter 53

Humanity's Tribulation

Inside Pangu Temple, the twelve titans gathered. Each one had a dark expression on their face.

"We were tricked," Di Jiang finally said.

"Let's go to Nuwa and demand an explanation!" Zhurong immediately said as fire spewed from his body, signifying his anger.

"It's no use," Gonggong said. "Nuwa fulfilled her end of the deal and established the earthly marriage. If there's someone to blame, then we can only blame the demons for being so insidious."

"I say we go to Thirty-Three Heavens and end them then and there," Zhurong suggested. "We can't wait for them to slowly pick us off. When another giant rises to become a gigant, are we going to let them scheme against him too?"

His words were met with rounds of approval, however, Jiuyin shook his head. "It's too dangerous. Many years have passed, and the demons' population must have increased more than before. If we rashly charge in, our losses will be far too great."

"What? I thought Gonggong was the coward, not you," Zhurong said, eliciting a glare from the Titan of Water. "Then should we wait for the demons to grow even more before charging? Screw Hongjun, let's get rid of the demons now!"

"Then can you defeat Yuanshi and Nuwa? If we break Hongjun's decree, only death will await us," Jiuyin said, silencing Zhurong. "I never said that we should let the demons grow stronger and kill us. Are there not humans? We should produce as many demigiants as possible to use as foot soldiers."

"Humans," Zhurong snorted. "I say this is all a trap. Who knows if something might happen at the critical moment? Nuwa created them, after all. If humans hadn't existed, Houyi wouldn't have been tricked. We should kill them all to prevent further trouble."

Zhurong's words elicited even more support, but it was Houtu who rejected his proposal.

"The humans haven't done anything wrong, they are innocent. We shouldn't kill them," Houtu protested.

"Houtu, you are kind, but sometimes too kind," Di Jiang said. "If killing the humans now could defeat the Demon Clan, and we did not do it, it would be too late to regret it."

"But Jiuyin's words are not without merit. What if the demigiants are the key to defeating the Demon Clan?" Houtu asked.

Houtu's firmness surprised Di Jiang until he remembered her position. The Houtu Tribe had the most integration with humans, and as such, demigiants made up a sizable contribution. "The Titan Tribe is split into twelve branches, and each branch can decide what they want to do with the humans."

Although Houtu was unhappy with the final verdict, she could only nod her head in acceptance.

"What about Xi Wangmu?" Rushou suddenly asked. "The demons could not have tricked Houyi without her help."

"It's an even worse idea," Di Jiang said. "With the demons, we can at least use the Pangu Genesis Formation to fight Nuwa, but don't forget that Xi Wangmu resides on West Kunlun. I refuse to believe that she has the courage to scheme against Houyi without the interference of those on Kunlun. Laozi and Yuanshi are both Saints of Heaven now. If we tear down the unwritten agreement between us, we will have to face three Saints. It seems our actions of yesteryear have come back to haunt us."

"Those bastards. Didn't they say that all grievances would end after the transaction?" Zhurong asked, reigniting the other tians' fury. Although they wanted to seek justice, none of them truly thought they could force anything from the Three Purities.

After this, Di Jiang also gave a verdict on the reason for the meeting. "We won't attack Thirty-Three Heavens for now either. From now on, the Titan Tribe will focus on subjugating and enslaving the rogue powers of the Great Desolation. Since they live on the land, they must obey its rulers, us. Furthermore, the battle between Heavenly Court and us will begin on the land. We will focus on whittling down their forces as much as possible before assaulting Thirty-Three Heaven."

Although some titans disapproved, they accepted their leader's decision. When they returned, all but Jiuyin, Jumang, and Houtu decided to kill the humans living in their tribes. Some of the demigiants rebelled, but that only reinforced the titans' resolve. They killed the rebellious demigiants and turned the remainder into obedient slaves.

Compared to the overall population of humanity that had reached a billion, the ones killed within the nine titan tribes were just a drop in the bucket.

After this, the Titan Tribe began capturing and absorbing the rogue powers that had not pledged their allegiance to a major force. Except for those with exceptional strength like Minghe or Kong Xuan, the Titan Tribe attacked them all. If they were not willing to submit, they would be killed.

Conspicuously, they avoided the area around Kunlun Mountain and Firesource Grotto.

While the Titan Tribe started a bloodbath on the land, Heavenly Court made plans of its own.

* * *

Di Jun glanced at the weak Earth Immortal demon bowing to him in Eminence Heaven Palace. He turned to Bai Ze, who had brought the creature here.

Bai Ze nodded and turned toward the demon. "Show His Majesty the weapon you showed me."

The little demon didn't dare to delay and brought out a plain copper sword. Di Jun waved his hand, and the copper sword flew into it. After inspecting it, Di Jun couldn't see what was so special about it. It couldn't be plainer and hadn't even reached the rank of an artifact.

However, Di Jun trusted his prime minister wouldn't bring something so worthless to his attention. He placed the edge against the palm of his hand, where the skin was the thinnest, and slashed. The sword didn't cut, but it left a white mark on his skin.

Di Jun's eyes lit up. Although his physical prowess wasn't as terrifying as that of the titans or giants, his flesh was still incredibly powerful. No ordinary weapon could have damaged it.

"Where did you get this?" Di Jun questioned.

The Earth Immortal demon lowered his head. "I refined this, Your Majesty."

"You did?" Di Jun looked at the demon, and he really couldn't see anything special.

"Tell his majesty how you refined it," Bai Ze prompted.

"Yes," the little demon said. "To answer His Majesty, I originally took the sword from a wandering human. After I took it and killed the human, I decided to use his soul to refine an artifact, but I never expected I would refine such a powerful weapon. Using it, I was able to kill Sky Immortals."

"Bai Ze, dispatch a squad of demons and capture some humans for Us," Di Jun ordered. Then he turned to the little demon. "If your words are true, We will handsomely reward you and even give you an official position."

Elation spread across the Earth Immortal's face. He quickly bowed, slamming his head onto the ground in the process. "Thank you for your grace, Your Majesty!"

A few months later, Di Jun held a sword in his hand. He had used Sunsource Iron, Undermoon Copper, and many other precious materials to forge this sword. Then, he'd used the souls of 10,000 humans to refine it, and now it exuded a misty, baleful aura.

Di Jun slashed the edge across his palm. The skin split, dripping blood onto the ground. "Haha, Titan Tribe, your good days will soon be over!"

The next day, Di Jun summoned all the demon officials and the demon emperors.

After announcing the news, Kunpeng immediately saluted Di Jun and said, "Congratulations to Your Majesty. Saintess Nuwa must have created humanity to propel the Demon Clan's rise. Not only can their souls be used to refine a powerful artifact, but I heard that demons who feast on their flesh can cultivate even faster."

The second part was news to Di Jun, but he still smiled. Truthfully, he had been displeased by the humans growing close to the Titan Tribes, but owing to them being Nuwa's creation, he had not taken action. However, now he could reap their lives to strengthen the Demon Clan.

"Your Majesty, I think you must not," Fuxi spoke up, stepping out at this moment. "Humanity is Southern Emperor Wa's creation. We mustn't use their souls as materials and eat them."

Di Jun frowned, displeased by his defiance. "Did you not hear the Demon Preceptor's words? Southern Emperor Wa's creation of humanity is for the Demon Clan. Why can't We? She will understand. Now, I order the full might of the Demon Clan to mobilize!"

Fuxi could only sigh upon hearing Di Jun's decisiveness.

* * *

In Wa Outer Heaven, Nuwa's eyelashes flickered as her gaze penetrated the Thirty-Three Heavens and peered at Di Jun. She moved to rebuke him, but the Way of Heaven stopped her. She frowned, but relented.

"This is a tribulation humanity must face in order to become the future masters of the world. Hmpf, Di Jun, don't think just because I won't take action, you won't have to pay the price." With that declaration, she closed her eyes and resumed her cultivation.

* * *

Humanity faced its greatest catastrophe yet. Everywhere, hordes of human settlements were slaughtered. Old, young, male, female, none of that mattered to the demons. Before, many had already discovered the benefits of devouring humans, but had done so in secret to avoid Nuwa's wrath.

Now, with the Heavenly Emperor's orders, they openly ate the humans to quickly raise their cultivation. Their mission was to collect human souls and not bodies, after all.

As more and more humans died, the wandering ghosts and phantoms inhabiting the Great Desolation dramatically rose. Usually, most of the remnant spirits would dissipate with time under the purifying rays from the Supreme Yang Star or go to the Blood Sea, but there were too many dead humans covering the whole of the Great Desolation in a baleful atmosphere.

The actions of the demons naturally caught the attention of the human ancestors in the East Sea, who held an emergency meeting. Sitting under Nuwa's statue, Suiren, Zhengyi, Youchao, Wutian, and the rest of the upper echelons gathered.

"Have you discovered why the demons have suddenly begun to assault us en masse?" Suiren asked.

The wisemen looked at one another and shook their heads. To them, this disaster had come out of nowhere.

"Even if we don't know, since the demons dare to massacre us, we must make them pay the price," Wutian said.

After gaining enlightenment from Laozi's sermon, he had entered the Golden Immortal Realm and created a path to both the Earth and Sky Immortal Realms using martial arts, exponentially increasing humanity's strength.

Now, he was focusing on perfecting the Golden Immortal segment. He had decided that he wanted to use martial arts to grow instead of Supreme Purity Scripture, even though it would be faster to cultivate to the Great Unity Realm using it.

After Laozi's sermon, although many people had started cultivating the Grand Purity Scripture Later Heaven Method, many still cultivated martial arts since it had a low entry requirement. Martial arts once again flourished with the appearance of more and more Earth Immortal martial artists.

Wutian had dispatched those Earth Immortal martial artists to settlements who didn't have any martial art inheritance or had lost theirs. Because of this, Wutian's prestige now overshadowed that of the first three human ancestors.

"I don't think that is wise," Zhengyi said. "Although humanity has grown stronger, it's still not enough to combat the Demon Clan."

"We don't need to beat them," Wutian said. "We just need to show them that killing humanity is not worth the effort. If the price for slaughtering us becomes too high, they'll stop."

"Wouldn't that price also be too high for us?" Suiren asked.

"What else can we do?" Wutian said helplessly. "We as a race are too weak compared to others. If we don't show a tough front, the Demon Clan and even the Titan Tribe will think humans are insects that to be squashed at their leisure. Don't forget that nine of the twelve branches exterminated the humans living in peace among them."

Hearing this, all the upper echelons' expressions darkened. One of them suddenly asked, "What about Mother Nuwa? Is she not doing anything?"

Suiren, Zhengyi, and Youchao closed their eyes. They had prayed arduously to Nuwa's statue, but there was no response. Clearly, she was unwilling to intervene.

Another member asked, "What about your master?"

Wutian hesitated. He looked around the room, and upon seeing the pleading expressions, he gritted his teeth. "I'll ask. In the meanwhile, gather all the immortals of humanity and plan a counterattack!"

"As the Martial Ancestor commands!"

* * *

In the Supreme Purity Hall, Tongtian opened her eyes. The Kongtong Seal appeared in her hand. Upon closer inspection, it was clearly trembling like it was crying. Tongtian, of course, knew the reason for its abnormal state. The current calamity of humanity had dramatically decreased their Karmic Luck.

Each human carried a little bit of Karmic Luck. No matter how little, together, it made up a terrifying force. Of course, humanity's Karmic Luck would diminish if their numbers dramatically fell. The one most upset by this situation shouldn't have been her or Laozi, but Nuwa.

Thanks to the Kongtong Seal, Tongtian had occupied a portion of the human luck, which greatly aided in her comprehension of the 3,000 laws. But recently, her comprehension had slowed. Nuwa, who occupied an even larger portion, would notice the effect even more.

Tongtian stopped as she gazed out of Three Purity Palace onto the base of the mountain, where she saw her disciple, Wutian. She summoned Baihe, a white crane Yuanshi had accepted as a steward for Three Purity Palace.

"Aunt-Master," Baihe said. Like Haotian, Baihe appeared like a child no older than ten.

"Go down the mountain and bring up my disciple."

Baihe blinked. He had not known that Tongtian had accepted a disciple, but he didn't question it. The Sky Immortal descended and was surprised to find that Tongtian's disciple was a Golden Immortal.

The one with the most advanced cultivation base among Yuanshi's disciples was Guang Chengzi, and he was only at the Profound Immortal Realm. The Heavenly Venerable of Primordial Beginning also had another Profound Immortal disciple, Antarctic Immortal Weng, but he was a nominal disciple accepted by Yuanshi after he established the Enlightenment Sect.

Baihe led Wutian to the Supreme Purity Hall before excusing himself.

"Master," Wutian said as he kneeled down and bowed.

"Rise," Tongtian calmly said. "Why have you come?"

"Master, humanity is undergoing a calamity, and we seek your aid. Please, help us."

Tongtian sighed. Although she had long stopped considering herself human, she still held special feelings for them. "Even if I wanted to help, I cannot."

Wutian furrowed his brows. "I don't understand."

"All I can say is that it involves the secrets of heaven, and I cannot lightly divulge it. All things in heaven and earth must undergo tribulation. Not even the Great Desolation is exempt. This is humanity's tribulation, and you must overcome it by yourself." Seeing Wutian's sorrowful expression, Tongtian continued, "However, it's not like it's impossible to help."

Wutian raised his face, his eyes shining brightly.

"Say, if the demons were to come to Kunlun Mountain, then I and your Uncle-Masters can naturally expel unwanted guests."

"I understand. Thank you, Master!" Wutian immediately left the hall, leaving Tongtian alone.

"I wasn't finished," she muttered. "If you were in danger, I could take action to save you since you're my disciple."

CHAPTER 54

The Martial Path

Di Jun slammed his palm onto the armrest of the Nine Dragon Throne, creating a thunderous boom in Eminence Heaven Palace. "What did you say?"

The demon official fell to his knees as Di Jun's overpowering aura crushed him. Still, he repeated his earlier report. "R-Reporting to Your M-Majesty, a squadron of fifty Sky Immortals perished while reaping a human settlement."

Although fifty Sky Immortal demons were nothing to the overall strength of Heavenly Court, Di Jun had never expected to lose a single one to a race he considered ants. "Did the Titan Tribe take advantage of our operation to attack them?"

"N-No," the demon official's voice grew infinitely smaller as he spoke his next words.

"Say that again."

The little demon wished a hole would appear under his feet and swallow him so he could get away, but he still obeyed the Heavenly Emperor's orders. "It was the humans. Over a thousand Sky Immortals suddenly showed up and massacred the squadron."

Di Jun slapped the Nine Dragon Throne's armrest again, causing the sound to reverberate in the court. "Such gall! Which general is willing to exterminate those Sky Immortals?"

"Your Majesty, please reconsider!" Fuxi said, stepping out. "Humanity is simply defending itself. We arbitrarily decided to harvest their souls, and we are already in the wrong. As the Heavenly Court, we must seek to regulate and manage heaven and earth, not cause needless bloodshed."

Di Jun's eyes scanned Fuxi. The latter's scalp tingled as he saw the endless hatred in the former's eyes. "Whatever We do is to manage heaven and earth. Humanity should behave like the livestock they are. To resist is to commit the heaviest crime! Western Emperor Xi, stay in Thirty-Three Heaven and guard against the Titan Tribe." Di Jun turned his attention to one of the Ten Demon Sages. "Fei Lian."

Fei Lian, the Soaring Leopard Demon, stepped out and kneeled. "Subject is present."

"Lead a squadron of Immortal Lords and exterminate those Sky Immortals and the four human ancestors!" Di Jun's voice resounded like thunder throughout the hall.

"Subject obeys!" Fei Lian said. He was the only Demon Sage still in the Great Firmament Realm, so he was the most suitable. No matter how powerful the humans were, they could never have a Golden Immortal of the Great Firmament, much less a Quasi-Saint.

As Fuxi watched Fei Lian, he closed his eyes and sighed. Unknown to anyone, Kunpeng's eyes flashed with elation as his plans came together perfectly against his expectations. He didn't even need to use the backups he'd prepared.

Fei Lian led a squadron of fifteen Golden Immortal demons down to the land where the thousand human Sky Immortals had appeared. When he arrived, he discovered that not only had the Sky Immortals disappeared, but the human settlement had also vanished.

The demon sage growled with frustration. "Search the surrounding million li. If you discover any humans, eliminate them and harvest their souls. If you see human Sky Immortals, kill them at will!"

The Immortal Lords accepted Fei Lian's orders and spread out.

Fei Lian and the Golden Immortal demons searched high and low for those Sky Immortals for the next few years, but the humans used guerilla tactics to attack and fled mostly unharmed. Furthermore, after piecing together the information over the years, Heavenly Court discovered that humanity had gained over 9,000 Sky Immortals.

As a result, the squadron of fifteen Golden Immortals grew to over ninety.

More and more humans were deserting settlements. Humanity not only used their Sky Immortals to attack the demon soldiers but also evacuated as many humans as possible. Finally, Fei Lian grew tired of playing hide-and-seek and decided to attack their home base near the East Sea.

When the demon sage arrived above the core of humanity, he saw thousands of martial artists scuttling about. At the center of it all was a magnificent temple. Fei Lian snorted and spread out his hand. A gigantic hand made of qi formed above humanity's core lands and pressed down, flattening everything in its wake. When the dust settled, all that remained was a small shelter glowing with spiritual light.

Fei Lian's eyes lit up as he saw the meritorious artifact.

Suiren, Zhengyi, Youchao, and the other upper echelons of humanity filed out of the shelter-shaped artifact. After witnessing the devastation and all the human corpses, their faces turned ugly as they glared at the demon squadron. Even if they knew that they had no chance of winning, they wanted to make them pay.

Fei Lian sneered when he saw them. The three ancestors of humanity were only in the Golden Immortal Realm. "Per the decree of the Heavenly Emperor, the four ancestors and leaders of humanity are sentenced to death for killing members of the Celestial Army!"

Just as Fei Lian started to attack, his expression paled as rainbow light erupted from the temple's rubble. The rubble was blasted away, revealing the statue of Nuwa.

"Wait, Emperor Wa, it was an accident! I didn't know your esteemed self was enshrined here!" Fei Lian screamed, but it was no use.

The rainbow light shot through Fei Lian and the rest of his army. They coughed blood by the mouthfuls, and their auras and combat prowess plummeted until it barely hovered between a Golden Immortal and Sky Immortal.

Suiren laughed loudly. "Haha, praise Mother Nuwa!"

Before his laughter could be heard, and when he turned around, the statue of Nuwa shattered into dust. Suiren and the other humans' faces darkened with anger.

"Kill them all, don't let a single one leave!"

Under Suiren's orders, the three ancestors of humanity and the other upper echelons swarmed Fei Lian and the Golden Immortal demons. Most of the Sky Immortals were out evacuating humans, but a force of a thousand remained in the core lands.

Over a hundred died when Fei Lian attacked unannounced, but most had been inside the temple, so Youchao had protected them with his meritorious spiritual artifact.

They lost over half of the Sky Immortals present, but they managed to kill Fei Lian and the rest of the demons. Still, that could not quell their wrath as Fei Lian's words echoed in their ears. Sentenced to death for killing members of the Celestial Army? Was it wrong to protect themselves against this unjust killing?!

This was the scene Wutian returned to. After hearing what had happened, he sighed. "You should have let one escape."

"What, why?" Suiren asked.

"If you had let one escape, then news of Mother Nuwa's action could have acted as a deterrent. Now, It's likely that the Heavenly Emperor will send an even stronger force to kill us," Wutian said.

"Can't we just tell them?" Youchao asked, scratching his head.

Wutian smiled bitterly. "If a demon told them, they might believe it. But if we said it, then they can call us liars. After all, no witnesses are left. Even if they believed our words, Di Jun would still call it a lie to make it easier for them to kill us."

"How about we build another statue of Mother Nuwa?" Zhenyi suggested.

Wutian hesitated a bit before nodding. "We can try."

The four ancestors of humanity tried to sculpt another statue of Nuwa, but no matter what they did, their efforts were in vain.

"As expected," Wutian said.

"What does Fourth Brother mean?" Suiren asked.

"Master told me that this is the human race's tribulation. During a tribulation, we cannot avoid it or rely on external aid. Presumably, this is the reason why Mother Nuwa can't actively aid us."

"Then what can we do?" Zhengyi asked, furrowing her brows in worry.

"Survive," he answered. "The Heavenly Emperor wants to kill us. We'll use ourselves as bait to draw them away while relocating most of the population to Kunlun Mountain or any place with a Saint of Heaven. I heard that Saint Redcloud of Firesource Grotto will take us in and repel the Demon Clan too."

Suiren, Zhengyi, and Youchao nodded, agreeing to Wutian's strategy. The three understood the risks, yet they still chose this option for the future of humanity. None of them had been contaminated by the negative emotions and thoughts of the later generation of humans.

They were still the pure and selfless humans Nuwa had created.

First, they recalled about 4,000 Sky Immortals. The four ancestors led their best combatants in the opposite direction of Kunlun Mountain with a noticeable trail. Second, they had the other Sky Immortals hasten the relocation efforts. Even if only one percent of humanity survived, it would be considered a victory.

Wutian and the other ancestors of humanity flew as far as possible, but Heavenly Court's reaction was much faster than expected.

"Killing one of the Demon Clan's sages is an unforgivable crime! For this, We sentence humanity to extinction."

Wutian looked up at the Celestial Army of Heavenly Court with sweat dripping down his forehead. He had never expected him to personally lead the army. "Heavenly Emperor Di Jun."

Di Jun raised his arm and brought it down. The legion behind him, composed of Profound Immortals, attacked.

The human Sky Immortals were the first to fall. Although they put up a valiant fight—especially with their martial prowess—the Celestial Army outnumbered them more than two to one. Even Wutian, Suiren, Zhengyi, and Youchao struggled.

"Haha, Di Jun, you purposely massacre life in heaven and earth for selfish reasons. You are not worthy of being the Heavenly Emperor!" Suiren shouted angrily.

Di Jun's eyes narrowed. He pointed at Suiren, forming a wisp of Solar Truefire on his fingertip. It shot toward the offending human and enveloped him. The Heavenly Emperor thought that would be the end of a mere Golden Immortal of Merit, but to his shock, Suiren didn't die.

Shrouded by the Solar Truefire, Suiren laughed even more wildly. His outline grew hazy in the extreme heat, but at that moment, his stalwart figure was imprinted in every human's mind.

"I am Suiren, the Fire Ancestor of Humanity. Although I may perish, my fire will not! I will transform my body into flames and protect humanity. So long as humanity exists, the Human Heartfire shall never be extinguished!"

Suiren's body merged with the Solar Truefire, turning it a warm red instead of its former golden color. Upon seeing it, any human would recall the warmth and protection it brought, while any of humanity's enemies who saw it would feel fear.

The Human Heartfire shot up into the sky and exploded. Wisps of fire rained down, nourishing the humans. When the flames touched demons, they writhed in pain and agony. Even a Quasi-Saint like Di Jun had to spare some effort to extinguish the flame.

"Eldest Brother!" Wutian, Zhengyi, and Youchao called out in anguish.

"Demons, you and humanity are forever incompatible!" Wutian shouted. "As long as a demon exists, we humans will slaughter them!"

"An ant like you dares to declare a feud with Our Demon Clan?" Di Jun's anger boiled over. He appeared in front of Wutian wielding a sword covered in a baleful aura.

Wutian leveled a lethal glare at Di Jun. Despite knowing his efforts were fruitless, he threw a punch. Even if it were to have no effect, he would carve his name into the Heavenly Emperor's memories.

Di Jun's eyes did not contain any trace of respect, only scorn. But before his sword could cut down Wutian, fine threads wrapped around the blade, stopping it.

Wutian took this chance and struck. It was nothing more than a punch filled with his heart and mind, but it reached Di Jun, even leaving the tiniest of marks. Di Jun couldn't believe that a mere Golden Immortal actually landed a strike on him. He growled and slapped

Wutian down to the ground. The human hit the ground hard, bleeding from all nine orifices. Di Jun then turned to the source of the fine lines wrapped around his sword, Zhengyi.

When Youchao had received his merits, the first shelter he'd built had become his companion artifact. Zhengyi's meritorious artifact was her clothing. She used it for both offense and defense.

Di Jun flicked his wrist, but to his shock, his sword couldn't cut through the threads wrapped around it. He had used millions upon millions of human souls to refine the spiritual artifact, yet it couldn't even cut mere thread. It had to be known that Di Jun had tested it on top-grade innate spiritual artifacts, and the sword had won each time.

The Heaven Emperor yanked the sword back, pulling Zhengyi over as well. Although he couldn't cut the threads, his strength still outstripped that of a little Golden Immortal. When Zhenyi neared, Di Jun burst her head with a single punch. Her remains splattered all over the land, and the threads loosened and fell off.

"Second Sister!" Youchao cried out. He knew that the chances of them surviving were slim to none, but each death still hurt. He began laughing, just as Suiren had.

"I am Youchao, the Shelter Ancestor of Humanity! Although I may perish here, my protection will not! As long as humanity is united, they will receive protection. The more humans of the same mind and heart, the stronger their defense!"

Di Jun frowned and appeared behind Youchao. He decapitated him, killing him instantly. But Youchao's body evaporated into a golden light that merged with his meritorious shelter-shaped artifact. The artifact disintegrated into dust and flew into the sky, raining down and merging with all of humanity.

"Second Sister, Third Brother!" Wutian roared as he flew back into the sky.

Pain wracked his body, but the suffering in his heart was even more unbearable. He glared at their killer. "Di Jun, you and I cannot coexist under the same sky!"

Wutian's aura shot up dramatically. The light from Youchao gathered onto Wutian, shrouding him in a golden glow; Zhengyi's robes flew onto his body and transformed into a battle robe; Suiren's Human Heartfire lit up his eyes. His aura shot up to the peak of the Golden Immortal Realm, the Great Unity Realm, and even the Great Firmament Realm. He even showed signs of breaking through to the Quasi-Saint Realm.

"Today, I, Wutian, establish the Martial Path for humanity! The Martial Path does not cultivate qi but refines essence into inner energy! Cultivate the body to refine the mind and improve oneself! This is the Human Way!" His voice echoed throughout the Great Desolation, aided by the Way of Heaven.

After Wutian finished speaking, endless merit descended onto him. He did not absorb it to forcibly raise his cultivation but condense it into a halo of merit behind him. Wutian turned toward Di Jun. Although his realm had not reached the Quasi-Saint, his combat prowess had. "Die, Di Jun!"

Di Jun's eyes burned with ruthlessness. He stored the sword and took out his Celestial River Diagram. A weapon refined from humans would not be effective against them, especially given their last answer to the Demon Clan. It would be better to kill Wutian with his diagram and nip the threat in the bud.

He formed the Starry Sky behind him and shot countless bolts of starlight. The golden glow around Wutian increased as he reared back his fist. Just as the two attacks were about to clash, a sword light descended between them and formed a ravine below.

Both Wutian and Di Jun looked up to see Tongtian. She sheathed the Qingping Sword and said, "Return, Di Jun. Humanity's tribulation has ended. You shall no longer massacre them."

CHAPTER 55

The Underworld

"What is the meaning of this?" Di Jun demanded as he looked at the slowly descending Tongtian.

"Exactly as I said," Tongtian said, flying in front of Wutian.

"Daoist Tongtian, don't meddle in business that is not yours. If you don't move, then don't blame me for being impolite."

Tongtian's lips quirked upward as she looked at Di Jun and his half-battered army. "Impolite? I really want to see how impolite you can be. Besides, Wutian here is my disciple. I won't let you kill him."

"Do you want me to stop him?"

Tongtian frowned when she heard Yuanshi's words. She glanced toward Kunlun Mountain and said, "Don't interfere."

Her anger had been building while watching the demons slay the humans. If she didn't vent her frustrations, they would stay with her for a number of years and disrupt her mood, slowing down her cultivation.

Di Jun frowned at Tongtian's declaration. He was wary of Tongtian not because of her strength but because of the two Saints of Heaven behind her. The Saints shouldn't take action if he didn't kill her.

The Heavenly Emperor focused on Wutian, and the killing intent within his eyes intensified. He feared Wutian's potential. Being able to form a different path like the Immortal Path cultivated by the majority of the creatures of the Great Desolation or the Strength Path cultivated by the Titan Tribe represented infinite potential.

If Wutian were allowed to grow, then it would be truly a disaster for the Demon Clan. He had to die!

"Celestial Army, kill the human!" Di Jun ordered.

After a moment of hesitation, the demon army charged forward while Di Jun occupied Tongtian.

"If it were Taiyi, I would have to be more careful, but you aren't him," Tongtian said. She waved her hand, and 10,000 swords appeared around her. "Arise, Myriad Sword Formation!" The 10,000 swords arranged into four layers and formed a field filled with sword light. Any demon who entered was instantly shredded. "Even Quasi-Saints don't dare to enter my Myriad Sword Formation, much less mere Profound Immortals. No matter how many of them enter, it's useless."

Di Jun frowned. He raised the Celestial River Diagram and started flipping through the pages one-handed. A miniature Starry Sky appeared behind him. He waved his hand, and 365 flags appeared and flew toward the 365 major stars of the miniature Starry Sky.

The miniature Starry Sky seemed to resonate with the true Starry Sky above the land, dramatically increasing its power. "Although your Myriad Sword Formation is powerful, do you think that I don't have a way to nullify it?" Di Jun asked.

Tongtian's eyes widened in appreciation. "I never expected you to merge the formation flags of the Starry Sky War Array with your Celestial River Diagram."

The miniature Starry Sky clashed against the Myriad Sword Formation. With the starlight occupying the sword light, the Myriad Sword Formation came to a standstill.

A black lotus full of cracks appeared above Tongtian's head; it was the Twelfth-Ranked Black Lotus of Destruction she traded from Kong Xuan. A black aura seeped out from the lotus and enveloped the Myriad Sword Formation and the miniature Starry Sky. Everything within disintegrated, breaking into tiny particles.

Di Jun covered himself in a protective layer of Solar Truefire, but even that was slowly withering under the destructive domain of the Twelfth-Ranked Black Lotus of Destruction. The Heavenly Emperor gritted his teeth, and after a moment of hesitation, he said, "Retrea—"

Before he could finish, Tongtian appeared in front of him and unsheathed the Qingping Sword.

Di Jun bit back a groan of pain as he retreated, covering the large gash on his torso. "You—!"

He still didn't get a chance to finish as Tongtian disappeared. This time, she reappeared behind him and lacerated his back. He screamed in pain. From there, no matter where Di Jun tried to flee, Tongtian would reappear in front of him, preventing his escape. He was helpless against Tongtian's superior strength and techniques. He could have shrunk down the miniature Starry Sky to defend, but that would have put the demon legion at risk.

However, Di Jun didn't have a chance to decide. Tongtian increased the destructive power formed from the black lotus, killing all the Profound Immortal demons.

"You bitch!" Di Jun shouted.

Tongtian froze for a moment, but soon, a smile more beautiful than any flower blossomed on her face. It was a smile that Yuanshi would flee from, no questions asked. Di Jun only felt the chill of death creeping up on him.

"GAH!" Di Jun screamed as Tongtian appeared in front of him and stabbed her sword through his chest.

She paused for a moment, allowing Di Jun to blast her away and put some distance between them. He pressed his palm against his wound, trying to stop the bleeding.

Tongtian halted her attack. She released the Myriad Sword Formation and stored the Twelfth-Ranked Black Lotus of Destruction. "Why are you staring at me like this? Do you wish for me to end you right now?"

Di Jun continued to glare at Tongtian, but he flew backward. When she remained hovering where she was, he stored the formation flags and the miniature Starry Sky and fled. "I'll remember this!"

Tongtian felt the corner of her lips twitch. *Do you want me to kill you that badly?* She shrugged. Even if she wanted to, the price would be too high. The Heaven-Opening Merits she possessed would likely disappear as punishment from the Way of Heaven. Tongtian flew to her disciple and asked, "How are you feeling?"

Wutian looked down at the land, where the corpses of his fellow humans lay. "Master, is there no way to save them?"

Tongtian sighed. "I don't possess the ability to resurrect them. Right now, you should lead the rest of humanity at Kunlun Mountain since the other human ancestors are dead. They need you more than ever now."

"How many are left?" Wutian asked, dreading the answer.

"Less than a million remain; at least 95 percent died."

Wutian clutched his heart and wailed in pain. "Demon Clan, you will have your retribution!" he roared into the sky. Thunder roared as if the heavens agreed.

Tongtian shook her head. "Let's go."

She carried Wutian home. During the journey, she taught him the rest of the Nine-Revolution Arcane Art and the method to sever the Corpse and enter the Quasi-Saint Realm.

Halfway there, Tongtian stopped. "You go back alone. In the current world, only Quasi-Saints can threaten you."

Tongtian left. She didn't worry about humanity anymore because the Saints of Heaven had already commanded Heavenly Court to cease the massacre.

Tongtian wanted nothing more than to return to Kunlun Mountain and improve her comprehension. Through her connection to the Kongtong Seal, she had realized that the luck of humanity had stabilized and even showed the potential to exceed its previous peak. Furthermore, as Wutian's master, she also gained a portion of the Martial Path's luck.

But she'd just received notice that Houtu had started to roam the Great Desolation.

Is it finally time to form the Underworld and Six Paths of Reincarnation?

* * *

After the Saints prevented Heavenly Court from slaughtering any more humans, Houtu decided to traverse the Great Desolation. For some time, her heart had grown restless, aching as if there was a hole.

After leaving Chiyou in charge of the Houtu Tribe, she left to wander the lands. Unlike the Great Desolation of a few eons ago, restless souls and ghosts filled the land. Their grievances condensed into miasma, damaging the land even more and making it unlivable for most lifeforms.

Killing and death had always existed in the Great Desolation, so for this unbelievable amount of miasma to form, a vast number of lives with spirituality must have been prematurely taken. Before Nuwa had created humans, all life that attained spirituality were at least Earth Immortals and above. However, they only composed a small percentage of all current life.

Humanity was different. Although they were Later Heaven life-forms, they were born with spirituality. After death, their remnant desires and emotions could form ghosts and phantoms. And humans had populated many lands and areas in the Great Desolation. Heavenly Court had slaughtered millions of them, causing the current dilemma.

The more Houtu saw, the more she sighed. All twelve titans had belligerent natures, herself included, but she possessed something the other titans did not: a heart of compassion for all life. Houtu could cast aside her compassion when fighting and killing the demons of the Heavenly Court, but a large loss of life still saddened her.

"If only there were a place for these lost souls to return to." As soon as Houtu said those words, her eyes brightened. She began to search for a place that could store remnant souls and ghosts.

She looked high and low but couldn't find a place to hold the lost souls. Everywhere, the Supreme Yang Star shone, which curbed and damaged the lost souls. Once they were completely burned away by the sun's rays, the soul would cease to exist forever.

Eventually, Houtu followed a trail of them leading to the Blood Sea. There, ghosts merged with the miasma of the crimson waters, but they lost all reason and only knew how to war with each other. Just like getting burned by the sun's rays, such an environment would lead to their destruction.

It was not the place she was looking for.

Houtu turned her head as the space next to her suddenly distorted. Moments later, a figure clad in red emerged, and space calmed down.

"Daoist Tongtian," Houtu greeted the Supreme Purity.

"Lady Houtu," Tongtian replied.

"I wonder why Daoist Tongtian is here?" Houtu asked. Although the Three Purities and the Titan Tribe weren't enemies, they weren't allies either.

"It's nothing. It's just that I felt a chance here."

Although her words were vague, Houtu's eyes lit up. Those who cultivated the Immortal Path understood heaven and earth better than those who cultivated the Strength Path. Perhaps Tongtian could enlighten her.

"Daoist Tongtian, do you feel that the Great Desolation is missing something?" Houtu tested.

"Of course," Tongtian said without hesitation.

Houtu's eyes shone even brighter. "Then what does Daoist Tongtian think is missing?"

"Reincarnation!"

Houtu felt her heartbeat quicken upon hearing the word. The fog blocking her thoughts disappeared. "So, it's like this..."

Tongtian watched Houtu mutter to herself. The titan ignored Tongtian and revealed her true form, dwarfing the immortal. She stepped into the Blood Sea. With each step, blood rumbled and parted as if awaiting Houtu's arrival. Houtu waded deep into the red waves but not toward the core area. Tongtian followed along and continued to watch Houtu. Not long after, she saw Minghe flying over.

"Daoist Tongtian, Houtu, what are you doing?!" he roared. He had noticed Houtu when she'd appeared, but he hadn't dared to reveal himself after losing his Twelfth-Ranked Red Lotus of Karma alongside the Yuanti and Abi Swords.

Minghe's wariness had increased when Tongtian appeared. He could no longer hide when he felt himself losing control of the Blood Sea despite being its master.

"Don't attack her," Tongtian said, blocking Minghe. "Don't worry. It's a good thing for the Great Desolation, and you as well."

Minghe gritted his teeth. Why would he believe Tongtian's words without any proof? Furthermore, he could feel the Blood Sea's level decreasing as it was absorbed by Houtu's body. Still, with Tongtian blocking him, there was nothing he could do without heavy retaliation. So, unwillingly, he could only watch Houtu continue to move and absorb parts of his precious sea.

Houtu continued to wade through the Blood Sea until she reached the edge. It did not connect to any land of the Great Desolation but to the chaotic boundary. Once there, she announced, "Heaven and earth lacks reincarnation. I, Houtu, will use my body to form the Underworld and Reincarnation to house all life that has died!"

Her words reached throughout the Great Desolation, carried by the Way of Heaven.

Houtu's body expanded, transforming into a dark and gloomy world that neither sunlight nor moonlight could reach. The newly formed Underworld had several landmarks, such as the Nine Nether Springs, Nether Capital Youdu, and the Bridge of Forgetfulness.

The River of Time appeared above the Underworld and started to change. It trembled as part of it split away to form the River of Reincarnation below. Tongtian stared at the River of Time and River of Reincarnation without blinking, engraving the exposed law of heaven and earth into her very soul.

Endless merits descended from the Way of Heaven. Ninety percent of the merits merged with the Underworld and River of Reincarnation, causing the speed of their creation to increase. The last 10 percent split in two and flowed to Tongtian and Minghe.

The Underworld was complete.

* * *

In Kunlun Mountain, Laozi and Yuanshi stood up from their

prayer mats and made a half bow in Houtu's direction. As the most exalted personage in the Great Desolation, Saints of Heaven did not need to bow to anyone, but Houtu was an exception. Her actions benefited the Great Desolation and perfected the world.

Even Nuwa, who held a grudge against the Titan Tribe, lowered her head. Alongside her, Redcloud Ancestor, Jieyin, and Zhunti also bowed.

* * *

Inside Eminence Heaven Palace, Di Jun looked away from his refinement of nascent artifact using human souls. At first, he furrowed his brows at Houtu's action but quickly brightened up. Houtu had used her body to form the Underworld and River of Reincarnation, which meant the Titan Tribe had one less titan, preventing them from forming the Pangu Genesis Formation.

* * *

In Pangu Temple, all the titans fumed. They didn't care that Houtu's actions benefited the Great Desolation because her actions sealed their ability to use the Pangu Genesis Formation. After a quick discussion, all of them decided to make their way to the newly formed Underworld.

Chapter 56

All is Pangu

Tongtian sighed as she transferred all the merits she'd just received to her Obsession Corpse, Lingbao. Although it was only five percent, it was the most merits she had ever received. Despite that fact, it was still far from enough to consecrate Lingbao.

It seems I have to wait until Buzhou Mountain shatters, Tongtian thought.

Far away, Lingbao placed the merit into the Allheaven Jianmu Tree. The more perfect the connate spiritual root was, the more merits would descend when it became the new heavenly pillar that separated the heavens and earth.

Back in the Underworld, Tongtian flew to Youdu, the Nether Capital. There, she sensed a drop of Houtu's presence. *Did Houtu not die?*

Unlike humans or other creatures, when titans died, their souls would dissipate and could not undergo reincarnation because they had no spirit to protect their truesoul.

Seeing Tongtian flying inside, Minghe followed after a moment of hesitation.

Tongtian ignored him and flew into the palace in the middle of Youdu. Deep inside, she saw a woman in a black dress sitting on a throne. Although her facial features were different, the woman on the throne reminded Tongtian of Houtu and someone else. "Are you Houtu or the Chaos Fiendgod of Samsara?"

The woman on the throne looked at Tongtian and smiled. "The Chaos Fiendgod of Samsara died when Pangu created heaven and earth. Houtu died when she incarnated into the Underworld. I am Empress Pingxin, but you can just address me as a fellow Daoist."

"Then, I've seen Daoist Pingxin," Tongtian said. She could tell that Empress Pingxin no longer possessed the body of a titan. In fact, her body appeared weaker than an average Quasi-Saint's.

Empress Pingxin closed her eyes, whispering, "Sever."

Tongtian felt the whole Underworld tremble as Empress Pingxin severed her Corpse. Her Corpse appeared like an old lady with a hunched back who still exuded a charismatic charm like an amiable grandmother or elder.

"Old Lady Meng, go and welcome the souls at the Bridge of Forgetfulness," Empress Pingxin ordered.

As Old Lady Meng left, Tongtian stared at her back. *So Old Lady Meng, who gives soup of forgetfulness to the dead souls, is actually Empress Pingxin's Corpse?*

"Fellow Daoist, I still have a few questions I hope you can answer for me," Empress Pingxin said.

"As long as I can answer them, I naturally will," Tongtian said.

Empress Pingxin nodded. "Although I have formed the Underworld and the River of Reincarnation, it isn't perfect. I wonder if Daoist Tongtian knows why?"

"I have a guess; the Underworld lacks personnel. No matter how powerful you are here, you cannot take care of everything. You can gather some of the giants to help you run the Underworld. Furthermore, you can choose some ghosts who do not want to reincarnate and have them become nether officials."

Empress Pingxin nodded.

"As for the River of Reincarnation," Tongtian continued. "From the moment they are born, all things bear karma and continue accumulating karma while they are alive. All souls should reincarnate into different lifeforms depending on their karma."

Empress Pingxin's eyes lit up. "And what should they reincarnate into?"

"If they bear karma for slaughter, they will be reincarnated into shuras; souls bearing karma due to excessive cravings and attachments should be turned into ghosts; souls with karma resulting from impulses and instincts should be reborn as beasts; souls with balanced karma should be reborn as humans; souls contaminated with only Karmic Sins shall not reincarnate until they are served due punishment for their actions. Together, they form the Shura Path of Reincarnation, Hungry Ghost Path of Reincarnation, Animal Path of Reincarnation, Human Path of Reincarnation, and Hell Path of Reincarnation," Tongtian said.

"Daoist Tongtian is wise indeed," Empress Pingxin said. She turned to Minghe to ask, "Daoist Minghe won't mind, right?"

"How can I mind?" Minghe said. He couldn't wait to beg Empress Pingxin to turn the shura race he'd created into one of the paths of reincarnation. A constant supply of merit would descend on him without him needing to do anything.

Empress Pingxin nodded and amended the River of Reincarnation, transforming it into the Five Paths of Reincarnation. The Way of Heaven sent down merits again the moment she completed it. Seventy-five percent flowed to Empress Pingxin and the Underworld; 15 percent flowed to Tongtian, and 10 percent flowed to Minghe.

"Fellow Daoist, reincarnation still is incomplete," Empress Pingxin said.

"That is indeed the case," Tongtian said. "Since there is a Hell Path, there must be a Heaven Path for all those who bear great merits and good karma. Unfortunately, such a race has not been born yet."

"So, that's the case," Empress Pingxin said with regret. "It seems that I can only wait."

Tongtian nodded and cupped her fist. "Since Daoist Pingxin is busy, I'll leave first. I still have many gains that I haven't digested."

"Then I bid farewell to Daoist Tongtian."

Not long after, Minghe also departed, leaving Empress Pingxin alone. She waited patiently for the titans to arrive.

* * *

Minghe returned to Crimsonsap Palace and summoned the four Shura Kings: Sakra, Bali, Kharakantha, and Vemincitrin. The four of them had grown stronger all these years, reaching the peak of the Great Firmament Realm.

However, their growth had come to a halt.

Minghe had reservations about the shuras, so he'd never taught them how to become Quasi-Saints. After all, shuras were bloodthirsty and even more belligerent than titans. They only respected him because of his superior strength. What if they pointed their fangs at him?

Although, even if he did, they would only become early Quasi-Saints. Due to the nature of shuras, they had no good thoughts, so they could only create two Corpses at most. Still, Minghe had no desire to face a group of Quasi-Saint shuras.

Minghe scanned the four Shura Kings. The one he feared the most was Sakra. Not only had he reached the peak of the Great Firmament Realm the fastest, but Minghe could see signs that he had started comprehending the Law of Lightning. Even if he didn't teach them the method to sever three Corpses, Minghe suspected the shura could enter the Quasi-Saint Realm by tempering his qi.

Feeling the deeply hidden killing intent from the shura's creator, Sakra lowered his head to expose the nape of his neck, showing his subservience. But the more subservience Sakra showed, the more Minghe wanted to kill him. Compared to the other shuras, who only knew how to kill head-on, Sakra's mind was too deep.

Minghe suppressed his killing intent. It was not yet time, and Sakra hadn't grown beyond his power yet. His eyes left the four Shura Kings. "Today, I have decided to establish a sect called the Shura Way."

The Shura Kings became excited. The establishment of a sect meant great merit, and if possible, they might be able to enter the Quasi-Saint Realm.

"The Shura Way will focus on war and killing to wash away the karma and sin of previous lives," Minghe continued. "You four will be the vice-masters of the Shura Way, commanding four forces each in your war against each other."

All four Shura Kings nodded and obeyed, especially Bali, Kharakantha, and Vemincitrin. Sakra had always oppressed them. If they obeyed their creator's order, couldn't they openly attack him? After years of being suppressed by Sakra, the three Shura Kings eventually learned what teamwork was.

Minghe nodded. "The Way of Heaven above, I, Minghe, establish the Shura Way! All shuras born from reincarnation shall war and fight to cleanse their karma and sins!"

Clouds of merit descended from the sky. As before, compared to when Nuwa had created humanity or when Laozi, Yuanshi, and Redcloud Ancestor had established their sects, the amount of merit he received was but a fraction. It couldn't even be compared to the establishment of the Liberation Sect.

Sixty percent flowed into Minghe, but even after absorbing it all, he could not merge his three Corpses and enter the Peak Quasi-Saint Realm, much to his frustration. Twenty percent split into four parts and flowed into the Shura Kings, while the last 20 percent was distributed among the shura race.

* * *

Minghe's actions alerted everyone in the Great Desolation. Some called him an opportunist, others called him a copycat while drowning in envy, but the eleven titans ignored this as they made their way to the Underworld.

Inside Youdu Palace, the eleven titans confronted Empress Pingxin.

"Houtu, what is the meaning of this?" Di Jiang asked. Although his voice was calm, a trace of barely contained fury could be heard.

Empress Pingxin sighed. "I no longer possess the body of a titan, so I can no longer use that name. The Way of Heaven won't allow it."

"So, you are abandoning your identity as a titan?" Gonggong asked, the sting of betrayal reflected in his tone.

"It's not that I want to, but I must," Empress Pingxin said. "I am now Empress Pingxin, ruler of the Underworld."

"Underworld, Pingxin, I don't care," Jumang said. "I just want to know why you did this. Why did you abandon the Titan Tribe?"

"Because it is Father God's will," Empress Pingxin said.

"Father God's will?" Tianwu repeated.

"When Father God formed heaven and earth, it was incomplete for various reasons," Empress Pingxin said. "Houtu was born to form the Underworld and perfect heaven and earth. That's why she was able to advance to the peak of the Quasi-Saint Realm so quickly."

"Bullshit!" Zhurong cried out as he pointed accusingly at Empress Pingxin. "There's no way Father God would want a titan to fall like this!"

Then, without warning, Zhurong covered his fist in flames and sent it toward Empress Pingxin. Before his fist could even reach her, the flames dissipated and coercion arose, freezing all the titans in their positions.

"Zhurong, stop," Empress Pingxin said. "It's useless. Not even Saints of Heaven can defeat me in the Underworld."

"Houtu," Di Jiang began but stopped when he saw Empress Pingxin's gaze. Unwillingly, he said, "Pingxin, let Zhurong go. You know he's always let his emotions go to his head."

The coercion receded back into the ground, freeing the titans. Zhurong still glared unwillingly at Empress Pingxin but said nothing and closed his eyes. When the coercion had appeared, it resembled when the Dao Ancestor had descended and stopped their Pangu Genesis Formation.

"Pingxin, what is the Titan Tribe supposed to do? Without you, we cannot form the Pangu Genesis Formation," Di Jiang said.

"I already thought of this," Empress Pingxin said. She waved her hand, summoning a large drop of earthen yellow blood. "Before my body incarnated into the Underworld, I extracted my remaining blood essence. Give it to Chiyou, and he can take my place as one of the twelve cornerstones of the Pangu Genesis Formation."

When Houtu's blood essence floated to Di Jiang, he looked at Empress Pingxin with a complicated gaze. Compared to before, her manner was far less compassionate. "I want to ask a question. You said that not even Saints could do anything to you in the Underworld. This means you must have reached a similar level, right? What are the chances of the Titan Tribe prevailing against Heavenly Court?"

Empress Pingxin closed her eyes and stayed silent. That was all Di Jiang needed to know.

"So that's the case." A powerful aura erupted from Di Jiang's body as his fighting spirit soared. He entered the Peak Quasi-Saint Realm.

Empress Pingxin opened her eyes and looked at Di Jiang and the rest of the titans with conflicting emotions. "If any of you want to retreat, you can always come to the Underworld."

Without hesitation, all of the titans rejected Empress Pingxin's offer. A titan could lose and even die, but they must never admit defeat, even in the face of certain death. She sighed and did not try to convince them, knowing it was useless.

"Send me some giants," Empress Pingxin said. "The Underworld is understaffed. Allow me some giants to help me manage it. The Underworld benefits heaven and earth, and even a minor position will grant immense merits over time."

"Pingxin's words are worth thinking about," Jiuyin said. "We can spare some giants to help manage the Underworld."

Although he called it helping, Di Jiang knew that Jiuyin meant they were leaving a retreat for the Titan Tribe in case Heavenly Court won. So, even if they lost, the Titan Tribe would still exist and not perish to history.

* * *

"Welcome back, Master," Wutian greeted Tongtian as she entered Three Purity Palace.

Tongtian nodded and moved to enter Supreme Purity Hall but paused at the last moment. "How are you feeling?"

Wutian froze for a moment but quickly responded, "I'm coping. The deaths of Eldest Brother, Second Sister, and Third Brother have motivated me to improve humanity's strength even more. I don't have time to overthink."

Tongtian sighed. "The River of Reincarnation has been created, so it's not impossible for the three ancestors of humanity to be reincarnated in the future and regain their memories."

Wutian's eyes shone with hope. "Please enlighten Disciple."

Tongtian shook her head. "With my current strength, I cannot calculate it. But they are people of great merit, so their reincarnations will not be lackluster. For now, go attend to the human race. Stay on Kunlun Mountain until the Titan-Demon War ends."

"Per Master's orders, I take my leave."

After instructing Wutian, Tongtian headed into the her hall. When the River of Time had created the River of Reincarnation, she had peered into the future and seen the end. At the end of the River of Time, Tongtian saw Pangu.

Pangu incarnates into all things. Thus, all is Pangu.

Her Law of Time had made a major breakthrough, and it was time to form her first incarnation. She had expected to sever her past or present, but never did she expect that she would sever her future first.

CHAPTER 57

The Eternal Cycle

The future was unpredictable. Countless variables contributed to the end result, just like how the flap of a butterfly's wings could result in a hurricane on the other side of the world. However, the Great Desolation was different.

Since Pangu incarnated into all things, weren't all things Pangu? After the Immeasurable Calamity, heaven and earth would collapse and return to Pangu. Tongtian's thoughts went deeper. *Is it possible that this isn't the first world created by Pangu?*

What if the process of Pangu killing the 3,000 chaos fiendgods was an eternal cycle? Every time Pangu created the Great Desolation, it would fail the Immeasurable Calamity and return to chaos. Then the chaos would birth the 3,000 chaos fiendgods, who Pangu would kill to create the Desolation once more. Creation and Destruction, an eternal cycle.

Tongtian's thoughts frightened her. Since everything returns to Pangu in the end, were her actions her own or driven secretly by Pangu?

"No, the Great Dao is fifty, the Eye of Heaven is forty-nine, and one escaped," Tongtian said. "I'm likely a survivor from the previous iteration of the Great Desolation. I likely stuck onto the Chaos Fiendgod of Time but was truly revived as the Supreme Purity."

Tongtian felt as if she had touched upon the truth and her destiny became clearer. "Even if I die and perish forever, I won't be absorbed by another person."

A pressure began to emanate from Tongtian's body, like when she'd broken through each stage of the Quasi-Saint Realm. It quickly reached and then surpassed 120 li.

"Sever!"

"SEVER!!"

"SEVER!!!"

All the Saints opened their eyes and peered into the River of Time. They saw it tremble, watching as a silver light flew out of it toward Kunlun Mountain. When they followed to investigate, a snort thundered in their ears.

Their eyes widened when Yuanshi destroyed their spiritual probes. Although they were unhappy, the Saints didn't take any action. After all, they had intruded into someone else's territory first, and they vaguely felt that Yuanshi's strength outstripped theirs by at least one level.

In Supreme Purity Hall, a hazy figure of silver formed in front of Tongtian.

Tongtian waved her hand, and twelve drops of blood appeared in front of her. The twelve drops emanated faint fluctuations of space, time, wood, metal, water, fire, wind, thunder, lightning, storm, rain, and earth. These were the blood essences from all twelve original titans.

When the Titan Tribe had asked Yuanshi to improve and repair the Titanomachy Flag, they'd paid him in blood essences, resulting in the Three Purities having even more titan blood.

The twelve drops of blood essences merged into the silver figure. They first formed the bones, then the organs, muscles, and finally the skin. When it was completed, a woman with 89 percent similarities to Tongtian stood in front of her. She wore fur instead of red robes, had untamed hair, tanned skin, and exuded a wild aura, slightly resembling Pangu.

From her Future Incarnation, Tongtian could feel the aura of a titan. Although the strength was only at the Great Firmament Realm, its source and origin were even more perfect than the twelve titans'. Since it was an incarnation, it had the same strength as Tongtian, but the Future Incarnation focused more on the Strength Path like the titans.

"Since you are born from my future, resulting in all things returning to Pangu, and are a titan, I shall name you Tonggu," Tongtian said.

"Tonggu greets Main Body," Tonggu said with a careless salute that suited her wild atmosphere. She turned into silver light and merged into Tongtian's body.

Tongtian closed her eyes and studied her changes. Her body felt lighter as if a weight had been lifted from her shoulders. Her comprehension speed did not necessarily increase like when she'd severed a Corpse, but she just felt... freer.

Under the influence of this wonderful feeling, Tongtian immersed herself in comprehending the Law of Time, ignorant of the world around her.

* * *

With Tongtian in a state of enlightenment, Yuanshi sealed Supreme Purity Hall and prevented anyone, especially Wutian, from disturbing her. Years passed. After the creation of the Underworld, neither the Titan Tribe nor the Demon Clan made any big moves. Both sides focused on amassing their power, waiting for the ten-eon time limit to end and rekindle the fire of war.

As the allotted time neared, everyone seemed to be preparing. Chiyou took Houtu's place as the new Titan of Earth. Although he had not inherited her innate ability to control the earth, he could still become one of the cornerstones of the Pangu Genesis Formation.

* * *

Di Jun sat atop the Throne of Heaven in Eminence Heaven Palace. In front of him floated a black sword, its blade swirling with the phantoms of dead human souls howling in agony.

"Refine!" the Heavenly Emperor roared as he concentrated the final batch of human souls into the sword. When the sword came to completion, a pillar of baleful qi erupted from Eminence Heaven Palace, attracting the attention of everyone in the Thirty-Three Heavens.

The completed spiritual artifact did not leak any aura, appearing much like a simple sword, but Di Jun caught glimpses of the howling phantoms swirling within the blade. He reached out and grabbed the handle. The moment his hand grasped it, killing intent flooded his mind, urging him to annihilate everything in sight. If there was nothing in sight, go seek it out and end all life. Sweat dripped down Di Jun's brows as he broke free from the sword's influence.

Had it not been for the Throne of Heaven fortifying his mind with the Karmic Luck of the Demon Clan, Di Jun truly might have become a mindless devil that only knew slaughter. However, that only made Di Jun happier. The more powerful the sword, the better.

Although the sword was only a top-grade acquired spiritual artifact, Di Jun knew it could rival cardinal artifacts in terms of pure power. "Good sword, good sword."

The hatred in Di Jun's eyes resonated with the negative emotions contained within the sword. "I shall name you Titanslayer!"

Titanslayer hummed as if resonating with its new name. After completing the artifact, Di Jun's eyes seemingly peered out of Eminence Heaven Palace and into the Great Desolation. Right at the Titan Tribe's location. "Oh accursed Titan Tribe, I'll have you accompany my sons soon enough."

* * *

Laozi also accepted a disciple during this period. To be more precise, it was his Saint Corpse, Taishang Laojun, who accepted a disciple. Although Laozi's way was the Way of Inaction, he had established the Human Way to consecrate his Corpse, so he'd had to accept a disciple to pass down his teachings.

While Laozi stayed on Kunlun Mountain to cultivate, his Saint Corpse roamed the Great Desolation. Along the way, he encountered a human kneeling in front of a mountain. He observed the human for years.

The human led a nomadic life, living off whatever berry or prey he could catch. Whenever he saw a majestic mountain, he would kneel for thirty days, hoping to find a master to lead him on the Immortal Path. When no one answered, he would move on to find the next mountain and kneel for thirty days again.

One day, Taishang Laojun appeared next to the human and asked, "Young man, what are you doing?"

"Hello, Mister," the young man said. "I am begging for an immortal to take me as a disciple."

"What if there's no immortal on the mountain?"

"That's fine. I'll kneel for thirty days. If there is no immortal, I'll search for the next spiritual mountain and kneel for thirty days again," the young man answered.

"What if you never find an immortal?"

"I believe that as long as I persevere, I will accomplish my goal."

Taishang Laojun nodded. He pinched his fingers and deduced that the young man in front of him had some fate with him. He no longer hid the aura on his body, revealing his holy aura. "I am the Heavenly Venerable of Virtuous Way. Are you willing to become my disciple?"

"Willing!" the young man cried as he tried to contain his excitement, kowtowing to Taishang Laojun. "Disciple Xuandu greets Master!"

After accepting Xuandu as his only disciple, Taishang Laozi brought him back to Kunlun Mountain, where he met Wutian.

"Descendant Xuandu greets Martial Ancestor," Xuandu said as he bowed.

Wutian had a strange expression on his face as he took in Taishang Laojun's newest disciple. Finally, he said, "There's no need to bow or call me Martial Ancestor. You are now Uncle-Master's disciple, you can just call me Senior Brother."

Xuandu hesitantly accepted Wutian's suggestion. "Greetings, Senior Brother Wutian."

With Wutian's presence and guidance, Xuandu showed remarkable improvements in his martial arts, but he displayed far greater talent with Laozi's Grand Purity Scripture. Within a thousand years, he entered the Earth Immortal Realm; within a hundred thousand years, he entered the Sky Immortal Realm; within the eon, Xuandu became a Profound Immortal.

Now, as the ten-eon peacetime came to an end, Xuandu was just at the cusp of becoming a Golden Immortal.

* * *

War began between the Titan Tribe and Demon Clan without any warning. It started as a minor scuffle when the demons of the

Heavenly Court could officially descend onto the Great Desolation once more.

The giants ambushed them and killed the first group of demons. In response, the Heavenly Court dispatched more demons to kill the giants. The Titan Tribe then sent even more giants, which only prompted the Heavenly Court to send out more demons.

The cycle continued, and without a word, the third and final war between the Titan Tribe and Demon Clan began. Unlike the first or second wars between the two forces, which were concentrated on Buzhou Mountain, this one spread everywhere.

With ten eons of recuperation, the populations of the Titan Tribe and the Demon Clan had exploded tremendously. The Demon Clan had grown more than a hundred times larger, but that included all demons, even those in the Earth Immortal Realm. Their top-level strength had only increased around five times.

Although the Titan Tribe's growth wasn't as massive as the Demon Clan's, their numbers still grew tremendously due to the titans using the blood pool to boost it. In addition, half of their population was made up of demigiants or their descendants born of the union of humans and giants.

On average, the Titan Tribe still had the upper hand, but the Demon Clan frequently teamed up against them. Even though the giants had also learned rudimentary teamwork, they could not compare to the demons. So evenly matched, both sides suffered heavy losses. It was as if they had entered a blind rage and could not see the increasing deaths of their comrades.

Their war shattered the land, split the seas, splintered rivers, ravaged the forests, blotted the skies, upended the mountains, and dyed the land red with blood.

* * *

"Leader, why can't we just rush up to Thirty-Three Heavens and crush them?" Chiyou asked. After absorbing Houtu's blood essence, he'd managed to break through and enter the Quasi-Saint Realm, but only the early Quasi-Saint Realm.

He and the rest of the titans were sitting inside Pangu Temple, directing the war. During these ten eons, only Di Jiang and Jiuyin had reached the Peak Quasi-Saint Realm, while the others had only managed to reach the Advanced Quasi-Saint Realm.

"Chiyou, there's no longer any need to address us with any honorifics," Jumang said. "You can address us by our names or just call us brothers."

"Have you forgotten about Nuwa?" Jiuyin asked. "Although she is in the chaotic boundary, you shouldn't underestimate the means of a Saint of Heaven. This war can only be won, not lost."

"Do you think it would be possible to lure Nuwa into the Underworld and have Hou—Pingxin deal with her?" Gonggong suggested.

Jiuyin shook his head. "It's no use. Pingxin refused. She said that Nuwa or any other Saint would not stay to fight her in the Underworld. Damaging the Six Paths of Reincarnation will decrease Karmic Luck and incur massive amounts of Karmic Sin. You've seen what luck could do, but if all our luck turned to sin, it would not be worth it. It's even more the case for Saints who follow the Way of Heaven."

"Merit and sin aren't important," Zhurong declared contemptuously. "As long as we defeat the Demon Clan, it'll only take time to restore our luck. By then, who would dare to fight us? Once we deal with the Demon Clan and Nuwa, the other Saints are next."

Although the titans didn't agree nor object, their eyes came alive with fighting spirit. They'd never considered Saints to be invincible. As long as they improved their strength, who would be their opponents?

The glory of the Saints of Heaven was only temporary.

"Enough," Di Jiang said. "Leave the other Saints for later. It would mean nothing unless we defeat the Demon Clan with a clear victory. We have to focus on minimizing our losses. Also, do not act independently. If we lose just one of us, we can no longer form the Pangu Genesis Formation."

All the titans obeyed Di Jiang's words. And so, the terrible war continued.

Chapter 58

Nuwa's Strike

In Thirty-Three Heavens, Di Jun glanced at the kneeling demon officials. Standing one level beneath him were the demon emperors Taiyi and Fuxi. Below them was Demon Preceptor Kunpeng, and after him were the Ten Demon Sages. Finally, there were the rest of the heavenly officials.

"Bai Ze," Di Jun summoned. "Tell Us how many demons have fallen."

Bai Ze stepped out, bowed, and reported. "Answering Your Majesty, it is currently the 9,747th year of the war. So far, Heavenly Court has lost 300 Golden Immortals of the Great Firmament, 3,000 Golden Immortals of the Great Unity, 27,000 Golden Immortals, over 400,000 Profound Immortals, over a million Sky Immortals, and countless Earth Immortals."

Audible sounds of cold breaths could be heard at Bai Ze's reports.

"Tell Us how much remains of Heavenly Court's army," Di Jun commanded.

"Reporting to Your Majesty," Bai Zei continued. "The Heavenly Court still has 800 Golden Immortals of the Great Firmament, 12,000 Golden Immortals of the Great Unity, 49,000 Golden Immortals, 70,000 Profound Immortals, eight million Sky Immortals, and countless Earth Immortals."

"Tell Us how the war will go if we continue to fight like this."

"Your Majesty, we cannot survive the war like this. We need to keep a force of at least 48,000 Golden Immortals in reserve to unleash the greatest power of the Starry Sky War Array. Soon, we won't be able to send out many Golden Immortals, and the Titan Tribe will hold an undeniable advantage over us. However, if we dispatch Golden Immortals, we will weaken the Starry Sky War Array by a level, and we won't be able to combat the Pangu Genesis Formation."

"Bai Ze has a point. Do beloved officials have any suggestions?"

The demon officials immediately began discussing different strategies. Each put forth their own suggestions, but the pros could not outweigh the cons.

Finally, it was Kunpeng who stepped forward. "Your Majesty, I believe we should attack the core of the Titan Tribe."

Di Jun raised an eyebrow. "And why is that, Demon Preceptor?"

"It isn't the weaklings that determine the victors in the war, but the top combat strength. As long as the titans fall, what can the rest of the Titan Tribe do?" Kunpeng asked.

"Beloved official has a point," Di Jun said. "But, what about the Pangu Genesis Formation? The Starry Sky War Array cannot guarantee victory over the Pangu Genesis Formation. Especially since the farther away it is from the Starry Sky, the weaker its strength."

"Your Majesty, delaying it will only prolong the inevitable," Kunpeng said. "Although the Titan Tribe managed to replace Houtu, the Pangu Genesis Formation requires balance. Chiyou's early Quasi-Saint strength will inevitably hinder its power."

Di Jun stayed silent as he contemplated Kunpeng's suggestion.

"Your Majesty, we don't need to defeat the Titan Tribe when we attack," Kunpeng added.

"Oh?"

The Demon Preceptor revealed a sinister sneer. "The titans are brash and reckless, fearing nothing. If we attack their core, would we be afraid of them not chasing us? We simply need to lead them back to Thirty-Three Heaven and deal with them here."

Di Jun's eyes lit up, and he looked appreciatively at Kunpeng. As expected of the sage who created the Demon Script.

* * *

After the war started, the twelve Titan Tribe branches: Di Jiang Tribe, Jiuyin Tribe, Jumang Tribe, Rushou Tribe, Gonggong Tribe, Zhurong Tribe, Qiangliang Tribe, Tianwu Tribe, Jizi Tribe, Shebisi Tribe, Xuangming Tribe, and Houtu Tribe all returned to the land around Buzhou Mountain near the valley containing the Pangu Temple.

The day was like any other. Numerous giants sparred against each other without mercy. Giants had powerful bodies. Even if they received a large wound, as long as they had enough vitality, they could heal within a few days.

Aside from the warriors sparring, numerous other giants were catching prey. Even in war, giants still needed to eat to maintain their strength. Unlike the Immortal Path or Martial Path, few giants directly absorbed essence. Instead, they received essence from the flesh they consumed.

Their favorite prey were demons. Since demons cultivated the Immortal Path, they had large amounts of essence compared to other creatures. Such a relationship also contributed to the current feud between the Titan Tribe and Demon Clan.

Suddenly, the sky darkened, and a myriad of stars appeared above the tribe. Of the 48,000 stars shining above, 365 shone the brightest—especially the silver-blue star, gold-red star, and purple-gold star.

The giants didn't have time to marvel at the beautiful scenery before the starlight descended. Each beacon crashed into the ground like a meteorite, cracking the land and blasting whatever unlucky giants directly under it into chunks of flesh.

Before the starlight could reign for more than ten breaths, a furious shout echoed over the Titan Tribe. A mysterious force dispersed the starlight and diverted their trajectory away from the giants.

"Di Jun, you stinky bird! Are you tired of living, daring to come to the Titan Tribe?!" Di Jiang's voice resonated over the 100,000 li surrounding the Titan Tribe.

Di Jun's laugh answered Di Jiang's wrathful roar. "I'm also helpless. I waited for you for nearly 10,000 years, but I didn't expect the so-called brave titans to suddenly lose their courage and hole up in their tribe. Since you won't come to me, I'll come to you!"

"You damn flat-feathered beast!"

Di Jun's words had thoroughly infuriated all the titans. Instantly, a massive humanoid figure with wild hair wearing a furred loincloth appeared in the core of the Titan Tribe. They had formed the Pangu Genesis Formation.

"Come!" The Pangu Genesis Formation raised its arm to summon the three Heaven-Opening Treasures, but just like the last time, neither the Taiji Diagram, Pangu Banner, nor the Chaos Bell could be summoned.

Two snorts rang in the air, and the Pangu Genesis Formation trembled for a moment but was otherwise fine. An illusionary ax appeared in the false Pangu's hand. It exuded a powerful aura, but it was akin to rootless duckweed in the Saints' eyes. It appeared strong but held no substance.

"Break for me!" the false Pangu roared as it slashed its ax down.

In response, the 48,000 stars of the Starry Sky War Array shimmered. The glittering lights formed countless layers of starlight to block the ax, but they shattered like glass on impact. However, the layers eventually slowed down the ax enough that the stars only dimmed slightly before regaining their brightness.

Di Jun commanded the Starry Sky War Array to retaliate against the Pangu Genesis Formation. Thousands of stars slammed against the false Pangu's chest. Although each impact sent ripples across the false Pangu's skin, they didn't inflict any noticeable injuries.

The two most powerful formations of the Great Desolation continued to duke it out. The Pangu Genesis Formation constantly attacked and weakened the Starry Sky War Array, while the Starry Sky War always managed to disperse most of the Pangu Genesis Formation's power and remain relatively unharmed.

However, that would not last long. The titans could see that the Starry Sky War Array was on the brink of collapse. They wanted to take this chance and get rid of Di Jun and the other top-level demons as soon as possible. Without the Starry Sky War Array, the Demon Clan would be easy pickings for the Titan Tribe.

At this time, the Starry Sky War Array focused all its effort on defense and fleeing. The false Pangu roared with frustration and chased after the fleeing demons. It constantly swung its ax, destroying the landscape with each missed strike.

The chase didn't last long, as they were already near Buzhou Mountain. When the Starry Sky War Array reached the mountaintop, the Pangu Genesis Formation unleashed a powerful ax strike.

Pangu Heaven-Opening First Art - Chaos Splitter

The Starry Sky War Array bunched up together, forming a ball of chaos. It flew under the incoming ax blade as if attracted by some unknown force. Finally, the ax touched the ball of chaos and split it in half.

"Hahaha, Di Jun the stinky bird has finally died!" Zhurong's voice jeered from the Pangu Genesis Formation.

"No, wait! Something's strange!" Gonggong said, his voice overlapping with Zhurong's laughter.

The Starry Sky War Array that seemed to have been split by the ax dispersed into a hazy black mist, but within that mist, countless tiny motes of light glimmered. As the lights increased in intensity, so did the aura of the Starry Sky War Array. It soon surpassed its peak strength from that first battle.

The Pangu Genesis Formation suddenly looked up, ignoring the hazy Starry Sky War Array below it. The real stars had descended and came incredibly close to the land of the Great Desolation. It seemed as if the sky would collapse into the ground, returning the Great Desolation to chaos.

This cosmic calamity led to numerous natural disasters. With the Starry Sky closer to the land than ever, the Starry Sky War Array reached an unprecedented level of power.

"Ancient Annihilation Constellation, form!" Di Jun's voice reverberated throughout the surrounding million li.

The hazy Starry Sky War Array rose from the ground. As it did, it merged with the actual Starry Sky. The 365 major stars and 48,000 minor stars blasted starlight that converged into a colossus of constellations equal to the Pangu Genesis Formation. Strands of starlight formed its hair, its right eye was the sun, the left eye the moon. Its robe appeared as if someone had cut the night sky and stitched it into a robe.

"Just a mere imitation!" Di Jiang's voice appeared from the Pangu Genesis Formation. The false Pangu raised its ax and attacked the star colossus.

In response, a giant bronze bell appeared in the star colossus's hand. It raised the bell and slammed it against the ax. The resulting clash sent bell rings echoing over ten million li, killing countless weak creatures.

The titans were shocked by the Ancient Annihilation Constellation's strength. The first time the Starry Sky War Array had appeared, it couldn't even resist. The second time, it could only delay the Pangu Genesis Formation. But during the third clash, it was able to trade blows!

The Pangu Genesis Formation should have had the upper hand, but any damage dealt to the Ancient Annihilation Constellation was instantly repaired by the starlight from the Starry Sky, a practically limitless source of energy. Dragging it out would only end in the titans' defeat. They needed to destroy the Ancient Annihilation Constellation and Starry Sky War Array as soon as possible. The false Pangu raised its ax above its head, gathering power.

Seeing this, Di Jun commanded the demons to blast it with as much starlight as possible.

Three hundred sixty-five dots shined on the Chaos Bell as it channeled the power of the Starry Sky. The star giant smashed the Chaos Bell onto the Pangu Genesis Formation. Bruises and injuries formed on its skin, as well as lingering starlight, but the false Pangu stood firm and unmoved.

Pangu Heaven-Opening Second Art - Open Heaven

The ax left a brilliant arc in the air, like a trailing sky, as it cleaved through the Ancient Annihilation Constellation to greatly injure Di Jun, Fuxi, Taiyi, Kunpeng, the Ten Demon Sages, and the rest of the Golden Immortals of Great Firmament that controlled the 365 major stars. The star colossus scattered the technique's dividing effect.

Di Jun's face turned grave as he saw the Pangu Genesis Formation raise its ax again to gather power. "Everyone, attack it with all your might! Detonate the formation flags if you have to! Destroy the Pangu Genesis Formation!"

Over 48,000 miniature stars appeared and smashed into the Pangu Genesis Formation. Many of them sputtered out of existence as the Golden Immortals controlling them died, unable to withstand the backlash. A few crazy ones gave up on surviving and self-detonated along with the formation flags.

The stronger ones who did this, such as the Golden Immortals of the Great Firmament, directly turned their stars into supernovas. These supernovas unleashed a single strike near the top power of the Starry Sky War Array.

The Pangu Genesis Formation faltered, stumbling back a single step. Still, it held firm even as more bruises, burns, and other wounds appeared on its body.

Pangu Heaven-Opening Third Art - Dividing Earth

The stars scattered and returned to high above the land as the false Pangu's ax sliced downward. The miniature stars charging toward the Pangu Genesis Formation fell and imploded on impact, making a crater out of the formerly mighty Buzhou Mountain. Even Di Jun, Taiyi, Fuxi, and the other Quasi-Saints fell onto the ground, spitting up blood.

The false Pangu gazed at the downed demons with labored breaths, obviously on its last legs. It swung its ax at the survivors, intending to kill them and cinch victory.

"This is the end!" Di Jiang's voice boomed from the Pangu Genesis Formation.

However, coercion descended at this moment. The titans bellowed while the demons rejoiced. A hand with milky-white skin appeared through a portal, reaching for the Pangu Genesis Formation.

"Destroy!" the false Pangu roared, changing the trajectory of its ax swing to target Nuwa's hand.

The hand phased through the ax and tapped the Pangu Genesis Formation's chest before disappearing. Moments later, cracks started to appear originating from the point Nuwa had tapped. Like shattered porcelain, the Pangu Genesis Formation broke apart, revealing the twelve titans inside. Although they weren't bloodied, their aura fluctuated wildly, revealing their unstable state and hidden injuries.

Di Jun rose from his collapsed state. His gaze locked onto Di Jiang's. As if they had a prior agreement, both of them roared, "Charge!"

Chapter 59

Madness

Inside Wa Outer Heaven, Nuwa observed the increasingly intense battle between the Titan Tribe and Demon Clan. She also detected the probes from the other Saints of Heaven monitoring the confrontation.

Her heart clenched when Fuxi and the other demons formed the Starry Sky War Array and engaged the Pangu Genesis Formation in combat. Every time the false Pangu swung its ax, Nuwa worried for her brother.

As the false Pangu chased after the Starry Sky War Array, so did the giants of the Titan Tribe. While the two most powerful formations clashed atop Buzhou Mountain, the giants and demons warred in the surrounding land. It was a terrible war; thousands of demons and titans perished each second.

When the demons died, their blood formed rivers that flowed endlessly. Their flesh rotted, leaving only bones behind. When giants died, most often, their lifeless bodies turned into mountains or other geographical features.

Giants from the Zhurong Tribe turned into volcanoes; giants from the Gonggong Tribe turned into lakes; giants from the Jumang Tribe turned into giant trees and forests; giants from the Rushou Tribe turned into metal veins; giants from the Houtu Tribe directly merged with the land; giants from the Di Jiang Tribe disappeared and merged with space; giants from the Jiuyin Tribe supplemented the River of Time; giants from the Qiangliang, Jizi, Shebisi, and Xuanming Tribe turned into storms; and giants from the Tianwu Tribe turned into tornadoes.

After the Pangu Genesis Formation destroyed the Starry Sky War Array, Nuwa's hands moved. Using her mastery of the law and the ability granted to her as a Saint of Heaven, her hand appeared above Buzhou Mountain to split apart the Pangu Genesis Formation.

Nuwa had wanted to kill a few titans so that although both sides would still lose, the Demon Clan could still preserve their numbers. However, this went against the Way of Heaven, forcing her to settle on injuring the titans and destroying the Titanomachy Flags. She continued to watch the battle with bated breath. When Nuwa saw Fuxi enter a dangerous situation, she wanted to take action again, but several Saints locked onto her.

"What is the meaning of this?" Nuwa asked with a dangerous flash in her eyes as Yuanshi appeared in front of her.

"Junior Sister should understand that we Saints cannot intervene in this war," he calmly said, ignoring Nuwa's look.

Nuwa's hands moved, but the incoming coercion from Yuanshi stopped her. It wasn't that she feared his strength, but the Way of Heaven's power overlaid with Yuanshi's coercion.

The Way of Heaven was using Yuanshi to stop her.

Left with no other choice, Nuwa could only play the part of witness. Even if she wanted to extract Fuxi from the war, she could no longer do so.

* * *

Blood leaked from Fuxi's lips as he dodged the Titan of Lightning's fist. Electricity exploded from the mass of lightning and struck

Fuxi, injuring him anyway. He didn't have time to recompose himself as Qiangliang, the Titan of Thunder, unleashed a sonic roar upon him.

Pushed to the brink, a decisive look flashed through his eyes. Two figures emerged from Fuxi's body. They were his Good and Evil Corpses.

Fuxi held the Fuxi Qin, his Good Corpse held a pipa, while his Evil Corpse had a flute at his lips.

All three instruments sang at the same time. Their song disrupted the flow of lightning in Jizi's elemental form, destabilizing it. The song also drowned out Qiangliang's thunder, overpowering him and causing blood to leak from his orifices.

Jizi pointed his hand at Fuxi and shot out a beam of lightning, interrupting his song and allowing Qiangliang to regain his bearings. The two titans and Fuxi reignited their battle.

Bai Ze's divining plate smashed into Chiyou's chest. The new titan coughed blood, reeling back. Then, Ji Meng transformed into his true form, a colossal white stag with crystalline antlers. He charged toward the pseudo-titan, impaling him.

Chiyou roared even as more blood spilled from his mouth and chest. He wrapped his barrel-like arms around Ji Meng's neck, slowly tightening them like a boa constrictor.

Ji Meng struggled, unable to free himself.

Chiyou ignored everything else, focusing solely on snapping Ji Meng's neck. Even as Demon Sages Ying Zhao and Qing Yuan assaulted him, he shut out their attacks. Finally, Bai Ze smashed the Titan of Earth's head with his artifact, loosening his grip. Ji Meng transformed into his humanoid form again, drastically reducing in size and slipping out of Chiyou's grip.

"Slippery bastards!" Chiyou roared. His voice boomed and ruptured the ears of the Golden Immortal demons surrounding him. He set his sights on Ying Zhao and tackled him into the ground, punching the demon sage until he was a meat paste.

After killing Ying Zhao, Chiyou's breathing became labored. He could tell that he wasn't going to live, so he roared again and charged at the weakest of the three remaining demon sages. In no time, he turned Qing Yuan into a second bloody smear on the ground.

Ji Meng revealed his true form to gouge out the earth titan's internal organs while Bai Ze decapitated him. Bai Ze and Ji Meng didn't have time to celebrate their victory, swiftly joining their fellow demon sages and Kunpeng in fighting against Tianwu and Jumang.

Taiyi faced Rushou, Zhurong, Gonggong, Xuanming, and Shebisi. Gonggong and Xuanming had merged their innate abilities to control water and rain to combat Taiyi's mastery over the Solar Truefire. In addition to Shebisi's storm abilities, they curbed Taiyi's advantage over Rushou.

When Chiyou died, the five titans roared. They fought with reckless abandon and disregarded all defense. Even Taiyi felt pressured by the increased onslaught and had to rely on the Chaos Bell to defend himself.

Despite ten eons passing, Taiyi was still only at the Advanced Quasi-Saint Realm, having never severed his obsession. However, he had not stagnated, and his power now comparable to that of peak Quasi-Saints. Unfortunately, collectively, the titans had progressed further than him, having all reached the Advanced Quasi-Saint Realm.

Rushou and Zhurong combined their abilities to form a giant molten metal spear aimed at Taiyi. When it struck the Chaos Bell, it forced Taiyi to take hundreds of steps back, but it wasn't done. The spear deformed into a molten sludge that started encapsulating Taiyi and the Chaos Bell.

Taiyi punched the Chaos Bell with a roar, causing the engraving of himself and Tongtian to light up. The bronze bell's rings shattered and dispersed the molten metal, but before he could catch his breath, a tide of water engulfed him.

An intense heat rolled off Taiyi's body, evaporating the water around him. Soon, fire started to burn around the Eastern Emperor, even as the water threatened to crush his body.

Suddenly, a hole appeared in the sphere of fire surrounding Taiyi. He doubled over as if something had punched him into the gut. As the holes multiplied, Taiyi convulsed with numerous gashes appearing all over his robes and body.

As he became more and more bloody, the phantom image of a three-legged crow appeared above him. The golden crow roared, unfurled its wings, and unleashed a wave of Solar Truefire that vaporized all the water. Taiyi fell to the ground, drenched in a mixture of blood and water. The remaining wave split into two, transforming into a weakened Gonggong and Xuanming.

Without waiting for them to recover, the Chaos Bell hurtled toward the downed titans. Rushou appeared in front of them and held out his arms, stopping the incoming artifact. He roared as he was forced back a thousand steps. When he finally stopped, numerous cracks covered both his metallic arms.

The Chaos Bell flew back but immediately aimed itself at the Titan of Metal again. Just in time, a fiery colossus appeared and punched the Chaos Bell, sending it careening into the ground with such great force it caused an earthquake.

Zhurong didn't wait for the others, charging Taiyi by his lonesome. A golden crow phantom appeared above Taiyi's head and merged with his body, covering him in fiery armor. He, too, charged Zhurong.

As the battle between Taiyi and the Titans of Metal, Fire, Water, Rain, and Storm raged on, Di Jun and Xihe battled Di Jiang and Jiuyin.

Di Jiang had transformed into an amorphous blob of gold radiating spatial aura. Jiuyin also took on an amorphous form, only he radiated a timeless silver aura.

Di Jun held the Celestial River Diagram in his left hand and Titanslayer in his right. The miniature Starry Sky he formed with the Celestial River Diagram appeared above his head and rained down starlight.

The light phased through Di Jiang's body, while it seemed to exist in a different time than Jiuyin. Di Jun tightened his grip on his sword and lunged at Di Jiang. Starlight gathered on his body, covering him in armor formed of constellations.

Xihe followed close behind. In her hand, a gray gourd appeared. She uncorked it, and it unleashed a torrent of Solar Truefire and Lunar Truewater that swirled around each other in a spiral but never touched. The empty space between the streams produced a unique power.

Di Jiang tried to phase through them, but to his shock, he couldn't. The two streams actually bound him in space. Taking this chance, Di Jun slashed with the Titanslayer, forcing him to revert back to his physical body.

"Di Jiang!" Jiuyin shouted as he rushed over. He punched Di Jun, forcing him to retreat lest he wished to test his physical prowess against a titan's.

Di Jiang recomposed himself and transformed into a spatial colossus again. Both he and Jiuyin stormed Xihe. She was the weakest of the four, but now that she posed a threat, they wanted to eliminate her first.

Starlight formed before Xihe and shot toward the two titans, but they ignored it. As the light phased through them, Di Jiang and Jiuyin punched Xihe. She unleashed her fire-water formation again, but under the combined might of the Titan of Space and the Titan of Time, it was ruthlessly shattered, and both hits landed.

The gray gourd dropped from her severed arm.

Di Jun screamed, "Xihe!"

Xihe acted as if she hadn't heard him and charged at Jiuyin. The Titan of Time grabbed Xihe in his hands and squeezed. Blood poured out of the lunar goddess's lips, but she didn't scream or cry. Two more figures appeared within Jiuyin's grasp. They were her two Corpses.

"Hmpf! Even if you add two more, the end result will be the same!" Jiuyin said as he used his other hands to tighten his grip. Di Jiang blocked a furious Di Jun.

As the life disappeared from Xihe's eyes, she revealed a ghostly smile.

Jiuyin felt an ominous premonition, but before he could react, Xihe self-detonated. The self-detonation of a Quasi-Saint could not be underestimated, and Jiuyin suffered immense injuries and lost his spatial form.

"Jiuyin!"

The Titan of Time looked in Di Jiang's direction, but all he saw was an incoming blade. The Titanslayer pierced his head, and the light of life faded from Jiuyin's eyes.

Titanslayer pierced the ground as Jiuyin's body dissolved into silver lights and merged with the River of Time.

Di Jiang roared and attacked Di Jun with all his strength. Di Jun lost an arm, but he ignored the injury. Retrieving the Titanslayer, he hurled it at Rushou.

The Titanslayer pierced Rushou's chest, causing him to revert to his physical form and fall to his knees. Taiyi appeared behind Rushou. Grabbing the sword's handle, he slashed upwards, splitting Rushou's head vertically.

"Rushou!" Gonggong roared. He rushed Taiyi and sent him flying with a punch.

Taiyi smiled. Although his injuries had worsened, he'd still gained the overall advantage since he only needed to face four titans instead of five. However, all was not well for Heavenly Court.

While Di Jun was distracted, Di Jiang appeared in front of the Heavenly Emperor. He exploded his spatial body, and numerous spatial blades lacerated Di Jun's body, turning it into a bloody mess.

Di Jiang reverted to his physical form and sneered. "Haha, Di Jun! Today you will die under my foot!"

"I will never be killed by the likes of you!" Di Jun roared and charged toward Di Jiang, emulating his wife's final act. "I'll be joining you soon, Xihe, my sons."

Di Jun's self-detonation resembled a supernova, brilliant and memorable but ultimately fleeting. When the explosion dissipated, neither Di Jun's nor Di Jiang's remains were left.

"Brother!" Taiyi screamed, but the worsening battle robbed him of the chance to grieve.

Fuxi's face paled as Qiangliang smashed him into the ground. He had transformed back into his original form, revealing the lower half of a snake. His Corpses had been destroyed, but neither Qiangliang nor Jizi could maintain their elemental forms any longer.

Jizi appeared next to Qiangliang and raised his foot, ready to stomp Fuxi to death.

"Kunpeng, save Fuxi!" Taiyi roared.

Kunpeng, who was fighting Tianwu, glanced over, and his eyes shined. Although Jumang had had seemingly endless vitality, he was eventually killed through sheer numbers. Nearly half of the demon sages and over 10,000 Golden Immortals fell, but Jumang died, his corpse growing into a gigantic tree.

The Demon Preceptor's figure disappeared and reappeared where Di Jun had sacrificed himself. He transformed into his true form, a great roc, and grabbed the Celestial River Diagram in his talons before fleeing north. His actions severely demoralized the Demon Clan, giving the giants the perfect opportunity to slaughter them en masse.

Fuxi laughed, and madness filled his laughter as he rushed toward Qiangliang and Jizi. Before they could react, he also self-detonated, killing Qiangliang and gravely injuring Jizi. The latter was quickly overwhelmed by the demon horde and executed.

Despite the deaths of so many of their leaders, or perhaps because of them, the Titan Tribe and Demon Clan continued to war, unable to extricate themselves from this bloody affair.

Tianwu eventually died, but at the cost of nearly all the demon sages' lives. Taiyi was riddled with injuries, but he had managed to kill Xuanming, leaving only Gonggong, Zhurong, and Shebisi. The Eastern Emperor would not last much longer in his current state and with his dwindling qi.

Taiyi suddenly stopped, and a calm silence dominated the battlefield for a brief moment as he stared at a certain location in the sky. He sighed and closed his eyes. When he reopened them again, his face paled, but his gaze never wavered.

With the Titanslayer in his left hand and the Chaos Bell in his right, the Eastern Emperor charged at the three titans. Gonggong,

Zhurong, and Shebisi exchanged over a hundred blows with Taiyi. Each time, more wounds appeared on Taiyi's body.

"Haha, you damn bird, the Titan Tribe is going to prevail in this war!" Gonggong shouted. He and the last two remaining titans surrounded Taiyi. All of them stepped forward to beat him mercilessly.

Taiyi blocked one of the punches and threw the Chaos Bell into the sky, attracting all three titans' attention. Then, a forlorn smile appeared on his face. "Farewell."

Zhurong was the first to react. He shoved Gonggong away and said, "Haha, cowards like you shouldn't die. Live, Gonggong!"

Taiyi's self-detonation enveloped Zhurong and Shebisi. When the dust settled, their remains were gone. Gonggong stared straight ahead in a mixture of stupor and disbelief. He suddenly awoke from his battle trance and stood up. His eyes scanned the surroundings and saw the bloody state of the Great Desolation. Both sides had dwindled to nearly nothing.

The titan erupted with mad laughter, much like Di Jun and Xihe. His cackles echoed through the surrounding million li, drawing the remaining fight to a halt. Then, Gonggong grew until he was over a thousand li tall. He raised both hands above his head, clenched them together, and smashed Buzhou Mountain under the horrified eyes of the giant and demons.

Chapter 60

Yuanshi Mends the Heavens

Buzhou Mountain shattered. Pangu's spine, which had supported the sky since the creation of the Great Desolation, had broken. The Starry Sky fell, and the land shattered as heaven and earth started collapsing into one once more.

The Celestial River was disrupted and flowed onto the Great Desolation. Celestial Starwater was one of the top ten truewaters of heaven and earth and carried the power of the stars. Wherever it flowed, countless lives were lost. No other race felt this more than the human race.

After their tribulation at the hands of the Demon Clan, humanity had been pushed to the brink of extinction. In a few eons, they'd repopulated the land once more, but they were several levels weaker than the humanity of yore.

Wutian had listened to Tongtian and ordered many humans to stay near Kunlun Mountain. As a result, their population remained small, and they focused on increasing their strength.

Elsewhere, pockets of human settlements had managed to survive and started to repopulate. However, they had lost the inheritance from their four human ancestors and lived like beasts. Without Laozi's Grand Purity Scripture or Wutian's martial arts, they couldn't improve their strength and remained at the bottom of the food chain.

Now, these human tribes suffered the most. As the world flooded, mountains and land masses floated up and crashed into the sky. The collision destroyed the stars, dimming the sky and unleashing a terrifying nova that pulverized the land even more.

All this happened in a few moments. If this continued, heaven and earth would return to chaos within the day.

The Saints of Heaven appeared and took action to halt the destruction of the Great Desolation.

Yuanshi summoned the Pangu Banner to suspend the descending sky. Laozi brought out the Taiji Diagram in an attempt to push it back. Nuwa also appeared and used the Mountain and River Diagram to aid Laozi.

Redcloud Ancestor appeared next. Under his control, red clouds appeared and diverted the Celestial Starwater and suppressed the land from floating up, allowing all life on the land to sigh in relief.

Jieyin and Zhunti appeared next. It had taken some time due to the distance, but they'd still arrived quickly. Embarrassingly, they didn't have any suitable artifacts like Laozi, Yuanshi, and Nuwa to prop up the sky. They could only rely on their spells to delay its descent.

"We managed to temporarily stop the sky from collapsing, but this isn't a long-term solution," Nuwa said.

Laozi nodded. "Junior Sister is correct. We need to find something to replace the broken pillar of heaven."

"Unfortunately, the West is too barren and does not contain any suitable materials," Jieyin said. If it had, he wouldn't have minded using them. Replacing the heavenly pillar was of great merit and could bring prosperity faster to the West.

Redcloud Ancestor furrowed his brows, and hesitation appeared on his face.

"Daoist Redcloud, do you know anything?" Zhunti asked. "Repairing the pillar of heaven is of the utmost importance for the Great Desolation."

Redcloud Ancestor sighed. "I have a friend who lives in the North. He possesses the power of a peak Quasi-Saint, but he can't transform because his body is too powerful. Just his size alone is over 100,000 li. His four legs should be able to replace the heavenly pillar."

Upon hearing this, all the Saints' eyes lit up.

Zhunti said, "Hurry and bring him over. We can't hesitate. What's one life compared to the whole Great Desolation?"

Redcloud Ancestor nodded with some melancholy, but he steeled his heart and prepared to fly northward. But before he could, Yuanshi spoke.

"Wait."

All the Saints turned to him but saw him looking westward. They followed his line of sight and noticed it too. At the juncture between East and West, a tree sprouted out of the ground. The tree possessed bronze-colored bark and iron-colored leaves. It appeared small at first, but in a few breaths, it grew endlessly until it touched the sky. The trunk thickened until it was around a tenth of the base of Buzhou Mountain.

The Saints sensed the Starry Sky halt in its descent, disentangling from the land below. The tree's branches held the remaining stars in place, and the leaves glittered like stars.

"The world tree is propping up the Starry Sky, but it's not enough," Yuanshi said with a frown. He looked towards Redcloud Ancestor. "It seems you still have to make the trip."

Redcloud Ancestor prepared to move, but just as he did, he stopped. He and the other Saints looked towards the North, where they saw a woman in red flying over. Behind her, four gigantic pillars followed.

* * *

Tongtian sighed. She stood with Lingbao next to the connate spiritual root. After the Allheaven Jianmu Tree had started to grow and support heaven and earth from merging, the Way of Heaven took over and guided the Allheaven Jianmu Tree's growth.

Alas, the Allheaven Jianmu Tree wasn't enough to support the sky alone. It had not matured enough, and it seemed Xuangui needed to fulfill his original fate.

Tongtian's figure disappeared as she teleported to the North, leaving Lingbao to look after the Allheaven Jianmu Tree. In the Darknorth Sea, she saw a massive turtle standing on its legs, looking up. The bottom half of the turtle's shell had completely risen above the water, and the legs were longer than the depth of the sea.

"Xuangui," Tongtian said.

Xuangui turned away from the sky and looked at Tongtian. "I finally know why I can't transform."

Tongtian wanted to smile, but she couldn't. How pitiful was Xuangui? He possessed a body stronger than the titans and was nearly invincible. Yet, his fate was to be slaughtered, his legs turned into pillars to support the sky.

"Go ahead, I'm ready," Xuangui said as he closed his eyes, ready to accept its fate.

"Wait," Tongtian said.

Xuangui opened his eyes and looked at Tongtian with some confusion.

"Although your body will be refined into four pillars to support the sky, you can still grab some benefits."

"What do you mean?" Xuangui asked as some spark returned to his eyes.

"If you willingly offer up your legs, endless merits will descend," Tongtian said.

"What use are merits if I'm dead?" Xuangui asked.

Tongtian shook her head. "Your body may die, but your soul will be reincarnated. The Underworld has formed, and all life that died can be reincarnated with a new life. As long as you cultivate back to the Quasi-Saint Realm, you can regain your memories. Even if you haven't awakened your memories, the Way of Heaven will continuously bestow merits upon you. In your new life, you won't need to be trapped in the North anymore!"

Xuangui turned silent before he met Tongtian's gaze firmly. "Thank you. I hope we can be friends in the next life too."

He looked up at the sky once more. "The Way of Heaven above, I, Xuangui, offer my body to support the sky from collapsing into the ground!"

Because the Way of Heaven was busy with the collapsing sky, Xuangui's voice did not reach all of the Great Desolation. Golden lights emitted from him. His body began to shrink, while his legs grew and thickened, becoming pillars. In the end, only a turtle shell and four pillars were left.

Tongtian sighed once more as she saw Xuangui's soul fly toward the Underworld. She waved her hand and stored the turtle shell, but she couldn't store the four pillars. Left with no choice, she carried the four pillars with her to Yuanshi.

"Third Sister?" Yuanshi called out.

Tongtian nodded. "Second Brother, you have the Qiankun Cauldron and reigned supreme in artificing. You should refine these into four heavenly pillars to aid the Allheaven Jianmu Tree in supporting the sky."

Yuanshi nodded in understanding and waved his arm, taking out the artifact. All the Saints looked at the Qiankun Cauldron with desire, but thinking about Yuanshi and Laozi's strength, hid their envy.

"Senior Brother, please wait," Nuwa said. She waved her hand, and several five-colored stones appeared in her hand. "While I was living in the chaotic boundary, I happened across these Five Elements Chaos Stones. If you add them to the pillars, it should increase their strength."

Yuanshi nodded. The Qiankun Cauldron expanded several times, and the four pillars and Five Elements Chaos Stones flew in. A gray and black flame lit under it, and Yuanshi started to refine the auxiliary heavenly pillars. The Saints observed this process as they continued to support the sky, aiding the Allheaven Jianmu Tree.

"Daoist Tongtian should retreat; it's not safe for non-Saints," Zhunti suddenly said.

Tongtian's eyes cooled as she lightly glanced at him. "Junior Brother doesn't need to worry about my affairs."

Zhunti smiled like the embodiment of compassion and clapped his hands together. "Unfortunate, unfortunate. If Daoist Tongtian had stayed away, Daoist Redcloud would not have lost his chance to attain merits."

Tongtian's eyes cooled even more. Was he trying to sow discord between her and Redcloud Ancestor? "Since when have you cared so much about Daoist Redcloud's affairs?"

"Daoist Redcloud is my great benefactor. Had it not been for him, I would not have become Master's disciple."

Tongtian sneered. "What a great relationship you have with Daoist Redcloud. But why did you stand by when he was in danger?"

Zhunti was not perturbed by her words. "Alas, I was in the West and could not sense Daoist Redcloud's situation. If I could have, I would have come to his side as soon as possible."

"As soon as he died, right?" Tongtian pressed.

"Daoist Tongtian, are you questioning my character?" Zhunti asked, finally losing some of the compassion on his face.

"Yes, I am, Junior Brother."

As the air between Tongtian and Zhunti turned tense, Yuanshi's voice echoed, "Enough."

Tongtian snorted and looked away.

"I'll respect Daoist Yuanshi and won't say anymore," Zhunti said as he closed his eyes and continued to support the sky.

At this time, Redcloud Ancestor spoke. "It's good that you took Xuangui's legs. Had it not been for Daoist Tongtian, there would be no Saint Redcloud today."

Zhunti's face stiffened for a brief moment, but he kept his smile and closed his eyes until they turned into crescents.

Tongtian nodded toward Redcloud Ancestor and said, "You don't have to worry about Daoist Xuangui." She would not elaborate. Who knew if Jieyin and Zhunti would kidnap Xuangui's reincarnation and take him as a disciple? Xuangui would receive continuous merits, which would increase the West's prosperity.

Although Redcloud Ancestor didn't know what Tongtian planned, he still trusted her. Aside from Zhen Yuanzi, he trusted Tongtian most of all the people he knew.

The Saints kept destruction at bay while Yuanshi continued to refine Xuangui's legs. Finally, he finished. "Form!"

Four streams of light shot out of the Qiankun Cauldron toward the East, South, West, and North. When they landed at the edge of the Great Desolation, massive pillars only shorter than the Allheaven Jianmu Tree appeared.

Tongtian noticed that a stray piece of the Five Elements Chaos Stone that had not been used had fallen out into the Great Desolation. She quietly made a note of where it fell and felt the changes in the Allheaven Jianmu Tree.

With the aid of the four additional heavenly pillars, the Allheaven Jianmu Tree successfully propped up the sky. The Saints stored their spells and artifacts once they detected the sky no longer falling. In fact, it started to rise, its stability more solid than when Buzhou Mountain was still the Heavenly Pillar. No longer could a force easily summon the Starry Sky so close to the land.

The Thirty-Three Heavens shifted until it was directly atop the Allheaven Jianmu Tree, while the Underworld shifted until it was connected to the roots. With this complete, the Great Desolation was separated into three realms: heaven, earth, and mortal.

Once the sky stabilized, the Way of Heaven bestowed merits.

The Way of Heaven used the essence of the Dragon Ancestor, Phoenix Ancestor, Qilin Ancestor, and Xuangui to strengthen the four supporting heavenly pillars. On the East Pillar of Heaven, the engraving of the Azure Dragon emerged; on the South Pillar of Heaven, the engraving of the Vermillion Bird emerged; on the West Pillar of Heaven, the engraving of the White Tiger emerged; on the North Pillar of Heaven, the engraving of the Black Tortoise emerged.

Then, the clouds of merits appeared above the Saints and Tongtian. To the Saints' shock, 60 percent flowed to Tongtian. Yuanshi received a quarter of the merit. Nuwa gained 5 percent, and the last 10 percent was split among the remaining Saints.

They didn't have time to question why Tongtian had received so many merits as they turned their eyes toward the ownerless artifacts. Predominantly the Titanslayer sword, but also the Chaos Bell.

Just as they were about to start to compete, a coercion emanated from the Allheaven Jianmu Tree. All the Saints recognized it as the consecration of a new Saint of Heaven. They turned toward Tongtian, but it wasn't her who was ascending to Sainthood.

She frowned as they did, but for a different reason.

From the direction of the Allheaven Jianmu Tree, a voice echoed through the Great Desolation.

"I am Lingbao, the Heavenly Venerable of Numinous Treasures! I am the master of the Allheaven Jianmu Tree, the Central Pillar of Heaven!"

Chapter 61

Saint of Heaven

Ignoring the Saints' shock, Tongtian closed her eyes and felt the changes in her Corpse. Of the six others present, only Yuanshi and Laozi noticed Tongtian's abnormality. They quietly flew closer to her, guarding their sister.

When Tongtian had received 60 percent of the merits, she'd transferred all of them to Lingbao, her Obsession Corpse. The immense amount of merit equaled or surpassed when Taishang Laojun had established the Human Way, and it triggered the Grandmist Violet Qi to merge with Lingbao's soul.

Tongtian's perception changed and merged with Lingbao's. What Lingbao saw, she saw too.

* * *

At the top of the Allheaven Jianmu Tree, Lingbao sat in a lotus position with his eyes closed. He didn't perceive the stars above him or the tree below. Instead, he found himself in a mystical space full of indescribable colors and abstract shapes.

Holding these colors and shapes together were 3,000 lines. In an instant, Lingbao understood where he was. This was the core of the Great Desolation, and the 3,000 lines holding everything together were the 3,000 laws that formed heaven and earth.

Some of the lines had already been claimed, such as the line representing the Law of Chaos taken by Yuanshi or the line representing the Law of Infinity taken by Laozi. Lingbao explored further and identified the line representing the Law of Karma taken by Jieyin and the Law of Dreams taken by Zhunti. Redcloud Ancestor had chosen the line representing the Law of Illusion, much to his surprise.

Of note, he couldn't discover what law the Dao Ancestor had used to become a Saint of Heaven. Logically, there should be traces, yet he couldn't find any. On another note, although no Saint had taken the line representing the Law of Samsara, it was no longer available.

Tracing the line representing the Law of Samsara, Lingbao could see it connected to the Underworld and Empress Pingxin, despite her not reaching the Primordial Origin Realm. Only in the Underworld could the nether goddess unleash the power of a Saint of Heaven. Though, that would change if she ever reached the Primordial Origin Realm.

Lingbao extricated himself from any extraneous thoughts and focused on finding the Law of Spacetime. To enter the Primordial Origin Realm, a cultivator needed to master a complete law first, but it was too difficult. Laozi would have taken much longer if his Saint Corpse hadn't taken the line representing the Law of Infinity.

When Lingbao emanated the fluctuations of the Law of Time and the Law of Space, two lines vibrated in resonance. The silver line represented the Law of Time, and the gold line represented the Law of Space.

Unfortunately, no matter how Lingbao searched, he could not find the line representing the Law of Spacetime. *Does the Great Desolation not contain the Law of Spacetime?*

Now, Lingbao was trapped between two options. He could either use the Law of Time or the Law of Space to become a Saint of Heaven.

And his time was running out. He could feel the Grandmist Violet Qi that had merged with his soul urging him to choose. If he didn't, it would assign him a law at random.

As the vibrations intensified, Lingbao made his decision. He grabbed the golden line representing the Law of Space. Once taken, he exited the core space of the Great Desolation.

Lingbao's senses returned to the top of the Allheaven Jianmu Tree. A golden sea emerged behind him, with three twelve-petaled flowers above it. The three flowers descended and merged into the golden sea and melted. The sea rose above Lingbao's head, releasing a rainbow light. Its color gradually faded into translucency and transformed into an aurora coated in gold.

The coercion disappeared, and Lingbao opened his eyes. He had successfully become a Saint of Heaven. So long as heaven and earth existed, he was imperishable. All at once, Lingbao—and by extension Tongtian—understood the stages of the Primordial Origin Realm.

The Primordial Origin Realm was divided into twelve layers. The Early Primordial Origin Realm consisted of the First Heavenly Layer to the Third Heavenly Layer; the Intermediate Primordial Original Realm consisted of the Fourth Heavenly Layer to the Sixth Heavenly Layer; and the Advanced Primordial Origin Realm consisted of the Seventh Heavenly Layer to the Ninth Heavenly Layer. Finally, the Tenth Heavenly Layer to the Twelfth Heavenly Layer represented a peak Golden Immortal of the Primordial Origin.

As a newly consecrated Saint, Lingbao stood at the First Heavenly Layer. Due to his previous accumulation, he soon reached the peak of the First Heavenly Layer. Had Tongtian become a Saint instead of her Corpse, she would have likely been able to enter the Third Heavenly Layer if she had chosen to control the Law of Time.

After stabilizing his realm, Lingbao rose from his lotus position, tore the space in front of him, and stepped through. He rushed to where Buzhou Mountain once stood to provide reinforcement.

* * *

When the coercion disappeared, the Saints moved. Whoever the new Saint was, they would be competition for the Chaos Bell.

"The Chaos Bell belongs to the Demon Clan. As such, it should return to the Demon Clan," Nuwa said, reaching out.

"How can that be?" Jieyin asked. "The Demon Clan and Titan Tribe caused untold devastation and almost destroyed the Great Desolation. How can they be worthy of retaining the Chaos Bell?"

A golden vajra appeared in Jieyin's palm to strike Nuwa's hand. Nuwa frowned and summoned the Red Hydrangea, which she used to smash Jieyin's Vajra Pestle.

When his artifact rebuffed hers, Nuwa's brows furrowed. With her other hand, she summoned the Mountain and River Diagram. In response, Jieyin summoned the other half of his artifact, the Divine Mortar, to tangle with the diagram.

Due to the higher quality of her artifacts, Nuwa held the upper hand against Jieyin's single artifact, but only barely. While the two entangled each other, Zhunti took action.

"The Chaos Bell has fate with my West," Zhunti said as he sent out his artifact.

Zhunti had been gifted the top-grade innate spiritual artifact, the Plain-Colored Flag of West Clouds, and the high-grade innate artifact, the Eight-Treasure Merit Pond, but the artifact he took out was neither of those. It resembled a tree branch with seven forks and exuded a wondrous glow. It was the Seven Miracle Treasured Tree, a top-grade innate spiritual artifact.

Before the Seven Miracle Treasured Tree could touch the Chaos Bell, a yin-yang symbol blocked it.

"As one of the Heaven-Opening Treasures, there is no one more suited for it than us, the Three Purities," Laozi said as he reached forward.

"Destiny is determined by strength," Redcloud Ancestor said as he took action. "Whoever can refine it is fated with the Chaos Bell!"

Jieyin and Nuwa also stopped fighting each other to team up against Laozi. No matter how powerful Laozi was, he couldn't face the combined might of four Saints. He enlarged the Taiji Diagram and maximized the defense to block the Saints' attacks but was pushed away.

This time, Yuanshi appeared and swung his Pangu Banner. Chaotic winds emerged and pushed the Chaos Bell toward him. Upon seeing this, the four Saints once again combined their might against him.

Yuanshi snorted and waved the Pangu Banner. Unlike Laozi, he wasn't pushed back, but the Chaos Bell no longer drifted toward him.

Jieyin formed a one-handed seal and pointed at the Chaos Bell. A golden glow encased the bronze bell, and it drifted toward him. However, to Jieyin's, Zhunti's, Nuwa's, and Redcloud Ancestor's surprise, Tongtian suddenly appeared in front of it.

"The Grand Purity holds the Taiji Diagram. The Jade Purity holds the Pangu Banner. Naturally, the Chaos Bell should belong to me, the Supreme Purity!" She grabbed the top of the bell, and the golden glow disappeared. Her beautiful face looked befuddled, but regardless of the abnormality, the Saints took action again.

Jieyin formed the seal again, but no matter how much energy he used, he could not establish even the slightest connection with Chaos Bell. Since he could no longer establish a link with his karmic technique, he attacked Tongtian with the Vajra Pestle and Mortar. Nuwa threw her Red Hydrangea and Mountain and River Diagram at her too. Redcloud Ancestor hesitated but still summoned the red clouds and sent them at Tongtian.

Yuanshi appeared protectively in front of his sister with murder in his eyes. He swung the Pangu Banner and repelled the Vajra Pestle and Mortar, Red Hydrangea, and Mountain and River Diagram. He used his free hand to slap the red clouds and disperse them.

Zhunti, who had not taken action yet, dissolved like a mirage. Next, he reappeared behind Tongtian and sent the Seven Miracle Treasured Tree out at her. "This isn't a battlefield a mere Quasi-Saint can interfere in."

Tongtian awakened from her daze and glanced at him. She rang the Chaos Bell, lighting up the engraving of her and Taiyi. Spatial energy reverberated out from it and wrapped around her, causing Zhunti's attack to fly through.

Four Saints widened their eyes as they saw this. They were shocked by two points. First, Tongtian seemed to have refined the Chaos Bell to an extremely high degree as if she had owned it for eons. The second, more shocking fact, was the profundity Tongtian displayed. The Saints could tell that Tongtian had completely mastered the Law of Space.

The difference between a Saint and a Quasi-Saint wasn't just the difference in the quality and power of their qi. More importantly, it was the difference in their mastery of the law. Now, Tongtian had displayed mastery that was equal to theirs!

Zhunti frowned, and the Plain-Colored Flag of West Clouds appeared in his hand.

"Eldest Brother, why aren't you taking action?" Yuanshi yelled as Zhunti attacked Tongtian again.

Tongtian activated the Chaos Bell again, and Zhunti found himself immobilized. He roared and forcibly broke free of the restriction, but it was already too late as the Taiji Diagram appeared in front of him and blocked his way.

Zhunti stopped and regrouped with Jieyin. They, along with Nuwa and Redcloud Ancestor, stared at the Three Purities. Tongtian, Yuanshi, and Laozi also stood together, facing the four Saints.

"I really admire you three siblings' relationship. Even though she is only a Quasi-Saint, you actually let her have one of the three Heaven-Opening Treasures," Zhunti praised.

"Zhunti, stop being so shameless," Tongtian directly called out. "Our relationship isn't something an outsider like you can butt in on. Besides, who said I was only a Quasi-Saint?"

At this, Tongtian and Yuanshi revealed queer smiles. While Laozi retained the same expression, his eyes held disdain as he looked at them.

The four Saints wondered what the Three Purities meant, but their attention was distracted as they turned toward the approaching unknown Saint. They could see it was a man unfamiliar to all except Nuwa. Realization dawned on her as the newly consecrated Saint flew toward Tongtian.

Jieyin, Zhunti, and Redcloud Ancestor wondered why Yuanshi and Laozi didn't take action, but they soon knew why. Their eyes widened in disbelief as the newly arrived Saint merged with Tongtian, and not a second later, she exuded the aura of a Saint.

The Saints weren't stupid and immediately guessed the truth.

"You turned your Corpse into a Saint?" Zhunti asked.

The four Saints stared at the Three Purities in horror. Saints became consecrated by merging with the Grandmist Violet Qi and mastering a law of the Great Desolation. As such, each law could only be mastered by one Saint, but the same didn't apply to those in the Primordial Origin. To become Golden Immortal of the Primordial

Origin, you only needed to master the complete law.

If Tongtian's Corpse was a Saint, that meant she could become a Golden Immortal of the Primordial Origin at any time. Thinking further, didn't this mean that Yuanshi and Laozi were the same?

All four Saints felt sweat drip down their heads as they thought of this possibility. Wouldn't this mean that even if they teamed up, they were still outnumbered by two?

Tongtian acted as if she couldn't see the gears turning in their heads and smiled at Zhunti. "Junior Brother, do you still think I'm unqualified?" Before he could answer, she continued, "You probably do. I just became a Saint and can't compare to you. Since that's the case, I can only do this."

Four swords appeared around Tongtian, and the four Saints' faces paled. They were the four Immortal Extermination Swords. According to the Dao Ancestor, only the combined efforts of four people in the same realm could break it. Theoretically, Jieyin, Zhunti, Nuwa, and Redcloud Ancestor could break it, but Yuanshi and Laozi wouldn't stand still and watch.

"How can that be?" Zhunti stepped forward and asked with a smile. "Senior Sister's might is unrivaled. I can only admit defeat and hope you can forgive my previous transgressions."

Tongtian felt her lips twitch at how fast Zhunti had changed his attitude. *Sure enough, shameless people are invincible.*

She stored the Immortal Extermination Swords and the Saints sighed in relief. They could only stare reluctantly as Tongtian stored the Chaos Bell. Who'd told them to be weaker than the other party?

The Saints searched for the Titanslayer sword. Although it couldn't compare to the Chaos Bell, it was still a powerful artifact, but they could not find it. Moments later, they saw Tongtian's smirk and understood. While they focused on the Chaos Bell, Tongtian had grabbed Titanslayer before obtaining the Chaos Bell. The Saints could only sigh again. Even if they asked, would Tongtian hand Titanslayer over?

Reason, logic? Those weren't worth anything in the Great Desolation. Might made right, and unless the Three Purities split, the other Saints could only remain below them.

Aside from the Chaos Bell and Titanslayer, the rest of the unowned spiritual artifacts couldn't enter their eyes. Only Redcloud Ancestor made a move to collect them. His entire net worth was actually less than that of Jieyin and Zhunti. Redcloud Ancestor didn't care for these treasures either, but he had to plan for his disciples.

With the distribution of the artifacts finished, the seven Saints turned toward the Titan Tribe and Demon Clan. The remaining giants and demons looked up at the Saints, awaiting their judgment. Gonggong was nowhere to be seen. When the Starry Sky fell, he was the first to fall, transforming into a sea upon his death.

As the strongest, Yuanshi spoke first. "The Demon Clan and Titan Tribe have failed in their bid for hegemony. During the war, they broke the heavenly pillar supporting the sky and became the Great Desolation's greatest sinners. As such, they should no longer appear in the Great Desolation and cannot contest for hegemony any longer."

"Although the demons are ridden with sin, the West is willing to take them in to absolve them, washing them of their Karmic Sins and bringing them salvation," Jieyin said as his body exuded a golden light. Any demons who saw this suddenly became filled with yearning for the West.

Nuwa frowned. She waved her hand and broke the golden light. "I am one of the demon emperors of the Demon Clan. They should follow me instead."

At this, the demons also looked at Nuwa. In the Demon Clan, only Di Jun had held higher prestige. Compared to the barren West, they were more willing to follow her.

"Daoist Nuwa is right," Zhunti said. "You are the Southern Emperor, but because of that, you also hold responsibility for the destruction of Buzhou Mountain. If they followed you, I'm afraid they wouldn't learn and would repeat their mistakes."

Nuwa turned toward him and glared. Zhunti only clapped his hands together and smiled. She turned toward Jieyin next to him, and her eyes flickered.

"How about this?" Tongtian asked, breaking the tense atmosphere. "We cannot forcibly take them. How about you let them decide for themselves?"

The three Saints nodded in agreement and waited for the demons' response. They looked up at the Three Purities, but the siblings closed their eyes. Obviously, they weren't willing to take the demons in.

Laozi practiced the Way of Inaction and did not want to accept disciples or followers. Yuanshi was even worse. He looked down on beasts like the demon clan. How could he be willing to accept them?

As for Tongtian, she felt a headache upon seeing a large number of demons. She didn't even want to establish the Interception Sect, which was destined to bring calamity to its founder; why would she accept them?

One of the ten demon sages, Ji Meng, gritted his teeth and stepped forward. His body transformed into his true form, a white stag with crystalline horns. "I am willing to become the Heavenly Venerable of Numinous Treasure's mount!"

All the Saints, especially those competing for him and his brethren, stared at Ji Meng. After the war, hardly any Golden Immortals, Golden Immortals of the Great Unity, and Golden Immortals of the Great Firmament remained, much less Quasi-Saints. Furthermore, for one to willingly become a mount was disgraceful.

Tongtian stared at Ji Meng's stag form. Although his fur was no longer shiny and pure due to the injuries, it was still incredibly beautiful. She nodded and waved her hand, and a white light descended upon Ji Meng and instantly reversed his injuries, returning his coat to its peak sheen.

"You can become my mount." Tongtian looked at the demons behind the stag. "The Deer Clan can also become my followers."

Ji Meng smiled and quickly flew under Tongtian, allowing her to sit upon him. His descendants flew behind the Supreme Purity.

With this, the rest of the Saints looked at Bai Ze with anticipation. When he flew behind Nuwa, they were disappointed. Furthermore, he was not willing to become a mount either. In terms of reputation and prestige, Tongtian's instantly rose due to having a Quasi-Saint mount.

The majority of the demons followed Nuwa, but a few followed the two Western Saints, and Redcloud Ancestor also accepted a few to become his disciples. With the demons dealt with, the Saints turned their attention toward the giants.

Nuwa's lips curled as she turned to Zhunti and Jieyin. "Why don't you accept them as well? Didn't you want to save all beings in heaven and earth? Then save the giants."

"Unfortunately, the giants have no fate with my West," Jieyin and Zhunti said. Who was Nuwa kidding? The giants only respected Pangu and had no spirit. They couldn't cultivate the Immortal Path, and having them in the West would only worsen it.

Although the demons were full of Karmic Sin, the two Western Saints had enough patience to slowly replace the sins with merits and turn them into protectors of the West. They did not need to worry about the sin contaminating them since Saints were unburdened by karma.

While the Saints argued, the ground suddenly trembled and split, swallowing up the giants. Tongtian, with her connection to the All-heaven Jianmu Tree, knew that Empress Pingxin had taken action using the power of the Underworld.

Since the giants had been dealt with, the Saints planned to return to their abodes. But then bell rings echoed throughout the Great Desolation. It wasn't the rings of the Chaos Bell, but the Purple-Gold Bell inside Violet Heaven Palace.

The Dao Ancestor had summoned them.

Thank you for reading a MoonQuill original novel. More exciting stories can be found on at www.moonquill.com.

We would greatly appreciate it if you could take a moment to leave a review. Each one helps the author and supports their ability to continue writing fantastic books for everyone to enjoy!

Scan the QR code below to subscribe to our mailing list and be notified of new releases. You'll receive 4 e-books for free!